Lingering
Poets

By Logan Lamech

ISBN-13: 978-1-9775-1453-0

DEDICATION

For Babe and my boys.

CONTENTS

Epigraph

The act of suicide is the loss of a battle. It's a battle that's fought by opposing sides of the same person, a battle that feeds on doubt, shame, anger and an overall treachery within oneself. Those trapped in this conflict must maintain unwavering strength in a never-ending siege. Losing is not the sign of a coward, nor the indulgence of the selfish, but instead may only require one moment of weakness against an unrelenting enemy. Even being victorious often leaves the survivor drifting and weary. Without ever achieving death, the battle still inhibits life from being lived. It inhibits growth, love, trust, ambition and can keep a romance from being a marriage, a job from being a career and a boy from being a man.

CHAPTER 1: GETTING ACQUAINTED

It was a deceptively sunny day. The day did provide the warmth and light it was expected to, but in its promise to deliver high spirits to the recipients of that light and warmth, it fell short, at least for one boy. The day marked the end of a long stretch of murky, rainy weather, following a far longer and more abusive winter. For many, this burst of sunshine was freedom from unjust imprisonment. It was a day that should conjure up a person's need to get outside and live their life. Athletes needed to compete, dancers needed to dance and lovers needed to love, but this boy was not athletic, nor a dancer, and no longer a lover—or perhaps he was better described as a lover with no one left to love.

So his slow trod down the sidewalk did not reflect the beautiful weather. Instead, it might cause a viewer to lose a portion of the goodwill the day had provided them with.

He had more reason than most to appreciate the lack of snow or rain that could slow him in his duties. Still, he maintained the same pace he had used throughout the hard winter, one that displayed a curious mixture of being both down-hearted and absentminded at once. His expression was that of a focused daydream. His thoughts were far enough away that he might well have been oblivious to his own sad state, blatant to any observer. He was a walking contradiction, both to himself and to his surroundings.

Still, despite his drifting eyes and broken stride, his attire was well taken to. His bright white socks matched the lettering on his bold blue tennis shoes. His just slightly large navy blue shorts were held tightly to his waist by a stern black belt. His baby blue shirt was properly tucked in, but just barely frayed back out to allow a subtle hang over the shorts. The shirt was neatly ironed. It was buttoned with all but the first two, which left the top open to expose the bright white T-shirt underneath. The T-shirt also matched the lettering, both on the shoes and on the outer shirt. He carried a hefty blue bag that read "US Postal Service" in broad letters on the outside.

His features helped him accomplish his attempts to avoid the residents on his route. His bold, dark eyebrows matched his combed-back hair, giving a ruffian-like quality that might slow anyone's desire to strike up conversation. His coal-black shields that served as eyes well covered the boiling emotions he hid behind them.

As his pace brought him to the last mailbox before returning to his truck, he pulled out a brown box about six inches wide, nine inches long and two inches deep. He opened the black mailbox, placed the package inside, closed it up and lifted the red arm. Then he continued down the sidewalk, passing his truck and taking rest on a nearby bench. There, he removed a blue zippered lunch pail from the mailbag to begin his noonday ritual.

As he pulled out his daily ham and cheese sandwich, he began yet another daydream. The subject of this dream was similar to many of those he used to pass the day. He wondered about the contents of the last package he delivered. It was commonplace for him to wonder about the packages, what was in them and who they were for. He read the names and tried to create faces. Even more, he would try to imagine what these people's lives consisted of.

James Fenton was the name on that box. It sounded like a distinguished name, perhaps that of an author. James received packages like that often, sometimes thinner, sometimes not. They were the right size for movies. He probably ordered movies very regularly. Maybe he watched lots of movies to jog his own imagination. Perhaps it would give him inspiration for his writing. One day, if he stuck to it long enough, he'd watch the right movie while in the right frame of mind while debating the right subject for a story and *poof!* It would all come together perfectly for the first time in his life. At last, James would know success.

"Pfff," he smirked as he snapped out of his own imagination. Though it was a constant practice for him, he still had to laugh at the baseless characteristics he had just given to Mr. Fenton. At times, his daydreams comforted him. That one he didn't like as much due to the obvious personal and self-serving undertone.

Though it was hard to deny, he didn't like the idea of all these daydreams really being a way to project his own fears and frustrations. But it went without argument that if he was on the verge of giving up, his addressees would face tragic loss and hardship. If he was feeling happy, there was nothing but good fortune for those people in his mind. Though that had not been the case for quite some while, he had to admit, there was a definite string of hope returning to his thought patterns.

He still felt covered with a relentless blanket of pointlessness and dread, but perhaps he was getting a second wind. Maybe the idea that he could find relief was returning.

It certainly was no coincidence that his mental James Fenton was a writer, a profession he had dreamed of pursuing since childhood. It was nice that things had worked out for James, instead of him dying a lonely, bitter old man who could never quite get his story the way he wanted it. That was the usual sorts of endings his daydreams had held for some time.

Why did I ever quit writing in my journal? the mailman wondered as he started on his tapioca pudding. *Ah, Susan—it seemed I never had time anymore, and she considered it feminine.*

In his younger years he had always felt that if he forced himself to write every day in a journal, about his own thoughts and events, that eventually a proper novel would present itself for him to write. Still, it was probably the fear that it would never work, as much as it was Susan, that caused him to quit.

"You're a dreamer, Samuel, that's what I love about ya," she'd always say, "but writing in diaries is for little school girls. I never even had a diary, so what would it look like if the man I'm going to marry was carrying one around all the time?"

Ah, Susan—without question, a pivotal turning point in his life. All his friends in high school told him not to take her seriously. She was Ms. Popularity and on the rebound from the school super-jock. She was just using the quiet boy in the back of the class to make him jealous. But what did they know? Of course, looking back, maybe they were right. They said it would never last and it didn't, though it was almost certainly longer than they had expected. But they had said she'd never really love him and she did. For a time Samuel believed she really did. It didn't last but she did fall in love with him, with his high hopes and free way of thinking.

So in a way it was his high expectations that brought him down. It was largely those expectations that enchanted Susan, and it was largely her that interrupted his life's natural progression. Though he kept a perfect grade point average with ease and boasted outstanding test scores with little to no studying, he did not continue his schooling.

Susan didn't want him to and she was a girl who tended to get what she wanted. She was head over heels for Samuel. She wanted to marry him. She did not want to wait another four years to start their life together. So Samuel quit giving school much attention and went on a hunt for a well-paying job. That's when his uncle got him in as a postman.

Sure it was the busybody, ant-mentality type of work he'd always preached against, but who cared? It didn't matter as long as he could make Susan happy. It didn't matter that they were complete opposites. That seemed to be a big part of what she loved so much about him.

He was something she never imagined nor expected. He was like a unicorn to her, a type of person she had heard about but could never believe existed. Plus, loving unconditionally and being loved was something Samuel had always wanted. He devoted himself to her and invested everything about himself into making her happy. But eventually, she got bored. It was not the type of lifestyle in which she'd been raised and it wasn't one she could live her whole life in. She was a woman of late nights, constant entertainment and short affairs.

"You drain me, Samuel," were her last words of consequence. "You're too much for me emotionally and spiritually. I can't keep up with your love of the world and constant imagination. I'm a down-to-earth sort and we both know it. I feel I'm holding you back and you'd be better off without me in your way."

It was a sweet, poetic farewell, but her noble intentions soon inverted when it came to the divorce proceedings. She was hoping to keep a free ride while obtaining a free lifestyle. She went after as much as she possibly could and more, assuming that when Samuel compromised on her request she would still end up with more than was reasonable. Instead, he didn't even resist the first offer. He just let her take everything. She lived better off her alimony than he did with the leftovers. He had a tiny hole-in-the-wall apartment and made just enough to cover his expenses. He worked every day to fund her life. But that really didn't matter to him. The problem with his life wasn't how much money he had, but that he spent the majority of his time doing mind-numbing work that he had no interest in or passion for.

The way he saw it, he had already given up his future. He'd have to continue working to live, and it wasn't a job that allowed him the freedom to live life the way he felt it should be lived. So what difference did it make? He had no need for excess money. She might as well have it. At least it would be put to use.

Now, looking back, he was somewhat grateful that she had been so nervous and uneasy about having children. He was glad there were no ties between the two of them. She had removed something very important from the center of his being. He didn't think he could handle seeing her on a regular basis.

He wondered if she knew even then that she was going to leave him, if that was why she didn't want to start a family. Maybe she knew she would leave him the shell of a man he was now; a drift-minded zombie walking the postal routes in his hometown.

He wondered if she still had contact with Carl the super-jock after all these years. Was it he who warmed her bed and heart at night? Susan was not one who could be alone for any amount of time. She needed constant affection from others to keep her own self-esteem in place. There was no way she left him before she knew where she would lie next. That was part of why Samuel didn't resist the divorce itself much. He knew if she was ready to leave, she had already moved on.

He looked back on that man being left as a confused, naive one. Back then he believed he'd be all right, that he could carry on without her. He underestimated the void she filled and thus the one she left.

He would never have imagined the longing for companionship that he was engulfed in almost immediately. It was those first six months after they separated, before the divorce was final, that he had maintained hope. He believed that since he'd only lived the life of a husband for four years, and the man he was before had lasted much longer, he would return and get on with his life. It was a nice dream, maybe even a reasonable one. Just not one he could bring to pass. One who has stayed in the castle can rarely find happiness back with the villagers.

It was during those six months he met the second love of his life, Leah. As short as his time with Susan was, his time with Leah was far shorter still, but for one afternoon.

It had been nearly two years but he still remembered it vividly. He was on the train back from a nearby town where his mother's funeral had just taken place. He had been very close with his mom growing up. Until his relationship with Susan had sprung out of nowhere, she was his closest companion. Still, she was very supportive of the two of them. He hadn't the heart to tell her about the split when her sudden illness arose. It would be telling her he missed her final years for no real reason.

Susan attended the funeral, and it was the first time Samuel had seen her since the divorce had been final. With the trauma of the loss of a dear loved one and having to interact with his lost love, Samuel passed the train ride with his natural response. He was far off in another world that was still based in the real one. He was making up deep, intricate reasons for the various expressions on the other passengers' faces. Despite his trauma he was in an almost euphoric state. Everything was wonderful for these people.

He felt the plump lady sitting opposite him with the miniature bag of peanuts, who kept eating one then closing the bag back up, was a very enlightened woman. She spent her days taking the time to enjoy each thing to the fullest. She was letting the sweet, honey roast flavor engulf her tongue before finally bursting it open with her teeth and releasing the buttery nut taste to join the mixture. Ah, what a wise woman. Most would wolf through the bag and have it finished before they even recognized the seasoning.

The man next to him with the briefcase open on his lap, shuffling frantically through papers, reading small portions and shuffling back through for more, was clearly one of the more successful men Samuel had encountered. He was the type who set day-to-day goals for himself on how much could be accomplished and was constantly breaking his own records.

The elderly lady asleep in her chair was almost certainly dreaming of her vast family and all the pleasant times they had together. Yes, it was still a wonderful world in his mind and he believed slowly but surely everyone else was realizing it as well.

It was while scanning these faces that he noticed another one looking back. She was smiling at the way he was studying everyone else. When his eyes caught hers, she quickly tried to look away. She giggled and put her hand over her mouth, embarrassed that she had been caught staring. She then looked back to see Samuel's reaction, which was a bright smile. She returned the smile, delighted by the moment they had just shared. Inspired by the immeasurable amounts of joy he felt surrounded by, Samuel hopped up and moved over to the seat across from the woman, never breaking his eye contact.

"Hello! My name's Samuel," he announced in a firm but cheery tone as he reached out his hand.

"Hey, I'm Leah," she returned as she shook it.

"Would you like to hear a funny story?" he asked in a tone that was humorously presumptuous.

"Well, I would love to hear a funny story," she responded in a similar tone.

He proceeded to tell an amusing anecdote from a recent day's work, which she couldn't help but giggle at. This led to a long and pleasing conversation that made the ride seem to fly by. They shared backgrounds and current situations. She was coming into town for business then heading straight back. He worked well to dodge his own purpose on the train.

They truly hit it off. She seemed to have no trouble keeping up with him intellectually and from the occasional long stare into each other's eyes while they were talking, it was clear they liked each other on a deeper level as well. The interaction contained an undertone of knowing that they would probably never see each other again. Their situations didn't allow them to pursue a relationship so they had no choice except to simply enjoy each other completely for the time being and not be concerned with anything more. That removed all the pressure and made for a very relaxing atmosphere.

As the attraction built and the signals were noted, Leah eventually explained that her business wasn't going to be for a few hours after they arrived. She really had nothing to do in the meantime. They briefly entertained the notion of getting something to eat, but they had both already admitted how long they'd been without a companion so it was awkwardly agreed upon that the time would be better spent if they were to rent a room.

Samuel's personality was at its height and his charm was unparalleled, right up until their plans for after their arrival in town were made. Though their situations and mutual fondness made such a rendezvous the perfect step, and it was indeed what Samuel wanted, his disposition fell a bit once it was set. He had never been with a woman other than Susan so he suddenly grew uptight. He tried to calm himself but it was as if another part of him was calling the shots. His uppermost consciousness still seemed at ease but he found himself fidgeting in his seat despite his attempts to stop. His wit dulled and the conversation stiffened. Though he couldn't admit it to himself, he was scared.

Once they arrived at the station they continued to Leah's car rental then drove to his car in the lot. They made a few dry comments about their difficulty finding the car and the traffic awaiting them outside, but nothing bringing the same ring of camaraderie they had on the train.

"You just want to follow me?" he asked when they reached his car.

"Sure. You're running the show here," she answered.

Samuel replied with a smile and hopped in his car. Due to traffic it took a good twenty minutes for them to reach the nearest hotel. He found himself trying to figure out exactly what he needed to say when they were reunited. He hemmed and hawed about how he should approach this sudden source of joy, a type of joy he had been without for months now. He started to feel the need to be delicate and careful, so as not to ruin what he had come upon—an approach that completely contradicted the way he had gotten into the situation in the first place. Eventually he became so nervous that the only solution was to block the predicament from his mind completely. The carefree, spontaneous man who had been on the train just a short while ago was gone, and he was sure she would be able to see that.

After they reached the hotel they found the nearest parking spots. As soon as Samuel got out of the car all the emotions he'd been pushing to the side hit him square in the gut so hard that he actually felt short of breath. He found himself grasping the few seconds he had before they were back together and the pressure was completely restored.

"Hey. You ready?" he asked senselessly.

"Sure. Lead the way," she answered with a confused expression on her face.

They continued into the hotel and straight to the desk clerk.

"We need a room," he announced proudly, in attempt to cover his uneasy feelings.

"Do you have reservations?" the clerk asked.

"No," he answered.

"Then I'll need a major credit card and a valid ID."

Samuel smugly pulled out his wallet and handed over both. The clerk then swiped the card and began typing on the computer. A few moments passed, along with some half-smiles and inane comments about the drive.

Then the clerk interrupted. "I'm sorry, it says this card is no longer valid," he announced as he handed Samuel's card and ID back to him.

Samuel immediately waved off the gesture, explained that there was some sort of mistake and that he should try again. He did, but there was nothing said during this wait, which ended the same way: rejection of card.

Samuel could almost feel his heart shrivel. It started to leak into his mind that he had never paid that much attention to what specifically happened to their accounts during the divorce. He had no idea if his credit card was still valid. It was the only card he had ever carried and he was unwilling to accept that he couldn't pay for this room. He demanded that the clerk try again.

"You know what?" Leah finally interjected. "The more I think about it, I really need to prepare for my conference anyway. I'd hate to go in there unfocused."

"Oh... are you sure? I know this is just some sort of misunderstanding."

"Yeah, I have some papers I really need to look over. How about we exchange numbers and we can talk sometime?"

"Well, that'd be nice," Samuel replied as calmly as possible.

They did. Then he stood broken as he watched her walk away for what would surely be the rest of his life. It was not only the pain of rejection he was feeling, but the cowardly shame that came with failing at something you knew you could have done better. It was his own fears and hesitations that made him incapable of handling the obstacles he'd just come across; that was perhaps the hardest part about it.

It was that drive home when he fell apart. When he lost that "everything is gonna be all right" feeling he'd had throughout his whole life. He finally let it truly enter his consciousness that he was alone. He was a man traditionally sheepish toward women who was now alone and might never have the courage to approach another one. The only person he had truly been close to was his mother, and she had just died after being somewhat neglected for the last years of her life. His best friend was in prison and there was no one to keep him from falling. He was stuck in a job that could never bring happiness and he'd thrown away his chances at the future he'd always wanted. What he was living for was nowhere in sight and he could barely keep his head lifted to watch the road.

A truly pointless existence—that was what he was living. His mind kept trying to drift to other things, like fictional characters from stories he'd written in high school and delightful people on his route he had never actually met. He knew he was trying to dodge his problems and he wouldn't let himself. He'd been dodging them too long. It was the first time he realized that his imagination had ceased to be an outlet for his creativity and had instead become a blockade to protect him from reality. It failed. Now reality was pouring down like a tidal wave on a rowboat.

When he arrived at his apartment he leapt out of his car without shutting the door and raced up the stairs to his home. Slamming this door behind him, he scurried through to his bedroom, where he began fingering through his dresser drawers until he found an old .38 revolver. He had figured out the only way he could solve his problems. There was only one solution to make this equation balance out.

He went to the bathroom, looked himself straight in the mirror and put the gun to his own head. He stared coldly back at himself. He felt no love for the person he was looking at. His idea of worth had always been derived from the affections of other people. His mother, then Susan, but now there was no one who cared what happened to him one way or another.

He fell to his knees with the gun still to his head. He could not pull the trigger. He hunched over in tears. He did not know what would come next after pulling that trigger and it terrified him. He could not bear to go on living but was too scared to take his own life. So the gun slowly slipped out of his hand and fell to the ground while he clutched at his own face as the tears continued to roll.

He continued sobbing profusely as he lay curled up on the bathroom floor. His body shook from crying so hard but still he just lay there. He couldn't remember how long he lay there crying. As he looked back he always felt like he could still hear his own moaning voice even while he dreamed.

When he awoke there in the morning, he cleaned himself up, got dressed and went to work. He kept up appearances and did everything he could to maintain a reasonable state of mind. Over the years to come, that's what he did, maintained. He felt fortunate that he had not taken off more time for his mother's funeral. If he had not had to go back to work the next morning, if he had sat alone in the apartment for any amount of time, he might not have made it. It was also an important decision to allow his imagination to continue to run wild. He hated the idea that it was a defense mechanism to avoid the real world, but if that was what he had to do to make it through, that was what he had to do.

He also had to cut back on the drinking and partying lifestyle he'd developed with Susan. He could handle it for periods of time but eventually he'd get too belligerent and spout off to uninterested people about how he'd lost the love of his life, or else he'd lose his grip and end up back in his bathroom with the revolver. When he drank it seemed to unleash all his deepest thoughts and feelings. He found it hard to hold in all the things he thought about but knew no one wanted to hear. When drunk he'd tell them anyway and start to dwell on the painful emotions he hid from. His social acquaintances had grown used to his occasional spells, but he knew he could only get like that so many times before something horrible happened. He cringed at the number of times he'd almost ended up on Susan's front steps. He tried not to think of the number of times that gun had been pressed against his head. Eventually he had to decide to stop drinking almost altogether. He still went out to see the boys or to play poker and had a beer or two, but he hadn't been drunk in years. He was fortunate to have made it through his binge days unscathed.

He made it through things one day at a time. He still had no feeling of purpose. He had no motivation to get himself out of bed in the morning. He just did it anyway. Occasionally his daydreams would offer thoughts of a mugger shooting him, or an out-of-control bus running him over. He'd always picture himself lying on the ground giggling. He'd thank the shooter or driver. They'd given him the relief he'd longed for. They'd relieved him the burden of living. He would be free at last from the relentless monotony of his pointless, inadequate existence. But then he'd snap himself back into reality. Moments of weakness like that would hinder his routine for survival. He tried not to think on them often.

All these memories swirled around his mind constantly. He hoped he'd learned and become a better man from all of it. But it was past time to be back to work so he zipped up his lunch pail, tossed it in his mail bag and started back to the truck.

CHAPTER 2: GETTING BY

It was a long work day for Samuel; Fridays usually were. His head spun from one thing to the next, which always helped pass the time. It made work he considered unbearable a little less harsh.

Amanda Parker was a reporter receiving paperwork on a top secret story about to break. Brendan T. Harden was an architect receiving a congratulations card from his mother for the completion of his first major structure. Joshua Cush was a retired firefighter whose wife had just passed away. He was getting boxes with complicated models that would help keep his mind off his recent loss. Benjamin Y. Lemon was a veteran from the Coast Guard receiving disability checks for injury on duty, a small consolation for a bedridden existence.

There was a large variety of situations for Samuel's characters. Some were ups, some were downs. This was not really the norm for him. They were usually more one-sided. Perhaps it was a mixture of happiness that the weekend had almost arrived but still sorrow because he knew it, as always, would pass in a flash. No change would have occurred to break the monotony by the time Monday had rolled around. He'd be right back there again, walking the same routes, wondering the same things to help him pass through the same unrewarding routine.

As long as the day was, it did finally come to an end. He rolled into the station around five in the evening.

"Hangin' in there?" asked his overweight and overly-concerned boss. Bob was the perfect superior. He worried about everyone. He was always trying to be helpful, even when it wasn't needed. His face was cherry red and his gut stuck out enough he could rest his arms on it. His good mood never seemed to fade, which sometimes frustrated Samuel.

"Yeah, another week almost in the books," he answered.

"You could call it quits now, take tomorrow off," suggested Bob. "Don't you got a poker game tonight anyway?"

"Yeah, but getting up in the morning will give me an excuse to leave before I lose all my money," joked Samuel.

"Well Samuel, I swear, you're trying to set a record for most vacation time saved. I can't remember the last time you took a day off. I'm just afraid one day you're gonna take it all in a row and I'll have to hire a replacement to fill in while you're gone."

"Ha-ha," Samuel chuckled genuinely. "They'd pro'ly get done so much faster you wouldn't want to take me back."

"Thank goodness for government-secured jobs, right!" Bob agreed in a razzing manner. He stared as Samuel headed into the locker room. He didn't remember the last time he heard a hearty laugh out of that boy. It struck him as a bit odd.

Once he reached the locker room Samuel immediately heard the bellows of his favorite coworkers, Brad and Jason.

"There he is!" announced Brad as Samuel walked in. "You getting twiltered tonight?"

"Yeah, maybe if he's drunk he can play better poker," added Jason.

"Joke while you can fellas, 'cause there'll be nothin' but tears when I'm leaving with your hard-earned funds," Samuel hollowly gloated. "Are the swine gonna be there?"

"You kno-o-ow it!" hooted Jason, clearly looking forward to their evening.

"Good. Maybe I can win back the money for my seat belt ticket last month," said Samuel.

That night, the poker game at Brad's house had trouble gaining momentum. Mark Harden, one of the police officers who was due to attend the game, was over an hour late and he was supposed to be bringing the other officer, Clint Hatcher. By the time they arrived, Brad had so many beers during the wait that he was talking about everything but the game. It was difficult keeping him focused enough to make his bet. To top it all off, Jason's wife and daughter were having a bitter ongoing argument about something trivial and repeatedly called his cell phone for him to referee.

After one of these calls became a particularly lengthy interruption, Samuel and Mark decided to step out to the back porch to have a cigarette.

"So how's the job treating ya?" asked Mark.

"Same as always, pays the bills. What more can you really expect? How 'bout the law enforcement world?" returned Samuel.

"Real good, actually. I've been puttin' in the hours, bringin' home the fat checks. This is the first weekend I've had off in over a month. Clint and I made a plan to get good and fucked up tonight to celebrate but it doesn't look like it's gonna happen at this pace."

"Yeah, I was planning on going home with a good portion of you boys' money but I haven't really got the chance," joked Samuel.

"You're dodging a bullet, you ask me," laughed Mark.

A few moments passed as they both stared up at the sky. Finally Mark broke the silence.

"Well, you ready to get this game going?" he asked.

"Yeah, I guess," answered Samuel in a faded tone.

"What's wrong with you?" inquired Mark.

"Man, nothin' really. Sometimes I just feel like I gotta find something new, you know?"

"How do you mean?"

"It just seems like nothin' ever changes. I just keep doin' the same shit with the same people making the same jokes. Sometimes I feel like I'm gonna drown in this endless circle of nothin'. I swear it's like my social life has less point than my work one does."

"What is it you want to happen?" asked Mark, still not sure what he meant.

"I don't know. Some form of happiness, I guess. Some break in the ice that'll let me feel like there is something to accomplish. I feel like I've been putting myself in some sort of protective shell for a long time and now that I'm startin' to feel ready to come out, there's nowhere to go."

"Well, maybe winning some money will help you feel better. Come on," said Mark as he headed back inside.

"I'll be in there in a minute," answered Samuel. The door closed, as did Samuel's eyelids as he felt himself losing grip. He had given up on anyone wanting to help. He had given up on people in general. But every once in a while he'd still try and reach out to someone. When he did, it was always the same, a quick fix or a blow-off, a complete lack of interest in him or his troubles. No matter how many times it happened, he was reminded that no one cared, and it still hurt like the first time.

He took a deep breath and clenched his fists to hold back the tears. He couldn't let anyone see him cry. The embarrassment alone would kill him. Finally he sighed as he felt the intensity of the moment pass and he started to regain his composure. He looked up at the black sky with the little pinholes of light. It was a helpful reminder of how small his problems were. There were others out there facing much worse. It wasn't some horrid thing that his friends didn't want to sit around and talk about what was wrong with their lives. It was natural. They came out to have a good time, not to get depressed.

Those were the things he'd try and remind himself as a way to put it all back on his own shoulders. It'd help him stop trying to find someone to share the weight. Though it brought him relief for now, it really just got the ball rolling. Trying to ignore his problems and negative thoughts would just put them into his subconscious, where they would start to build and build until a month from now, three months from now or even a year, when they'd catch up and hit him square between the eyes. Before he knew what hit him, he'd be back on the bathroom floor. Even knowing that, he had no other way to cope, so he did it anyway.

Now that he was relaxed again he decided it was probably a good time to make his exit. He headed back in to see the drunkest two in the room, Brad and Jason, arguing over the upcoming season in basketball and now Clint on his cell phone bickering with his wife about something. Mark looked up at Samuel immediately and started shaking his head at the fact that the game was still nowhere in sight.

"Yeah, I think I'm 'bout ready to give up this elusive poker game," Samuel announced.

"Fuck you!" hooted Brad. "You're not leaving here till you're signing over your paycheck."

"Well, as appealing as that sounds, I do got a route to run tomorrow."

"You got more excuses than a sixty-year-old virgin," snapped Brad.

"Ahh, I think I'm with Samuel on this one," joined Jason. "I do need to get home before Quinn strangles Courtney."

"Well, what's everybody got going tomorrow?" asked Mark. Everyone's faces remained blank as they looked around.

"I'm free," offered Samuel, eager for another chance to get out of the house.

"Beautiful. You guys all down to try this again, then? We'll get started early to avoid all these problems," suggested Mark.

Everyone agreed, including Clint once he got off the phone, and they headed home.

The next day Samuel went to work as usual. He slept well the night before. He didn't let his momentary weakness at Brad's bother him. It was routine, like everything else in his life. Occasionally something set him off. All he could do was try to focus, clear his mind and get back on course. It was a reminder not to attempt to get close to anyone. If he did eventually, if not immediately, he'd be disappointed or hurt again.

So he went to work and delivered the mail like he was paid to do, all the while daydreaming of anyone's life but his own. Occasionally he couldn't help but think about what he said the night before. How he really did feel like he might be ready to try and live life for real again. Then of course he got a small reminder of what it was like, and knew he couldn't risk getting close to anyone.

CHAPTER 3: GAINING A FRIEND

Thinking of friends made him wonder about David. If ever he had a friend, David was it. You never had to worry about getting too close to him, though. He was tough as nails, not exactly the sentimental type. But he was one who would listen to Samuel's problems whenever he'd get up the nerve to talk about them. Samuel had learned to be cautious in doing so. David wasn't one to hold punches. Sometimes his advice was a little too real for Samuel to handle.

It seemed likely that his life might be different if David was around. He would never have let Samuel mope through each day the way he did. He was the type to look out for everyone he cared about, and he cared about Samuel. He had kind of developed a big brother relationship with Samuel. It was odd since he was almost two years younger, but he lived the sort of life that made you grow up quick.

Samuel could still remember the day they'd met. It was soon after his relationship with Susan began. So it was soon after his dive into the party lifestyle.

After meeting Samuel, Susan almost immediately began taking him to all the social events. She was part of the "in" crowd, the type who never missed an opportunity to get high and/or drunk. Overnight Samuel went from a couch-warming homebody to a fast-paced socialite. This new world was exciting and intriguing to him, though at times he had trouble keeping up with the others. He didn't have the years of experience the other kids had, but his final months of high school were winding down and he wanted to enjoy every minute he could before it was over. Unfortunately, this attitude commonly resulted in an incoherent evening he'd need others' help to remember the next day. It was one of those evenings he'd met David.

Samuel, Susan and a few others were supposed to meet some friends at their house. Samuel couldn't remember who was driving that night, but he was certain none of them should've been. When they arrived at the house it was dark and there was no answer at the door. Susan went around to the back while the others went climbing through the bushes, knocking on windows. Though it should have been obvious their friends had not yet arrived home, the bunch were sure someone was there and were determined to be let in.

On nights like these, when there was a lot of trafficking from one place to the next, Samuel just followed the rest of the crowd. He didn't bother paying much attention. He just enjoyed the drunken state he'd entered and talked the ears off anyone who'd listen. He didn't concern himself with much else. Susan would shuffle him into the car or into the house as needed. It sometimes made for confusing mornings. Not having taken part in any decision making, Samuel had trouble remembering how he got from one place to the next. It was almost magical the way he seemed to just appear in new surroundings with new company. It always struck him as humorous when he looked back.

When the dilemma of getting in the house arose, Samuel remained in his usual role. He left it to the others while he stared aimlessly at the stars.

That's when he noticed a shadow flicker through a nearby streetlight. He scrunched his eyes to try and improve his blurry vision. There was a shirtless boy approaching with his chest puffed out in gloating fashion. Before Samuel could make out any other facial features he could already see the wicked blue eyes piercing through the dark. As the figure got closer Samuel could see he wasn't especially big. He couldn't be more than a hundred and sixty pounds. His ragged blond hair was messed into every direction and you could somehow see in his face a love for the mischief he had either just gotten into or was planning ahead for. More than likely, it was both.

"You think you could give me a ride?" the figure asked. "This isn't really my part of town. I was just at a party around the block. We had a misunderstanding, so I had to leave in kind of a rush."

As the young man reached him, Samuel noticed marks all over his exposed body. There were at least ten welts in the shapes of fists covering everywhere except his head.

"Man! Who'd you have a misunderstanding with?" questioned an astounded Samuel.

"I told you, 'the party,'" returned the boy matter-of-factly.

"The whole party!?"

"Damn near. They were pussy, though. Many of 'em as there were and they didn't even get me to the ground. Got me out the back door, though. I was swinging the whole way out. Caught the big one real good. He was the one who started the whole thing. They were lucky I was by myself. They'd've really been in for it if Kris and the rest of the boys had been there."

"Kris?"

"Yeah, Kris Caine, my older brother. That's what the whole thing was over. The guys there don't much care for him and they were stupid enough to come tell me about it."

"Oh yeah, Kris Caine—I remember him. He used to go to school with us, real good guy. Whatever happened to him?"

"He's around. Followed in the Caine tradition. Start a family, drop out of school, get a factory job. He still be hangin' out though. I can't wait to tell him 'bout this. He's gonna flip."

"I don't think anyone's here," Susan called out as she came back around the house.

"Hey Susan, come here. I want you to meet someone," returned Samuel. "This is . . . well, I guess I didn't get your name . . . but it's Kris Caine's brother."

"My name's David Caine," boasted the boy, proud to be known by his own title.

"I know who it is," she answered Samuel as she rolled her eyes.

"Well, he just got in a huge fight and needs a ride," explained Samuel.

"A fight—well, that's something new for you," stated Susan sarcastically, "Where're you going?"

"Over there in Post Edition. You think you could take me? It's a short drive but a hell of a walk."

"Yeah, why not. Maybe they'll be here by the time we get back."

David made a strong impression on Samuel that night. He was good and drunk and kept telling everybody he saw about how he was just standing there when a guy appeared out of nowhere with fist prints all over him, how this guy fought the whole party and all they really accomplished was ripping his shirt off. The next morning it was one of those memories it was hard to believe he got right. It was so weird to him the way David just popped up out of nowhere. He was amazed by the nonchalant way David referred to what he'd just been through. He continued to bring it up for days after. Susan was not nearly as enthused.

She knew David from the social scene. He was like most of the boys from the Post Edition neighborhood, always into trouble. The neighborhood probably consisted of about twenty blocks and it had a reputation like a slum. The difference here was that the houses weren't in bad shape and most of the families had paying jobs. The whole neighborhood just seemed to hold a common way of thinking, mainly among the youth. It was always mischief and action over there. Fights, shoot-outs, early pregnancies and a lot of prison terms. Post harvested trouble among their young the way farmers harvested cash crops.

The kids there were lifelong partiers. They came out of the womb with a cocky smile and wisecrack waiting. It was their constant jokes and tough-guy attitudes that kept them from saying anything sincere. It left them withdrawn for verbal affection, which might be prodded and made fun of if expressed. The affection instead made its way to the light through their actions. The quickness to take up arms for one another showed the brotherhood of the Post Edition.

It contained the real concentration of the factory rat population. All the kids in school who were too wild to keep their grades up or dropped out early could always get a decent-paying job in one of the countless factories in the city and continue their unproductive lifestyles. They birthed kids into single-parent, bar-hopping families who usually developed the same sort of lives, lots of liquor, occasional drug experimenting and a low respect for schooling. Most of the kids around there couldn't stand the idea of giving up the ongoing party. Some also couldn't stand the idea of wasting away in a factory. Those were the ones who usually ended up as the drug dealers or low budget thieves. David was a shining example of the "what we got to live for," "go out in a blaze of glory" mentality that seemed so common in his neighborhood. That made Susan uncomfortable with Samuel being so enthused with him.

She didn't know Samuel well enough yet to realize that it was a type of lifestyle he could never really adopt. That was why he was so intrigued by his glimpse of it. It was sort of like her intrigue with him. It's easy to be impressed by a person you know yourself incapable of being.

That wasn't the last time David made such an impression on Samuel. In fact the next time they met was quite similar. It was at a party on the outskirts of town, far enough out that the music could blaze without fear of police being called. The DJ was posted up just inside a barn in the backyard of the residence. His records were spinning, the speakers were roaring and it was hard enough to hear your own voice over the music, let alone over the screams of the massive crowd, bouncing up and down.

Samuel and Susan were nestled up close at the very back of the crowd. They were about as far from the DJ as possible without being antisocial. They commonly avoided being in the center of the mix at the big gatherings. There were a lot of over-opinionated people who didn't like Susan being with anybody but the super jock, Carl. Many people thought of them as the textbook couple. They in turn considered Samuel an unwanted obstacle to what was "meant to be."

She could usually avoid bringing Samuel around the wrong people but it was harder at the really large parties. Anything this large had everyone there, including Carl. She didn't think Carl himself would have the nerve to confront them out of fear of Susan's verbal wrath, but with all the alcohol around she didn't want to push her luck and knew there were others who wouldn't hold their tongues.

As they stood there safely on the outskirts of the party, Samuel felt a tap on the shoulder. He turned to see David, smiling deviously as ever.

"What's up, man!" he hollered as he gave Samuel five. "How ya been?"

"Well, I'm good. What 'bout you? Shouldn't you be fightin' somebody?" cracked Samuel.

David's face grew attentive while maintaining his smile. "Oh yeah, sure, I just got done." He pointed over his shoulder with his thumb, without even turning his head to look. "Now I can go start drinking for real."

Sure enough, about ten yards away was all the makings of a recently finished party brawl. A crowd of people were huddled around, all clearly excited. Some looked angry, others were laughing, but all were talking about what had just taken place. There was even an added cherry of a rather large guy crawling on the ground, holding his face to slow the blood spurting from the bridge of his nose, while a bunch of his crew girls tried to help him and show concern.

Then, there in front of the two of them, was David unscathed. His thin half-trench leather coat was still on and didn't have so much as a brush of dust. He stood calm, cool, collected and making chit-chat as if nothing out of his ordinary routine had taken place.

"Geez man, I was just kidding," said Samuel in a vacant voice, struck by what was intended as a sarcastic statement turning into an actuality.

"Hey David, come on! Somebody called the cops!" a voice called out from the crowd.

"Up. Sounds like my cue," explained David. "You guys want to join us for few drinks?"

"Nah, I think we're gonna stick around here yet. We'll catch up with ya another time," answered Samuel, still sporting a half-smile that was one part dumbfounded and one part delighted.

"All right, but this'll be getting broke up in the next few minutes anyway." With that he turned and began a half-sprint back to the car where the rest of his companions were already waiting.

Again Samuel was amazed by the encounter and couldn't stop talking about it. He'd start out with his initial meeting weeks ago, then lead into his joke that started the sequel. With each telling of the story his wording improved and the listener laughed harder.

"Man, if I had to hear you talk about David Caine one more time tonight I was gonna scream," said Susan as they made their drive home that night.

"I'm sorry. It just really cracked me up," apologized Samuel. "Hey, I didn't see Kris there. Did you?"

"No, you'll never see David bring Kris to handle some Penfield boys. It'd have to be something more serious than that. He can't stand being stuck under his big brother's shadow. He's put together his own group of flunkies to go around causing havoc with. I tell you, Post boys are like a virus. I can't even remember how many great parties I've been to that got broken up on account of them," preached Susan.

"Yea-a-h, but David's all right. He's just a little rambunctious," defended Samuel.

"Oh please! He might be the worst one. He's like five and a half feet tall and is always getting referred to as Kris's little brother. He's the epitome of having something to prove. It's that short man's disease that'll get him locked up or killed one day. Mark my words."

Samuel nodded, somewhat surprised at his own girlfriend's knowledge of his new favorite subject. She was almost right, though, just a little off. David was a natural-born big brother, strong-willed, protective and always helpful to those close to him. Unfortunately, socially, he was known as a little brother. It drove him nuts and did result in a lot of unnecessary trouble, but it was the big brother mentality that got him locked up. He always tried to control the world as it affected his people. That caught up with him eventually.

CHAPTER 4: STANDING UP

Samuel's friends nowadays saw him as meek. They would figure him likely to go out of his way to avoid a confrontation. To some degree they were correct. He would go to great lengths to avoid trouble, but more as one who felt he had nothing left to prove than as one who was intimidated. They would surely be surprised if they ever saw how he responded if backed into a corner. The ferocious attack would leave their jaws unhinged. Though emotionally Samuel was a pussycat, he had no fear when it came to a physical dispute. That was almost completely thanks to David's influence. It was he who first got Samuel to stand up for himself.

It was another crowded party outside of town, just after graduation. The guests included sort of a who's who of the youth's social scene.

Now that school was out and the sports were done, Carl the super jock didn't have the flock of groupie girls ready to please him as before. Now he was looking more to the future. He didn't like the idea that he couldn't include Susan in that future, especially since she was taken by some bookworm turned cool. As his frustration over this grew he made a habit of badmouthing and threatening Samuel through the grapevine.

Susan had grown accustomed to Carl's ranting behind their back without the nerve to confront them. She liked that Carl was intimidated by her temper. She let it balloon her ego into believing that he'd never dare approach Samuel, even if she wasn't around. So she didn't give it a second thought when a friend invited her to attend a liquor run while Samuel was busy talking to David on the back deck. She let him know that she was leaving and asked if he wanted anything. Samuel just waved her off and continued the joke-cracking and laughter he and David were partaking in. This was the first time they had ever got to have a real conversation. Samuel wasn't belligerent and David wasn't in the midst of battle.

Carl, who couldn't go more than five minutes without glancing over at the coveted couple, made quick note of Susan's departure. He rounded up his usual backers and fellow jocks then made his way to the deck. What quickly became a mass of people flooded the beginning of the yard and the stairs leading up to where the two were talking.

Certainly large portions of Carl's herd of backers were more than ready to take up his beef. But in a situation like this, exactly how many of the boys were truly willing to get involved was hard to determine. There were always a number of half-friends who would bunch up with a team just to look involved. Once anything actually popped off they backed away and watched the show. Later they would give the play-by-play and state that they would have gotten involved but it wasn't really their place. On the other hand, should the dispute remain verbal they would hold their ground, then later give the play-by-play and instead state that they were right up there in the mix to support whatever team had already won. The winner, of course, was usually easy to determine before the ruckus actually started.

In this case all these people were crowded around Carl, smiling playfully and waiting to watch what would surely be either the verbal or physical abuse of Samuel, eager to get the juicy details so later, they could be the one to tell the story best. Carl had been in a few fights, always coming out on top. He had also checked countless people. In both cases he only took on easy challenges but to the kids in those circles he was an undisputed champ.

The entire swarming of the opponents was so swift that Samuel hadn't noticed it until Carl had already begun insulting him. David caught it from the corner of his eye before Samuel. The size of Carl's entourage, along with his showboat barks, got the other guests' attention soon after. That resulted in quite the audience.

Anyone from their school could figure what was going on almost immediately. Fights like these brewed behind the scenes in whispers and predictions long before they came about. This one had been in the making longer than most. Everyone expected it the second Susan took on the unknown smart kid loner as her new boyfriend. Carl wasn't the type to pass up the chance to swing his dick around and look tough, especially not when it was a chance as unthreatening as this one.

When Carl first heard of the new couple he had been genuinely relieved. He had figured tossing Susan to the side would result in a lot of late-night nagging for him and harassment for whoever he was courting. When Susan instead decided on what he figured to be a ploy to make him jealous, he was delighted. He knew it would make all the last-chance, end of high school bedding he wanted to do run a lot smoother.

As time passed and it became clear that Susan's lack of heartbreak or even interest might indeed be genuine, he became furious, not just with the idea that he might really be losing his longtime girlfriend. Even more than that, he might be losing a competition. To him, everything was a competition.

He nailed most of the prospects he set after. Now he was ready to have Susan back. Though, knowing Susan, it didn't make any sense, he couldn't help believing that by making a fool out of Samuel and proving himself the better man, he would in turn win the prize of Susan back.

Making a fool of Samuel and showing him for the pussy Carl assumed him to be was all he really planned to do. He was the type who had always been praised by his elders, through sports and school accomplishments. The negativity that surrounded an actual all-out fist fight wasn't really his thing. Threats and showboating were more his style. It was not that he couldn't handle himself in a fight; he was a wonder when it came to physical activity. It just wasn't the way he usually handled things. He figured he'd flare his temper a bit, maybe even get some tears out of the kid, and the point would be proven.

Samuel remained running at the mouth right up until he was completely surrounded. There were sliding glass doors behind him, deck rails to each side of him and an event-craving mob in front of him.

". . . by this time I had no idea how much alcohol we'd killed or where we were but . . ." explained Samuel.

"Looks like you got company," said David as he pointed with a sideways nod toward Carl.

"Huh?" replied Samuel, caught off guard by David's interruption.

"So I heard you had some things to say about me you little punk!" began Carl. How he was going to approach Samuel was a touchy situation. He didn't want to make it obvious that this was over Susan, even though it was. It would be admitting someone currently had the better of him. He decided to pretend he heard Samuel had been badmouthing him, when it was actually the opposite. This allowed a verbal attack without losing face and without appearing to be a bully.

Samuel's head whipped around attentively to see who was yelling at him. The second he saw Carl, he froze like a deer. The realization of what was taking place swarmed over his brain. He had daydreamed about the possibility of a confrontation with Carl but never took it seriously. Susan always brushed it off as foolish talk among busybodies. Samuel had witnessed many of these party disputes. He talked about them countless times but he'd never been at the center of one. Everyone was watching. The embarrassment mounted with the pressure to save face was surreal.

"Did you hear me, you little bitch?! Why don't you talk some of that shit now, now that I'm in your face!" roared Carl, as he stepped closer to Samuel.

David was enough paces back that he appeared to be just another onlooker. He bent back calmly and picked up a can of beer from the cooler at his feet. As he waited to see how things played out he stared coldly at

Carl and shook the beer with a subtle, methodic pace.

"What the fuck you staring at!" hooted the huge black 250-pound lineman standing to Carl's right. It was obvious David's reputation was not yet widespread or the jock might not have been so quick to call him out. It was common for the disputer's "best man" to start something with whoever was standing with the opponent. It was a way to show their support for their friend. Sometimes the opponent didn't even have anyone there supporting him, but there was always someone nearby watching the show like everyone else. The stare could be used as cause to insult and bring into the mix this pawn that would serve the best man's purpose. David, standing at 5'9" and weighing about 170 pounds, must have seemed a fine candidate.

David remained calm, just smiled and waved off the attack. "I'm just watching the show, man. It ain't got nothin' to do with me."

Hearing a friend's voice snapped Samuel out of his daze, but hearing David back down made him all the more frightened by the sudden situation. Not having been involved in anything like this before, he didn't know that there was only standing up or backing down. There was no room for explanations or clarification of misunderstandings. Even if the misunderstanding was genuine the opponent would take an explanation as a sign of weakness and more than likely up the degree of his assault. If the opponent didn't look ready to fight the instigator could continue to look like superman without the inconvenience of a real brawl, thus making the explainer's situation worse.

"I-I-I don't kn-know what you're talking . . ." stuttered Samuel.

"Da-da-da!" laughed Carl at how obviously nervous his opponent was. "I don't want to hear no bullshit like that! All I want to hear is why you think you can insult me and say I ain't shit when I'm not around, but don't think it's gonna come back on ya! 'Cause that leads me to believe you might really think I'm not 'bout shit! And I know that's not what you think, now is it!?"

"But I never-r . . ." Samuel began again, now even more frustrated. He hated Carl already. He'd heard too many stories of how he'd treated Susan. He hated him and had always wished he'd get his, but Samuel was scared. It was a mixture of speaking in front of a crowd, having to perform without warning and threat of severe bodily harm all rolled into one. He couldn't help it. He was just scared.

"NAW, FUCK THAT!!" roared Carl. "You're not talking your way out of this shit! The only thing I want to hear out of you is 'I'm sorry, Carl, I should have never done that dumb shit and it won't happen again!'"

Samuel stood there, still frozen. There was no way he could bring himself to say something like that. He finally realized it wasn't a matter of what really happened; it was just a matter of Carl wanting to make a fool out of him. He was too scared to stand up for himself but he was too strong to cave completely.

"I'm waiting! Ya fucking punk!" beckoned Carl.

Then David very slowly and calmly walked the three paces to Samuel's side. Turning slightly so most of his back was to Carl and the crowd, he leaned over slightly and began to whisper into Samuel's ear. Carl's face curled up in outrage at this intrusion.

Samuel listened attentively to what David said. "I don't know what you think this big faggot motherfucker can do to you, but I swear on my mother, my sister and everybody I ever knew, that if you don't hit this pussy right now, I'll be the one fucking you up myself."

At the sound of David's voice Samuel knew he meant every word. His eyes sprang open wide with an entirely new level of fear. Without another thought his fist came from all the way back with a step behind it and landed directly on Carl's chin. His whole weight was into it and Carl dropped like a brick in water.

Immediately David stepped to his left and gave a Nolan Ryan worthy pitch of the shaken beer can square between the eyes of the massive lineman. Without bothering to watch the knees buckle, David grabbed up the nearby deck chair and charged into the approaching crowd as he screamed out, "K - K - R - R - I - I - I - S - S!"

At the sight of Carl and his lineman collapsing, every letter coat and wannabe jock charged the deck. At the sound of his name being screamed Kris realized his brother was on that deck. He, his immediate crew and every other Post boy at the party charged Carl's backers. As the crowd of jocks turned to see who was approaching them, their mouths dropped open at the recognition the Posties had part in this fight. Most tried to stand their ground. A handful actually removed their letter jackets and went into full sprint as if involved in their grand finale track meet.

When Carl dropped from Samuel's swing he was able to catch himself on all fours. Unfortunately for him, that was a perfect position for Samuel to deliver the field goal kick he was sending to Carl's face. The broken bones it caused in his foot may have made Samuel regret that choice the next morning, but at the time it had the desired effect.

Carl rolled to his back. From his shoulder blades on up was now hanging over the stairs of the deck. Though surprised and dazed, he remained conscious. He tried, somewhat in vain, to fight back. He leaned forward and grabbed Samuel's legs at the knees. This brought Samuel falling to a squatting position on Carl's chest. That gave Samuel useful momentum as he was thrusting another fist to Carl's head. The force to Carl's upper region started him sliding down the steps on his back. Samuel rode him down like a sled. He was able to average one solid stroke to the face for each step. Carl's eyes rolled around but there was no conscious thought left. Samuel kept swinging. He didn't stop swinging until David pulled him off.

When the fray was over it was deemed the largest brawl most had seen. Though the Post boys were outnumbered in participants, and severely outnumbered in pounds, it remained an almost completely one-sided massacre in their favor. Many of the jocks, including Carl, needed medical treatment; even those who didn't still discontinued attending parties in their hometown for fear of having a run-in with the attackers.

It was all different after that. David was a lifetime friend and Susan's opinion of the boys from Post Edition couldn't help but change. They had been there for her Samuel when he needed them. To her and Samuel both, the entire group moved from acquaintances to friends. They spent the rest of that evening partying in Post Edition, recapping what happened. In fact that was a good description of the rest of the summer. Even the preppy girls from school became accustomed to hanging out in Post. The guys they were used to spending time with didn't come out much anymore and Susan was always over there. It didn't take long before it was everyone's hangout. The Post boys enjoyed the new female element.

Overnight, Samuel went from a chick easing out of its shell to a full-fledged rooster. His psyche, personality, and relationship with Susan all flourished. He was so high on everything if his writing habits had still been intact it was likely he'd have produced an award-winning novel. Instead there was a lot more partying, laughs, smiles and memories he wouldn't trade for the world.

Very few challenged him physically after that. He had an instant reputation. A few guys may have thought he just got lucky and still considered him a mark they could use to make a name for themselves. But in time he was put to the test and the results were the same.

After a while, the joy of the after-fight hype wore off. Eventually it got so he didn't even like all the attention for such a negative accomplishment. At that point fighting became more of a last resort than a way to liven up an evening, but he always knew he could handle himself if he needed to. That made for a confidence he never had before.

CHAPTER 5: SOMETHING NEW

It was hard living without a friend like David, especially after he lost Susan. David was the type of friend who was always there when needed. He wasn't like the friends Samuel had now. It was hard to even call them friends. They were just the guys he spent his free time with when he couldn't stand to be alone.

He had lost track of the rest of the Posties. He hadn't spoken to David in some time. He knew David would likely ask more from him than he could provide. He'd tell Samuel to get out there and live his life. David would be disgusted with the way he'd shut himself off from the rest of the world, the way he moped through his days.

He had continued visiting and kept up the front for a while, but he could only fool a friend like that for so long. He had run out of fake stories to tell. He could sense David was on to him. He was starting to prod a little too much. So Samuel's visits turned to letters and his letters became few and far between. Now it was just one more thing he felt bad about, the way he'd neglected a dear friend.

Perhaps it was time to rectify that. He'd wanted something to break the monotony. Maybe a visit to David was just the thing. The next parole hearing was coming up soon. It was past time Samuel got in touch with him to find out the plans for his release.

For now it was time to get on with the route. Walk the sidewalk, drive the truck, and deliver the packages. Tonight he had a poker game. His disposition had risen a bit with the plan to visit David. He was actually looking forward to hanging out with the guys. Perhaps he'd pick up some fine cigars for the occasion.

As always, once back on the move his mind drifted from the game tonight to the packages in the bag. There was a large envelope for Edwin Andrews. Maybe it was the return on a patent for a new invention. Soon he'd be able to market it and make a fortune. Then he'd have the freedom to spend his time with his trinkets and gadgets. He'd be doing what he loved, trying to create.

Cecilia Harris was receiving a small box with the word "delicate" in red print. Delicate indeed—Samuel decided her high school sweetheart was in the military overseas. He'd finally got up the nerve to propose. Since he couldn't do it in person he sent her a gorgeous wedding ring in the mail with a small note that read, "Would you be mine?" It was probably a ring that his grandmother had worn for her marriage and passed on to his mother, who passed it on to him to give to the person who gave his heart the joy she had given his.

Corey Gristini had a small envelope mixed in with the junk mail. It had classy penmanship, obviously from a woman. The return name was Melinda Megan Gristini. It was probably his grandmother. Every year she sent him a card with a check for twenty dollars on his birthday. Even though he was a man now she continued the tradition for sentimental reasons and he appreciated it.

Ah, Monique Romano—it was her regular monthly envelope. This was one of Samuel's favorites. With her slightly exotic name and an orange-tan envelope, two and half inches tall by six and a half inches wide, Samuel always imagined her as married to some criminal mastermind. The envelopes were about an inch thick and could give the impression they were filled with money. There was never a return address.

Two weeks ago Monique had hired movers but she didn't move. Samuel saw them come and start boxing up her stuff but she was still there the next day. He could see in the windows when he delivered mail. Almost everything in sight had been boxed up. All the furniture was in boxes. Then, a few days later, it was shipped out UPS. That must have cost a pretty penny. She lived in a large, expensive house, yet she always seemed to be home and he'd never delivered mail for any other resident. It all played into Samuel's crime fantasy nicely.

She was prepared for a quick move but hadn't left. Samuel decided that her lover had pulled a big score a while back and was just sending her enough to get by on until the heat was down and he could make his move. When the coast was clear he'd send the whole score. It'd be easier for him to travel if he didn't have to be concerned about concealing the large quantities of money. No one was on to her. She could take the money and meet him at the rendezvous point where she had already sent their stuff. Then they could be together at last, living the good life. Now she was just waiting on the package. Then she'd be off in a hurry.

As Samuel made his way up to her house he looked into his bag to see who he'd be delivering to next. Deon Benton was receiving numerous letters from movie and music clubs. He was probably a trendy type of guy with a knack for all things considered cool. He certainly had a large collection of music and DVDs. Samuel figured Deon's friends to view him as a sort of connoisseur of such things.

Samuel made his way up the steep hill that was a driveway and halfway across the sidewalk that went parallel to the Romano house. He opened up the mail slot to drop in the envelope when the front screen door burst open and out came a young boy barreling down the hill; then came his mother chasing after him.

"Cullomine! Cullomine, you stop right there!" she hollered. It was the recipient of the envelope, Monique. She sprinted to catch up with her son. Her long, deep brown hair was in a braid and followed her stride like a snake. She caught up with little Cullomine before he was too far down the hill and scooped him up, laughing all the while.

"You little hon-yok. I can't let you out of my sight for a moment." She turned to head up the hill when she noticed Samuel standing there. "Oh!" she yelped, a bit startled. "I'm sorry, I didn't see you out here. I guess it's good timing, though. I wanted to talk to you."

Samuel stood there dumbfounded. He had seen Monique from a distance and noted her to be a pretty woman, but he had never seen her up this close. He was stunned by her engulfing beauty and the fact that she was speaking to him. She had a golden tan complexion that set off her deep brown hair and clear hazel eyes. She spoke with a thick but understandable Latino accent that emphasized her exotic appeal.

After an instant Samuel came to his senses and replied, "Well, what can I do for ya?"

"I have an urgent package coming here soon. In fact, you might have noticed I am all packed up to move, but I can't leave until it arrives. It should be a black cardboard box about the size of a briefcase. Would it be too much trouble for you to keep an eye out for it? I'd like to know the instant it arrives. I'm always home and I'm usually out by the pool in the back here," she explained as she pointed to the side of the house that was lined by a trail leading back. "If when it arrived you could bring it right back to me, I would be extremely grateful. In fact, if you just wanted to start bringing my mail back there, that'd be really great. Then I know you'll be in the habit and won't forget."

Samuel was again paused in place, this time for a completely different reason. What she had just said correlated perfectly with his daydream. His head spun between reality and his own make-believe world. It caught him completely off guard. He'd always thought that as much as he dreamed about people and their lives, it stood to reason that he would be right sometimes, but this still struck him as an outlandish coincidence.

Taking his pause as resistance she started in again, this time in a cuter, more desperate tone. "Please, it'd only be a few more yards for you but a huge help for me."

He snapped out of his daze. "Oh yeah, sure. That would be no problem at all. It'd be nice to do something a little out of the same old routine."

"Well, good. I can't thank you enough," she said as she headed into the house. She turned to see Samuel off. "So I'll probably see you in the next day or two?"

"Count on it," he said confidently, hiding his nervousness at conversing with a beautiful woman.

How could this be? It was natural for him to tie her delay in moving into something related to him, the mail. Still, what were the chances that after thinking she was waiting for a package before she could leave, that would actually turn out to be the case? Was he right about all of it? Was she waiting on a shipment of money? Could he have actually nailed it that square on the head? The curiosity brought a level of intrigue he had not known in what seemed like a lifetime. His mind was racing. It felt great.

How could she afford a house that nice in a neighborhood like this one, yet she said herself she was always home? There was no sign of a job. Wouldn't it be even more outlandish for him to deduce from his evidence a reason for her to be waiting for a package of money, then to have it only be half-right? To have her waiting on a package before she could leave, but it was containing something else. She said "the size of a briefcase," the typical container for large portions of illegal money in any movie or novel.

I must be crazy, he thought. There's no way he could be right about all this, but those envelopes did have the ring of money. They were the perfect size and a dark color so they couldn't be seen through.

Now he was a little frustrated. He knew the curiosity would consume him, and how could he ever find out for sure? He had to know if he was right. There was no real reason. He just needed to know.

He would get to see her more often now, after agreeing to bring her mail directly to her. Maybe there would be some clue to tip the scale as to what she was waiting for.

What does it matter? he tried to tell himself. It was a very trivial thing. If he had something in his life he enjoyed, he was sure he wouldn't be nearly so interested. But he didn't have much of anything in his life. He always tried to tell himself he didn't need any hobby or people in his life. Everyone else just used things like that to distract themselves until the day death caught up with them. He tried to tell himself he wouldn't live that way. He tried to tell himself he only needed the basics in life to get by. It was agitating whenever it became so apparent that he was wrong.

He knew he was going to dwell on and look forward to her deliveries to no end. The small mystery was the most interesting thing to crack the mold in years. On top of that Monique had quickly taken the role in Samuel's mind as the most beautiful woman he had ever met. Just to look at her, let alone talk to her, was sure to brighten his day without fail. He could already feel himself becoming addicted to this situation. It would be worse for him than a drug addiction was for some. It would consume his thoughts. Even the few things he enjoyed now would likely become an obstacle of time until he was talking to her again.

". . . something out of the routine." He thought back on what he said with animosity. She was probably considering what a silly thing that was to say right now. What did she care if it was out of his routine? He was very frustrated with himself. Just a small statement like that was a sign of him reaching out. He was trying to tell someone about his life. He'd spent countless hours convincing himself that no one cared about him and here he was trying to tell someone about his life. He thought it important to remember that no one cared so that he could avoid being hurt. He looked at himself as hopelessly stubborn when he tried to pretend that people had anything but trivial interest in him.

She doesn't care that you don't like your routine. She's probably wondering why you brought it up, he thought to himself. Then came an all-too-familiar wave of self-loathing. One that always put him back in the niche he'd found in life. This sinking feeling usually rode on different memories of neglect. He'd go down a spiral of pity as he pictured an assortment of things that ranged from his wife leaving him to being cut off mid-sentence by someone who was clearly not listening to begin with. Every little detail he could come up with to remind himself that no one cared. As sorrowful a state as this was, he had grown accustomed to it. There was something empowering about accepting that you were in things alone. If no one was concerned with you, you didn't have to concern yourself with anyone else. It was the removal of any and all responsibility toward your fellow man.

This wave of sorrow commonly came directly after a glimpse of hope. This was a perfect example. He liked this girl on his route, liked the idea of getting to know her, an opportunity presented itself and he started to think about what it'd be like. Within a few minutes, as if preprogrammed to do so, in came a reality check that told him that it was not really going to happen. He was just hoping for something he was not going to receive. So rather than risk disappointment, he cut right to it. He reminded himself that he was all alone in things and it was pointless to think of anything else.

He'd continue to think of all the times in the past he'd been let down. As many as it took until he remembered that was the only reality there was. At that point he was so depressed he couldn't keep his head from staring directly down at the sidewalk in front of him. Thank goodness for his daydreams, which could now be fueled by the extra intrigue in his life. They were all that kept him out of the gutter.

He continued down the sidewalk in his duties and drifting thoughts. Lonnie Cotton was a lonely, bitter old man without a friend in the world.

He was constantly sending his second cousin from Wisconsin letters of no consequence. His cousin was the only person left who was still nice enough to respond. He wouldn't answer Lonnie's calls but did write back occasionally. He really didn't have anything to say but the human contact was appreciated.

Adam Joseph was a formerly successful stockbroker. Unfortunately for him, he got cocky on a bad hunch and invested the bulk of the stocks of the bulk of his clients. It went through the floor and he ended his career in record time. The letter from Brenda Joseph was a response from his mother after having received a letter from him explaining such. It had been six months since his downfall and he'd been too nervous to inform his demanding mother. Now that he had he was sure to receive a written lashing that would accentuate what was already unbearable.

Samuel continued pumping out thoughts of this nature for the rest of the day. He had sunk into rare depressed form. When he stopped for his lunch he had no appetite. He didn't eat; he just sat on his traditional bench, thinking.

Later he passed a hungry derelict woman on the corner. She was carrying a sign that read "will mow lawn for food." She was one of the typical walkers of this town. Between crack and heroin sales, the war vet hospital and all the halfway houses in town, there was no end to people like her wandering the streets. There was no neighborhood off limits to these decorations to the local sidewalks. He glanced down at the lunch he hadn't touched, but he didn't give it to her. He didn't want to help her. The world had rejected him so many times that he felt obligated to reject it back.

When he reached his truck he thought about the woman. In truth, he didn't care what was wrong with her. He had no desire to help. If he'd given her his lunch and she had shown the least sign of joy it would have been a smack in the face to him. To see a glimpse of what his life was so completely void of would have been too much to handle.

He smirked as he thought what a far cry he was from the Samuel in high school. He could remember going to the airport on the occasional weekend. He'd sit by a gate amongst the people waiting for the arrivals. With each person stepping off the plane he'd see another person or group of people hop up, smiling brightly. They'd exchange hugs and greetings. It overwhelmed Samuel with a sense of contentment and peace at the sight of all that genuine pleasure. He would watch the similar scenes repeat themselves. He'd hypothesize, based on the greetings, how long it'd been since the two parties had been together. He'd describe some of the reunions in his journal, while others he'd just let soak through his mind. Some days he'd spend hours at the airport just watching the joy of others. His eyes would gloss over and he'd enjoy a euphoric daze that could last for hours.

What different times those were. He wished he could go back and talk to the Samuel of old. Maybe that boy could tell him whatever it was he'd forgotten, remind himself of what it was like to enjoy living. Of all the people to end up where he was, it didn't make sense sometimes. What was even worse was that feeling that somewhere inside he knew the answer and just couldn't bring himself to see it.

CHAPTER 6: A LITTLE SHOVE

That night Samuel was looking forward to the card game. Once he accepted his life philosophy of being destined to be alone, he would usually feel resolved. Within a few hours he'd feel free. He was untouchable by the reckless hands of man. It was the rainbow after his storm of depression. This time he had the interest in today's strange circumstances to set his mind on as well. Now he was going to the game with a chin up. Perhaps he would actually win some money for once.

When he reached Brad's he saw that though a little early, he was the last to arrive. That was a good sign. It meant everybody was ready to get a game going. When he stepped in the back door he was greeted with a synchronized "He-e-y-y!" followed by Brad announcing that the game could begin.

"Grab a beer and pull up a chair," added Brad.

"Yeah, and don't forget your wallet," cracked Jason.

"We got poker chips again?" Samuel asked at seeing them stacked on the table.

"Yeah, but we're paying first to avoid anybody running off after losing their ass, and then blaming it on the alcohol," explained Mark.

"Probably a good idea. We all know how you get," Samuel returned.

"Oooh," applauded the bunch.

Mark just raised one cheek in a genuine smile and blew it off. "Oh, we'll see. Let's let the cards do the talking."

The game went well. There were a lot of wisecracks, followed by hearty laughter, with surprisingly few interruptions. There was plenty of beer to go around. After a few hours of play the shirts began to unbutton and the faces began to glow red. Samuel always figured this should be his time to flourish since he was the only one who kept his drinking to a minimum, but it never worked out that way. Someone would always start an off-topic conversation that would slow the game. The fellow drunks would start to pay more attention to it than the card play. Still, Samuel never seemed to get to capitalize.

Clint's face was particularly red. His hair had taken on an interesting style. He had a typical short-haired cop cut but it was still long enough for him to pull at when he was thinking. Unfortunately, it wasn't much of a tell. Once he'd had a couple of beers he pulled at it every time he got his cards, good or not.

Being the drunkest, it was he who started the first off-topic conversation. "Did I tell you about little Clint Junior?" asked Clint, making reference to his son. Everyone looked up attentively, gesturing that they didn't know what he was referring to. "Well, hell if the wifey didn't find a sack of marijuana in his sock drawer."

"Ahh, don't give it much worry," reassured Brad. "All the kids do it nowadays. It's even more popular than when we were his age."

"Well, it's not just that he had it. I guess I expect it here and there. It's that the dumb shit left it in his sock drawer," explained Clint. "I think I got a full-fledged, certified idiot for a son. If he gave it a half a second's thought he'd've known his mom would find it."

"That's true," added Mark. "Under the bed, in a hat—anywhere would be better than in your sock drawer."

"Shit yeah," started Clint again. "It wasn't even in a sock or nothing. Just sittin' out where she could see it. Now he's got wifey all in a huff, so she's stressing me out. I don't like that shit. It's like he's either an idiot or he wasn't worried about me finding out. Either way he's gonna end up with a night stick up his ass. That tends to get the head screwed back on straight."

"I bet you he's shaken now that it's missing," added Samuel.

"Speaking of drugs," began Mark, changing the subject, "guess who the fuck's up for parole in a few weeks?"

"Who?" asked Jason. Samuel's ears perked; David was up for parole in a few weeks.

"Cullomine Torreo!" announced Mark.

"That piece of shit!" roared Clint. "They should have thrown the key away as soon as they got him in there."

"I think I heard of him," said Kyle.

"I got no idea who you're talking about," said Brad.

"Never heard of Cullomine, huh?" began Mark. "He's pretty much an overrated middle man. We're dead center between Detroit and Chicago. That's why we've always had such a drug problem. But as bad as it was, it got considerably worse when Cullomine hit town. He's part of a prestigious drug cartel that makes up a large portion of the key players on both coasts. His staking claim here was the beginning of their operations here in the Midwest. You can pretty much guarantee the second he gets out, the streets are gonna be flooded again."

"What are the chances he's getting out?" asked Clint.

"They say it's pretty much a sure thing," explained Mark.

Samuel listened closely to the explanation. Before he knew it his private puzzle boasted another potential piece. Cullomine was the name Monique had called that boy. It was an original name. Samuel had never heard it before, yet now he heard it twice in one day. He tried to keep himself from connecting the dots. *It is too perfect,* he thought, but it wasn't long before his mind was racing again.

Here she was waiting for a package, all prepared to move, and a man carrying the same name as her child was up for parole. It even fit with the original theory, though a drug dealer wasn't exactly the criminal mastermind Samuel had anticipated.

That was it. It was too juicy for him to ignore. He had to try and figure out more. What better place to start than the prison? Surely David could tap the prison grapevine and could probably find out everything Samuel wanted to know. He already wanted to visit David so this sealed it; he was heading up north.

CHAPTER 7: LOSING A FRIEND

A week later the arrangements had been made and he was on the road. He was nervous about seeing David. Looking back, he couldn't believe he'd remained absent so long, the fruits of this endless circle of depression. He wasn't sure how David would treat him after all this time.

Samuel hoped he hadn't really noticed, but he knew better. David didn't allow any other visitors. To see family or old Posties would be hard on him. He didn't like getting sentimental. His only contact with them was over the phone. Samuel, however, he did let visit. He liked to hear Samuel's insight on things. It helped him with his own decisions. Plus, seeing him wasn't so much a slice of home. He was his outsider friend.

Samuel felt guilty for having not been more respectful with his visiting privileges. He couldn't help it, though. He wasn't capable of maintaining a relationship with anyone at that point. David's stern tongue made it all the harder. He could see Samuel backing into the emotional cave he was now in. He tried to keep him from it. Samuel needed that cave to survive, and David was an obstacle to it. He hoped he could understand without having to be told. Samuel was sure he would. Maybe he'd have to vent with some harsh words first, but he'd come around.

It was time for him to come back to the real world. Deep down, Samuel hoped the return would help bring himself back as well. That was the strongest motive for the visit. The gumshoe curiosity was just lubrication helping him get there.

It was strange to think of David in a cell, such a free spirit confined. He hoped it hadn't taken its toll, that David was still the same man who went in.

Perhaps he had been too free-spirited but it wasn't the only thing that got him where he was. No, he was locked away for another part of his personality. Despite being a wild one he was the type who believed certain things should be a certain way. He was willing to do whatever was necessary to make them that way, especially when it came to his loved ones. He would protect them to the death, or to confinement, as the case was. It was that big brother philosophy and his free-spirited application of it that put him behind bars.

Samuel could still picture perfectly the day of the arrest. He had just finished his route and Susan was off visiting family. He headed over to pay David a visit on Wendell Street, right in the heart of Post Edition. When he pulled to the house and got out of the car, he was startled by a barking dog jumping energetically in the neighbors' yard. It was a big dog. It was part Great Dane, but not full-blooded. Post boys loved their dogs. They always had stories to compare about whose dog was the most vicious. It was usually Pit Bulls, Rottweilers and other purebreds though. It was out of the ordinary to see this mutt out barking. Its front paws were resting on the fence while large amounts of drool oozed from its wide open mouth.

Couldn't blame him for drooling; the day was a scorcher, one of those humid days where the fan just made you hotter.

When he entered the front gate Samuel could hear David hollering in the house. He still lived with his mom and sister. His sister was enrolled in school but she had reached the age where she didn't bother attending often. David and his mother worked at the same factory. They did pretty well for themselves. His mom owned the house and he paid the utilities. It allowed plenty of leftovers.

It was a fun time for Samuel. He was just out of school and bringing home real paychecks. He had a car, his own residence and the girl he loved. His friends all worked so it wasn't like before when they had to scrounge up drinking money. It was more like they were playing grown-up than actually being responsible. It was entertaining to him. He liked meeting the boys after work for a brew, then going home to his "wifey."

David came out the front screen door and slammed it behind him. He looked up to notice Samuel approaching from the front steps. "Ah, what up, man?" He opened the door back up and screamed like it was an insult, "Hey Ma, bring me out another beer."

"You just got one," she responded.

"Don't fuckin' worry about what I got."

He let the door close and turned his attention to Samuel. "Fuuuuck!" he squeaked as he shook his head. "The fuckin' women in this family." He took a seat on the top porch step and sprawled out. He had his button-up factory shirt undone and hanging to the sides. His white undershirt was dingy with sweat and they were both untucked, hanging low. His belt too was loosened and his overly baggy jeans were barely staying up.

His mother came out to the porch with a beer. David tipped back his own for a drink and gestured to Samuel to indicate the recipient to his mother. She handed it to him and started back in on David.

"It's not my fault what she does. You don't have to take it out on me."

"Oh yeah, you're just her mother. You ain't responsible at all," said David sarcastically.

"As if I ever had control over any-a you kids," she returned.

David just waved his hand at her like he was swatting a fly. "Just take your ass inside and leave me the fuck alone," he ordered, more like the parent than the child. She did.

Samuel opened his beer to take a drink and went halfway up the steps, where he leaned back on the porch railing. "Man, what they got you so worked up about?" he asked.

"Shit, really it ain't even her. It's Missy's punk ass. She just ain't here so I gotta take it out on Ma."

"What her little ass do now?"

"What she doin'. As in right now, as we speak. How many times I told her about dude and she's out eating with him right now. She shouldn't have been so dumb as to tell Mom. Should have known she'd tell me."

"Who she with?"

Just then, the dog next door interrupted with resounding and meaningless barks.

"Fuckin' mutt!" roared David. "Luke! Hey Lukas!" he screamed at the house. The side window opened and Little Lukas Bailey's head popped out.

"What!"

"Why the fuck you gonna get that mangy dog, then leave her outside all the time, so we gotta listen to her bark?"

"Him. It's clearly a him, and I ain't got the money to get him fixed and he tries to fuck anything he gets close to. I caught him trying to slip it to my grandmother while she was asleep. Look at the fuckin' thing. It's got a constant nonstop hard on. I swear he's gotta be breaking some kind of record."

Samuel and David both laughed. Sure enough as he was up resting on the fence you could see plainly he was prepared for any action that might come his way.

"Yeah, laugh it up. If you want to pay for him to get fixed, then I'll bring him inside," explained Lukas before slamming the window closed.

"He might as well get rid of the damn thing. What good is a mongrel like that anyway? Ike-o in there would tear it in half," said David as he gestured inside to his hefty Rottweiler. "Anyway, what the fuck were we talking about?"

"Missy."

"Oh yeah, she's out with Tim Russell right now."

Samuel's eyebrows rose. This was an issue. Tim Russell was a small-time drug dealer who lived four houses up. He was a cliché in this neighborhood. The type who would never get a job and took all the rap music he'd listened to over the years way too seriously. He made his lifestyle obvious, which kept the authorities watching Wendell Street. That got everybody pulled over on a regular basis. It frustrated the boys that driving down to the corner store would be risky with a beer in hand, due largely in part to Tim and his ilk. Tim stayed in and dealt out of his grandmother's house. Another thing David found despicable.

None of those details really mattered, though. David hated dealers in any situation. "Cats who are too pussy to rob and too weak to work deal," he'd always say. That wasn't really the problem, though. Kris had a different dad than the younger two. Their dad had been a career drug dealer. He left 'em high and dry when they were young. The only memories he did have of his dad were the beatings he and the rest of the family took. The only thing he had to remember him by was a scar on the top of his chest. If the collar on his shirt was low enough you could still see it.

His dad took manipulating their mother as almost a sport. One time when she hadn't behaved as he told her, he put his cigarette out on their baby David's chest as punishment. She was holding him at the time, leaving her with no way to stop it. To try and resist or struggle would have risked dropping the child. She knew he wouldn't hesitate to make him fall. She watched in horror as the hot box fused into her three-month-old child's flesh. It had the desired effect. She did as she was told for long after.

She didn't stand up to him again until she became pregnant with Missy. He insisted she have an abortion, but she refused. She contended it was her choice and she wouldn't do it. He gave her a beating to remember but both she and her unborn baby survived. She didn't waver and he, uninterested in having another "screaming piece of shit" running around, finally left the family altogether. As soon as he was gone Mother Caine went out and had both her children's last names switched to hers. When Missy was born she was given the same and they became the Caine family. She swore never to let another person in. It would just be them from then on. She wouldn't risk having another person tear at them the way he had. She stuck to it. It was the only strong thing she had ever done.

But for her it was too late to prevent the damage. Any self-esteem she had started out with was ripped from her. She still woke up with night terrors. Her kids were young and vulnerable again and it was her job to protect them from something stronger than her. It took its toll over the years. She didn't go out much and really only associated with a few of the local girls she grew up with.

It was at that young age David accepted his dad wasn't coming back and he couldn't rely on anyone else to take care of him or his family. Because of his dad's abandonment, his abuse and the broken woman he'd left as David's mother, he always hated drug dealers. Kris felt the same way, not so much because of his mother or the beatings he'd taken; it was really because his brother felt so strongly about it. When it came to David, Kris didn't care whether he was being unreasonable or completely in the wrong, Kris was just interested in what was going to make him feel better. Whatever it was, that's what he would do. He'd bust open the head of every dealer he came across if he believed it was what David needed.

So for Missy to befriend a dealer, let alone date one, was not something either of the Caine boys would bear. To top it all off, Tim was almost as old as David, which made him entirely too old for Missy.

"Shit," replied Samuel, "I can't believe he's dumb enough to try and rub up on her."

"Dude ain't got no sense."

"I knew he was dumb but not that dumb. She's a smart girl, though. She won't get in over her head."

"Fuck . . ." began David as he scratched the top of his head, "I hope not."

Before they could say another word a girlfriend of Missy's pulled up to the house and Missy got out of the car. She didn't look at either Samuel or David while attempting to march right by them. Before she could get to the top step David calmly grabbed her ankle. She looked down at him with a beet-red face.

"So did you have a good time?" he asked condescendingly.

With that Missy flailed into a frenzy. She kicked her leg free from his hand and threw her purse at his head, screaming all the while, "It's none of your fucking business! You're not my daddy! You don't worry about what the fuck I'm doing!"

Her hollers came from the back of her throat with a passionate curdle in her voice. Her eyes quickly welled up with water and tears rolled down her cheeks. David didn't give much response, just a wide-eyed expression, followed by a quick hop to his feet. It went without saying that Missy would get mad, perhaps even blow up at him, but not with the type of screams she was using. It wasn't the words she used, but the tragic tone behind them. Missy wasn't the type to shed tears easily, and if she was going to cry, rest assured, she wouldn't let anybody see.

She turned and ran into the house, slamming the door behind her. You could almost see the gears turning behind David's eyes as he tried to make sense of what had just occurred. Then he must have realized, because there was a sudden burst of energy as he shot into the house and up the stairs where both the women were.

Samuel at first expected to hear screams and bickering when David went in. But when he heard nothing his gears, too, began to churn. The silence seemed to be explaining more than words ever could. It wasn't just a lack of talking. It was that thick stillness that is experienced at funerals or car accidents. Slowly Samuel started to realize what must have happened. Though he didn't want to accept it, he also realized what it meant. After he waited what seemed like an eternity, he could finally see David descending the stairs. He had a calm urgency in his pace. Samuel could see him fiddling with something in his hand. As he grew closer Samuel could see it was his chrome .44 caliber revolver being loaded. He stuck it in the front of his pants and pulled his T-shirt down over it. When he came out the door and down the porch steps, Samuel didn't say anything. There were no futile attempts at logic or reason. He just followed him out the gate.

To Samuel's surprise he didn't turn left, but instead right toward Lukas's. He began petting the hound softly on the head.

"Mouse!" he yelled. "Mouse, get your ass out here and bring a leash."

After a brief wait Lukas stuck his head out the window again. "Wu'd you say?!"

"I said, get your ass out here and bring a leash!"

"We taking the dog for a walk?" he asked.

"Just hurry the fuck up!!" roared David as his face went white.

In what seemed like almost instant response Lukas burst out the front door with leash in hand. He recognized the urgency David displayed and reacted not out of fear, but like Samuel, wishing to show support.

The three, accompanied by the pouncing mutt, headed in the opposite direction up the street. The same mission pace as before was used by David, and so by his companions, until they reached the residence four houses down. The road took a slight curve so Missy and her mother could see perfectly out the window as the four entered the gate.

Once inside David handed Lukas the leash.

"All right, you stand here waiting with the dog until I tell you otherwise. Samuel, I need you to go to the door, knock, and ask for Tim. Once he comes to the door I'll take it from there. Make sure you stand directly in front of the door so they don't see Lukas. Once he comes out you go outside the gate and wait. From then on, you just happened to be passing by and stopped to watch the show. Don't get involved again unless completely necessary. Lukas, once I give you the okay you're gonna join Samuel outside the gate," David explained his plan quickly and clearly so his friends could understand. They nodded their heads and obeyed like well-trained soldiers.

As Samuel walked to the door to knock, David followed close behind until they were on the porch. He then stood with his back against the wall just to the left of the door. Samuel could see someone begin to rustle in the kitchen as soon as the porch steps squeaked. They were already on the way when he knocked. It was Tim. Before he even reached the door he spoke up.

"Do I know you?" he asked suspiciously. He continued toward the door until he reached and opened it.

Samuel began to respond divertingly, "Yeah, I live just up the street and been meaning to ask you . . ."

Before he had to finish making something up Tim stuck his head out the door, which was all David needed. David grabbed him by the collar of his shirt and yanked him out on the porch. Tim spun around to see who it was. By the time he turned, David had pulled the gun out of his jeans and pressed it against the center of Tim's forehead. Tim's face dropped. Though he'd probably spent a lot of time imagining it, it was clear he'd never been in a situation like this one. He stood speechless, looking into David's sharp blue eyes. Before David had a chance to say a word, Samuel had already made his way clear and was waiting outside the fence as instructed.

"Turn around and head down the steps," he ordered so only Tim could hear.

Once they got about halfway between the porch and fence, David told him to stop and he began new instructions. "Drop your pants and boxers to the ground."

"Fuck that!" responded Tim, who had apparently gained some courage. David responded by firing a shot in the air. Tim responded by dropping his pants. The crackle of the shot was as frightening as was needed, but since David obviously had no fear of getting caught and going to jail, Tim had to figure he might not be worried about killing him. As soon as the pants were down David thrust the butt of the gun into the back of Tim's head. He fell to all fours.

"Come here," said David to Lukas. Then he pressed the gun against the back of Tim's head and began speaking to him again. "If you move any one palm or knee from where they are right now it's the same as killing yourself." Then he kicked Tim in the ribs as hard as he could. Tim coughed and spit but didn't move. "Yeah! I think you got the picture," said David with a smile. "So I'm really curious. Did you really think you could rape my little sister and have no repercussions? Did you have that little respect for me that you thought nothing would happen? Did you have that little respect for my brother? I don't understand that. A little punk like you, never made no real bones round here, livin' half your life off your grandma's Social Security, and you think you can do whatever you want, like you're the don or somethin'. That's disrespecting me, my family, and this whole fuckin' neighborhood. But make no mistake, that's not why this is happening to you. This is happening because you raped Missy, and I'm an 'eye for an eye' sort."

At that he gave another kick to Tim's ribs. There was now a puddle of urine underneath Tim's midsection. The dog was still frantic, running back and forth, erect as ever. Tim didn't move a muscle while Lukas and David helped Butch into position. He was so scared he'd been humbled to the point he wanted to take his punishment if it meant he got to live. It didn't take much coaxing. All they really did was get Butch's front paws on Tim's back and the dog quickly figured out the rest. As soon as he started working his hips David nodded to Lukas and Lukas went out the gate with Samuel.

Both of them smiled as they saw their friend bring justice to the situation. They had both known Missy for some years now and even if they found it hard to get along with her spunky attitude, the idea of someone forcing themselves on her small, fragile frame was unbearable. David didn't smile. He just stared coldly as he watched the dog lay into Tim like he was the prime poodle up the street. He didn't have to point the gun anymore. He knew Tim wasn't moving. Besides, Tim's eyes were squeezed shut with tears dripping out the sides. He couldn't see that David had his hands crossed at the waist with the gun resting against his leg.

The shot had brought most of the neighborhood out. Now they were all watching and gasping at what was going on in the Russell front yard.

It didn't take long for the police to arrive. They weren't in time to thwart David's plans. He had degraded Tim in the same way his sister had been. He threw the gun to the side and put his hands in the air. Tim had his eyes open to see that and immediately rolled over and began kicking at Butch. Butch wasn't done and continued trying to get at Tim, barking ferociously when he couldn't. The spectators couldn't help but laugh at the bickering lovers. The police rushed into the yard, broke them up and arrested David. Samuel and Lukas backed away like they had only been there to watch.

When the cuffs were slapped on David's wrists he made no attempt to struggle. There was no offer of explanation or even any sign of emotion in his face. He had accepted how this would end before he came down those stairs. To him it was simply the price he'd have to pay for obtaining justice.

When it came court time, Tim was too embarrassed to testify. Still there were enough disgusted neighbors and a terrified grandmother who witnessed it to give David time. It was a strange case, the sort of crime with no real precedent. When it was all said and done David was sentenced with 15 months to five years. It was said by some that the judge was lenient due to sympathy toward David's motive.

CHAPTER 8: GREEDY JUSTICE

It was almost time for David's first parole hearing when Tim decided to retaliate. Like David expected, Tim disappeared after the incident. Missy never heard from him. He stayed out of all Post circles, apart from his closest friends. Some believed him to have moved away altogether.

He had no choice but to hide. He had raped Missy Caine, which in turn got David thrown in jail. Remaining easy to find would have made Kris a terrifying threat.

Over the years Kris Caine had become the reigning champ of altercations. So much, in fact, there was really no one who would take up a beef with him or his entourage. Besides that, he was likable. He was never too good to talk to anyone about anything. He was Post Edition's answer to the star quarterback everyone was rooting for. To see him get into a simple bar brawl was looked at like Sugar Ray's long-awaited return to the ring.

Anyone who knew Kris, as most of the city did, held him in high regard. The vets of Post Edition gave him almost kinglike status. David, as the younger version, was thought of as a prince. He put forth great effort to evade Kris's shadow, thus not spending much time with him in public. Still, everyone looked at him as the little brother. They would want to be good to him just to be respectful to Kris. To wrong him or Missy would be like an assault on the royal family.

The whole neighborhood was outraged when what happened got around. Everyone was very eager to be the one who helped bring about Post justice. Between fear of running into Kris himself and knowing that anyone who saw him would get word to Kris, Tim couldn't show his face in public.

That the Caine family was so respected was probably much of what originally motivated Tim's actions. It was a cheap way to gain credibility in the streets. Disrespect the most respected that he might be held in the same league. That motivation came back and stung him. Irony seemed to have it out for Tim as well.

His name did become known, though not likely the way he'd hoped. It was months before a pet could come into conversation in those blocks without a Tim Russell joke following close behind. In turn that made Tim more dangerous than he was given credit for. He was now a shamed thug with no standards, nothing to lose and all the more to prove.

By the time the 15 months had passed, Tim's obligated absence gave him a useful distance from everyone's thoughts. He was usually only remembered in the occasional joke, or in spitefulness toward David's whereabouts. So when he walked into Snickers with his ball cap pulled low to the brow, no one noticed him.

Snickers was the local bar and billiard on the outer edge of Post Edition. All of the old bunch used to frequent the place. It was Kris's official hangout. Though most of the boys could be found there on the weekend, Kris was a regular during the week as well.

When Tim walked in that Tuesday evening, Kris should have known something was up. He was likely blinded by his anger and the unlikeliest of moments. He looked around the bar. He could tell he was the only one who noticed. Even the other Posties there hadn't seen Tim arrive.

Tim didn't look like he'd grown up much, still inordinately skinny, clothes laughably big and walking like he was revered by all.

Kris was mid-shot in a pool game when his attention was caught. He didn't stop what he was doing. He continued the shot like a lion not wanting to spook his prey.

Tim didn't seem to be paying him any mind. He went directly to the girl in the booth behind Kris and began speaking eagerly.

Kris continued under the assumption that he hadn't been noticed. After he missed his shot on purpose, he set down his stick, turned and smoothly walked up next to Tim. He put his arm around Tim like a long-lost friend with old times to reminisce.

"Hey pal. How ya been?" he whispered with venom in Tim's ear. Tim looked up, somewhat surprised. He didn't say anything so Kris started in with his old renowned speech. "Now I don't know what the hell you're doing here. But I gotta assume that havin' been out the loop and all, you weren't aware that this was my spot. 'Cause I can't believe that you would be so shit-ass stupid as to come in here if you knew there was even a slight chance of seeing me. But none of that matters now. The way I see it, me and you got some personal problems we need to take care of, man to man. Now if we start raising our voices and swinging our dicks around in here, it ain't gonna take no kind of time before everyone starts stickin' their nose in. It'll stop being man to man. People'll be breaking us up and the cops'll get called. Instead, me and you could step out that back door there, real calm and collect, and no one'd be the wiser. Then it'd be just the two of us. We don't need to put on a show for no crowd. Me and you can just handle the business that needs to be handled."

Only a portion of this speech was already famous. It was the part where he invited Tim to sort of sneak out the back with him so they could fight privately. Most people around there really got in fights to show off. They were trying to make a name for themselves by beating their chest in public. Regardless of motive, it was customary to start hollering and flaring tempers. That, of course, brought an audience. An audience limited the amount of time to inflict any real damage. Not a whole lot of blows would get thrown before people would intercede. A crowd also made it possible and quite likely that a person could scream and act crazy without actually providing real action in their performance. The spectators, wanting to be involved in the drama, would hold the participants back. They'd try to break it up and cool things down before it got out of hand. It was bad enough at a party. A bar was even worse due to involvement of bouncers and quicker calls to the police. Essentially the behavior allowed people to appear tough without actually having to back it up.

That's why it was so amusing to people when they heard how Kris usually approached a genuine beef, one where he truly wanted to duke it out. The idea that he was willing to go in private to fight an individual made it clear to that individual he had no fear of them. He didn't feel there was a need for others to be there and break it up because he knew he wouldn't be the one getting hurt. It also displayed the fact that he wasn't concerned about impressing anyone. All he was concerned about was beating on that individual until he felt appeased. The no-nonsense approach undoubtedly struck fear in the opponent. It was commonly referenced and laughed about when Posties described what a hard-ass Kris Caine was.

Tim played it cool. He paused, stared coldly into Kris's eyes, as if cocky enough to believe he could handle him, then answered, "Fuck it, man. We can do that shit. We can do that right now. I don't give a fuck who you are. I ain't scared of nobody."

Snickers had the perfect back exit for the boys' plans. There was a door not ten paces from the pool table Kris had been using. Once through that door, there was a small entryway with another door on each side. The one on the right led to a private party room that was rarely used. The one on the left opened to the very back of the parking lot.

At hearing Tim's reply Kris smiled brightly, amused by his ignorance. "Follow me," he instructed cheerfully.

Once through the second door Kris's eyes widened and he tried to turn back. Before he'd gotten back around he felt a forceful push from Tim that sent him through the door off-balance. That set him up well for the home run swing of a baseball bat by one of the five boys waiting for him. It landed square on the top of Kris's head. A stream of blood immediately shot down his face. He staggered back but didn't fall.

At this point, had Kris yelled, things might have turned out differently. Even if the people in the bar didn't run to his aid, which they would have, there was a good chance that his rookie opponents would have been spooked and scattered. Kris wasn't the yelling type. After he'd been struck, there was no amount of opponents that would have scared him off. There was no piece of reason persuasive enough to talk him out of what he was in. He had never backed down from a fight. He wasn't capable of it.

At least three of the six attackers were born and bred Posties. They were considerably younger, so they had grown up looking at Kris Caine as a sort of legend. After the first blow came, there was a synchronized pause of anticipation to see how he would react. Had he multiplied into double their numbers and stomped the whole group it might not have been enough to surpass their expectations of him. Instead he focused his eyes on who had hit him. Without lifting his head to give himself away, he took a step into a right hand he was launching to the chin of the swing-happy boy. Kris was dazed by the head-splitting shot he had taken. His retaliation might not have been all it could have been, but it was enough to drop its receiver to his ass.

With that, two more of the bats hit the small of Kris's back and his shoulder blades. He grabbed onto the bat to his left and used it to pull the holder into the right hand he had for him. It caught the corner of the boy's eye and drew blood, but Kris's off-balance stance prevented it from having much effect. At the same time as the hit, he gave a yank on the bat. To his attackers' dismay, he was now armed as well.

Before he got a chance to use it, another bat hit the side of his left knee, forcing it to snap. Kris fell to his good knee and the palms of his hands. He was trying to keep his left leg elevated as he looked back at it with a snarling expression of both anger and amazement.

It was then he must have realized the intentions of his attackers. A blow like that could have quite likely rendered his leg useless for the rest of his life. He had to realize that these boys hadn't just come to get a little attention and act tough. They were too fearful of him for that. They had come with the intention of killing him. The bats were in place of guns to avoid the noise. There was murder in their hearts, but still there was no yell from Kris. He could never give them that satisfaction.

Once Kris was put in a vulnerable position, Tim picked up the bat waiting for him against the building. He pulled it back over his head as far as he could and brought it down with all his scrawny body into the back of Kris's head. He collapsed limp to the ground. It was likely he was dead then, but they were not leaving any room for chance to play a part. All six of them were on their feet, raising their bats and bringing them down repeatedly with ferocious speed. All the bats landed in assembly line style, giving a rhythmic sound of pounds to flesh. When it was clear that no life could possibly remain, the boys fled the scene of their ambush, leaving the Postie king lying motionless on the cold, wet pavement.

When the body of Kris Caine was examined it was said to have over two hundred separate contusions covering it. The skull had been caved in three different places. His murder was a regular fit for a typical Eastside tragedy, the futility of the motive in a low-budget drug dealer trying to save face. The poetic injustice in Kris being so much stronger, smarter, more talented and honorable than his opponents, yet not being granted victory. It was all too typical of the traditions in the chaotic streets of the Post Edition neighborhood.

The timing of the assault was especially bad for David. His first parole hearing was less than a month away. It was likely that he would have been released, but when he was informed of his brother's death, he went into a wild frenzy, swinging and attacking everyone and everything in sight. There was a total of eleven guards involved in detaining the relatively small man. Three were injured in the process.

The regrets of time with his brother sacrificed to the cage he was in and memories of pointless bickering over the years weighed heavy on his soul. Perhaps not so heavy as the countless times a big brother had come to the aid of an overly proud recipient, too tough to show his gratitude.

When the parole hearing had come around he still hadn't completely calmed himself. He wasn't released. David always made hollow sermons about the board wanting to protect Tim's life from a brother's wrath. In truth it was David's outburst that kept him there. A guard with a broken jaw is not the sort of thing the board could ignore. Though his behavior before and after was flawless, it would be a good amount of time before David's release could be seriously considered again.

That time was at hand. His good behavior had continued and it would be hard for anyone not to sympathize with David's motives in both incidents. He stood a good chance of being released this time. Though he might not show it, he was optimistic.

CHAPTER 9: REUNION

It was a two-hour drive to the prison. When Samuel arrived he had to wait all the longer before he actually got to see his old friend.

He sat at the small table, trying not to fidget. He didn't know how David would respond to his leave of absence. He hoped there would be no grudge. More than that, he didn't know how he was going to answer some of the more personal inquiries that would occur.

When David finally did come through a door about twenty yards away Samuel didn't notice him at first. It was like when you're being picked up from the airport by a friend or family member you haven't seen in a while. Whether you mean to or not you develop a mental picture of what they are going to look like, or where they are going to be standing. When you actually see them it takes you that extra instant to make recognition.

As he stared off into the distance, waiting impatiently, he was taken aback when realized he was staring directly at what he was waiting for. It was the cocky half-smile that caught his attention. He started to wonder why this man was smiling at him when he suddenly realized it was David. Then he returned the same cocky curled lip that was typical to the East side of their hometown. Though Samuel hadn't lived there, he'd picked it up from association. It was a smile that suggested they knew something about the other that the other wasn't aware of. Though that wasn't true, it was the attitude they brought to any situation.

He was comforted to see the smile. It told him that if there was any anger, it would be overcome. Samuel felt numb all over. In that instant he was flooded with fond memories and comfort. He might have felt uneasy in a room full of criminals but when David came in, all that was gone.

David had the same pushy bounce in his pace. Although he was almost certainly shorter than the majority of his fellow inmates, it didn't faze his "stronger than the world" attitude. His shirt was tucked in but pulled back out to hang over the top of his pants, which rode low under his hips. His ragged blonde hair was shaved on the sides and stood about three quarters of an inch on top. It was pointing in many different directions but looked like it was supposed to do so.

Once he reached his seat and the guard escorting him left their side, he leaned back smugly in his chair. His half-smile couldn't help but give way to a full-fledged one that put his cheeks against his eyes. Samuel, too, was overwhelmed and had to return the boasting smile, though he usually tried to avoid them in hopes of hiding his dimples. They sat smiling, nodding their heads, reminding each other of every drunken laugh and triumphant conquest they shared over the years, without saying a word, until David finally gave way.

"M-a-a-a-n, where the fuck you been?" he said in a tone that failed in hiding his delight at seeing Samuel.

"Fuck man, I'm sorry. You know how it is in that hellhole. As shitty as it is, it's hard to tear yourself free sometimes."

David gave a now-condescending smile, as if disappointed at the poor excuse for an explanation. "Yeah, I know how it is. So what's the haps over there? You still walkin' the routes? Got any dish for me? What's the deal?"

"Shit, you know I ain't got no dish. I don't be seeing none of the old crew around, and you know I'm still walking those fucking routes."

"Wh-a-a-t? You ain't seen nobody? What kind of shit is that? You can't just not see nobody. City ain't that big. And all you got to do is go down to an Eastside bar and you would see plenty of old timers. You know what that means to me? You saying you ain't seen nobody. That means you still wasting your days, and especially your nights, in that same apartment, sweatin' over that same ol' tramp, trippin' bout the same ol' shit. That's what that tells me."

Samuel just rolled his eyes and looked up while shaking his head like he knew it was coming. "Yeah, yeah, I heard it all before. You're not saying nothin' new. All these years in here and you're still saying the same shit."

"'Cause you still doin' the same shit. How can I be saying different shit about what you're doing when you doin' the same shit?"

Both the men giggled at a conversation that displayed the tendencies of the days of old. David then sobered up a little bit and spoke again. "It is good to see you, man. Whatever it was you was dealing with that kept you away so long, I got to respect that, but I'm damn happy to see you here now. Shit, you had me thinking I was on my own come next month."

"Ah hell naw. You knew I was gonna be the first face you saw out the door. Only way I wasn't gonna be waitin' for you out there was if I was in here."

"Shit, you better never let me catch your ass in here. You ain't built for this bitch. It might taint that one-of-a-kind mind of yours."

Samuel repeated the eye roll to show he didn't want to hear compliments about his potential that he didn't take seriously anyway. Then his eyebrows curled down and he changed the subject. "What you mean on your own, anyway? What's up with Ma and Missy?"

David's face became even more sober and he shook his head as he replied, "Man, from what I hear Missy is a junkie. I try to talk to Ma about it. She just downplays the whole thing and makes excuses. I can't stand that woman."

"Damn, dude! What the fuck? I swear one out of ten peeps we went to school with is a head now. Don't tell me she's gettin' sucked down too. It's this fuckin' city. It sucks it out of everybody."

"Yeah, I guess. And I'm 'bout to be right back in that bitch. I don't know, though. I can't say for sure I can rack that one up to the city."

Samuel gritted his teeth. He knew, of course, that everything that went wrong in that family or anyone's life, to David, somehow came back to him. He didn't trust anyone's shoulders to hold the burden but his own. Samuel tried to hide his anger as he asked David to elaborate. "What you supposed to mean by that?"

"I don't know, man. It's like sometimes I think she'd've been a lot better off if I hadn't responded to what happened. At least not the way I did. My trying to fix the situation got me in here. So I think she feels responsible for her brother in jail, so in turn she feels responsible for what happened to Kris. Shit was too much for her to handle. So it kind of comes back on me. If I hadn't run off half-cocked the way I did, none of this shit would have happened. I wouldn't be in here. Kris would still be alive. My sister wouldn't be a junkie. It's hard not to feel responsible."

"Surprise, surprise. You're taking responsibility for everything. It's like I always said. You're always trying to be big brother to the whole world. What the fuck, man! You was handling what needed to be handled. You did and was always doing what you thought needed to be done. And you did it the best way you knew how. There's not many people nowadays that can say that. What? You was supposed to let everything slide for fear that faggot might come back on Kris? Wasn't nobody supposed to have to worry 'bout your big bro's well-being. That was one motherfucker who could handle himself. That little dog lover got lucky as a bitch. I never heard all the details of how it went down but I think it pretty much goes without saying that at least a couple of the motherfuckers involved got permanent mementos to remember Kris Caine by. You can't put that shit on you. The whole fuckin' thing gets racked up as another one for the city."

David nodded approvingly in appreciation for the words that his friend had given him. "Yeah, I hear ya man. But fuck talking 'bout all that bull shit, though. I want to hear about the first stop after you pick me up. Tell me you got something planned."

The two old friends reminisced about old times, and made high-hoped plans for the future. There was many a hearty laugh and many a joke at each other's expense, much like old times. It did both boys' souls well to spend time with each other and they were both fully aware of it.

Eventually Samuel remembered what had prompted him to make the visit in the first place so he directed the conversation there.

"So you ever heard of a guy named Cullomine Torreo?" he asked.

David pulled his head back with a startled scowl. "Whaddya know about Cullomine Torreo?"

"I asked you first."

David smiled, amused by the childish retort. "He's a bigwig drug dealer. Scum of the Earth like the rest of 'em. Why would you be askin' about a guy like that? You better not be into anything involving him."

"No, no, it's nothing like that. You know me better. It's just that there's this girl on my route. Beautiful woman, actually. She's been all packed up to move for weeks but no departure. Then she tells me that she's waiting for this urgent package before she can leave. Plus her son's named Cullomine. It's a rare name. I hear this Torreo is gettin' out soon. I think, hey, maybe there's some connection."

David paused, staring at Samuel wide-eyed, then began to giggle profusely. Samuel rolled his eyes and shook his head again. David continued to giggle incessantly, only interrupting with an occasional attempt to talk which was overpowered by more giggling. Finally he gathered himself enough to speak.

"B-o-o-o-y, you ain't changed a bit. Still wasting your time daydreaming about other people's lives instead of living your own. I'm actually happy to see it. I'm glad to see that steam engine imagination of yours is still intact. I'd hate to think you'd lost it."

"Yeah, yeah, I just was curious if you knew anything."

"What you care about this? Why would you care if they are connected? Who cares? What would it have to do with the package anyway?"

"I don't know, man. It's just . . ." Samuel paused, hesitant to invoke more giggling at his expense. "It's just that every week or so she gets these little thick brown envelopes. They're just the right size for sending a stack of bills. I guess reasonably there could be anything in there. It's not the only time I've seen envelopes of this size. It's just usually my theories vary from day to day. But these envelopes—all I can ever picture inside them is money. So I figure no legitimate people get letters full of cash. Maybe she's got some beau sending her loot. She is waiting for an urgent package before she can hightail it out of there. Maybe it's a big shipment of loot."

David still couldn't wipe the superior smirk off his face but the mere mention of large amounts of money forced him to take things at least slightly more seriously. "Come on, man, you can't start taking your own imagination too seriously. That's like one step away from the san. Besides, what are you gonna do if it was a big shipment in cash? I don't see you acting on it. Opening other people's mail is a federal offense, let alone for a mailman—there's gotta be some kind of extra charges involved," joked David.

"Like I said, man, I'm just a little curious. What's the big deal?" Samuel put on a somber face that struck a nerve.

"All right, all right. You don't gotta pout. I'll ask around a little bit. Fuck, what else I got to do to kill time?"

"Good shit, man. I mean, 'cause it does all kind of add up, if you ask me. It'd suck if there was something to this and we let it slip by . . ."

"Yeah, yeah!" David interrupted. "I already agreed; you can quit selling me. I just hope I don't get shanked for askin' the wrong questions. I hear he's a real bigwig."

"Well, don't go out on a limb or something. It's just novel interest. It's not worth any trouble." Samuel was a little taken aback at that statement. It was always a little weird when he brought something that had grown in his mind for so long out into the open. The idea that there could be dreadful consequences was a little too real for him.

Their time was about up. They made a few more plans in the direction of his release, then said their farewells, and Samuel departed. The drive home went by fast. His head raced with variations on how the Cullomine situation would play out, all the possibilities. Each time his head mulled over it, there was a new twist. Some instances ended with him and David sipping margaritas in the Caribbean. Others had him taking a heroic bullet in place of Monique, who was in a damsel-in-distress predicament. He hadn't had that much energy in a long time. He noticed some of his old creative tendencies returning. Once he was about halfway home he developed a massive appetite. He stopped at a fast food restaurant and ordered more than was reasonable and ate it all. He hadn't been that hungry in a while. He hadn't enjoyed his food that much in a while either. To an extent the edge was taken off and he actually looked forward to getting up in the morning.

CHAPTER 10: TROUBLESOME JOY

Over the next few days, Samuel's rapport with himself continued to improve. Having someone else involved in his personal mystery made it all the more intriguing. Even better, it made it all the more real. Now it was something to occupy his mind which was no longer completely in his mind, no longer strictly fantasy. Someone else was thinking about it too. Plus Monique was due to get a letter soon as well. That just gave him all the more to think about: what would be said, how he would speak to her, what he could say to try and pry a little information. It had been days since he had a suicidal thought or even considered how wretched the world was.

When the day finally came he was a little groggier than usual. He had rented a video the night before and it kept him up a little late. Video renting was an old habit he hadn't partaken of in a while. He'd actually been thinking about the different possibilities so much that he wanted something to take his mind off it. But groggy as he was, his attention focused sharply and his mouth went dry when he saw the little brown envelope with the name Monique Romano written on it. She hadn't been sent mail since their last encounter. Not even some junk mail that would allow him back to talk to her. Here it was, another one of those envelopes. His curiosity was in full swing.

He examined the package like a kid on Christmas Eve, trying to figure out what he was getting. He felt at it, firm but flexible. He even pulled out a bill from his wallet to compare sizes. It was a perfect match.

He'd probably have been better off not to notice it until later in the day, 'cause now all he could think about was delivering it. Truthfully, that was all he thought about anyway. But this put things in overdrive. Every time he thought about it he got nervous, even to the point of sweating. It was a warm day but not that warm. How could he start up a conversation with her? The last thing he wanted was a quick 'here's your letter, talk to you later.' But he knew when he got there, he would panic and it was exactly what he was going to try and do. If he thought of something now to say that would spark conversation, he could force himself to say it when the time came, and things could go from there. If he left it to his wits at the moment he would surely cop out and it would be back to dreaming about his next visit. No progress was a dreadful thought.

He couldn't take his mind off it. His excitement made the day drag on. It was like waiting for Christmas morning when you couldn't sleep. It's like the batteries have run low in the clock. Finally he thought he would inquire about the origin of her last name. If he got her talking about her heritage it would give him a little time to pull himself together. That would in turn improve his chances of finding out something of consequence.

When the time finally came to deliver the letter his brain felt numb. When he passed the row of bushes that served as a barrier to the left of the house, he could finally get a full view of his coveted destination. The cream white rock exterior house reflected the blazing sun to give it kind of a glow. The freshly trimmed lawn also glistened in the sunlight. Though the house was clearly an expensive one it was only one story. It maintained high square footage by being a bit wider and longer than the average abode. The fence went from the side of the house to the row of bushes and then turned to begin surrounding the back yard. Its gate was left open invitingly. He assumed it was to remind him to come back there and deliver the mail personally. He figured since she had no way of knowing exactly when her mail would arrive, the gate must have been open quite regularly for him. That was a nice thought. The idea of a mail recipient giving him thought made him feel appreciated. A pleasant change from the unnoticed city worker vibe he got from most his residents.

Now that he had arrived his butterflies were out of control. He had been in such a rush to get here, and now he'd like some more time to dwell on it. He had skipped his lunch in the rush to arrive. Maybe he could go eat now to delay. Then he thought perhaps she had already noticed him, in which case it would look kind of strange, him walking off now. Instead of cutting straight up the yard to the gate he decided to walk to the driveway on the opposite side. This would avoid him having to walk on the well-manicured lawn, and give him a few more of the seconds he was clinging to so vigorously. The house rested on top of a notable incline that made him slouch when he walked up the driveway. Upon reaching the top he turned left and started down the sidewalk that led to the gate. Along the side of the house were many windows. They didn't even have drapes on them. She must be in a rush to leave, he thought. She was probably growing impatient for the package she was waiting on. He hoped she wouldn't be disappointed when he wasn't bearing it.

As he cornered the house the trail opened up into a lavish, vast backyard, in the center of which was a large swimming pool. As stunning as the yard was, Samuel was far more transfixed when he noticed Monique face down in an open lawn chair sunbathing. Not having had much contact with the opposite sex in quite a while, he found the sight excessively pleasing. Her tan body was covered in a light gloss of sweat that made her skin glisten more than the grass did. Her deep purple bikini was a little on the skimpy side but not to the point where it might be considered slutty. It properly accentuated her plump, well-rounded backside that was sticking in the air. Her legs were thick, firm and to Samuel's eyes rather inviting. He might have wished she was lying face up but the picture was so appealing he didn't give it a thought. Once he got closer he started to feel a little awkward. He hoped she wouldn't be embarrassed being in a bikini and all. He hoped she had remembered asking him to come to the backyard to give her the mail personally. He started to feel out of place, like he was trespassing. Obviously she didn't think about this moment as much as he had. Perhaps she had indeed forgotten and would be startled or even offended to have him back there.

He took a deep breath and tried to gain composure by speaking to himself. *Pull it together, Samuel. She's just lying out by the pool; it's nothing to get worked up about. Surely she's not. Even if she did forget her instructions she's sure to remember when she sees you. She seemed like a very nice lady; there's no reason to be tense. Just speak up.*

He got about ten paces away when he opened up his mouth. "Excuse me, Ms. Romano."

Her head lifted calmly to see who was addressing her. "Hey, how's it going?" she said cheerily. "I was beginning to think we didn't have a mailman anymore."

"Yeah, you haven't gotten much lately, have ya?"

"Nothing is more like it." She hopped up, clearly not giving her attire the same weight that Samuel did. "What you got for me?" she said as she approached with her hand out. Samuel, taken aback by the full frontal view of Monique in her purple bikini, was at a loss for words.

"Ah, just the one letter," he muttered absentmindedly. She took it from his hand like she was going to open it but instead just looked down at the front as if studying its origin. Samuel decided to take the moment of silence as his opportunity to start conversation. "So Romano, is that your last name?" He then froze in embarrassment at the miswording of his question. Monique looked up, nose scrunched and smiling brightly in a confused manner.

"Yeah, that's why I put it right there after my first one," she smarted off in her thick Latino accent. Then she giggled in a way that made him feel like his slip wasn't that big a deal. Her playfulness toward his embarrassing moment made him feel a lot more at ease than having said something debonair would have. Samuel shook his head and started to explain, "Not what I meant to ask. What I meant was . . ." Then a young voice came from the house.

"Ma! The buzzer is ring-ging." Her son was hanging out the back door hooting to her. She turned, concerned, to hear him, and then looked back to Samuel.

"Up, could you . . . What's your name?"

"Oh, I'm Samuel," he answered.

"Could you hold that thought for one second, Samuel? I don't want to burn lunch."

"It's no problem at all."

Monique turned and headed back to the house in a half trot that caused a bouncing Samuel had to pretend to ignore. He stood patiently, smirking at his verbal error. He felt more relaxed now than he would have ever expected he could in this situation. It was finding bliss through expected failure. He'd already done something very embarrassing and it wasn't that bad. It temporarily tore down his inhibitions about the moment. After a short wait, Monique now stuck her head out the door and addressed him.

"Do you want some fajitas, Samuel?"

"Ah..." Samuel hesitated as he debated how to answer.

"Come on. I'm a good cook and I want to thank you for giving my mail delivery special attention. It's the least I can do."

"Well, to tell you the truth I haven't eaten yet and I am pretty hungry."

"It'll be right out. You don't mind hot foods, do ya? It's kind of spicy. That's the way Cullomine likes it."

"Nah, that's fine."

"Good."

Samuel again smirked, this time at the cuteness of Monique's accent. After a few more moments she emerged from the door with a tray of food in her hand. She was now wearing a silky white robe that cut off about mid-thigh. "Take a seat," she ordered as she gestured toward one of the lawn chairs. Samuel did and when he looked up he saw her folding out legs from under the tray to turn it into a small table. Monique pulled up a lawn chair to within reaching distance of it.

"Well, that's a nifty little contraption there. Where did you pick it up?"

"Flea market," she answered simply. Samuel nodded his head with his bottom lip out to signify that he understood. Then he picked up one of his fajitas and bit into it like he hadn't eaten in a week. As he chewed his eyes opened wide and his mouth slowed. Monique looked up and smiled as she realized he had overestimated his tolerance for Latin spice. He immediately swiped his punch and began to guzzle in hopes of cooling his palate's fire.

"No, no, that won't help much," explained Monique. "Try this." She scooted a small glass of milk toward him. "I thought you might need it."

Samuel dropped the glass back like it was a shot. He swirled the cow nectar around his mouth and his eyes rolled over as he found relief. Once he had drunk the milk he began laughing hysterically.

"Geeeeze!" he hooted. "A little hot! This'd intimidate a firefighter." He continued to laugh at the way he'd been affected by the food. Monique joined in but tried to hold back her amusement with a hand over her mouth, which in turn made the moment all the more amusing.

"I'm sorry. I guess I'm just used to it. Here, try dipping them in this first." She pushed over a dish full of liquid cheese. "It dilutes the spice."

"I don't know, it sounds a little risky." With that he stuck the end of his fajita in the dip and attempted another bite. Monique watched intently for his reaction. Samuel looked up as if studying the flavor. He then began to nod in approval. "Yeah, that's a lot better. Yeah, actually that's the bomb." He repeated the action to take another bite while continuing to nod his head.

"You like it now?"

"You weren't kidding."

"About what?"

"Being a good cook, a damn good cook. I might need a doggy bag."

Monique giggled, happy to hear her food was appreciated. "So... Samuel, right? Do your friends call you Sam or Sammy or what?"

"No. They don't really call me anything but Samuel."

She looked pryingly into his eyes. "Yeah, I guess they wouldn't."

"So Cullomine—is that your husband?" he asked, in hopes of sparking a conversation and digging up clues.

"Cullomine?" she repeated inquiringly.

"You said Cullomine likes these spicy."

"Oh, I was talking about my son."

"Oh, I see."

"No, I'm actually not married," she explained honestly. "How 'bout you?"

"Yeah, I been married, if you could call it that. It didn't last too long."

"I guess not. You look too young to be divorced."

"Huh. I am." Samuel looked around the grounds. "So this is a real nice place you got here."

"Thank you. I like it real well. It's a shame I have to leave it. Guess that's the way it goes."

"Yeah? Why do you have to leave?"

"It's my mother; she's not well."

"Oh, I'm sorry."

"Oh, don't worry about it. It's not a new thing. It's just my sister has a job offer in a different city than where my mother lives so it's kind of my turn to take care of her."

"I see."

"We've always been a real close family, though I haven't got to see them since my dad died. But they keep in touch. In fact, it is they who send those brown envelopes regularly. There's a letter from each of them and a few of my old friends. That's why it's so thick, plus there's usually some negatives in there for me to get developed. I don't always do it though—reminds me of the old country too much. I'm kind of torn. Missing it there, in so many ways, yet loving it here. Ah well, I guess the decision got made for me."

"Well, at least that takes the pressure off. So where is the old county?"

"Chile," she answered in a tone that suggested it should go without saying, "but I'm boring. What about you?"

"Ah, I think I got you beat when it comes to boring."

"Oh yeah, sure. You're not fooling me. You probably got more friends than you can count and probably go home with a different girl every night."

"Hah, I don't know about that. There ain't that many worthwhile girls in this city," disclaimed Samuel, unwilling to completely deflate the myth.

"Sure, likely story. I bet you don't have a steady girl though."

"No, you're right about that. Haven't had a steady girl in some time."

"Yeah, you get around. Be breakin' them hearts, don't ya? That's probably what happened with you and your wife."

"Nah, if there was any extramarital activity goin' on, it was on her part. I was the perfect husband."

"Oh, I see. So now you take what she did out on all the innocent ladies out there."

"That's kind of an oxymoron, isn't it?"

"Oh, that was harsh," she said while laughing at his ill-placed joke. Samuel laughed as well but was suddenly struck with concern of what time it was.

"Ooh, I'm sorry, I'm going past my lunch allowance here," he said as he looked at his watch.

"I understand," she replied earnestly, "duty calls. It was nice chattin' with ya though."

"Yeah, you too. It's nice to get to know one of the people on my routes."

"Well, next time you see I got mail don't bother eating lunch again. I'll try and have something a little less spicy."

"All right, it's a fair deal. Thanks again though; the food was delicious."

When he left the yard he was smiling ear to ear at how well everything had gone. He could not have hoped for as much interaction. Both feet were in the door and there were even plans for the next meeting. But as soon as he had reached the sidewalk and restarted his route, monotony and dread regained their thrones. For one, the news about her mother poked all the air out of his hopes for some scandal to unfold before him. She had explained what the brown envelopes were and though he still had no explanation for the package she was waiting on, the foundation for his theory was destroyed. Unfortunately, Samuel knew that was not the real anchor to his mental state. Though he didn't want to accept it, he was already depressed to be away from Monique. He tried to pretend he wasn't that pathetic, like a puppy dog begging for attention. But deep down he knew it was the case. As small as it was, he hadn't received that much attention from a woman in what seemed like ages, let alone a woman as striking as Monique.

The only way to ease his lonely sorrow was to dream of her. He tried to avoid it. He knew the more he thought about her the more he'd want her but she was outside his grasp. Try as he might, he still found himself staring at the sky picturing her face. It carried him through the next few days. Soon her beauty became less like a picture and more like a poem. Not just her voluptuous hips or darling smile or innocent giggle—it was the whole package coming together to make an overall vibe or feeling that seemed to ease him no matter how frustrated or uneasy he was. The sound of her Latino accent rolling her R's, the idea of her simple beginnings in Chile, the glow from her golden brown skin made a fantasy that seemed to be the engine fueling even the simplest of thoughts or tasks for Samuel over those days. Finally he seemed to have a weapon to combat the dread that had made him its slave for so long. But he feared his weapon. He knew that eventually it would leave him and the dread would make him pay for his rebelling. Now that he was up, coming back down would be that much more painful.

Still, as much as he tried to tell himself that, it seemed every little thing that happened to him would be formed into a description for him to tell Monique about. Even though they were usually such small, insignificant things that he had no intention of really sharing them, it was as if nothing that happened to him was complete until he had envisioned it in a conversation with her.

CHAPTER 11: TRADING PLACES

Every morning Samuel would shuffle through his mail, hoping to find something going to her. Then he'd scold himself again for letting himself become so addicted to something he couldn't have. The idea of her being a criminal's mistress with some fortune in the middle of legal turmoil had almost completely eluded him.

It eluded him until about a week and a half later, when he found himself sitting at the same table waiting for the same person as he had been the day his imagination went into full swing in regard to Monique and her mystery. When David did emerge from the door he didn't have the same cocky smile he'd boasted before. Now his eyes were wide and his expression attentive. He approached the table in a power walk almost worthy of exercise.

"What's up, man?" he greeted Samuel when he arrived.

"Not shit. What you so worked up about?"

"What you mean?"

"You just seem a little anxious is all."

"Well, I got some interesting news about what you had me look into."

"Ah, don't even worry about that, man. I came to try and make some more concrete plans for when you get out. What you're gonna do and all."

"Well, depending on how all this pans out, maybe we won't need to."

At that moment Samuel realized that this mystery fantasy had begun to serve the same purpose for David as it had for him just weeks ago, something to dream about and keep his hopes up while passing the time. David, however, used it to get through the days of being imprisoned within those walls, whereas Samuel's prison seemed to follow him wherever he went. As David's potential release grew closer his excitement grew with it, thus the days began to drag. He'd latched on to this theory to make the time move and to keep his mind off the anxiety of wondering what he was going to accomplish once released. Samuel realized that and thus didn't put much interest in the clues that David had found. He blew them off as desperate, unrealistic hopes.

"Nah man, I talked to her. I really don't think there's anything to it. Don't even sweat it."

"Well, can I at least tell ya what I found out? I've been bursting to tell ya. I almost called but decided I'd prefer to wait and tell you when you were here."

"All right, go ahead and lay it on me," said Samuel, slightly amused at his friend's childlike excitement.

"All right, so I asked around about Cullomine Torreo, trying to find out his story: what he's in for, what he was into out there exactly. It turns out they got him in on some bullshit charges. Don't really got a whole lot to do with what he does out there. It turns out he's not just your average dealer; he's like a Tony Montana, full-fledged scum of the Earth kingpin. But not just him alone; he's a member of this elite group full of Tony Montanas called the Dragon Clan. I don't really know how the dragon or the clan comes in 'cause it's all out of Mexico and South America. I usually associate both those words with Asian origin but anyway, that's the name. They've been heavy movers into the country for years. Started out along the West coast. Eventually they were even big in New York. Over the last decade or so they've moved here into the Midwest. Cullomine is the head of operations here, or was. It seems he had some kind of falling out with his alma mater. The details on that are fuzzy too but it's something like he had an old beef with someone who got moved up in the ranks and he knew he'd be getting took out the picture soon. So he tried some sneaky shit." As the story poured out of David's mouth at an excessive rate Samuel's interest slowly aroused. He was now sitting up, attentive in his seat, hanging on his old friend's every word.

"I guess these guys are so big they got business arrangements with high-up law enforcement groups on a massive scale. So Cullomine's supposed to make the payoff but never shows up with the money, somewhere in the amount of twenty million dollars. Unfortunately for him, he gets nabbed on this other bullshit by the local authorities and he doesn't get a chance to split. All that's kind of hazy. Some people think taking the money was the only way he could survive in here because they would have to keep him alive to find out where it's at; others think he just got caught up in the middle of the plan. Regardless, I guess the tension is building. His parole hearing is coming up the same time as mine, and they think he's gonna get it. The second he steps out that door everybody's watching for him. Seems the Dragons said retrieving the money was the law's problem 'cause they should have never let dude get arrested in the first place. Not only do they pay these fucks off, they get dirt on all of them, like blackmail shit, and make sure they know it so if the law gets pissed about something the Dragons can tell 'em to go fuck themselves. So he'll have all sorts of Johnny Laws following him waiting for a sign to where the loot is, he'll have his own cartel looking to kill him for stealing and whatever else. Fuck! Talk about the pressure being on. This guy's a mouse in a maze. Everybody says he's a slippery one so they're waiting to see what's up his sleeve. The people who know about it are placing bets on how it's gonna unfold. I can't believe anybody thinks he's gonna weasel out of it. I just wish I could be there to see him get nabbed."

"Well, as interesting as all that is, I don't think it really relates. I mean, I ran into two Cullomines—it's not that huge a coincidence."

"Oh damn, I left out the most relevant shit. My fault, man—this is how it plays to what we're dealing with. Let's imagine for a moment that Torreo hooks up with some skeeze, no one he ever marries or nothing. They just got a baby; that's why the law don't really know anything about her. So if he can just get the money sent to her, she can make off with it. He can slip away 'cause nobody's ready to kill him until they find out where the funds are. Then she can take off with the money and the law, who're the ones really concerned about the loot anyway, don't know nothin' bout it. Then they can rendezvous later."

"I don't know, man; it's shaky."

"Yeah, but this guy ain't really in the sort of situation where he has the luxury of non-shaky plans. And here's where the real evidence comes in. I guess this Dragon Clan is more like a brotherhood with illegal funding than it is a cartel. They have all sorts of rules and regulations on how they have to handle each other and shit. One of which is that when a member is imprisoned their family has to be taken care of by certain standards, that vary, based on your status. The family gets money sent to them every week or so. An allowance is set. A guy like Cullomine's mistress could be gettin' something like five thousand a week. They're very strict about their rules. Even though they're looking to kill this guy they still gotta send his girl money as long as he's in jail. Crazy, huh! That's probably what them envelopes you always thought were full of money are about. I don't know how, man, but I think you might have hit this shit on the head."

Samuel sat quietly, still mulling over all the information he'd just been given.

"You don't seem as positive as you did before," pointed out David.

"Yeah, I don't know, man. I still don't really think she's involved in all this. But it is all adding up a lot like I thought it did. Gotta admit it's fishy."

"There's gotta be some way to find out for sure. I got a course of action we can take. But we gotta be sure before we can go forward with it. But that leads me to my real question. If this does turn out to be the way it sounds, if this money is in the mix, are you gonna be willing to take it? That's a line of involvement I can't say I'm sure you're ready to cross."

Samuel sat quietly for a moment, and then looked across the table. "Would I be willing to take myself out of this dead-end life at the price of taking a dealer's fortune? Yeah, I'm willing. I'm more than willing."

"Hah-hah! That's what I wanted to hear! Man, if I could see the dumb look on the prick's face while he's waiting for the slut to show up with the money," David hooted as he kind of pounced out of his seat. The nearby guard looked over sternly to see what the excitement was about. David noticed and purposely cooled down. It was weird for Samuel to see anyone have that sort of authority over David Caine. But he knew he was trying hard to get out and had to become accustomed to appeasing the guards. In a way, it was a testament to how strong he really was.

Though Samuel's level of intrigue had risen again, his level of excitement had not. It was now replaced with weariness. He no longer liked the idea of this girl, who was a source of such joy for him, being tied up with a notorious drug dealer in the middle of a dangerous web. He also didn't like the idea of her lying to him. It would undermine all the affection he had built toward her. So now his stance had come full circle and he wished the entire Cullomine situation would turn out to be a figment of his overactive imagination.

As much as his affection for Monique contrasted his desire to get his hands on that money, even that was eclipsed by his wariness towards David's sudden interest in the situation. He was far more comfortable with David being skeptical than excited. When it was just Samuel's personal mystery, he was free to back out whenever he wanted. Now that David had taken a real interest, each bit of progress made it more likely that he would be unwilling to let go. Even if Samuel became uneasy or a threat arose, he would still be stuck in the situation as long as his friend was involved. Once David got his eyes fixed on the prize, there was no telling how far he would take it. It'd happened too many times during their friendship. They'd all get drunk and think up some exciting mischief they could get into. It would come time to see it through and they'd discover an added risk or something unexpected. The stakes would have become too high and everyone would be ready to let it go, but David couldn't do it. He could never back away from the challenge. Samuel, being among his true friends, would take his side in whatever the incident was and before he knew it they were running from the police, or face to face with a bunch of steroid-popping bodybuilders, or any number of other instances. Samuel had to admit they always came out all right, but none of those events had been as high grade as this. They had just been the result of overgrown children having too much time and far too much resolve. This was a different situation entirely. It was dealing with a nationally known criminal and FBI agents' money. It struck fear in Samuel knowing that none of that would impress David.

Samuel was kicking himself now for not seeing the potential problems putting this in David's head might bring. He was too antsy in that cage not to mull it over time and time again. He'd start to think of all the things he'd done wrong and tragedies he felt responsible for. He'd start to think of all the good he could do with that money and how he could right the wrongs he'd done. He could buy his girl, Jamie, something that let her know he never forgot her. He could whisk his mother and sister away from that leech of a city they lived in. Surely beautiful beaches, relaxation and quality time with the family could cleanse Missy of her drug problems. Eventually he would be convinced, not consciously, but in the back of his mind, that getting that money would give him the chance to make up for having cost them Kris's life. Once he got that in his head, there would be no backing him off, no matter the circumstances.

Perhaps worse than that was the involvement of a drug dealer in this. David had never tried to hide his hatred for them. He'd always just see the lazy, heartless, waste of a man his dad was. He considered the way they built their life by taking advantage of other people's problems and weaknesses to be a portrait of who his dad had been—someone completely caught up in even their smallest short term desire and uninterested in the damage it did to anyone else.

David wasn't one who could leave a score unsettled. Deep down he always felt he would catch up with his senior and break him in two. Every time a beef arose with a dealer or even a good chance to confront one came up, he would take out a small dose of the aggression he saved for his dad out on them.

David had more than enough reasons to hate the very man that gave him life. What made it worse was that Kris's dad had been around now and again. He was not perfect by any means, but his child support payments were made and he usually showed up for birthdays and holidays. That was enough to rub David's nose in his own dad's absence. David never resented Kris for it; he just added to his hatred for dealers. Rather than accept that his dad specifically was worse than Kris's, or that his dad specifically didn't really care about him, his mother or sister, he just blamed it on the genre. He decided they were all soulless scum. In a strange way it was like telling himself deep down that his dad had no choice but to act that way. It helped him deal with the knowledge that his dad was a horrible person, or even worse, that there was some good reason for him not to be loved by one of his parents.

As far as Kris was concerned, his brother hated dealers from square one, so he would hate them and any friend of his would have to as well. So it was a family tradition to hate dealers and it eventually became kind of a group motto for their circle of friends. As Kris and his followers grew in popularity it was a byproduct that the majority of the neighborhood began to feel that drug dealing was a lowly profession. Reasons got added to the list over the years. Heat it brought to the neighborhood, simplicity of the crime and making money off others' problems were just some of the frequently used reasons for hating them. It was part of the strange sort of self-righteousness for a group of people with few to no morals. No one who ran with Kris's crew would deal. It was left to the dregs of the neighborhood. Watching the dregs do it for long enough reinforced that it was a disgraceful way to earn an illegal living. They almost all smoked weed, but anything heavier than that was frowned upon and anyone who made a living dealing was barely associated with.

David's hatred for drug dealers was potentially the worst thing about him having taken interest in the Cullomine situation. All that time spent alone with his thoughts those years in prison had almost certainly built his anger toward his own dad to new heights. Having merged all dealers into one person the way he had, causing any problems or discomfort to Cullomine Torreo would be a chance to get back at his own dad. Once he'd gotten a taste for that satisfaction on his mind, it would take something quite powerful to get it off. Even if the whole thing came up to be a vicious rumor and there was no pot of gold involved, Samuel could see David being too tied up in the idea of hurting Cullomine and wanting to do it anyway. Who knew what that might lead to?

Unfortunately for Samuel, no matter how poor he realized his decision had been, there was no turning back now. What was done was done. David was a part of this thing now. Samuel would be better off setting his mind to damage control, rather than dwelling on a mistake made.

Now he was wondering what David meant by "a course of action." He decided not to bother himself worrying about that either, at least until he found out what he needed to and it became more relevant.

CHAPTER 12: GETTING CLOSER?

Samuel was back to the waiting game again, waiting for more letters—a sad irony that it was the delivery man who was stuck waiting for the delivery. Every day he got in the truck hoping to find mail addressed to Monique Romano on Emerald Boulevard. When there was nothing, he tried to pretend to himself he hadn't been waiting. He still attempted to convince himself he wasn't completely hung up on her. Being able to maintain any doubt at all was a testament to his ability to delude and manipulate himself. She occupied the majority of his thoughts. He was constantly swirling around different fantasies with her worked into the middle. Even the regular day-to-day things led to her. If he was angered by a long wait at the drive-thru it would be passed with him verbalizing his complaint to her. Picking out something at the grocery store might be accompanied by explaining to her why. She was the most important thing in his life, though he'd spent less than an hour of total accumulated time in her presence.

Unfortunately, now most of his fantasies weren't as happy as they'd been before. Now they usually contained an undertone of deceit and tragedy, ranging from her admitting to a past sex change on their wedding night to turning out to be a serial killer locking him away for torture at her amusement to finding out she was using him, making him fall in love so she could be married and stay in the country, then filing for divorce as soon as possible. No matter how well-intended his fantasy would seem at its beginning, it would always take a sudden turn for the worse midstream.

After a relentless stream of blatantly distasteful endings, he finally gave it some thought. He realized that his meeting with David had placed a sour apple in the middle of his thoughts. David's evidence suggested Monique had already lied to him, though he tried to tell himself that if David's information was right, it would be natural for her to lie about that situation.

He tried to convince himself it wasn't that big a deal and not worth worrying about. The truth was that he hated the idea of Monique having ever been with Cullomine Torreo and he feared the idea of their real relationship having started on such a deceitful note. That fear was arising now, as his fear usually did, in his daydreams.

Finally the day came when his closet hopes came to pass. There was a bit of junk mail addressed to Monique. There were a few different letters from local businesses giving out coupons and advertisements. He filed through the letters and was relieved to see that the traditional brown envelope wasn't there. As much as he'd been hoping for it, so he could pay a visit, he was also torn by knowing how much he would want to open it and bring closure to his mental debate. This was the best of both worlds. He got to visit and he didn't have to argue with himself over whether he should take a peek into her private property. Now he would have to resort to prying verbally in hopes of some tip as to the truth behind Monique Romano.

He hoped she wasn't waiting as impatiently for that envelope as he had been. If so, she would certainly be disappointed with the poor excuse for mail he was delivering. It was the type of stuff most people didn't bother opening. Samuel thought himself likely the only person to have ever been happy to see junk mail.

As he thought on that, he got an idea. It was crafty and unethical in his job, but not a big deal in the scheme of things. She certainly didn't care about these letters so it wouldn't hurt to hold on to one and deliver the other. That way he'd get his visit today, then he'd be able to pick exactly when in the next few days he would make his next visit. This would remove all the horrible waiting he'd had to struggle with lately.

By the time his route had brought him to Monique's stoop, he was again feeling sheepish about actually making the journey up her hill. He skipped lunch due to his anxiousness and her request to do so. Still, he again felt unwelcome, like he was imposing somehow.

When he sluggishly reached the backyard it was déjà vu as he became intoxicated by her glistening tanned body sunbathing by the pool. This time, facing up in a bright assorted-color bathing suit, she looked to be asleep.

"Monique," he whispered, not wanting to disturb her. She didn't respond. He walked up slowly. When he reached the side of her lawn chair he could see that she was unconscious. He looked at her luscious surroundings. He was envious. How pleasant it must have been to doze off under such circumstances. The light trickling sound from the motion of the clear blue pool water. The smell of freshly cut lawn off set by the peach-scented tanning oil covering her body. The last sight before closing her eyes was probably the big-leafed trees in abundance around the yard, serving as an extra fence. She must lead a pleasant life there on Emerald Blvd.

Not wanting to interfere with her blissful nap, he quietly tucked the envelope between the bar of her chair and the concrete beneath it. He backed up in long, slow paces then turned and headed back out of the yard undetected.

He had mixed emotions about leaving the way he did. Partly he was relieved. It was a blameless copout from the pressure he felt when he knew a visit was coming. On the other hand, he had genuinely wanted to spend some time with her. He had looked forward to getting to see her again, as well as obtaining information to take back to David. He took comfort in having his letter back at the truck. That kept the door open for his next visit. Without that, leaving might have felt like a complete failure.

As always, Samuel reached the last house on the street, crossed to the other side and started back in the opposite direction, where he would eventually return to his truck.

As he reached the house labeled 5004 he heard a voice calling from 5001. He looked over to see Monique standing on the front porch in a pair of khaki shorts and an oversized white T-shirt.

"What do you think you're doing?!" she called.

"Delivering the mail. What do you think you're doing?" returned Samuel jokingly.

"I mean, what do you think you're doing delivering my mail then sneaking off without a word? I'd expect better manners from you."

Samuel was a little embarrassed having this beautiful woman screaming to him for everyone to hear. He felt like all his feelings for her were apparent to anyone who might be looking out their window, which to him was certainly every resident on the street. To lower her tone he started across the street as he answered and hoped his face didn't look as red as it felt. "Well, you looked so peaceful lying there, I didn't want to interrupt just so you could shoot the shit with me." Samuel startled himself a bit, thinking better of having called out profanity while wearing his postal uniform.

"Well, I take offense at that, let alone you didn't stay for the lunch I made you. It's been wrapped up in my fridge for three days just calling your name. Makes me think you didn't like my cooking or company. Well, which is it?"

"Well, you'd be a crazy lady indeed for letting any thought like that cross your mind. I already told you what a stellar performance you had on the stove last time I was here." By now Samuel had reached the end of her driveway and was debating whether he should continue up it or not. Being caught off guard prevented him from having the chance to develop butterflies. As soon as he heard her voice and replied, he fell right back into that comfortable rapport they'd developed those weeks ago. Still, he wasn't sure if his company was wanted after already having delivered the mail.

"So have you eaten yet or are you standing me up altogether?" she asked, bringing an end to any such questions as to how he should behave.

"Well, I skipped lunch again when I saw you had a delivery. Then you didn't look prepared for guests, so I was just about to finish this street and then start on my sack lunch."

"You'll do no such thing. Get in here. Eating a lunch out of a bag when you have a perfectly good meal waiting for you in here—that's ridiculous," she commanded.

"I'm not gonna argue with that." He started up the hill and was brought through the front door this time.

"Have a seat. I'll have it right out," she directed as she gestured toward a modest kitchen table. He watched attentively as she soldiered around the kitchen like it was her personal battlefield. She pulled out the food from the fridge, took off the covering and put it in the oven, which appeared to be already heated. She then started toward the glasses to get him a beverage. She was dressed plainly and comfortably. Her white shirt was thin enough he could tell there was a swimsuit underneath. The shorts came down about mid-thigh and were rather baggy. It was a style Samuel was accustomed to.

Her house was beautiful inside as well as out. The area he could see was all wood floors and oak trim. The kitchen counters were a brown-based marble and were accompanied by lavishly carved cupboards. In contrast he sat at what was probably originally intended as a portable card table with a folding chair on each side.

As Monique brought him his drink he feared what he was thinking was obvious because she offered an explanation. "Sorry about this table. Everything has already been sent back home to Chile, but my son has to eat his meals at the table," she explained as she bustled around the kitchen gathering up spices. "I'll never understand you Americans, letting your children eat in front of the TV or wherever else they choose. What kind of family life is that? Not my boy, so I just grabbed something disposable to fill the purpose in the meantime. It's about the only furniture in the house. There's a couple of mattresses, some dishes. All stuff we can leave when it's time to go. Like that TV in there," she explained as she pointed to the adjoining room connected by a half wall. In it was a little portable TV that was likely capable of running on batteries. Little Cullomine was lying on his belly, watching intently while wagging his legs back and forth. "Heck, that's probably considered child abuse around here, making a child watch their programs on a television that small. If it's not yet it probably will be," said Monique.

Samuel chuckled lightly at her critical opinion of American culture. He was enjoying her company but was still antsy to make an inquiry. "So what is holding up your departure?"

"I told you, a package," her voice called back. She was crouched down behind the counter that separated her from Samuel, looking through cupboards.

"Right. But you're all ready to go; you've already sent everything else— what package could be so important?" Samuel was happy to have finally been able to ask about the package without sounding suspicious, but there was no reply. For a moment he thought he hadn't been heard, then she answered.

"Well, you see, I have some important memorabilia that was my padre's. Carvings my grandpa had made and things like that. My mother was so distraught when she found out I was moving to America that she wanted me to have something meaningful to remind me of home. So she gave me a cigar box full of these—well, it's just an assortment of different knickknacks with stories behind them. Junk to anyone else but more important than money in my family. My brother is the man of the house now that my padre has passed, so he was resentful, thinking he should be entitled to these heirlooms, but nobody argues with mi madre."

As she told her story she carried over the food, along with another glass of punch. He assumed the second glass was for her but she set it right next to his other glass in front of him. Slightly confused, Samuel put his finger up, asking permission to interrupt. She stopped talking mid-word and widened her eyes as to ask what was wrong.

"I'm sorry, but I'm curious to a fault and I gotta know why you brought me two glasses of punch," he asked pleasantly.

"W-e-ll," she began to explain, "last time you ate here you finished your drink before you were halfway through your meal. I figured you are one of those guys who have to drink a lot when they eat. Rather than getting up for a refill in a minute, I figured I'd bring you two glasses now. Save me the trouble."

Samuel smiled ear to ear, delighted by her observation. "Why thank you!" he pronounced genuinely. "You're right. If only the waitresses at restaurants would ever notice. I can never get the refills fast enough. The glass is mostly filled with ice to begin with. It's a real pain."

"Well, you need to stay well hydrated doing all that walking in this heat," said a sympathetic Monique.

"You're right about that. This all looks delicious, by the way," he complimented as he looked down at his plate full of well-decorated tacos and tender wild rice.

"Thanks. I was gonna make you my killer taco salad but I didn't know when you'd be here to eat it. I didn't want the lettuce to spoil."

Samuel almost instinctively told her he'd likely be coming back tomorrow so she could make it then, but he bit his tongue in time. He, of course, couldn't admit to what now seemed the immeasurably petty behavior of holding back her letter. He decided to redirect things back to the package. "That would have been nice. Maybe another time. So finish the story you were telling."

"Oh yeah," she began again, "anyway, so when I first moved to America I lived in California. There I put the stuff in a safe deposit box to make sure it was safe 'cause Mama would have my hide if anything happened to it. I figured it was fine there, so I didn't see the need to get it out when I moved. Now I gotta go back all of a sudden, so I've sent for them but the bank is taking its sweet time about sending it to me—paperwork and such. My family is impatient for me to get there but I gotta keep making up excuses 'cause Madre wouldn't like the idea of me putting that stuff in a box as opposed to keeping it at my bedside. And if I showed up without it… Ah! I wouldn't like to see Madre's reaction, let alone how my brother would respond. So the second you bring me that package I will bid you farewell and head straight to the airport."

"I see. That makes a little more sense. Like I said, I'm a curious person and I was having a little trouble putting it together. I couldn't understand why you would want to wait around after you had already sent your stuff," he explained as he finished up his food in record time.

"Geez, are you in a rush or what?"

Samuel looked up with a confused expression. "Oh! Nah, I'm just a fast eater."

"I guess so."

"It's good, what'd ya expect?"

"You didn't finish it off like that last time."

"Yeah, I was out of drink. I get stomachaches if I eat much without washing it down with a beverage," explained Samuel.

"Well, you should have said something. I would have gone in and got you another drink. Man, I've never seen anyone eat like that, though."

"Yeah, I get that a lot. See, my ma was always on a diet when I was a kid so she'd give herself minuscule portions while loading my plate up. She had this weird attitude, though. It was like she convinced herself that the calories didn't really count if they didn't come from her plate. She was always dieting but she could never really stick to it. She'd finish off her food then before too long she'd get to pickin' at my plate. She wouldn't order anything at the restaurant but I'd see her looking at my food as soon as it came. So since I didn't want to give up my grub I ate fast. I picked it up kind of subconsciously. I don't even realize I'm doin' it. Here it is all these years later and I still do it."

"That's funny."

"Yeah, it got so she'd eat faster, so I'd eat faster. We never talked about it out loud but we both knew what was going on. Now it's just habit."

"So were you and your ma close?"

"Yeah, we were till a couple of years ago. She passed."

"Oh! I'm sorry, I had no idea."

"That's all right. Well, you know what it's like, your dad and all."

"Yeah, but he was an old grizzly bear. He had us late in life so it wasn't exactly a surprise."

"Right. So what's the order on you kids?"

"My brother Franco is the oldest. He was always tryin' to look out for us like a second padre. Then comes my sister Lita, who's about four years older than me. Then I'm the baby of the family."

"Ah, how was that?"

"Pretty nice in a lot of ways. It's nice to be spoiled and pampered but then it's like they won't give you any room to grow. That's why I had to get away. But I've had my fun, expanded my horizons, and now I'm going back."

"So you're happy about going back then."

"Yeah, kind of. I'm mean I'm gonna miss my house and all, and I love it in America but it's time to go back to my roots. I miss my family. I mean, I sit around here all day by myself and the only person I talk to is my son. I need some grownup conversation. Plus I want Cullomine to get to know his family and culture. They've never even met in person. I show him pictures and tell him stories but that's not the same."

"Yeah, I think it's good for children to be brought up close to their grandparents. It helps them learn about life in a lot of ways."

"True, but what about you? All we ever talk about is me. I wanna hear about you some more."

Samuel smiled slyly to one side and kind of rolled his eyes like he didn't want to let out the secret details of his elaborate life. "Well, I'd love to tell you the nitty-gritty but unfortunately my lunch period is up. Perhaps another time."

"Oh, I see how it's gonna be. I'm gonna have to pry you open with a crowbar." They both laughed. "Speaking of next time," began Monique, "it occurs to me that every day you don't come here you eat out of a bag, probably all by yourself. If you're gonna be on my street delivering mail anyway, you might as well come here. That way I get to talk to someone about things not regarding cartoon characters and you get some actual nutrition."

"You sure that wouldn't be too much trouble?" he asked politely.

"Nah, I like to cook."

Samuel nodded his head and rolled his bottom lip out. "I don't see a problem with that then. I'm certainly not gonna turn down delicious food and the company of a beautiful woman," agreed Samuel coolly, not wanting to show his enthusiasm.

"Great. Well then, I'll see you tomorrow. You can just come to the front door. Will it be the same time?"

"Yeah, thereabouts."

Samuel left his encounter on cloud nine. Not only had his visit gone smoothly, not only did he get what he considered to be the last nail in the coffin on the Cullomine connection, he also got an ongoing invitation. It was perfect. There would be no more presorting the mail in search of her name. There wouldn't be any false hopes or anticipation. He knew when he'd get to see her and he knew it was every day.

He didn't feel the need to research anymore. Of course, that wasn't the real motive for his visits any longer. He was entranced by her and though she was leaving soon, he would enjoy her all he could in the meantime. He knew it meant eventual heartbreak when she left, but in a way that made things easier. Knowing things could only go so far was a safety net. She would never have a chance to reject him. It was wonderful and safe. He was in heaven.

It was no longer just about her beauty, or even just about her social handout to an emotional beggar. He was truly taken by her observations of him. She noticed how much he drank when he ate. Even more, she took it into consideration when making his lunch. That wasn't the self-centered behavior he was accustomed to. She was a kind soul amongst a vast field of petty self-indulgence. He hadn't had female contact in ages, let alone with one so attractive. Just to look at her was food to an appetite long neglected. That's who she was to him in many ways: food to a starving soul.

It was like time flew until the next meeting. It was no longer just a matter of dreaming in vain about talking to her. Those dreams were always undermined by knowing they were make-believe. Now he had the opportunity to truly tell her anything he saw fit. He tried to keep it in check, with little success. Now even the smallest event in his life was incomplete until he pictured telling it to her, and having the freedom to really do it removed the bitter taste it left before.

When he finally did arrive, he composed himself. Having the freedom to tell her everything was enough to take the edge off. He didn't have to put her through the monotony he himself was usually strangled by. So once he got there, he just played it cool, like the visits didn't matter much to him. As much as he might want to share things with her, he wouldn't. He didn't want to do anything to taint her image of him and telling her about running out of toilet paper at an inopportune time might not really maintain the image he tried to project.

"Hola!" she greeted the next day when he arrived, knocking on the screen door. "You know where the knob is, don't ya?"

Samuel let himself in the front and approached the counter that separated the kitchen from the dining area. "I got a letter I'm sure you were anxiously awaiting. It's not your package, mind you, but I know it'll be a close second," he joked.

"Oooh. Sounds interesting. What is it?" said Monique, playing along.

"Well, it's probably risky telling you standing up, but it's double coupon day coming up at the mini-mart and near as I can tell they sent you a whole envelope full."

"Ah! My hero!" she gasped sarcastically as she reached over the counter and threw her arms around his neck for a hug.

"I thought you'd be excited."

"You were right; just for that I'm gonna feed ya. Pull up a chair."

Samuel did as he smiled at their amusing conversation.

"So do you prefer punch? I just realized I never asked. It's just what Cully always takes. Not that there's a lot to choose from. It's either that, milk or water. Sorry, I don't usually keep much in the way of soda in the house."

"Actually no, I prefer punch. I've never been much for carbonation. It makes it hard to guzzle and as you know I love my liquids. 'Course on the other hand, punch turns my lips bright red, making me look girlie the rest of the day, so sometimes it's hard to decide."

"Ah well, I'm sure everyone can make out your gender."

"Well, I hope so. That's why I risk it. So what delicacy will I be fortunate enough to partake of this afternoon?"

"Well, actually I made that taco salad I was telling you about."

"Lovely. Just like your ma used to make, I'm sure."

"Ah, don't let her hear you say that. She never thinks either of us girls' cooking is up to her standards. Parents are your worst critics sometimes."

"Yeah, they expect the most out of ya."

"What about your parents? Were they hard on you?"

"Well, actually no. I never knew my dad. He died when I was just born. Some kind of auto accident. My mother was always worried I'd feel cheated not having a dad so she gave me everything she could and let me get away with murder."

"Did you? Feel cheated, I mean."

"No, not really. As a kid I was just so enthused with everything. It was hard to make me upset or to even stop me from being intrigued. I didn't take the time to notice what I was missing. She said I had my dad's same poetic spirit. He was always just happy to be alive. She said it was what fueled the debonair style that swept her off her feet. Said I had his same passion for life. That's why she was always so supportive when I wanted to be a writer." Samuel froze, biting his tongue. He considered his desire for writing to be as private as it came. He didn't like telling people about it. He didn't want their opinions.

"A writer, huh? I knew there was something about you. You don't really strike me as the mail delivery type. So what the heck are you doing walking these routes? Shouldn't you be out signing autographs?" asked Monique, showing blind support of his abilities.

"Ah, it was a childish fantasy. I never really had the knack for it. My mother was a real tough woman but she was kind of at a loss when it came to raising a child. She just tried to be supportive of about anything that wouldn't get me killed."

"Ha-ha. I hear that. I can see myself doing that with my little one in there. That is part of why I want to get back home. My mother is one of those natural born types who always know what they're doing even when they don't. She'll probably take one look at my Cullomine and know just what he's gonna do in life. Something tells me if she looked at you, though, she'd see a writer." Samuel smiled stiffly in response. Noticing his distaste for the subject, she changed it. "So I bet you picked up those debonair qualities from your padre as well, huh?" She smiled slyly, as if she had caught his hand in the cookie jar. "Come on, I know—you give a few lines from some poem you wrote in high school and the women just melt in your hands," she continued as she laid Samuel's food in front of him. It was complete with salt, pepper and both glasses of punch.

"Nah, it's not really like that. It's just I had a marriage. I liked it. My wife didn't. So she left me brokenhearted. Tragic tale I know, but now I'm not really up for something serious again, so I keep my relationships short and sweet."

"Sounds like an elaborate excuse for being a gigolo if you ask me," joked Monique.

"It's not that. It's just I'm a man. I need a woman in my life. I just don't want to get attached or anything. I'm not up for the responsibility that brings."

"You're sure it's just that, right? I mean, you're not like out there trying to hurt other women, taking out what your wife did to you on the rest of the gender?"

"No, no. Nothing like that," Samuel chuckled.

"Good. I don't think it'd be right me feeding a woman hater like this. It'd be like I was a traitor or something."

"Aha, I'm not even doing anything and you're already siding against me," laughed Samuel.

"I know it. Can you ever forgive me?"

"You know, I don't think I could, except . . . you're right, this taco salad is killer. I think it's enough to win me back over."

"I figured it would give me some extra leeway when I made it."

Samuel smiled brightly at her sense of humor. "You know, you speak the language real well. How long have you been here—America, I mean?"

"Ah, let's see... I'd say about eight years now. I was always interested in America, though. I used to order American movies as a child and watch them even before I could understand what they were saying. My padre kind of spoiled me. Anything I wanted he'd get me. TVs and VCRs weren't real commonplace in our part of the country, but I had them."

"I see. What exactly brought you here anyway?" asked Samuel.

"My husband," she explained. "He was a large business man in Chile, also a well-respected friend to my family. He was considerably older than me but when he began to court, my parents both wanted me to marry. Looking back, I guess I was kind of pushed into it. But it all turned out okay. It was his work that brought us to America, a place I'd always wanted to come to. Plus I ended up with my Cullomine here. I can't imagine life without him."

"Where's your husband now?" asked Samuel, a bit taken aback by the mention of him.

"He died of a heart attack about three years ago. He was always a very large man. He ate like he was a bear preparing for winter."

"Oh, I'm sorry."

"There's no need. I can't say I ever loved him. He was a cold man. He got or took everything he ever wanted but I don't think he knew how to enjoy it. He left me with a lot, though. I have to appreciate that. I never have to worry about Cully's future."

"So you just decided to stay here in America?"

"Yeah, I figured I'd stay and see the country until something else came up. Now it has."

"You picked a weird place to dig in if you wanted to see the country. There's not much for sights anywhere around here."

"Hee. No matter where I live in this country, the people there always hate where they're at. They all act like the rest of the country is great but where they're at is the one place that stinks. I'll never understand your people. But you've changed subjects back to me again. I want to hear about you. Why do you want to go around hating women?" she joked again.

Samuel laughed at her humorous assault on him for something she had made up in the first place. "I didn't say I hate women, or go around hating them. I said I don't want to get in a relationship so I sometimes have to cut things short to prevent problems."

"So in other words you put forth enough effort to get them in bed, but then you won't call them or return messages. Breaking hearts with no remorse—how do you sleep at night?"

Again Samuel grinned. "Something like that, I guess. I don't know why you're so sympathetic; we both know good and well you've never had any problems getting your calls returned."

"Well, that was quite nice of you to say," Monique smiled brightly. "That's probably the charm that helps you to use and abuse all those poor local girls, huh?"

Again they shared laughter, then Monique began again, "But actually I've never really been a part of that game. Where I'm from there aren't a whole lot of phones and intentions are still commonly brought through the parents. And I was married throughout a lot of my time here. Then I've been like a hermit ever since. Everything I know about you guys' relationship habits I learned from movies."

"I thought you wanted to see the country. How can you do that as a hermit?"

"Well, it was a goal I set but it just never seemed to fit in with things. I can't say I've seen much."

"Ah, waiting for things to happen instead of getting up and going after them. You're practically a full-fledged American."

"Yeah, maybe you're right. It was easier just to watch movies. That's not even as enjoyable as it once was. It was a bigger deal to watch American movies back home. Now I can understand them all on top of having access to more than can be imagined. It's kind of nice in itself. I sent some of my favorites back home already."

"Oh yeah, what are your favorites?"

"I have a lot of favorites. *Dirty Dancing*, umm, *Romeo and Juliet*, *Wizard of Oz*. Oh, *Casablanca* has always been one of my favorites. I love the original *Annie*, and the *Sound of Music*."

"There're a couple of those I like. Not really my genres, though. I lean toward gangster flicks."

"Oh, *The Godfathers* are great movies. I have all three."

"Ha-ha, now we're talking. Three of the greatest movies ever made. The third one always gets a bad rap because of a few minor flaws, but I think people let those small things blind them to what a great movie it is. What about the Pacino version of *Scarface*? That's a classic."

"Oh no, that's not really my kind of movie. It's too violent and depressing. I don't care for all the guns and such in the *Godfathers*. It's just the big family going through hardships together that's appealing to me."

"I see, I see. Susan never really liked my obsession with gangster movies but luckily anything with Al Pacino she'd tolerate."

"Susan? Was that your wife?" asked Monique.

"Yeah, Susan was the other participant in my short-lived marriage," said Samuel, successfully masking the frustrations and emotions that festered just by saying her name.

"Do you ever see her anymore?"

"Nah, I haven't seen or heard in years," smirked Samuel. "Can't say I care to. Alimony is still coming out of my checks so I know she's still out there," he explained as he looked at his watch. "Shoot, it has been a pleasure as always but unfortunately, it's about that time."

"Yeah, I was starting to wonder. I swear it's been longer than your usual lunch period," she agreed.

"Yeah, I think I went a little over. I'll just have to walk faster I guess," he smiled. "All right, well, are we still on for tomorrow?"

"Certainly," she answered, returning the grin.

CHAPTER 13: CONFIDING

Samuel left, caught up in the same euphoric spell Monique had cast over him the day prior. He was about as happy as he was capable of with this new routine. It was almost scary feeling this good. He felt like he was walking a tightrope, predestined to fall off at any moment. But he couldn't concern himself with that until it happened. He was just going to enjoy everything to the fullest in the meantime.

Also like before, the time between visits passed in a flash. Life just seemed like distractions until he could be back on her step. Until he was back, knocking on that door, everything else was pretend. And once she let him in, it was like waking up from a deep sleep. Life became real again. If he thought back on the day before, the only things he remembered were while he was there. It was as if everything in between hadn't really happened.

"Welcome back," she greeted kindly as she let Samuel in. The front door had been closed due to the cool wind the day had brought.

"Thanks. Looks like we might get a storm before the day's out." Monique had to agree as she looked out the window. The sky had the foreboding stillness it commonly did just before letting loose the commotion of a thunderstorm.

"I hope you brought a rain coat," she said, concerned.

"I did. It's in my bag. I bet I'll need it by the time I leave."

"Yeah, I'm surprised because it's supposed to be nothing but sunshine tomorrow."

"Well, the sun always shines a little brighter after a storm."

"Good point. I didn't check the weather for today 'cause . . ."

"*CRACK!*" interrupted a resounding smack of thunder. The sound clearly startled Monique a bit, as she jumped slightly at the sound of it.

"Not scared of storms, are you?" asked Samuel as he was handed a large plate boasting a burger and fries. "Whoa. Not exactly a Latin dish here, is it?" he observed, somewhat surprised.

"I learned a few things here in the States as well," she answered with a smile as she joined him at the table.

Samuel bit into his burger and agreed, "I guess so. This is great." He took a few more chews. "Whatever that spice in the meat is, it really sets it off."

"Thank you and no, I'm not scared of storms. I was just caught off guard." The end of Monique's sentence was accompanied by the sound of rain landing on the roof. The gentle hum came abruptly and filled the room. It made the house feel cozy as it protected its inhabitants from the weather outside. "I was always scared as a little girl, though. My brother would comfort me."

"You don't strike me as the type who needs comforting," he suggested.

"Well, I'm not a little girl anymore," she agreed.

"I always loved storms. My mom would take me to the porch and we'd watch them together. It got so I would look forward to them as a kid. If there were clouds in the sky I knew we'd soon be on that porch listening to the splashing rain. Even the smell brings back a lot of memories."

"You and your mother must have been close. Just the two of you and all."

"Yeah, we were, until Susan entered the picture. Then I never had time. That's what made it so hard about her passing at the same time we were splitting up. It was like I missed my time with her for no reason, ya know."

"I'm sure she didn't feel that way," reassured Monique.

"She didn't have a chance. I never told her about the breakup. She got sick so suddenly. I didn't have the heart to let anyone know. I probably would have broken down and confided in her at the end, but I didn't make it to the hospital in time."

"Oh, that's so sad."

"Well, not seeing her off was sad but having it be my own fault is just shameful."

"How could it be your fault?" she asked with such warm sincerity that it opened a door Samuel considered welded shut.

"Well, I got the call saying she might not make it through the night. I was supposed to go up to see her, but as I opened the door I got scared. I sat in the chair next to me, just so I could think things over. The next thing I knew it was morning. My mother was always such a strong person. She had a way of making me feel safe no matter what was going on. When I started to picture her weak and on her last leg, it was terrifying. I just wanted a moment to try and regroup. When I woke the next morning and realized what I had done, I bolted out the door to the train station. Somehow the whole ride up there, I already knew I was too late. I can't tell you how hard it is knowing I was the one person she wanted to see . . . and she didn't get to 'cause I was too pussy." Samuel hadn't spoke of things so close to his heart to anyone in years. In spite of that he kept himself well composed while doing so.

"You can't be so hard on yourself. You were scared. That's natural," replied Monique, trying to come up with a quick fix to heal the wound.

"Being scared wasn't the problem; it was how I responded to it," replied Samuel solemnly. Monique didn't have anything to say to that. It was a hard point to argue. After a proper moment of silence she spoke again.

"Well, we all have things we've done we wish we could do differently. The nice thing about heavy regret is that we can learn from it. Perhaps next time things get too real or emotional and you want to back away, you'll remember that day and make a better decision. I'm sure your mother would be proud at having that be the final lesson she got to teach you."

Samuel nodded his head in approval. Hearing that actually made him feel a little better about something so shameful he hadn't even allowed himself to think about it, let alone speak of it, since it took place. "You're a real sharp one, you know. That's a better way to look at it." Samuel waited a moment, then attempted to lighten the mood. "You know, I've never talked about that with anyone before. I hope you don't mind me bringing up such a heavy subject."

"No, not at all. I'm glad you did. I read you as someone who holds a lot in. You should start trying to be more open, try and find an outlet for all your built-up… stuff."

"An outlet, huh. Well, what about you? What's your thing?"

"My thing?"

"Yeah, everybody's got a thing. Something they just loved as a child and could never explain why. Whether they're good at it or not, everybody's got what they gotta be doing to be complete. Builders build, painters paint, singers sing and so forth. So what about you? What's your thing? What do you just love to do?"

"Well . . ." she paused coyly, "as a kid I loved to dance. My mother got me in classes and stuff. It was great. In truth I still love the idea of it. I think that's why I love musicals so much. They get carried away by the music and all; it brings back memories of when I danced a lot."

"Well, there you go. You need to be dancing."

"I think I'm a little old to take up lessons."

"Never too old. But I'm not even saying that. Turn on a radio and dance by yourself in the kitchen if that's all there is. Anything's better than nothing. You got to do it. You can't neglect that one thing. Otherwise what's the point?"

Monique nodded her head like Samuel had made a good argument. "So what about you? What do you gotta do?" she said using his terminology against him.

Samuel looked at his watch. "Me, I gotta get back to my route."

Monique laughed at his dodge of the question. "Okay, I suppose I'll let you off the hook for now."

"Well, I guess I'll be seeing you Monday."

"Oh. . ." she paused, seeming displeased with the comment, "is it Saturday already?"

"Yeah, it sneaks right up on you, don't it?" said Samuel.

"Yeah, it does. Listen, I don't want you to take this the wrong way. I mean as a girl talking to a guy, I don't want you to think I'm trying to come on to you or anything like that. I mean, I'm leaving soon and all. It's just I really enjoy having someone to talk to and I don't have any friends around here. I thought maybe you could come over tonight after work sometime. So our visit wouldn't be rushed like it always is. I don't know if that's inappropriate, me being on your route and all. I'm just so antsy waiting to leave I can't stand sitting around this house by myself all the time," asked Monique, obviously feeling a little nervous about the invitation.

"I'm sorry, I'd really love to and appreciate the invite but I got this poker game with the fellas tonight."

"Oh well, that's all right, don't worry about it," answered Monique quickly, trying not to look rejected.

"Don't get me wrong, I'd really like to . . . well, what you got going on tomorrow?"

"Um, I don't have any plans. Yeah, actually tomorrow would be good if you want to do it then."

"That'd be great. What time do you think?"

"Oh, whenever. You know I don't go anywhere, so whenever suits you. I'm sure you got plenty of other things going on," insinuated Monique.

Samuel smiled slyly as if to falsely admit guilt. "How 'bout early afternoon?"

"That sounds good. When I heard early I was scared I was gonna have to get up before eleven. But afternoon is good. I'll be looking forward to it."

"Yeah, me too," agreed Samuel pleasantly.

When Samuel arrived home his mind wasn't racing. He wasn't even really daydreaming. He was too content to put forth the energy. He walked in and checked the clock. He wouldn't have to be ready for the game for hours. He hit play on the answering machine then proceeded to heat up leftovers. After the typical bill collectors and salesman voices played through, he was joyfully surprised to hear David coming through the speaker. Samuel sat down in his sofa chair while starting in on the spaghetti.

"All right, how often do I get to make these phone calls?" complained the voice. "Here's one of those times and you're not even gonna be there to pick up. I see how it is. A-h-h, just fuckin' with ya. I figured as much. I'm sure you're still out there, peddling the mail. I wanted to remind you, though; you should let me know what's up on that situation we've been looking into. If you remember it was your turn to supply some info. You got me boiling in my seat over here. I guess that's not all bad; it's been making the time move by. Anyway, let me know what you found out. The more I think about it, and the more I talk to people here, I'm almost convinced that you've really stumbled on to something. Like I said, I got a course of action if it turns out to be we're right. I'd like to fill you in. You could get things rollin' before I even get out. Anyway, let me know. Oh yeah, I gave Mouse your number so he can get hold of you. He's gonna be the one you'll need to talk to if things move ahead. I figured you might as well get reacquainted now. Not like you got something better to do," accused David, who was always angered by his friend's 'bump on a log' attitude. "Besides, I thought you guys might want to make some plans for when I get out. I know you haven't been around the old crew much. All right, well, I'll be waiting to hear from ya. *BEEP*."

"Hey, hey. Samuel, it's me, Lukas, Lukas Bailey. How have you been, motherfucker? I just assumed you had moved to Egypt or some shit, having not heard anything from or about ya in so long. Then David gives me a call yesterday and says you been right here in town the whole time. What kind of shit is that? Too good to make it over to the East side or something? Well, even if you are, you're gonna have to bite the bullet and give me a call. David says he should be getting out in the near future and we gotta make some plans. Plus I wouldn't mind hearing from your punk ass. 660-1482. Holler!"

Damn! thought Samuel. *Talk about a blast from the past.* Little Lukas Bailey, also widely known as Mouse due to his squirmy size and anxious attitude. He was the other one there when David got arrested. It was his dog that was put down after the incident. Samuel hadn't heard his voice since David was sentenced. Mouse was the only other person from Post Samuel might consider a real friend. They weren't close like with David, but they shared plenty of good times. Still, it was more like two guys who had a mutual friend than it was an actual bond between them. Regardless, Samuel still liked hearing from him. That sadistically perky voice that made him sound like he had something devious up his sleeve in even the most innocent of conversations brought back countless memories of Samuel's days in Post Edition.

Mouse had been a wild one out of the womb. Like a mouse, he was always getting into something. He was a typical rowdy Post boy who could make the gloomiest day fun through his own mischief. He wasn't all that small; he was just wiry. He was considerably younger than both Samuel and David. He was next-door neighbor to the Caine boys his whole life. Over the years he had become like a protégé. There were countless stories of a young David and Kris using Lukas to entertain themselves. As a little kid, Mouse would do anything to impress the older boys. Whether they told him to kick the next passing car or to break out a neighbor's window, he would always do it without hesitation. What started out as an easy way to get a laugh became a point of pride. If someone new came around David would invent a prank for Mouse to do, as a way to show him off. No matter how many whippings or scoldings Ms. Bailey handed out, Mouse wouldn't think twice about doing it. As he grew to a teenager himself he followed and mimicked David to no end. David took more interest in him than Kris and usually didn't mind him tagging along. Eventually an impenetrable bond had grown. You'd never know it to hear them talk to each other. It was always insults and jokes but all in goodhearted fun. If David asked him to, Lukas would turn his back on family and country. Knowing that, David would spare no expense to look out for his sidekick, and he had for some time.

Samuel finished up his food as he wondered how to handle the situation as it pertained to David. He was sure Monique had nothing to do with Cullomine Torreo. The description of her mother alone made you realize she would never have been allowed to get mixed up with that kind, but convincing David of that would not be easy. Even David himself had stated how convinced he was without additional proof. Samuel decided that the best route was to treat it as if it had been a small topic all along. Not responding right away and talking nonchalantly about it would hopefully bring David to his own conclusion that he'd blown it out of proportion. Samuel would also return Lukas Bailey's call so they could make plans for David's release. Getting David hyped on his exodus from prison might help him forget about Cullomine Torreo.

As his inhibitions about David resolved, his mind started to wander on to other things. Wandering, of course, brought him back to Monique. He laid his head on the back of the sofa chair and closed his eyes as she gently made her way into his thoughts. It was different this time. She didn't come in a fantasy. There was no self-serving story line surrounding his portrait of her. All there was now was the feeling of contentment he had felt when in her presence.

He wasn't picturing her face or even her body. He tried to recreate the sound of her voice in his head. Just thinking of the things she said to him, no matter how inconsequential, made him feel a warmth all over his body. It was a warmth he'd almost forgotten existed. In recent years he could remember being so envious of others going home with a girlfriend or even a local floozy in the bar. He hated the idea that they would go home and have sex and he would go home to a deep emptiness. Envy was nowhere near his mind now. Now he felt sorry for each of those men who never had the chance to spend time with Monique. To be in her good graces was his own personal paradise.

When in her presence he was covered in a warm glaze of comfort. It was a comfort that had long been missing in his life, one that made him feel almost complete again. It was that warmth that carried with it the memories of his first kiss from Susan, learning her affection was genuine, of being a sick child with his mother at his bed side petting back his hair, allowing him to doze off. This blissful haze made him feel ready to face the world again. She was the spring to his long winter that made him feel the need to just get out and live life again.

Dwelling on the joy she returned to him made the emptiness and dread that had long dictated his life feel miles away. In the recent weeks, growing closer to Monique and knowing of David's approaching return made him think maybe things would soon be better. But it hadn't taken intercourse with Monique or the arrival of David for that to happen. Just establishing this rapport with Monique suddenly made the sun shine again. He didn't feel happy. He wasn't smiling. It was a nourishing relief that tingled all over his body and as he lay there thinking on it, it slowly drifted him into sleep. Things hadn't felt like that since high school.

CHAPTER 14: GO WHERE YOU'RE HAPPY

It was a few hours later before Samuel awoke. At the opening of his eyelids he was looking directly at his wall clock, which informed him he was behind schedule for the poker game. He rustled himself out of the chair and into the shower. Behind as he was, he didn't rush. He thought of how he'd waited on each one of them before. It was fair for them to do a bit of waiting. Though he wasn't thinking of Monique, there was still the settled feeling she had given him.

He was exactly one half hour late when he stepped onto Brad's back porch. He was interested in seeing if the boys had given up on him or waited as it was tradition to. Stepping in the back door brought an onslaught of hoots and hollers.

"Woo-hoo! Look who decided to bless us with his presence," razzed Mark.

"Samuel, we didn't know you cared," added Brad.

"Why would you guys be in such a rush to lose all your money anyway?" replied Samuel in a playfully cocky fashion.

"UUHHOO!" hooted the boys in synchronization.

They had waited for him, and it was obvious how that wait had been spent. Looking across the table, there wasn't a face that didn't look at least on the verge of belligerent.

Samuel smirked at the sight of them, and then joined them at the table. "Well, let's get those cards dealt."

"Don't you wanna grab a cold one?" asked Clint.

"Naw, I'm all right," demurred Samuel. He was in too pure a mood to risk altering it with alcohol.

"Oh, too good to drink with the boys, huh. Make us wait all night then you won't even tip one back. I see how it is," slurred Kyle in an accusing joke.

"Ah, it ain't like that. I've just had an upset stomach lately. I don't want to irritate it. Plus you know I like an unfair advantage whenever I can find one," returned Samuel, deflating the accusation.

"Yeah, we know," agreed Kyle.

The cards were dealt and Samuel's newfound happiness was apparent in his luck. In spite of his repeated gloats he had a reputation for always finishing on the losing end. This time he was, instead, a noticeable amount ahead. It could be attributed to his opponents' highly and continually growing drunken state, but they had been drunk before without him gaining advantage.

Despite his lead Samuel was growing restless. His traditionally drab life suddenly had some enjoyment but he didn't feel comfortable sharing with them. His affection for Monique had not been consummated and so was of little interest to this bunch. His best friend David would most likely be released before the week was out, but his overly opinionated law enforcement friends would not likely have anything good to say about a released convict.

Samuel leaned back in his chair and thought of who these men were to him. There wasn't a real aspect of his life he would be comfortable sharing with them. Just the same, he knew they wouldn't be interested in hearing it. He wondered why he was wasting his time with them when he had received such a lovely invitation from Monique. Still, he hadn't accepted and was here now. If David and Monique were off limits the only thing left of interest to him was the Cullomine situation. He really considered the subject a dead horse but knowing that Mark and Clint were interested, he decided to bring it up.

"So have you heard anything more about that drug dealer?" asked Samuel. The heads rose at the new and unusually interesting conversational topic. "You know, that Torreo fellow you guys were goin' on about a few weeks back. Is there any word on his release?"

"Fuck! You had to bring that up, didn't you? That son of a bitch's release has already been approved. I swear somebody's gotta be greasing the wheels for that prick. Don't make no sense," complained Mark.

"Yeah, but supposedly it won't be as bad as we thought. Word I get is it's a safe bet that Cullomine will be on the first jet out of the country," continued Clint. "'Course that would violate his parole and the feds have a real hard-on for him. So everyone's figuring he'll get picked up at the airport and they'll put him back in a cell before the end of his first day of freedom. As far as I'm concerned, he'll either be in a cell or out of the country. Either way we win."

"That fuck doesn't deserve to lead a free life, in this country or any other. I hope they snag the son of a bitch," asserted Mark. "Better yet, I hope he resists and gets shot square in the chest."

"Yeah, that'd work," agreed Kyle.

"Well, I'll have to watch the news and see how it all turns out," said Samuel, trying to bring an end to the conversation he started. They weren't saying anything about Cullomine that interested him, and just talking about him made Samuel think of how much he hated the idea that his darling, innocent Monique could be wrapped up with Cullomine Torreo's kind. Samuel was sure that couldn't be the case but if it somehow turned out it was, he'd rather remain in ignorance. When she walked out of his life, Samuel didn't want to picture her anywhere but her mother's arms.

The boys continued to play cards and Samuel continued to win the majority of the hands. But with each dollar he won he was just reminded of how little it mattered to him. The more he thought about it the more restless he became. Monique was almost certainly sitting at home lonely and bored; he was sitting there wishing he was with Monique. It didn't make much sense.

"Hell, man! Are you in or out?" asked Brad sternly of Samuel, who was in a daze.

"Ah shit. What time is it?" wondered Samuel as he snapped out of it and looked at his watch. "A-h-h, I think I'm out, man. It's about time to get home."

"Fuck man, it's only 8:30! Don't you feel bad always being the one to break up the games? Especially tonight—you were the last one here. Now you're the first one out," complained Brad.

"Y'all can keep playing. I just said what I was gonna do. I didn't make no comment on what you guys should be doing. All I said was I was about to go," explained Samuel.

"Yeah, but you know damn well how this works. One person gets up and heads home and suddenly everybody else gets to thinking they should be leaving and it's like dominoes from there. I just don't see why it's always gotta be you that starts knocking them over," preached Brad some more. "Fuck it. You just finish off this hand. Let me get a chance to win some of my funds back, then I'll leave you alone."

Samuel chuckled, amused at Brad's irritation. Summing up the patterns that people and events followed was a common source of drunken amusement during Samuel's days with David and the Posties. Brad was very right with his description of the usual demise of their poker games. Pointing out the senseless routine of it brought back memories for Samuel. "All right, that's fair. But after this hand, I'm out," agreed Samuel.

He played the hand as they had agreed, but instead of Brad recouping some of his losses it was another win for Samuel. He smiled slyly, as if there was never any real doubt of his approaching victory, and then he departed in an obvious rush. As predicted, the rest followed close behind.

CHAPTER 15: A LONG NIGHT

As Samuel drove he didn't feel any of the apprehensions he usually had when approaching Monique's. He was sure he was wanted there; he knew he wouldn't be comfortable doing anything except going to her house. So he made one stop and then was there before nine o'clock.

He knocked at the door holding a freshly rented DVD player hiked up on his shoulder like a pizza delivery boy. In the other hand was *Moulin Rouge,* an innovative musical he hoped she had never seen. She had expressed her love for movies but she had been without them for a good while now. It would be a perfect gesture to bring both player and DVD to help her presumed withdrawals.

"Samuel!" she said, delighted at the sight of him. "I thought you had a poker game?"

"Well, I thought instead of losing my money to those clowns I should try and get something out of it. So I rented us a flick."

"And a DVD player, I see."

"Well, you said how much you liked movies and I knew you sent everything home already, so I brought equipment."

"Great!" she responded enthusiastically. "That is so sweet. I've been dying watching the poor excuse for entertainment on television."

"I thought you might be. I figured I owe you for all those lunches so I rented this from Holly Video. You get 'em for a week there."

Monique shook her head, smiling. "Well, I hope you don't think this gets you out of tomorrow's visit."

"I'd be happy to come over tomorrow. You'll be the one gettin' sick of me, though."

Monique just rolled her eyes in response.

Samuel hooked the player up, started the movie and joined Monique in leaning against the wall. She provided pillows to keep them from sitting on the hard floor.

"What's this movie again?" she asked as the previews began.

"*Moulin Rouge.* I think you might like it. There's a lot of singing and such."

"You know me so well already," she boasted.

As the movie played both had their eyes on the screen but neither was paying much attention. They enjoyed their chance to talk to each other and rather than focusing on the movie, their minds kept drifting to things they'd like to say. Neither wanted to interrupt the other's viewing but after a time Monique was the one to give in and break the courteous silence.

"So do you like musicals a lot too?" she asked, wondering if the choice was purely for her benefit.

"Yeah, kind of. They're not something I'd usually rent. I'd feel girly watching them by myself. It works out, you liking them. It gave me an excuse to get it," reassured Samuel, not wanting her to feel like a burden. "I'm not all about singing or anything. It's just when you watch the characters sing in these movies, you can see they're putting everything they got into it. That voice is coming from way down deep. They ain't holding nothing back. You don't see that kind of passion in much these days. Nobody comes from the heart anymore. Everybody you meet either seems like they're putting on a show or just going through the motions. I swear it's like I get withdrawals for anything genuine. Like a baby's smile, the epitome of genuine. You don't see that much with us adults."

Monique shook her head with an appreciative smile. "You're one of a kind, Samuel."

"Well, I can't really argue with that. It's a curse my mother gave me."

"You think it's a curse?" asked Monique.

"Yeah, but truthfully, as hard as it is at times, I'm still grateful. A lot of people just roll on through life not tasting their food, not even taking the time to look at what they really want. It's safer that way. You don't have the risk of disappointment. They keep everything really bad out, but in doing so, they block out what's good as well. I can't really blame 'em. It's gotta be easier that way. I'm just not capable of living like that. I don't know. Maybe that's just the way I see it."

"No, I know what you mean. Most people do strike me as . . . withdrawn, I guess. You talk to people about their lives and it's like all they do is focus on what are really just distractions. Why do they even bother if that's all they're in it for? Who wants to rehash what kind of deal they got on strawberries or how many miles they get to the gallon? Don't they have anything better?" agreed Monique. "So I take it your mother was like you."

"No, not really. It was the way she always protected me from her parents that she gets the credit for. When my dad died my grandparents had us move in with them so they could help pick up the slack. My grandpa was a real 'by the book' type of guy. He liked everything to be planned out, done in its proper way. It infuriated him when my mother fell for a guy who he described as having his head in the clouds. My dad always loved his poetry. He read it, wrote it and lived it, more or less. Gramps could never understand that. He liked to break down everything like it was a math equation. He loved and lived by reason. As Mother told it, Dad was an instinctive type. He did what his heart told him. My mother loved that about him, so when he died, and she saw his ways in me, she decided she'd do everything she could to keep me that way. It was the last thing remaining of my dad and she nurtured it as such. My grandparents wanted to pick exactly what I was gonna do in life. If they had their way the college I went to would have been chosen in elementary school. They wouldn't have allowed a make-believe movie or book in the house. My mother didn't give into them, though. She read me all the great fairy tales, she encouraged my writing and basically anything else I showed interest in. She wouldn't bog me down with a prescheduled life. She wanted me free to do what I wanted when I wanted. It drove Gramps nuts."

"She sounds like a wonderful woman," said Monique.

"She was. She had so much to give. She should have had ten kids. They still couldn't have sucked up everything she had to offer. There was not much she didn't have figured out. She kind of left me holding the bag, though. That passion she helped fill me with doesn't work so well out in the world."

"I don't see how you can call passion for life a bad thing. I see that sparkle in your eye when you start to really describe something. It's the same gleam I see in Cully when he's talking about his favorite big-time wrestler. It amazes me how a kid can feel so strongly about something so trivial. Most grown-ups have far more important things going on but not even a percentage of the enthusiasm. Somehow you still have a child's gleam. You should be grateful to your mother."

Samuel smiled lightly. He loved Monique's observation and if for only an instant, he had to wallow in the pleasure of it. His stare thanked the compliment before he attempted to explain his point. "It is nice being able to see what you want out of life, and seeing the joy in things, but it makes it all the more painful when you can't achieve it or when you no longer have that joy. It's still the way I think people should be, but it doesn't really work when only a few are. People need people to be complete. It makes it hard when no one is on the same page as you. But I hate the way most people do things so I can't change." Monique scrunched her face a bit still, not really following Samuel's point. He attempted again to elaborate. "You know those guys in the wars you hear about who don't even duck when the bullets are whizzing by their heads. Those guys come from the heart, you know. Somehow they just know whether they're gonna be all right or not and they don't base it on anything as trivial as random shrapnel or stray bullets. It's a deeper sense of things. Even the other soldiers can look at them and just tell they're gonna be fine. They might even be jealous. Those are the type of people I always had the most respect for. That's the way I've tried to be, but it's a lost breed. I don't think there're many left like that in the modern world. I'm sure people in modern wars only do things based on their training. They just think about properly acting out what they were taught. There's no room for the heart to serve as a compass. They think and plan and pre-decide and practice so much that their heart's drowned in it all. Then the second things don't go as planned they're at a loss. A simple unexpected occurrence can throw them off completely. That's a trivial way to base your life. Training is good but you gotta give your instincts room to breathe. That's how I see regular people nowadays. They traded their hearts in for a good plan. They're bogged down by all their schooling and over-thinking of everything. The idea of making a decision by any means but their brains is absurd. Their hearts are stifled by all that inane thought. So people base their relationships on who has the most stable job and who's easy to get along with but their marriages can't ever last 'cause they're still missing that passion that a person really needs. That passion that they never weighed in their choices because the heart wasn't there when they made it. It's the same with their jobs; they want what's practical and good pay, not what they enjoy doing or get some personal reward from. I don't think I know anyone who's happy overall. They're all just going through the motions. Their marriages never last. They complain about their jobs. I can't help but think it's because they never took the time to feel instead of think. But after years of it, they forget what their heart even sounds like. I . . . oh, I'm sorry. Once I get going I can rant on endlessly. Just be happy I'm not drinking. Then there's no shutting me up," said Samuel, startling himself with his flood of personal thoughts.

"No, no. I want to hear it. Finish what you were saying," reassured Monique.

Samuel was pleased to have someone who actually wanted to hear him. "Well, I was gonna say how I can remember asking my grandma for a ride to the movie theater to meet some friends. It was a short drive, wouldn't take long. A friend's mom was gonna bring us back home. She was making dinner, nothing out of the ordinary. She didn't need to be in any rush, but she wouldn't take me. I can remember being so frustrated when I couldn't talk her into it, but after a while I was just hurt. I couldn't see why she wouldn't take me when I wanted to go so bad. That can be hard on a kid when things they feel so strongly about are so easily neglected. Whether it's a bike you always wanted or a crush they blow off as childish, it can hurt to have what you think important considered worthless by your loved ones. Now, looking back, I know it was just a matter of it not fitting the schedule she had in her head. She had set an agenda for herself, though there was no real reason for it, or importance to it, but she had built it up in her head and couldn't tear it back down. She had things so figured out that the fact she was leaving me out of her equation didn't ever click. I think most kids forget how much that hurts. Then over the years they pick up the same habits, and then end up doing the same stuff to their kids, remaining just as oblivious as their parents had been. Looking back, I know if she could have just taken a moment to see how I felt, she would have taken me up there. It wasn't that she was selfish. She just had too many years of being wrapped up in her own head.

"I don't think we as a people can work that way, wrapped up in our heads. I think that's much of what keeps people in close relationships from getting along as they should. It's why so few people I see have found contentment. It's their hearts that're hungry but it's their brains they feed. But still people seem to be systematically strangling the heart without ever seeing it. Take how people raise kids nowadays; they're not supposed to spank 'em. Instead they tell them it's wrong, or it's naughty to misbehave. Now you tell me what lasts longer, a physical pain or emotional. A spanking brings tears, parent reminds the child they love them and it's over. But when they misbehave after being told it was wrong, and then they are left with that guilt and feelings that they might actually be bad. Which one is gonna last longer? I swear people must not remember what it's like to be a kid. I can remember looking at a toy in the store and wanting it more than I've probably wanted anything in my entire adult life. That's the passion in a child. I don't know too many adults who don't do something they really want based on whether it's right or wrong. So how are kids supposed to keep themselves from misbehaving simply because of words said? People don't realize how long those words can stay with them. But when a kid knows there's gonna be a whooping coming, then they second-guess whether they should be doing something. Then not wanting that spanking keeps them from doing it even when they wanted to. It teaches them how to control their emotions. They can be stronger than the feelings they feel. Then there's the guilt. Whether people want to accept it or not, there is a part of everyone that wants to atone for what they've done wrong. A good punishment wipes the slate clean but when there is nothing but a strong reminder that they misbehaved, the guilt is left to linger. Eventually it becomes easier to just ignore the heart altogether. To me it's like a whole system to keep people from having a soul. Maybe they can pointlessly work their lives away easier if there's no passion in them.

"Then there're some kids who continue to feel but are just convinced they're a bad apple when they can't behave like the other kids do. It's not their fault that no one really gave them what they needed to learn how to make themselves behave, but they don't know that when they give up on being good and start holding up liquor stores. Then you got those who tried to be good but still had traces of heart they just can't seem to put a muzzle on. That's me. We're like those lingering Japanese soldiers from World War Two that hid out in the caves for twenty years. We're the real casualties. We're left with all the wrong instincts from a war that's already been lost. It makes it harder to get along like everybody else. We don't understand when people are so selfish and cruel to each other. We can't get with the program. You take a teen who's still got that lingering heart but doesn't have any real control over it. It's a dangerous thing in incapable hands. It's like giving a toddler a machine gun. Then this teen has some kids insult him so deeply it's beyond him. His pain is stronger than him. He can't help but retaliate, and no one can understand how he did something so heartless as to come in the school shooting those classmates. I believe that's how a lot of those real heinous crimes occur, when people are left with un-nurtured emotion. If they can cut out their heart completely with their constructed look at life it's one thing, but when there's some left hiding in the crevices it can be real dangerous.

"I'm not saying I'm dangerous. I can just sympathize. I feel like I'm left behind enemy lines sometimes, like I'm the last living poet. That's why I spend so much time alone. The last few still out there trying to live life the way it should be lived are suffocated by the endless masses on top of us. These few can't pick up the slack for everybody. When no one else is doing things the same way it seems to make our intentions backfire. When you reach out a helping hand and it gets bitten, you're left feeling like it was your desire to be helpful that resulted in your pain. I don't know, maybe I'm just so wrapped up in the way I see things and it's easier to just see everyone else as soulless. Sorry, I know people don't like to talk about stuff like that. Like I said, I can rant on for hours if you let me."

"I see where you're coming from. I guess you're right in a lot of it. But you can't let that stop you from trying. You can't let other people block you from living your life. They might not act the way you want them to, but you got to keep trying. There's never any sense in just accepting unhappiness, no matter how hard it is otherwise."

"True. I guess I've always been kind of a mama's boy in that way. I loved the thrill of victory, like when we'd be out playing football or something. But I was also the one who used to quit when he didn't win his first tryout. I'd love to play as long as we were winning but if my team lost, I'd usually take my ball and go home to my mom. If things weren't how I liked them I didn't want to play no more. I never played through till we got better and won. I'd just go home where I could have things the way I wanted them immediately and without real effort. But now home doesn't do for me what it once did. That's the thing about writing a lot of stories, too. You get spoiled by being able to control the world. Then you're frustrated when you can't do it in real life."

"Well, it sounds to me like you got it good," said Monique happily. Samuel's face contorted with confusion at her statement. "You have the luxury of knowing what you're doing wrong. You just have to put forth the effort of fixing it."

Samuel nodded and smiled appreciatively at the insight. All he had to do was show her a glimpse of the anchors weighing him down and she knew just how to cut them loose. There was no problem that caught her off guard. In his experience most people either had no advice to give or were spewing it out too often. They hardly ever let a person finish describing their problem before they were tossing out a solution. They seemed to have the opinion they already had the world figured out and everyone else's problems were a small opponent against their all-knowing minds. She was the better of both worlds. She took things at a deliberate pace. She listened to what Samuel had to say completely. She dwelled for a moment, trying to see how he must feel. Then if she felt she had something worth saying, she shared.

Monique began again. "That's beautiful, the way you described your family though, poetry versus math. I think to get along properly a person needs to learn how to balance the two."

"They both have their place. There's just such a lack of poetry today. It's brushed aside like a pointless hobby instead of the way life should be lived. I think that's why I became so fond of the Posties. That's their natural way over there. Coming from the heart, I mean."

"Posties?" inquired Monique.

"Yeah, Post Edition is a neighborhood on the East side of town. There's a lot of bad-asses over there I got to be friends with. The last of the heart-led soldiers. From breathing to walking to loving, they don't hold nothing back. They don't know how. To me it was like all the crime that took place was a small price to pay to see people still living with soul. Those were fun days out there."

"You hung out with bad-asses? I can't see you as the type to get in trouble," said an interested Monique.

"Well, I never really got caught for anything, but I did my share. Sometimes if we didn't have the money or we couldn't find anyone old enough to buy, we'd just go in the grocery store, grab all the liquor we could and run out. Full sprint with a week's worth of good times in your hands and security hot behind ya—you know you're in all sorts of shit if they catch ya but it's all worth it. It wasn't even all the free drunkenness, or the gloating you got to do as you got everybody twisted that night, it was. . .you were just so alive in that moment. Stealing and running from the law is so ugly to most people but at the time it was beautiful to me. Scary as it was, we'd be laughing so hard there'd be tears in our eyes. Once Mouse, this younger guy who hung out sometimes," Samuel situated himself in his seat, visibly excited about reliving these days. Monique smiled at seeing the recently referenced gleam. ". . . he was running next to us with fifths in each hand and as we were rounding this corner the gravel under his feet started to roll. Before he knew it his feet came right up from underneath him and he was flat on his face. At the same time I'm still in full sprint and these two elderly women were coming out of the tanning salon, I'll never understand what some elderly ladies was doing in a tanner—one had a walker even— well anyway, they stepped right out in front of me. I had to jump on this picnic table to my left to keep from running them over. There was no time to think, I just reacted. With one stride I was up on top of the table; with the next I was down the other side and still running. By then the lady from the store had quit chasing. She just yelled 'We got you on tape.' Didn't matter, though; we were gone and knew better than to think some shoddy recording of a petty crime would ever catch up with us. Mouse had dirt all over his clothes, all his liquor had broke open and he had a deep scrape on his chin. I swear I never laughed so hard in my life, though. It was all I could do to keep running. You know how you can laugh so hard you gotta pee? For a minute, I couldn't even remember which direction the car was in. It was rare to see one of those boys mess up. He was so much younger than us it wasn't a big deal but you never saw David slip, whether running or anything else. I don't think him or his brother were capable of it."

"Well, don't you keep in touch with those boys?" asked Monique, not understanding how someone with such bonds could speak of being alone.

"Well, David's in jail, his brother's dead and I haven't heard from Mouse or any of the others in years."

"Whoa," said Monique, slightly startled by the group's unhappy endings. "That's too bad. So even knowing the way things have turned out, you don't wish them to have lived differently?"

"You mean get a degree and spend their whole lives being upstanding just so other people can talk highly of them? No, I couldn't bear to see them like that. I wouldn't have changed them if I could've. It's like seeing a cheetah caged at the zoo. What is a cheetah if it doesn't have its eighty mile an hour sprints across the fields? That life the media and schools tell us we're supposed to want, I just don't see anyone getting rewards out of it. I'd rather those boys enjoy the time they had the way they did than to be another zombie. Besides, David will be out soon. He's got life to live yet."

"Hmm, so tell me another story of a fun time you had together," requested Monique.

"Well, they weren't always that exciting. Just drinking, running at the mouth telling stories was a wonderful evening to me. David and his older brother Kris didn't hang out together that much but when they did it was always memorable. Anytime they came up with an idea, like the first time we made that liquor run, or when they'd get an uptown girl to put a hotel room in her name so they could have a party, those times were the best. They were such a perfect team. The fact they didn't do things together all that often just made it better when they did. There's a famous story about when Kris was eight and David six. They got fed up with the local bully and headed up the street to take him on. Kid was like ten but he got the shit kicked out of him. He held 'em off for a while but with the two of them coming at different angles he couldn't keep up. My point is they were a great team from square one. It was a shame they weren't together more often. If the two of them planned something, it always went down without a hitch. I never saw 'em mess up. That's the way they were. There was this time when Kris got us a house to party at. Actually, it was just few blocks from here. The owner of the local roller rink's wife had a crush on him. She had to be forty. She was gunning to get with a youngster still in his prime. Kris wasn't gonna hook up with a married broad but he never told her that. He would milk her until she gave up. She had this house her husband rented out and the tenants had just left. Kris talked her into letting us throw a party there. To us it was great getting to throw a party in the preppy neighborhood. It didn't get that big a turnout. Mostly just the immediate crew. Didn't make a lot of difference though. We were still drunk and cracking jokes. That was always enough for me. Later, when most everyone had cleared out, the stragglers started a game of strip poker. I wasn't playing. I was kind of blasted, sitting on the floor leaning against the wall daydreaming. Then I looked up; the lady who owned the roller rink was down to her panties and both the other girls weren't doing much better. Then I look at Kris, David and Mouse and they hadn't taken a thing off. Not one thing. Mouse still had on the fisherman cap he was wearing. I don't think they were cheating or anything; it's just how those boys were over there. They seemed so flawless at times. They never had shit, society might consider them low on the totem pole, but somehow they were always on top. It was beautiful to me. They would never even notice it, the way they won so completely. It was just natural to them. I had to cover my mouth when I giggled. I wouldn't have been able to explain what I was laughing at if they asked."

"I know what you mean," added Monique. "My brother was like that. Whenever I would compete with him growing up, I couldn't even come close. Even in simple games he would always have the better of me. I could never figure out how or why. It was like he was untouchable. A person can seem so mighty in that light. Eventually though, from having played him, I was better than most others. It made it worth all the losses."

"I know just what you're saying. Man, I miss them days; everything was ahead of us then. We could just play and have fun till we decided to get for real. There was no rush, no pressure. Then suddenly it was all over. I love thinking of anything from growing up, really. Days past always seem brighter. Even early childhood was great. All you did was play. You didn't need an alarm to wake up in the morning, you didn't want to sleep in, you didn't even know what you were gonna do but you were in a rush to get started. It seemed like there were endless options of ways to enjoy yourself. The only problem was picking which one for when," remembered Samuel.

"Yeah, I get to see that in Cully, and I'm envious. But we had our time as children. Couldn't last forever, I guess. You know, I never would have guessed you as someone so unsatisfied with their life. After talking to you tonight, there seems to be a lot you're unhappy with. I guess I just never got you to talk about you before."

"I guess there are a lot of things I wish were different. 'Course, your enjoyment of life is commonly in the perspective you use. My ma used to tell me how when my dad was young and his family didn't have much money they would eat the same tuna casserole five nights a week. Because of that, in his mind, tuna casserole was what a real meal was supposed to be. He was always asking her to make it. Then his brother, because they had it all the time, never wanted so much as to see tuna casserole again. He wouldn't even let his wife buy tuna. Two people in the same situation with completely different results. One focused on what they had, the other on what they wanted. Your own perspective is very important. My ma used to explain that to me. I guess I lose sight of it sometimes."

"It's easy to do. I find myself dwelling on missed opportunities a lot. Sometimes I feel whenever something good comes along, my circumstances won't let me grab it. It's frustrating if you let it be." Monique looked soberly at Samuel.

He returned the look. Samuel couldn't help but think there was some reference to him in that statement. He hadn't a response for her. They both had the same quiet passion in their eyes. Her expression showed a genuine affection Samuel had always longed for. He enjoyed it for what it was, and then let it pass, as it had to.

"I was thinking today of what you said about a person needing to do certain things, about that passion you had as a child," said Monique. "I can remember being a young girl and singing along to a song. I would feel so strongly about the words when I didn't even know what they meant. Then I'd just twirl around, dancing and dancing till I could hardly breathe. Happiness or sorrow, it was such an outlet. It was what a yell is to being angry but for other emotions. Maybe I should make it a point to dance sometimes. Maybe it would help when Cully gets me really worked up over something. I guess he's my real passion in life now. Things are different with your children. With most things you get out what you put in, but when he smiles it makes me feel wonderful regardless of my effort. Feeling accomplished has nothing to do with it. It's deeper and more natural than all that work versus reward. When he does something good I'm bursting with pride, no matter what. It's like a child's joy in things."

"He's lucky to have such a loving mother. I think a lot of parents aren't real sure how to love that deeply. Either they don't remember how or they're bothered by not being able to control emotions that big. They feel that passion when their child is born but they're not used to it. They're scared of anything in them being that strong so they instinctively muffle it or push it away. They replace love with rules and regulations because it's easier and they have a handle on it. I guess there're countless ways to mess up as a parent but when you care as much as you seem to, it's bound to work out."

She smiled, happy to hear Samuel didn't feel the same way about her that he seemed to about most people.

The mood had been somewhat heavy for a while so Samuel attempted to lighten it. "So these two guys walked into a bar... then the third one ducked."

Monique smiled widely at the uncharacteristic telling of a joke, and then they both laughed, more amused by his shameless attempt at humor than the actual punch line.

They continued talking into the early hours of the morning. Samuel repeatedly got up to leave for fear he'd overstayed his welcome but she'd reprimand him for trying to abandon her in the middle of a conversation. It made him feel welcome.

When the sun came up their speech had grown sluggish and their eyelids hung lower than usual. They both closed their eyes for a moment, feeling relaxed in each other's company. Startled by his obvious ability to fall asleep there, Samuel roused himself to his feet and suggested that it was finally time for his departure. Monique agreed she should get a few hours' sleep before little Cullomine ran her ragged.

He could see the morning mist out the glass doors and there was a forgotten smell of early day coming in through the open window. He hadn't been up at that hour in years. He'd forgotten what it was like to hear the birds chirp. He'd forgotten what a pleasant mood the early morning could have, one of new beginnings. He looked over at Monique for his final goodbyes. She was looking back with want in her eyes. He didn't know how he should take the look. It was frustrating not knowing how to behave. They'd become friends, but he'd like to kiss this friend goodbye. He wasn't sure if that was what she wanted as well. She had already explained that she'd be leaving and was not interested in him romantically, but her stare seemed to say otherwise. Still, it wasn't a risk he was willing to take. He smiled honestly. "Well, I'll see you tomorrow, or later today, I guess." They both smirked and nodded their heads. Then he was gone.

As he stepped out front to see the newly lit sky, he took a big whiff, letting in the morning air. He knew the memory of the smell, the color and most of all the feeling of that moment would stay with him till the end of his life. It was the kind of moment he'd spent hours trying to recreate on paper in his youth. He was overwhelmed with a feeling he'd almost become convinced was a myth. He felt happy. It was rejuvenating. It seemed as though he had the world ahead of him, as it should at the start of a day. He'd long considered happiness as something already having passed him by. Now was like a new morning to his entire life.

His groggy drive home was made bearable knowing he'd soon be in bed with thoughts of Monique relaxing him into slumber. There was a relief in him now. He believed it must be comparable to the resolution an alcoholic feels when they accept they have a problem. He was in love with Monique. There was no longer any denying it.

When he arrived home he went directly to his bed. He felt almost giddy as he snuggled himself under the covers. Falling asleep was now an exciting proposition. When he closed his eyelids to let the warm image of Monique seep in, it was not as hoped. A dark, foreboding creature lay at the edge of his thoughts. Its presence compromised the garden oasis Monique supplied him. He tried to disregard it and focus on what brought him joy but he was unable to shush the questions that had suddenly returned. He couldn't help thinking of the fiend Cullomine Torreo and the possibility of her involvement with him. Samuel did not want his perfect Monique to have anything to do with a drug dealer, especially one of his status. The doubts sparked by his poker buddy's comments rolled mercilessly through his mind. The fear of this possibility was too strong to keep that doubt at bay. Before, it had been easy. He had added up the evidence and reached the conclusion that there was not likely a connection between the two. Now logic and evidence were nowhere around. The only means he seemed able to try to use to again convince himself was the fact he didn't want that connection to be there. Not wanting it to be so was not a proper fence to keep the beast from his garden.

CHAPTER 16: A DATE?

After a while of rustling around, turning back and forth, trying to get comfortable, Samuel finally fell into a restful slumber. In turn, he eventually found his way back awake as well. After a moment to clear his head, he remembered what his day had in store for him. He felt like a child awaking to remember it was the morning of his birthday.

It was earlier than he might have expected, considering when he got home. But now he was too excited to sleep. He roused himself out of bed and into the shower.

As he prepared for his day he tried not to think of what his visit would be like. He didn't want to give himself preconceived notions of what would take place in hopes of avoiding disappointment. Even worse than disappointment, he might try to force things into the direction he imagined. He considered trying and enjoying to rarely work well together. Things had taken a natural progression that was working out wonderfully. He didn't want to taint that by putting his hands on it.

In spite of his efforts, it wasn't long before he was picturing the two of them kissing romantically on the couch after a potent scene in the movie. He reminded himself that those sorts of things couldn't and shouldn't take place. He could only imagine the state he'd be in once she left if they even kissed. On top of that, she made it clear she did not wish to pursue romantic avenues. When inviting him over she stated plainly that she wasn't coming on to him. He was not going to mess things up by letting thoughts contradictory to that into his head.

Finally, in what seemed like the snap of a finger, noon had passed, and he found himself heading up the steep driveway that led to her house. The day had the extra glow that came with a recently resolved storm. The dry grass and sidewalk gave no signs of the rain that had dominated it just hours ago. Samuel was happy, rested, had acquired the classic *Singing in the*

Rain and was now knocking on the door with a confident grin on his face.

The front door was left open, allowing Samuel to peer through the screen door. He didn't see anyone and in spite of his knock the house was quite still. Then he heard a rolling noise that brought his attention to the sliding glass doors on the opposite side of the house. There was Monique in typical casual attire of loose fitting denim shorts and a hot pink T-shirt with some sort of advertising on it. As she came his way, Samuel couldn't tell for sure, but she looked wet.

"Hey Samuel!" said a genuinely pleased Monique. "Come on in. I guess I didn't realize it was that late yet. This son of mine didn't let me sleep much. We've been playing in the back yard. I was trying to wear him out so he'd take a nap but I'm starting to think he's gonna outlast me."

"It's a sad day when a child first starts to outdo their parent," said Samuel as he came in the door.

"Well, I think you're getting a little ahead of yourself," laughed Monique, not yet giving up on victory. "Did you bring something else?" she asked, looking at Samuel's hand.

"Yeah, I stopped and picked up *Singing in the Rain*," he replied triumphantly.

"All right! I love that one. I haven't seen it in years either."

"I thought it'd be up your alley."

"Yeah, yeah, you're pretty much always on target, aren't ya? Let me round up my boy, then I'll be right in so we can watch it."

Samuel set the movie on the table and watched as she headed back to the door. The second she stepped out she was greeted with the splash of a water balloon square in her stomach. Samuel smiled, realizing why she looked wet.

"Oh, you little sneak. You wait till I'm not looking," she bellowed as she bolted in the direction the balloon had come from. Not wanting to miss out, Samuel quickly made his way out the back door to watch. As soon as he reached the patio he saw little shirtless Cullomine giggling profusely and running like his life depended on it. As he crossed Samuel's path there was another scream.

"Look out!" he heard coming from his left. Out of the corner of his eye he could see a bright blue blur soaring in his direction. Before he had a chance to react, the balloon splashed against him and he was soaked. He looked in the direction it came from to see an astonished Monique standing with her hand over her mouth. There was a bucket full of water balloons at her side. Samuel looked just to his right where Cullomine was standing, smiling all the more at his mother's bad aim. There next to him was a second bucket, also full of balloons.

While she was still trying to figure out how mad her guest was gonna be about being drenched upon arrival, Samuel trotted the few steps it took to reach the bucket and grabbed a balloon of his own.

"N-o-o!" she screamed as he unleashed the balloon in her direction. She made a quick sidestep to miss the assault but when she looked up to see her success she was greeted by a second balloon right on target. *Swalsh!* She was soaked all over again, this time by Samuel.

"Ah! Is that how it's gonna be?" she said as she headed back to the bucket. Before she could reach it she saw an onslaught of raining balloons. She had to quickly turn her attention to dodging them. Samuel, noting there were more balloons in the air than he had actually thrown, looked to his side. Little Cullomine had joined his team and was also throwing balloons at Monique. Samuel smiled brightly, and then continued tossing, assembly line style. Monique tried to dodge them while attempting to make her way to the bucket. Unfortunately, for her, the boy's placement was wisely used to guard the bucket as much as to try and tag her.

"Okay," Samuel whispered out of the side of his mouth to his newfound partner, "you keep throwing them to make sure she can't get to the bucket. I'll run up on her with a couple and get her while she's unarmed."

"Okay mister," agreed Cullomine. Samuel took a balloon in each hand and raced toward her. He was about halfway to her when she noticed his charge. Her eyes and mouth got big and she turned to flee. Samuel tossed one immediately but it landed just behind her running feet. He bolted back into pursuit. Monique was approaching the corner so she zagged up the end of the yard sharp enough that when Samuel followed he almost lost his footing. Her maneuver added to her lead and Samuel was unwilling to risk using his last balloon until he was in surefire range. As they approached the next corner Monique tried to round back at an angle that would keep her out of his reach but instead she did lose her footing and plummeted to her palms and knees. Seeing his chance he slid toward her and spiked his balloon in the square of her back. She squeaked as the cold water burst in every direction on her body. They both were laughing heartily and Samuel reached out a hand to help his opponent to her feet.

It was probably their laughing that masked the giggle that had clearly grown closer. Just as Monique made it back upright she had to let out another squeak as they both received the biggest splash yet. They looked up to see Cullomine setting the bucket back down after heaving all its contents on them.

"You backstabber!" accused Samuel as he began a chase of his new attacker.

Cullomine's continuous giggle rose to new heights as he returned to his life-threatened sprint toward the back end of the yard. Monique followed close behind, eager to join in the fun-loving abuse of young Cullomine. As the boy reached the edge of the pool in his run, he attempted to stop abruptly, as if surprised by its presence. He flailed his arms as he fell head-first into the water. When Samuel reached the edge of the pool he saw Cullomine's head pop up and he heard a bloodcurdling shriek. "A-a-g-g-g-h!!! Help! I can't swim! Help me!"

Without hesitation Samuel turned his sprinting pace into a dive, swooshing him under water. He frantically rushed himself back to the surface to locate young Cullomine. When he did he saw a happy little boy smiling ear to ear, out of arm's reach, and dog paddling quite calmly.

"I can't believe you fell for it," said Monique as she gasped for air from excessive laughter. "That boy swims like a fish."

Samuel smiled at his loss to the youthful opponent. "You got a clever one there," he said as he made his way back to the side of the pool.

"Yeah, don't feel bad. He outsmarts me all the time. I don't know where he gets it. He's smarter than me and his padre put together. Yup, we'll never have to worry about this one."

"That's gotta be comforting," added Samuel as he put his hand up for help getting out of the pool. As soon as Monique gave it, Samuel clasped her wrist, paused, and smiled brightly, taking a moment to relish his victory. Immediately, Monique's eyes got big, realizing what she had got herself into.

"N-o-o . . ." she began as she was yanked to join Samuel in the pool. She emerged from the water and pulled her hair back while curling her lips, clearly kicking herself for her foolishness.

"You caught me slipping on that one," she admitted.

"Yeah, well, I didn't want to be the only one who got it head to toe."

As they both climbed out of the pool they were heckled by Cullomine's giggles. He was standing at the edge of the yard, hunched over, holding his gut and pointing as he laughed incessantly.

"Yeah, well, it's your nap time. Try laughing at that," aced Monique.

Cullomine's face crinkled as he realized he didn't want to go take a nap and even worse, he had no way to combat his mom's victory. "So!" he said simply. Then he marched into the house and up to his room as if unscathed.

When they reached the living room Samuel waited as Monique got a handful of towels. They each dried their legs and clothes as best they could, then she wiped up the drip spots.

"Geez! That kid left a wet streak all the way to his room I gotta wipe up. He does that stuff on purpose," she explained. Her voice faded down the hallway as she wiped up the mess. "Hey, put that movie in would ya?"

"Yeah, I got it," he answered. When she returned she had more towels. She went to the wall opposite the TV and laid them out to give them a sufficient place to sit.

"I'm really sorry about the whole lack of couch but well, you already know."

"Oh, don't even worry about it. I'm used to it after last night," said Samuel as he looked back at what she put together. "It'll be like a picnic."

"Yeah, good idea. Hanging out on blankets, the sun shining in the sliding doors, only this is better 'cause we get to watch the movie. Oh wait, I need to get the food," remembered Monique.

"You don't have to go to the trouble," said Samuel.

"Don't worry, I already made everything. I just gotta heat it up. You know I don't have nothing but time on my hands. That's why you should have known I already taught Cully to swim," pointed out Monique.

Samuel playfully curled a smile as he was reminded of his recent gullibility. "Yeah, he got me good on that one. I bet you got your hands full with him," he said, making his way to a sitting position on the towels with his back leaned up against the wall.

"Yeah, he keeps me busy. 'Course on the other hand I don't know what I'd do without 'im."

"Sort of a love-love relationship then, huh."

"Exactly," she smiled as she went back down the hallway. She returned with two pillows and tossed them right into Samuel's face.

"Ah, good to see these again," said Samuel, putting the pillow vertically behind his back, making himself much more comfortable.

"Why don't you start the movie so you can skip through the previews?" she asked.

"Skip!? Are you kidding me? The previews are my second favorite part."

"After the movie, you mean?"

"Yeah."

"Well, I guess that makes sense," she giggled.

"But really think about it. It's like watching a bunch of little movies. They basically introduce the characters, let you know the premise, then give you a darn good idea if not flat out tell you how it's gonna get resolved. All the while they play emotional music and clip through all the most dramatic or amusing scenes. Plus it helps with the endless line of crappy movies out there nowadays, 'cause even the crappy ones are usually enjoyable in the preview. You don't have to wait through the boring parts or be frustrated by plot holes or simple dialogue. I figure movie makers usually just come up with the basic important points to hook the potential viewers, then kill the rest of the hour and half with meaningless scenes that waste time. Those movies are better off as previews anyway."

"I'm sold. Let's watch the previews," she agreed enthusiastically.

Samuel crawled over, slipped the movie in and crawled back. When he arrived back he was greeted with Monique handing him a tray full of lunch to put on his lap. He noticed he only had one glass and was wondering if she had forgotten until he saw her returning with her own tray and the entire jug of punch hanging from her hand. Samuel then looked down to see the famous fajitas from his first visit.

"You sure I won't need milk?" he questioned.

She smiled. "No, I didn't make them so spicy this time. Plus you got the cheese dip. It's good with those chips too." Samuel looked down to see the dip and a bowl of chips on the side of his tray.

"What's this?" he asked as he pointed toward the orange noodles next to his fajitas.

"Macaroni and cheese," she answered simply.

"More of the American influence leaking out."

"It's not that. I just wanted to remind you I have some range," she giggled. "'Course usually it would be kind of hot. 'Cause actually everything I cook is about as hot as those fajitas were the first time. Now I just make yours separate."

"Well, I appreciate you going to that effort."

"It's no problem at all. Like I got anything better to do."

Samuel started on his meal. It was as enjoyable as ever. Midway through, he refilled his glass with the jug. Then, after completing the lunch, he poured himself another, to wash down the food.

"You really do like your beverages," commented Monique.

"Yes, I do, and that was delicious. I tell you I haven't eaten in years like I have these last weeks."

"Glad to hear it. It being delicious, I mean. The other part's too bad. I can't believe you don't have anybody cooking for you. I'm sure there are women lining up to do it, if you let 'em."

"Naw, naw. You get in a relationship and let a girl start cooking for you on a regular basis, you give her room to believe it's a real-deal relationship. Like I said before; I don't play that 'real-deal' game. It's just not for me no more."

"What about me? I cook for you on a regular basis," pointed out Monique.

"Yeah, but we don't have that kind of relationship thing going. It's the combination of the two that gives you problems. Besides, a girl like you will make a fella reconsider his regulations."

"Yeah," she agreed sarcastically, considering it an unrealistic statement. "But I really want to know what could have been so bad. What could have made you completely give up on the idea of a genuine relationship?"

"It's hard to say. I guess honestly, even when I was young I always thought about a fulfilling relationship like that. I just didn't think it was a reasonable possibility. People are so self-involved. A real relationship like that, to me, has to involve putting someone else's needs before yours, plus being able to trust that they will hold your needs in the same regard. Nowadays you're lucky to get your own mother to hold your needs in that regard. Having someone else prepared to take things to that level is barely possible. So if that person does exist, what are the chances of you finding them? If you do find them, are you gonna get along? Are you even gonna like each other? So I was never too optimistic in the first place. Then believing that I found somebody, believing we'd taken things to that point—and then she leaves. It just made me realize I was right all along. It just drove those points in all the harder. Now, to me, it's like it's not worth it to put forth the effort. It's easier not to. Why try when you already know it's not gonna work? I just need the occasional fling and I'm happy."

"So you're not really the whole destiny, every person has someone they're meant to be with type of guy, huh," observed Monique.

"Well, it's a nice concept. I would probably be able to take it a little more seriously if I had ever seen it. The only time I ever see those relationships is on that square screen in front of us. I might sound like a pessimist, but I gotta consider it to be a hoax. I don't know one couple fitting that description, or even one that really lasts."

"Well, what about me? Do you think I'm the type of person that could put another's needs before my own?" asked Monique, catching Samuel a bit off guard.

"Based on the short time I've known you, I'd have to say you are one of those rare types."

"And do you enjoy my company?" she asked again.

"I do. I definitely do."

"Well then, you have to admit that we do exist. If we exist you can find us, if you try hard enough. Maybe if you let one of those flings pan out, instead of pushing them away all the time, you'd be delightfully surprised. As far as there not ever being those truly 'meant to be together' relationships anywhere outside that box, I have to say they do exist. I've seen them myself. You just have to be patient and open-minded. Even after you find them it's not as easy as the happily-ever-after-storybook endings. It still takes work. But that's just my opinion. You're entitled to yours. Whatever floats your boat is fine with me."

"Well, you make an interesting point. I'll have to give that some thought," said Samuel, trying to be nice but unwilling to give up his opinion. Monique gave a faint half-smile, showing she felt sorry for the person she was looking at, though she maintained affection for him. They both leaned back on their pillows to pay attention to the movie.

Samuel tried to ignore the sudden frustration altering his mood. That conversation got him a little worked up. He hoped it didn't show. Relationships were the one part of his life he had been dishonest about. Originally he had liked leaving the illusion that there were plenty of girls for him to choose from. He had liked her believing he had the occasional fling, though the closest thing he had ever had to it was Leah. He didn't want to admit the truth about his embarrassingly lonely life. But now, sitting there, he was reminded he hadn't the option to let someone love him. It was fun to portray himself as a jilted lover who snubbed the opportunity to love again. But if that had been true he would have had to agree with Monique's point of view. Instead, hearing it just accentuated what his life was really like. He was all alone and didn't seem to have any ability to change that fact. There were no flings in his life, or even anyone who showed him interest. If there were he wouldn't have the strength to snub them. Deep down he had that same desire to love and the same need for affection that he had always had. In truth, he knew he wouldn't hesitate to try again if he had a chance. That was much of what scared him.

He knew it was a possibility that he was so scared of being hurt that he instinctively avoided any social situation that might allow him to meet somebody. That thought brought him no comfort now. All he was sure of was his own loneliness.

He could almost feel the pain of loneliness swirling around him, starting to seep back in. He could remember as early as middle school painting a portrait in his head of what a truly anguished soul was. To him it was someone who was overwhelmed by the world, hanging their head in pain, and having no one there to care. He was always scared of ending up that way, of hurting his knee and not having a mother there to hug him, of having a bad day at work and having no one at home to sympathize. That was the life he was leading.

Since his divorce he had tried to convince himself that he didn't need other people to get by. He tried to go without their affections, but now, after the way he had emotionally latched on to Monique, he had to accept that it was his fear that he would be denied those affections more than it was not wanting them that fueled his philosophy. He didn't believe there was anyone out there capable of truly loving someone. That was the wallpaper in the shell where he'd been living. Remembering it was returning emptiness back to its authority from which it had just recently been removed.

Then there was Monique. Looking at her showed him just what an over-generalization of people his philosophy was. She showed him interest. She did seem genuinely concerned about his life.

Ah, Monique. She could battle that tyrannical lonely feeling that had ruled him for so long. He knew when she left he would have to return to his shell and he would be punished for ever leaving, but until then he would take her up on the relief she could provide.

A relaxed grin crossed his face, signifying the return of the good spirits he had been in when he arrived. If someone as wonderful as her could care about him, he had to be worth something. Here she was sitting on these blankets watching a movie with him. Perhaps he had been hasty with the idea of a temporary relationship between the two of them. Maybe believing that he wasn't looking for something long term was part of what she liked about him. She too had been alone for a long time. With her leaving soon, maybe a final American fling before departure was what she was after.

As he enjoyed his feeling of contentment, he looked over to the object that supplied it. There, her mouth hung open slightly and her eyes were shut. Her late evening, early morning and hard play had gotten the better of her. She was sound asleep. Before long her head slid over and Samuel's shoulder became her pillow. It was heaven to him. Whether things could be taken farther or not disappeared and that perfect moment became all Samuel ever needed. He was sitting on the floor cuddling with the gorgeous girl of his dreams. Sex and relationships were moot in comparison.

It wasn't long before Samuel met with the same late night, the same early morning and the same roughhousing that Monique had come across. Slowly and blissfully he joined her in slumber.

The next time Samuel opened his eyes he saw Monique in a fetal position with her head on her pillow, and himself in the same position pressed against her. Paradise had left his mind and found its place in the real world. He couldn't bring himself to roll away for fear life would never be that good again.

He closed his eyes again and tried to concentrate on enjoying the moment. He wanted to hold on to it so he could have it next time things got bad. He tried to think of how much he'd love the idea of this if he were delivering the mail right now. Doing so seemed to deflate the joy a bit. Focusing too hard on what was going on made it all seem fake.

Then the time passed. She rolled her body over without backing away. Samuel kept his eyes closed, not wanting to admit he was already aware of the position they were in. Though he couldn't see he could still feel how close her face was to his. He opened his eyes slowly, pretending to be just waking up. There she was, beautiful as ever, close enough to feel his breath, noses almost touching, and eyes plainly open staring back deeply into Samuel's. They were both aware of how close they were and neither was backing away. Samuel was enmeshed in the intoxicating moment. Thought was nowhere around. The butterflies in his stomach were like none he'd ever felt. Still, he lifted his head and leaned it toward hers. When their lips met, to his delight, she was kissing him back. The passion that had carried Samuel's lips to Monique's was now exploding as they held their kiss, brought their lips back, then pressed again. They held it for an instant of utopia that seemed eternal. Then Samuel felt a hand on his shoulder as Monique pulled herself away. She looked confused, blinking her eyes and shaking her head.

"I'm sorry. I don't know if I've given you the wrong idea or . . ." she paused as if trying to make sense of the situation she was in.

Then Samuel came to her rescue despite the horror he was feeling. "No, that was my fault. I don't know what came over me; it was just kind of all of a sudden."

Monique pulled up to a sitting position. "It's not that I don't like you, it's just . . ."

"No, no. Don't explain; it's not necessary," reassured Samuel, who really just didn't want to hear any patronizing.

Monique dropped her shoulders and gave a sympathetic expression. "I know, it's just . . . I don't want this to ruin things. I enjoy having you around and I don't want you to stop coming over because we've shared this kind of awkward moment."

Samuel smiled condescendingly to give the impression she was foolish to think that. "Don't worry about that. Do you think I would let something as silly as this come between me and your cooking?"

Monique smiled. "I hope not."

"Listen, the truth is I like talking to you too. It's nice to get to hear the thoughts of a woman every once and a while. Plus knowing you're not looking for a relationship means I don't have to worry about impressing you. What just happened was something silly. We were barely even awake. I'm not going to give it another thought, and you shouldn't either," reassured Samuel.

Monique gave a sigh of relief. "Good. I'm glad to hear that. Too bad we fell asleep, though. I was really looking forward to watching that movie."

Samuel looked down at his watch. "Yeah, I know and I am supposed to meet the guys here in a bit," lied Samuel, "otherwise we could watch it now."

"Darn. Well, maybe another time. Really, I'm surprised Cullomine isn't down here messing with us."

"Yeah, well, this will just give me an excuse to come over next weekend. I'll just leave it here till then."

"Good, that way I know you'll have to come back to avoid all those late fees."

"Well, I got my route tomorrow. You're not trying to get out of making me lunch, are you?"

"It'll be waiting for you," answered Monique with a smile.

Samuel returned the gesture. The idea of someone preparing anything for him was still nice regardless of all the embarrassment and rejection he was trying so hard to hide.

CHAPTER 17: PARADISE LOST

After Samuel left he took pride in his performance. He hadn't shown any sign of how much it hurt when Monique pulled away. He downplayed his feelings and allowed her to think it didn't bother him and things wouldn't change. In truth his emotions felt like a brewing inferno that he wouldn't let blow. When he heard the door close behind him his guard dropped and it became hard for him to walk. His spirit that had finally began rejuvenating was again broken in half. It felt like he would crumble to pieces before he could reach the car. He was almost dizzy, creating a wobble in his pace. No matter what she had said he still felt worthless, like his presence had always been a burden to her and he was just fooling himself to have believed otherwise.

Once in the car and on the road, his misery gained a hint of nostalgia. It brought back memories of his afternoon with Leah. He looked at himself like a rookie then. At that time he was completely surprised when he broke down. He didn't understand the delayed reaction. The emotions in general were new to him. He was unaware of his natural defense for his mind to keep his thoughts and emotions at bay until in the safety of privacy. Now he'd had years to study his habits of self-loathing. He knew exactly what was going on.

He'd spent his last few days in a lavish temple of Monique. Now the once-beautiful walls of that temple were crashing down. Though he applied pillars of logic to hold them up, it was little help. He reminded himself that he never wanted a relationship with her anyway. He just wanted to enjoy her company. He was happy enough with her just showing interest. But none of that mattered now. He tried to have her in a deeper sense and it was thrown in his face that he couldn't. That ripped the foundation from underneath the walls and now they were pouring down like an avalanche.

He was alone in the world. No one really cared what happened to him one way or another. Few people even acknowledged he existed. At times, when delivering the mail, he wondered if the people could see him at all. Now, having felt good the day before was another smack in the face. He was just jealous of the Samuel of yesterday. Thinking of his good feelings that morning made him feel pathetic for getting so worked up over nothing.

He thought of all the people going home with women from bars. All the one-night stands and dating that he wasn't a part of. It was as if the whole class had been given cupcakes but there wasn't enough for him. He hated them for it. There was no helping it. His envy was un-caged. The entire world was an insult to him for not feeling the pains he felt. Even the Samuel from years ago was a part of it. He hated himself from the years past, the same way he hated the rest of the world. The way he had once been in love, with a woman on his arm. The way he could go out with the guys and have women flirt with him, but wasn't interested because he was content with Susan. The way he could pass up on those flings then was an insult to him now. He once had that attention he now craved and had taken it for granted. It was like dumping out food while one of those starving children was actually in the room. How could he have snubbed then what he so longed for now? He needed the love of a woman, and thinking he had it with Monique was a tease.

He could again feel the sorrow rushing over him. The pain was swelling up into tears, and the tears were beading up in his eyes. His emotions were trying to manifest themselves into the real world, but he'd have no part of it. This time he wasn't going to let loose. This time he'd hold himself together. He took hold with a merciless strength. He heaved his chest up and squeezed all those emotions into a little ball. He pushed that ball down deep and swore to himself he'd never let it out. They didn't deserve to be let out. They shouldn't exist in the first place. He even giggled as a tear rolled down his cheek. He took a big breath and let it out slowly to gain some relief. He giggled a bit more considering his behavior foolish.

See, he said to himself, *I was on the verge of slipping up. I was starting to think I should love again. Yes, I'm grateful for this reminder. Hell, I still obviously have some charm or I'd never have got in the door. Maybe I just need to get out and have some of those meaningless flings. Thanks to this I now know better than to try to get something that doesn't even exist. I can trust myself not to get too serious. I'll get what I need and be on my way. Simple as that. It's time to get an active social life again and this embarrassing moment will be my life preserver, keeping me from getting over my head.*

He felt empowered by his sudden control of himself. He would have thought an event like this would be the end for him but instead he had a newfound strength. He would be invincible by turning off the part of himself that could get hurt. If he was safe in that aspect, he'd be free to acquire his needs. He decided the first chance he got he was going to get out of the house and back on the social scene.

The next morning he got up on time and went through the motions in his old zombie form. Before he was out of his early morning daze he'd already finished his inane first of the week conversations with the boys and the boss and was out on his route. In fact, he was still in this daze when he was sorting through his deliveries. Then, suddenly, his eyes opened wide and his full attention was aroused.

He still desired to think about her though he tried not to. It was that struggle that made him sort ahead to see what she was getting. He tried to stop himself due to embarrassment. He was like the old girlfriend trying to stop herself from driving by her ex's house to check up on him, but of course she'd give in, cut down his street and try to see what cars were there and anything else she could without slowing down. He was ashamed of his inability to stop himself from caring about something he shouldn't. When he broke down and did it, he considered it a harmless failure on his part. He didn't take into consideration the dilemma it might bring when he found her mail.

There, amongst a Clearing House letter and a rent-to-own advertisement, was a little manila envelope. Suddenly the dark creature that had invaded his paradise was a valuable ally. Perhaps the Cullomine situation still had room to pan out. Now that his blinding love for her had diminished, the prospect of her being involved with Torreo wasn't so absurd. There was the possibility she had lied to Samuel to cover up the truth about herself. If so it was likely that the envelope held the money Samuel had often imagined it to. So now the question for himself was whether he should open it or not.

His position was torn. Regardless of whether she would kiss Samuel or not, she still seemed too sweet and innocent to be tied up in the drug rackets. On the other hand, Samuel considered sweet and innocent people to be like a fairy tale or legend. Perhaps they existed once, but were extinct in the modern era. She said herself she was a contradiction to the way he believed women or even people in general to be. He believed her then. Perhaps he wasn't wrong about people after all. Maybe she tricked him, much the way Susan had. There was no question in his mind that there were plenty of people who appeared to be decent and caring. He just believed it to cover the surface. It was the way they got along socially. In truth they were trying to make things as good for themselves as possible. Being nice was simply the way they had learned to do it. They weren't actually worried about how things were for anyone else. It was a front. He thought Monique had proved him wrong in those opinions. If there was money in that envelope he would prove himself right. She would be just another liar.

On the other hand, he wasn't completely ready to give up on the beautiful picture he'd painted with her in the middle. He didn't want to lose the possibility that she would have come to her senses and would dive on him when he got to her door that afternoon. Also, what if he was wrong? What if it was pictures and things just like she said? He would have invaded her privacy for no reason. He would be the only villain in the situation.

For hours his decision would lean to one side, then back the other, a frustrating teeter-totter with the letter, his love for Monique, and his view of the world all in the balance.

If she was lying the disappointment might be more than he could bear. It would be an exclamation point on the end of the destruction of his short-lived paradise. If it was not the money, not only would he have betrayed one of the kindest people he ever knew, but he would have to accept that he was rejected by a flawless person. At least with things up in the air he could tell himself it was her own shortcomings that made her not want him.

He finished another street, got back in the mail truck, sat down in his seat, removed his bag from his shoulder, pulled out the envelope and began another in a countless series of stare-downs with the envelope. He had set the end of this street as the deadline for his decision. His next street was Monique's and it was almost lunchtime. He couldn't stop his fingers from tapping one at a time on his thigh. His hand longed to open it but feared its contents.

It was down to crunch time. A choice had to be made but there was still the dilemma of his not liking either of his choices. Delivering the letter and going on with this unbearable friendship left things too open-ended for him to accept. Whether he could fool her or not, he was going to feel awkward. Seeing her would just rub his nose in the fact that he couldn't have her. But opening the letter was giving up on a dream. Every time he got up the gumption to tear back the seal, he would remember the sunny paradise he had been in just days before. Opening it would be throwing away the small fragment of hope he held for them to be together. Whether it was finding out he was lied to, or himself betraying her by not believing, it would be a blemish on the fantasy he still clung to. Throwing out that hope would be throwing away all the childlike hopes he had about the world, that it could ever be as pretty as he dreamt.

It was no use. He wasn't ready to decide. He came up with a temporary solution; he would break that delivery rule once again. He would hold on to her personal property until he decided what to do with it. He would take the letter home. It was better that way. If he opened it now he might not be able to deliver it and would have to claim it was lost. At home he would have the proper tools to open and close it without leaving a sign. If he couldn't bring himself to do so before the night was over, he would just deliver it the next day, no harm done.

When lunchtime arrived Samuel wasn't plagued with the nervous feelings he usually got about that time. He was too angry for that. It was a rare type of anger. It was calm, cold and bitter. It was enough to make him consider not even showing up.

In spite of those feelings he reached her front stoop, but it was all he could do to force himself to knock. He was hoping that something had come up. He hoped that somehow she had forgot and wasn't there, but after just a moment's wait, the door swung open. There she stood, same casual clothes, same warm smile. Her upbeat expression showed she was prepared for the awkward feeling but was ready to get past it. She might have been able to accomplish that, if Samuel was open to it in any way. But he wasn't. He was too angry to even feel the awkwardness, so it could not be resolved.

"Hey, how's it going?" she asked.

"Not bad."

"Well, come on in. You know where the table is." Samuel nodded and stepped past her into the dining area. She hesitated at the door and looked out at the sky. "Well, how can it be such a gloomy day out after that beautiful sunshine yesterday?"

"Yeah, it's been like that. It's got that look and smell like it's gonna pour any minute but it just hasn't let loose quite yet."

"Yeah, well, I'm glad I'll be gone before fall hits. It's beautiful with the leaves and all but I just can't stand that chill in the air. Your winters are one thing I won't miss much either. They were cool at first but boy, I got over that opinion."

"Yeah, it's pretty much the same for us locals. As kids you start out mesmerized by the snow, but after some years you grow fed up with it like everybody else."

"Speaking of me leaving, I'm getting impatient for my package. You're not hiding it in your truck so you can keep your free lunches, are ya?" she joked. For a quarter instant Samuel was panicked. He thought she somehow knew he had her letter. Then he realized she was talking about the mementos the bank was sending her, if that's what they really were.

He hesitated, and then laughed at her joke. He wondered if there was some hidden meaning to it. *Suddenly she's in a hurry to leave?* She had fun leading him along but now things went a little farther than she planned so she'd just as soon get off the continent? Why did she even start up a friendship with him in the first place? She was only worried about that package. She figured if she befriended the mailman he would take special care that nothing happened to it. He would get it to her with no delays. That was the reason behind all these smiles and meals.

Samuel swirled down this spiral of negativity at the expense of Monique's character until she spoke again.

"Do you like rice?" she asked, actually curious about the silence.

"Oh yeah, it's one of my favorites."

"Good, you're having burritos and rice. Just in case you were wondering."

"Sounds good. So where's Cullomine?"

"Oh, it's his nap time right about when your lunch is. Lucky you. He'd be gloating over having got you in the pool yesterday."

"Yeah, good point. Hard to enjoy a meal when you're getting harassed," Samuel chuckled.

"So do you got a rain coat or something if it does start a downpour?"

"Yeah, you know the motto, I'm sure. Rain, sleet and so forth. I got one in the car with a nice big postal symbol on it."

"Sounds snazzy. Speaking of rain, I couldn't resist watching *Singing in the Rain* this morning. Didn't want you to be upset when it came time to watch it. We didn't really get to pay that much attention to *Moulin Rouge*. We could watch that this weekend, if I can keep myself from putting it in. It's hard to resist with the choices you have on TV."

"That's all right; I'll just pick up something else."

"Oh no, don't bother. I don't mind watching *Singing in the Rain* again if it comes to it. I love that movie. I just didn't want to pretend I still hadn't seen it in years if we end up watching it. 'Course there's a good chance I'll watch it a couple more times before the week's up. Maybe you should start thinking about something else," laughed Monique.

"Yeah, I expected you to watch them. I've already been giving some thought to another good choice we might both like."

Monique brought over the plate, and then came back with two glasses of punch, as was the tradition. It just added insult to injury. As they carried on in conversation, Samuel put on a show and pretended everything was the same. As it progressed, he knew he was doing a good job because he could tell she was getting back in the groove they had recently shared. She likely assumed he was doing the same, but it was too late for that. She rejected him; that now served as the engine in a train of thought that included his divorce, the way no one wanted anything to do with him, which eventually led to the caboose: there was nothing about him worth a damn.

As he ate the food he was all the more angered by how delicious it was. Was she trying to point out how wonderful life would be with her? A life he clearly wasn't good enough for. She brought him two drinks, like she cared about his thirst, as if anyone cared. He could tell his contempt was growing out of control as he found such ill motives to her simple deeds. He tried not to let his mind wander any further.

He ate, spoke, and waited till it had been a polite amount of time before he left. Once he did, it took great effort not to run out the front door. It was freedom to be out of that house.

He finished the deliveries on that street, got in the truck and drove to the next. The whole time he kept mulling over his new opinions. She was a hoax. She wasn't the person she made herself out to be and he was going to prove it. He couldn't even remember what they had talked about during lunch. All he could think about was exposing her for the fraud he was sure she was.

The second he got to the next road on his route he pulled over and grabbed the tan envelope. He took the lighter from out of his pocket. He ran the flame slowly back and forth over the seam. Once he had the glue warm he used his key to wedge the corner open without ripping it. He worked the key along slowly, pulling the envelope up, bit by bit. Every time it got stopped up, he put the lighter to that spot to loosen the glue some more, then returned to moving the key. In no time, he had the envelope open with minimal signs of tampering.

He hesitated for a moment, trying to bring into perspective what he'd just done. But he didn't care; all he was interested in was seeing the contents of that envelope. He lifted the flap to look inside. There it was. As he had suspected for some time, there was a neatly wrapped stack of money. There were numerous pieces of strange-looking tape wrapped tightly around it. It made it feel like a brick. Samuel sat there in awe. Now that he saw it, it was even harder to believe. Somehow he had been right in the beginning.

He'd been telling himself for hours that she had been lying to him, but until now, in his heart, he never accepted it. These weren't pictures from home. She hadn't been married to a rich businessman, at least not a legitimate one. More importantly, she wasn't waiting for mementos. Now Samuel had no doubt anywhere inside him, she was waiting for a shipment of money. A shipment far larger than the one in Samuel's hand. She was waiting for the missing bribe money. She was waiting for twenty million dollars.

As the amazement at the money wore off, the heartbreak set in. How could he have believed her to be such an angel when it was so far from the truth? Though he could have easily been devastated, he had pushed it all to the side like it wasn't important. He just shoved her betrayal down with everything else he didn't like.

It wasn't as hard as usual. There were plenty of other things to think about. These new events were just what he needed to permanently crack the shell. It was high time to get his cards back on the table, to start living again. This was a better chance to do that than most people ever saw. There would be no more wasting his days away. It was time to set his sights on higher things.

It would be simple. He'd kill time until the package arrived. Then, when the morning came that it was waiting in his truck, he would steal it and head to the airport. David would be getting out at near the same time as Cullomine. So he should be released before Samuel had acquired their fortune. They could make their plans ahead of time for where they would go and who they would take. David would be getting a sizable chunk for the information he provided. He'd likely want to take his mother, Missy, and Jamie wherever they went. It would be nothing but the good life from then on out.

In the meantime Samuel was ready to get back on the social scene. If he would be living the good life soon, there was no reason not to get started. When David got out there'd be plenty of partying to do. He might as well get back in the mix.

He didn't consider the thievery of Cullomine's money to require much more thought. It would be hard to mess up and once he had it, it would be smooth sailing from then on out. The whole idea had been too good to be true, but there it was. He had all the proof he needed. Now it was just a simple matter of waiting until a far more real paradise than yesterday's would be his. He had fumbled into a perfect position. No one interested in this money had any idea about Samuel and his knowledge. There would be no way for them to stop him from making the snatch. As long as Cullomine Torreo was successful in getting the money into mail circulation, Samuel would be successful in taking off with it.

When Samuel got home he felt like king of the mountain. Every weight that had been on his shoulders these past years was instantly removed. He knew he would soon be free from his dead-end job. He'd be able to purchase any affection he needed and life would be his to control.

He decided it was time to return Little Lukas Bailey's phone call. They needed to make the plans for David's welcome home party. Lukas would almost certainly want to meet somewhere to make those plans. It was the perfect opportunity for Samuel to get out of the house. It would be a nice first step back into the world.

"Yeah?" answered the voice on the phone.

Recognizing the tone, Samuel went into his accustomed smartass mode from years ago. "I'm looking for a sorry motherfucker who goes by the alias of Mouse." There was a pause on the other end of the line.

"M-a-a-n. I don't know who the . . . oh wait, is this Samuel?"

Samuel responded by laughing wholeheartedly.

"Ah shit, man. I was about to flip the fuck out over here," chuckled Lukas. "Fuck dude, you can't be gettin' me all worked up like that."

"Why's that? You gettin' too old for the shift in blood pressure?"

"Fuck! I'm gettin' there quick. Ever since I reached the legal drinking age I haven't been so healthy. Well, what the hell's going on, man? David tells me you been in town all along and you don't ever make it to the East side. What's up with that?"

"Ah shit, man. I just don't be gettin' out like I ought to. I couldn't even tell you the last time I been to a pub."

"Well, I'm thinking it's about time to fix that. What do you say we meet down at Snickers for a drink or two? We got to make plans, man. Your boy's gonna be home soon."

"Yeah, you're right about that. What time you wanna be down there?"

"Shit! I can be down there in fifteen minutes. So it's really what time you wanna be down there."

"Fuck it. I ain't got no plans. I'm leaving right now."

"Cool shit. I'll see you in a few."

Carried away by the moment, Samuel was dressed, in his car and on the road in no time. It was great to hear an old friend's voice. It hearkened back to a time that was full of laughs, parties and good memories. It was also nice to have someone happy to hear from him. Going and talking about the old days would do him some good.

When he walked into Snickers restaurant and pub, he immediately saw Lukas waving his arms from across the room. Just seeing him was a reminder of countless good times Samuel had in that nearby neighborhood. It was a smile that was in the background of most every gathering and social event Samuel participated in. Mouse had always tagged along, laughing at their jokes, trying to be tough. He did pretty well, for as much younger as he was. He even bagged the occasional party girl who was too drunk to note his age.

He didn't look like a kid anymore. It was the same rugged face; he'd just grown into it. It was the same cocky smile; it just wasn't as needy. His style of clothes was the same but cleaner and a little more expensive. He wore them the same. Neither button on his two-button shirt was done. The collar being left open and the lack of undershirt left his chest exposed. The symbol in the shirt's corner was the only way one would know it to be valuable clothing. Its being oversized, and the nonchalant application, was certainly no clue. In years past the symbol served to show what a capable thief Mouse was; now it showed that Little Lukas Bailey had come up in the world.

When Samuel reached his chair he saw that Lukas had already ordered them each a beer and a shot that was almost certainly Jack Daniels. He'd already started in on his beer but the shot was awaiting Samuel's arrival.

Lukas hopped to his feet and smacked hands, curled his fingers into a clasp, then threw his arm around Samuel's back for a half-hug. That was customary when greeting a friend not seen in a while, or during special occasions. A friend you saw on a regular basis would receive the smack and finger curl, without the arm around the back.

"Fuck man, it's good to see you!" opened Lukas.

"Yeah, you too, man. I see you got the drinks already," observed Samuel.

"Hell yeah. Figured we gotta do a shot together. It's been a long damn time."

"A-h-h-h. Yeah, I guess you're right. I can handle one but I don't put 'em back like I used to," explained Samuel.

"Are you kidding me? I didn't think you'd ever lay off. You used to drink like it was a sport."

"Yeah, it was just the same old thing all the time though, ya know."

"Yeah, I know. It's this fuckin' city, man. There ain't shit else to do. We all bring home these paychecks and what else do we got to spend it on but alcohol and trees?"

"Exactly, and my paychecks ain't what they used to be so I was like fuck it and chilled out."

"Right. Well, don't worry about that. These are on me."

"Good lookin' out," Samuel thanked him.

They both picked up the hefty shots. "To the old days," toasted Lukas, then they dropped them back like the long time pros they were. Neither made an expression, they just nodded to agree they had felt it go down. "Yeah, I heard about Susan stickin' it to ya when ya split up. That's crazy."

"Yeah, she went no holds barred with it. I didn't really fight it but shit, I didn't know she was coming like that," explained Samuel.

"Fuck! I can't believe she'd do you like that either. Hell, I can't believe y'all ever split up in the first place. Seemed like you two were always together. I thought if anyone was gonna stick with it, it was Susan and Samuel."

"Yeah, we had everybody fooled, even ourselves."

"Fuck it though, you're better off. 'Course this is all old news to you. It's probably like ancient history. I just never got the chance to ask you about it," said Lukas, seeking more explanation.

"Right. It was like we did great when we were out partying and shit, but when we got home, just the two of us, and there wasn't as much to do, we kind of fell apart. I guess she just wasn't the settling down type in the end."

"See, that's why I won't put a ring on no girl's finger. I figure if you two can't make it, I ain't got no business trying. Here I got two kids and another on the way and I still ain't even considering that shit."

"Damn, I didn't know that. You're a daddy and shit. Are they all the same mama?"

"Nah, I wasn't that lucky. The first one's by Mira. You remember her?"

"Yeah, you two were always back and forth with it. I should have known y'all'd end up with a kid," said Samuel.

"Yeah, they call that motherfucker Little Mouse. He's always into some shit. I see him a lot, but me and Mira ain't kicked it since he was born. My second and this one coming are by my girl Lacy. I don't think you ever met her. She was after your time."

"Naw, I don't think I did. That's cool though. So how you feeding these young ones?"

"Shit, I'm out there in the factory cove. EPL. I've been out there for a while," explained Lukas.

"I know Mira is hittin' them checks up for the child support," figured Samuel.

"Yeah, she do. But I still got my toes stuck in the Post Edition underbelly. I probably make as much off the bones Lorenzo throws me as I do workin' out there. It's just that friend of the court don't see no part of that."

"Yeah? There's that much to be made? Shit, that's cool. Who's Lorenzo, though?"

"Fuck! Are you kiddin' me, man? Shit! You probably wouldn't know, would you? That was just after you stopped coming around. Damn, you really have been out the loop."

"Sounds like it," agreed Samuel.

"Lorenzo Cole is like the Vito Corleone, Al Capone, motherfucker of Post now. He flipped the whole script; we make money citywide. Shit, outside the city if there's money to be made. He's the son of some bigwig in New York. There was a beef he got into that his daddy couldn't squash, so he got sent up here till it cooled down. This motherfucker started puttin' some old Yorker ways to use around here. There was no organization until then and he really got something going. Everything's organized now. Not just a bunch of cowboys runnin' around snatchin' shit. You don't steal a candy bar without breakin' Mr. Cole off a piece. That's no bullshit. And nobody goes to jail like they used to. He sees to that."

"You're makin' this up as you go along. Nobody can tame the East side. It wouldn't be Post Edition no more."

"Hey, I'm with you, man, hold on. Hey Trish! Bring us a couple more brews and those sides of Jack's, will ya?"

"Ah shit naw, man, I can't handle another," protested Samuel.

"Ah, come on; we'll do it in honor of David Caine's release from the penal institution."

Samuel thought for a minute and then caved. Getting out and unwinding was just what he was after. What was the harm in getting a little drunk, as long as he kept an eye on it? All this remembering the good old days was bringing back out the drinker inside him. Every smile he thought of from those times included alcohol on his breath. It was hard to think much of them without having a drink in hand.

"So anyway," Lukas began again, slightly under his breath. He lowered his head down closer to the table, causing himself to resemble a mouse. "Shit ain't like it used to be. I try to sound happy about the changes 'cause most people are, but it's just like you said, it ain't Post Edition no more. I mean, don't get me wrong, this motherfucker has done a lot of good around here, but there's plenty of downside too. It's like back in the day there was a Post law or guidelines everybody abided by. We were like a huge rowdy-ass family. We were allowed to piss on each other but nobody else was. Somebody who didn't live around here walked down one of the streets and everybody was lookin' at him, even grandmas and shit. You know what I mean. You probably got that for a while. Or like when the Espinosas and their crew robbed Keith, Jonah and the boys. Three days later they were all brawlin' together against a bunch of them Harper Creek rednecks at the Barker's party, all of it on Keith's behalf. Then, a couple days later both groups are back at each other's throats in the middle of the street. We got to take care of each other, and respond to each other how we wanted. Nobody even called the cops over shit like that. There was an understanding between most all of us. That's all gone now. If there's a beef it goes straight to Lorenzo. He makes a decision like he's a motherfuckin' King Solomon or something, ruling the land. Plus every decision usually has some nice benefit in it for him. That always takes precedence over what's fair. Back in the day, when Kris was the man on the block, didn't nobody want to deal. Dealers were looked at like sellouts. Shit didn't take no brains or guts so we didn't give 'em no credit. Lorenzo Cole pushes for cats to deal. He provides that shit for anybody who wants to move it. He'll front it to 'em. He just takes a fat cut. Shit, he's gonna do that even if he don't front it to you and you're movin' round here. You might as well go through him and save the hassle. The amount of shit in this neighborhood has tripled. In fact . . . M-a-a-n, can you keep a secret?"

"Yeah sure," answered Samuel, interested in hearing more.

"I mean you gotta swear on everything you don't pass it on to David. I mean, trust me, it's for his own good."

Samuel paused for a moment. "Yeah, sure, I swear."

Lukas turned his head back and forth as if someone was listening. "I think, in fact I'm pretty sure, he had something to do with what happened to Kris right behind this bar."

Samuel's eyes got as wide as they could. "Are you fuckin' kiddin' me? What the hell kind of shit are you telling me right now?"

"I know, man; it's crazy. I don't talk about it with most people but I figure you I can trust and it's one of those things you gotta talk about with somebody. Just think about it, man; he knows Kris is the man and he wants to be the man. There's one reason to get rid of him right there. Then he wants to make big moves with drugs and he knows how Kris feels about that and the way everyone follows Kris. There's another major reason right there. Then you think about how it happened. There's no way Tim Russell's dumb ass outsmarted Kris, no way. Plus from what I hear only a couple of the guys in on it were Tim's boys. The rest were some burly unknown types. Ever since then, Tim's been one of Lorenzo's main errand boys. I'm telling you, this guy's a real fuckin' serpent. He's a sicko with power. Doin' some conniving shit like that is right up his alley."

Samuel's eyelids rose up again. "Tim's still in town?! I thought nobody could find him!"

"Naw, naw man. That's just what we've been telling David 'cause we didn't know what else to say. No one could ever get to him. He's one of Lorenzo Cole's favorite puppies, has been ever since Kris got killed. He moves a lot of dope nowadays and he's always at Lorenzo's palace. Always doin' shit for him. He's like untouchable. I wouldn't be too surprised if they're fuckin'. We haven't wanted to tell David 'cause we knew all he'd think about in there was trying to take on Lorenzo, and it can't be done. He's got too many people. Too many resources. Plus he keeps his big ass crib on lockdown like Fort Knox. Cats with rifles all in the crib and shit. Armed guards at all times. Just looking at his place you know he's into something non-legit. Too bad cops don't work like that. I wouldn't have no problem seeing dude out the picture. He's a real fuckin' nut, you ask me. Let alone the fact that he had that shit done to my boy. Kris didn't deserve that shit. He was the most honorable thug I ever knew. I don't know if Lorenzo had it done to protect Tim or if he protects Tim 'cause he had it done, but there's too many big fuckin' coincidences for me not to believe he did it."

"Whaddya mean fuckin'? This Lorenzo's a homo?" asked Samuel with a queasy expression.

"I mean, he's not really a homo in the typical sense. He's just twisted. He has them drug-infested pool parties and shit, I've heard stories about him getting bored and yankin' down one of the tough guys' shorts. Just sticks it to them right there in front of everybody. I don't think it's about attraction as much as it is likin' to show how much authority he has and freak everybody out at the same time. Nobody will even say shit to him. He gets off on things like that. It's not like the other dude wants any part of it, there's just nothing he can do. You fight off Lorenzo, or even piss him off, you're likely to never be heard from again. If he knows you're not the type to care about that, and he is the type to know, he'll kill friends, family or do whatever he needs to. He keeps everybody's number and he makes sure they know it. Another night there might be a busty young hottie and he'll peel off her suit and give it to her. You never know; it just depends on how the liquor struck him. Even if she liked him it don't matter; he never has a significant. That ain't his way. I can't believe people will even risk being around the twisted fuck. You never know what he's gonna do. He just loves the authority. I guess they want the parties and drugs and think it's worth the risk. He's always into some twisted shit. Hearing stories about Tim and Butch pro'ly got his interest if anything. He's crazy and he has no limits. As much as I don't like 'im, I gotta say, he's the strongest individual I ever met."

"Man, this is shitty news. How long do you think it will take before David starts puttin' things together?"

"See, I don't know, man. That's part of why I'm telling you. That and I've had a couple of drinks."

"Here you go, boys," interrupted the waitress.

"Oh shat!" exclaimed Samuel.

"Yeah, we better take 'em before we get a whiff of the smell," suggested Lukas.

"Yeah, you're right," agreed Samuel as he lifted the glass. "To David." They clinked just before dropping 'em back.

"I mean, we'll have to tell him Tim is around, I always knew that. I just wanted him to be on the outside so he could see for himself what this fucker is all about. That's the only way he might keep chilled. It wouldn't do no one any good for him to be thinking about it all them years. If he came out fuming we could all end up dead. I mean fuck, if he's going after Tim I'll be right next to him, but it's not the smart play. Maybe we should tell him as soon as he gets out. That way he doesn't find out on his own and get pissed at me. I mean, he's gotta realize he wasn't told for his own good. If me and you tell him, and he knows about Lorenzo and all, hopefully we can keep him from trying something crazy."

"Hopefully," said Samuel plainly.

"Well, one thing we got going for us is that David wants to do business with him." Samuel's attention was caught again as Lukas explained, "Yeah, he told me that the two of you got something brewing and if things proceed as he thinks they will, you might want Lorenzo's help."

"No, no. Things do seem like they're proceeding as David thought, but I don't know why we'd need his help, or anybody else's for that matter. Shit should be simple; we got no reason to be mixed up with the likes of him."

"Huh, sounds kind of juicy. Anyway, he said after you guys talked again that I might need to introduce you to Loco."

"Well, I sure hope not to have to take that route."

"You don't know how true that is," began Mouse, easily enticed into speaking more on the intriguing topic. "It's crazy just being around him. He tries to analyze everybody as he meets 'em. He thinks he's some kind of philosopher-slash-gangster. When he was first gettin' a name around here you would always hear about him quoting poetry and shit before he killed somebody—actually, before he'd let a flunky kill somebody. He's always quoting old poetry and shit. He really trips me out. I try and talk with him as little as possible. He seems to know what he's doing. I don't know, it's just not my kind of shit I guess." Lukas chattered quickly and moved around a lot. Samuel liked seeing the antsy behavior that earned him the name Mouse. Somehow, without knowing it, Samuel had missed him.

"Sounds like he needs to go back where he came from."

"Yeah, but I don't see that happening. He's done too well for himself now. You ever heard of Alexander Cole?"

"Naw, I don't think so."

"That's his pops out there, well known in Jersey and NY. It's not real talked about but I guess the real reason they sent Lorenzo out here was because he developed some sick obsession with his aunt. His real-deal aunt, his mother's sister. He was like fifteen and ended up deadin' some dude she started dating. I guess sending him up here was as much not wanting to face what a sicko he is as much as it was hiding him from the law. He spent most of his years here getting tutored and studying different shit. Now he's something to be reckoned with, like I said, a serpent. It's a bad combination. I bet he's got a genius IQ, he's got all the means to put it to use, wicked as fuck and he's bored. He's always trying to come up with something new to entertain himself. I'm impressed with what he pulled off and all but there's too much authority for somebody so off balance. He could massacre a whole family just on a whim."

"Yeah, I don't know what David's talking about. I don't see why we'd have to get entangled with that dude. So how's this welcome home party gonna go down?" asked Samuel, ready to change the subject.

"Well, if it's cool with you, I already talked to the owner and he says we can have it here. Everybody already comes here all the time. It's like the crew bar so David might as well get reacquainted with it."

Samuel looked around. They were sitting in the large open restaurant area. There was a window-filled wall behind Mouse that separated them from a large billiards area. It was a nice spot for the party, right off the edge of Post Edition, plenty of room for everybody to mingle, pool for entertainment and judging from those shots, they were pretty generous with the drinks. "Hey, sounds good to me," agreed Samuel.

"Yeah, I thought you'd be cool with it. There's a private room in the back for parties but I told him we didn't need that. I figure everybody will wanna be out here."

"Now we just gotta let people know," said Samuel.

"That won't be hard. By this weekend I'll have let the whole squad know. If there's anybody particular you want here just give 'em a call. If you don't know how to get in touch just ask me. Chances are I will have already told them." As Lukas finished his sentence his eyes scanned up until they met a definite target, which brought on a smile. "Hey, hey! I didn't know you were coming too," said Lukas.

"Yeah, well, the boys told me you located a relic so I thought I'd have to come see for myself," returned a lady's voice from behind Samuel's back.

Samuel turned to see a handful of old faces coming toward him. His mind slowly recognized each one, bringing a smile to his face as well. The woman talking was Sheryl; they called her Déjà due to a false rumor she had once danced at a strip club by that name. She was closer to Lukas's age. She grew up wishing she could get to hang out with David and the older boys. She did occasionally in Samuel's day, and they had developed a real rapport at one time. As he continued to scan back and forth over the faces he quickly gathered together their names. It was Kurt, Jerrod, Harold AKA Muskrat, and Billy Howard. They were all old friends who frequently hung out with David and Samuel back when. Samuel was never close enough to any of them that he would have tried to keep in touch, but he shared some good times with each. It was nice to see their faces.

Samuel quickly hopped to his feet and started handing out clasp hugs to each of them. "Oh shit!" he hooted. "Look at this fuckin' posse of ruffians. Is it legal for all y'all to hang out together at the same time? There's gotta be some guideline or something against it."

"If there ain't it's just 'cause the chigs ain't got around to it," agreed Kurt as he gave his respects.

"Not that we'd pay it any mind if there was," added Jerrod as a hearty smile cracked through his jet black face.

The night proceeded, bringing drinks in excess. If one person wasn't buying a round the next was; even Samuel bought a few. As ready as he was to drink, he still wouldn't have done it to that extreme if he'd had time to think. It seemed whenever he turned around he had another of the old friends with their hand on his shoulder, bringing up a fight or amusing story they'd been through together. Each time they'd commemorate the memory by buying him a shot.

Eventually they were all in the pool area together laughing and making jokes at each other's expense. Every so often there'd be another shot toasted to David's pending return or how great the welcome home party would be. No one had the heart to pass.

As they made fun of each other's drunken stance or poor shooting, Samuel was overwhelmed with nostalgia. He remembered a time that didn't seem as long ago as it was when this was all his day-to-day routine consisted of. All their friends would find a place to get together, get drunk, smoke weed and still attempt to retain the ability to make witty comments against each other's character. Each insult was enough to bring a tear to his eye as he looked back on the lost perfection of it all.

He wished he had known then how important it would be to him now. That time, as time did once it had passed, now seemed flawless. He could taste how badly he wished he could return to those days. Telling himself he would appreciate them the way they deserved to be appreciated made him feel like he was worthy for another chance. Deep down he almost felt like he was gonna be able to make it back to them somehow. It was like a vivid dream that you were just sure would come to pass even after you were awake.

As these thoughts festered and his desire to be standing dwindled, he had to take a moment to consider how drunk he actually was. He giggled as he looked around; everything was very blurry. He was listening to people talk but he was no longer sure what it was about. He had to admit to himself he was drunk. There was nothing he could do now; he might as well lay back and enjoy it.

He looked to a nearby table. There, Kurt and Sheryl were playing touchy-feely while laughing and exchanging whispers. "Are they a thing or something, Muskrat?" he asked Harold, who was sitting next to him.

In a sluggishly drunk motion Harold turned his head from watching the pool game in front of him to looking in their direction. "Them? Nah. They just fool around every once in a while. Sheryl has pretty much made the rounds through the crew. I'm sure you could have predicted that. Now she just takes attention from whoever'll give it to her. That pretty much comes down to whoever gets the drunken hornies first."

"Right. She still looks good, though," observed Samuel.

"That she does," agreed Harold.

Samuel tried not to stare at them. He knew Kurt. He knew how this routine went. Kurt would be able to have whatever he wanted from her whenever he wanted, without the burden of any of the responsibilities a relationship usually involves. Samuel could practically taste the envy in his gut. Then he thought of the fact that were he given the chance to have a fling with her, there was a good chance he'd get emotionally involved. Then he'd be mocked behind his back. He'd be the guy who fell in love with the local slut. In those circles, there were few bigger signs of weakness in a man than one who took such a desperate girl seriously.

Samuel could feel it coming over him. It crept up slowly at first, like a cautious predator, careful not to upset the herd. Then it shot all over his body, rapidly taking control. The more he tried to fight it, the more insurmountable it seemed. It was the all-too-familiar dread that had prompted him to stop drinking in the first place. How quickly he'd forgotten the way the alcohol broke down his walls. They were important walls. They kept out the things too hard for him to deal with. Once drunk the walls disappeared. Every emotion or thought he had was free to come pouring in.

There was no goal or direction in his life. This world had nothing good enough to go after anyway. Samuel felt like he was at war. The battle line was drawn between his feelings of dread and his feelings of contentment. They had changed control at least three times in the last twenty-four hours. Now the dread was regaining its throne.

He looked again at the frolicking couple. That was what the modern-day relationship consisted of, jokes and sex. The idea of a loving, emotionally beneficial relationship was so far from these two, one had to wonder if they had ever heard of it in the first place.

He looked at Harold next to him, then Jerrod and Billy playing pool to his front. He thought about it. Neither he nor any of these friends had made one real step of progress in their lives since the day they'd graduated high school. Here they were doing the same stuff they had done back then. Telling stories from years ago just like they had weeks after the stories took place. Only now the details were distorted with time and it was just a matter of who started to tell the story first as to how it would take place. He felt like a bunch of war vets trying to relive their glory days. Whatever this lifestyle had to offer had long been dried up.

He looked across to another pool table where Mouse was bickering over the details of a game with a thuggish black guy who looked familiar from high school but definitely wasn't from the East side. One of the guy's friends was standing nearby laughing at their argument. Their whole group was so high they could barely open their eyes. Another of their friends was sitting on the bench staring blindly at the ceiling. His eyes were brick red all the way around, with a notable liquor gloss as well. He was so inebriated he was no longer capable of socializing. He would make it through his night by trusting his friends to lead him where he needed to go. He would be lucky to remember where they had been tomorrow. He was a shining example of this town they lived in. Samuel used to describe it as one big blackout. He figured they had likely set the record for most citizens simultaneously not remembering a particular night. Everyone hated their dead-end factory job. All there really was to spend their money on was babysitters and drinks. Everyone was always in a rush to get off work and get to the bar by a designated time. Then they would drink themselves stupid. They wouldn't have to think about their lives being so devoid of real value. Years might pass without them being able to tell you anything of consequence that had taken place. All they really had stored in their memory was who had been fucking who in recent months and any beefs that might be brewing.

Samuel felt nauseous. The all-too-familiar spiral of negativity was back in full swirl. He felt like everyone was spinning down it but he was the only one cursed with noticing. He never heard anyone else complain about these things. It was like whatever goal that had caused generations of old to persevere was never passed on to this one. Something was missing. Worst of all, Samuel was deemed narrator of the horrific monotony they were all a part of.

It was near that moment that his own blackout spells, which had plagued his party days, came into play. It seemed as if whatever part of his mind that was used to retain information would take a rest. His memory skipped from sitting in front of the pool table philosophizing to their whole group standing near the entrance discussing something. His brain had blinked and missed some of what happened. Now, as happened occasionally during these spells, his head was attempting to break free from the stupor it was in. Whenever this happened he was left with a brief image in the middle of an otherwise blank period of time.

After his mind cleared, just a bit, he tried to concentrate on the conversation taking place. Someone was upset and speaking rapidly about it. He looked over at Kurt and Sheryl. Still together after whatever had taken place, they were giggling the same, but now staring directly at Samuel while they whispered.

He decided to put his attention to figuring out who was talking. Despite his groggy mental state, he calmed himself and listened. After just an instant he came to discover it was his own mouth chattering so fast. He was the one worked up, speaking to Lukas, who also seemed agitated by the topic. They were a lot drunker than the rest of the group. Kurt and Sheryl, who were drunk but not belligerent, were enjoying watching the intoxicated conversation.

Samuel then tried to focus on the issue being discussed.

"I'm telling you, dude. This is our bar," Lukas explained in an inebriated voice, better suited for outdoors. "If you want a fuckin' bottle they'll sell it to us right now."

"Look, man. They might do that shit all the time, but it's illegal and they don't know me so I don't think they're gonna sell it to me. I don't see why you can't go get it," argued Samuel.

"'Cause I don't need it. I'm fine with the beer we've got at the crib. I don't see why you can't drink beer. You've been drinkin' 'em all night."

"'Cause I hate beer. If I'm gonna stay out and drink it's gonna be some liquor I like, but I'm not gonna go ask some total stranger to break the law for me, so I guess I'll just head to the crib," stated Samuel.

"Man, it don't matter if he's a stranger; you've been with me all night . . . you know what, fuck it, come on, we'll go together, you big baby!"

Samuel, now having forgot his separation of character, smiled like a kid who finally got his own way and bounced along, giving Lukas's head a rub of gratitude. Lukas laughed, shaking his head at an old friend's amusing behavior.

It took little time after Samuel received the bottle before his memory gave way again. It didn't return until the next morning.

CHAPTER 18: REPERCUSSIONS

He woke to a familiar, bitter gnawing in his stomach. His whole body was weak. His mouth was laced with a thick goop that had replaced his saliva. His brain, too, felt exchanged for an inadequate replacement. Each breath brought back the taste of a senseless number of cigarettes.

Worse than any of his physical ailments was a feeling like something awful had happened and he couldn't remember what it was. A thick mixture of regret and embarrassment was wedged into the depths of him.

He stood up, dragging himself to the bathroom, trying to minimize the spinning of his head by squinting his eyes.

He tried to piece together what his prior evening had consisted of. It was a moment before he could even recall where it began. Then it clicked: he had visited Mouse at Snickers. That was what had started things off. He and Lukas Bailey had shared some drinks, and then some old friends showed up. He remembered being happy with everything going on. That distracted him from how much he was drinking. He took note of that as the folly in his ways, to remind himself for next time. He struggled to recall what followed, but it was a blur. He could remember talking to his friends but their faces were hard to make out. They were just smudges of color, no detail. He couldn't even be sure which one he was addressing. He could only really remember people being amused with him.

Then he focused on some of the things he was saying. He could hear himself going on about the state of his life, the way Susan had left him. He was asking these hardcore men's opinions on things far too personal to bring up in casual conversation.

The embarrassment flared. He had been making a fool of himself. After not seeing these people in years, he gave a tainted impression.

He had certainly given the wrong idea about his current feelings toward Susan. They probably thought he was still carrying a torch after all this time.

He could picture himself again and again, sitting down with someone new and with no lead, diving into something no one could be comfortable talking about. He left them no choice but to laugh. He had made talking to him awkward. He knew his friends must have been trying to avoid getting stuck in one of his conversations. He could only hope they were drunk enough not to give it much thought the next day.

He wished he could take it all back somehow. He never decided for any of this to happen. It was like he had tripped on something and all this stuff was just there. A small mistake, taking one too many shots, removed his control. Once the control was gone he continued to take too many shots and now here he was, punished with these events having taken place.

He tried to justify them by telling himself it was a reminder not to drink. It didn't help much. Finally he was calmed by accepting that it was useless grief. There was nothing he could do now but try not to think about it. He had to roll with the punches. The regret would fade. It always had in the past. No matter how nauseous it made him feel at first, his friends would forget how obnoxious he had been, and he would eventually let it go as just one of those things. The only downside to that was that the door was left open for it to happen again. He could remember in those early years after high school, embarrassing nights like that taking place and him trying to cut down to prevent them recurring. Eventually, if things went well long enough he'd let his guard down and it'd happen again. If it happened too often in a short period of time, he might cut out drinking altogether, but it wouldn't last. A month, month and half later, and the pain of regret would be gone and he'd be boozing it up again. It had become routine back then. Still, knowing that didn't reduce the sting now.

He looked at the clock. He was already late for work, but there was little he could do about that either. He would just have to get ready and apologize when he got there. He was in desperate need of a shower. There was no way he was giving it up.

His mouth was too parched to ignore so he put it under the bathroom faucet for a small drink, just enough to provide some needed moisture. But once the water touched his tongue he couldn't help lapping it up like a hunting hound after a long day's tracking. He kept telling himself to stop but he couldn't help it. He was far too thirsty. After sucking down the water, he straightened his stance, then was greeted with the feeling he'd been trying to avoid. The water hit his gut like a heavyweight boxer. Before he knew it, he was on his knees spewing it back up, along with much of the prior night's acquisitions as well.

After the vomiting was complete, he felt a bit better. He showered, dressed, skipped breakfast and was on his way to work.

When he arrived, his boss was standing just inside the door. He was without his usual sporty grin. The cherry-colored face was instead white with uneasiness. His look resembled how Samuel felt. Samuel figured him feeling out of place due to the scolding he would have to give for tardiness. That was surprising, though. He didn't figure Bob would make that big a deal out of it.

"Hey, I'm sorry, man," began Samuel as soon as he was close enough. "I don't know what happened. Usually I wake up before the alarm goes off."

"You feeling all right?" asked Bob.

"Yeah, I'm good," answered Samuel curiously.

"I was wondering if we were gonna hear anything from you at all."

Samuel just nodded his head, hiding his confusion. Somehow Bob's words insinuated he knew Samuel's situation. His mind raced, trying to figure out how Bob could possibly know anything about the night before.

"Well, I better get a move on," suggested Samuel.

"Actually no, Jake has already taken off on your route. I need to talk to you in my office," explained Bob.

Samuel's eyebrows scrunched down in surprise. He couldn't believe someone had been sent out on his route already. If they had reached that point he thought they would have called his house. Something wasn't right. Without speaking he followed Bob to the office. He kept trying to picture himself communicating with Bob or any of his coworkers in his drunken state. It just didn't click. Even if he had talked to them, it still didn't make sense. Getting drunk and acting a fool after hours was none of his work's business.

As Bob opened the door to his office an unhappy thought occurred to Samuel. Jake would be delivering Monique's mail today. She would think Samuel was trying to avoid her over Sunday. Even worse, she might not have mail, keeping anyone from showing up at all.

The second Monique entered his mind Samuel's weary eyes flung open. The gnawing ball of regret and embarrassment suddenly burst open like one of their water balloons, covering his body as such. He had been to her house last night. When he got that fifth at closing time, he started thinking about how angry he was with her. Instead of following Lukas and the rest, he decided to give her his two cents. He wanted to scream as the memories leaked in. It was like it was all just happening that instant but there was still nothing he could do to stop it. He couldn't believe what he'd done. He wanted to sit there and figure out just what he'd said but before he could, Bob was sitting behind the desk, beckoning Samuel to have a seat.

"Well Samuel, this is kind of hard for me to address. You've been a great employee here for years. You're like the iron man of the postal service. That's what makes this so difficult," he explained to a slate-faced Samuel. "It seems we've got a complaint from one of your stops on Emerald Boulevard. A Ms. Monique Romano called early this morning. Before I had even gotten in today she had called and left a message. Before I had a chance to return it she had called again. It seems you went over to her house last night."

Samuel pictured himself knocking on her door. He could only picture a flash of her confused face when she opened it.

"She says you were pretty drunk, acting out of control. She's not comfortable with you delivering her mail anymore. That in itself would be a touchy enough situation, but she also said you tampered with her mail. That you had one of her letters last night. That you had opened it."

Samuel didn't respond. He could see himself with her envelope in his hands. He was yelling, on the verge of tears. He threw it at her. The money scattered everywhere. He turned and ran down the hill. He could remember her calling after him. She was begging to explain. He wouldn't have it. He remembered the frustration he felt when he slipped on the dew-covered grass in her front yard. She had almost reached him, wanting to give aid, when he got back to his feet. He wouldn't stop and listen to her. He just yelled more accusations and ran to his car.

"You must know how serious these accusations can be," began Bob again. "Do you have anything to say in your defense?"

Samuel paused, trying to think of what to say before he started muttering. "I don't know what happened, Bob. I went out with some old friends. We had some drinks. I guess we had too many. Everything's a blur. I've been trying to put things together since I woke up. I don't know. My head just hasn't really cleared enough yet to say much of anything for sure."

"Okay. That's understandable. But all I can really tell ya now is that you're taking some time off. I've been telling you for too long you needed a vacation. In my opinion this is a result of you being wound too tight. You need to let loose. Get your head on straight. I'm not sure how far she's gonna want to pursue this. All she really made clear at this point was that she didn't want you on her route any longer. I don't imagine that when you return you'll be going to the same route. The important thing now, though, is that we can get you back."

"So I'm suspended?"

"Look, you know I'll back you up. As far as I'm concerned no one else needs to know about this. She didn't seem like she wanted you fired. She seemed more caught off guard by the whole thing. So don't look at it like a suspension. Just look at as a long-overdue vacation. I'll keep you posted on everything. Hopefully I can put you back on the clock real soon. But I'll have to let you know when that is."

"All right. All right, man, I appreciate your understanding. I'm gonna get some sleep. If after that I can put a better handle on things to tell you just what happened, I'll let you know."

"Well, I'd appreciate that," he said as Samuel started out of the office. "Oh, and Samuel! Take care of yourself. I want a refreshed man when I get you back here."

Samuel nodded appreciatively.

Walking out, he tried not to look at his coworkers for fear they'd ask what was going on. He considered all the times he'd been upset with Bob's perky attitude. He was now grateful for the type of person Bob was. It was making a very hard situation much easier.

Samuel was a zombie the whole drive home. He couldn't believe how stupid he'd been. He should have known how prone he was to blow up. He couldn't block out all the emotions that came with Sunday's events if he was drunk. Again, he had to apply the same philosophy. What was done was done. He couldn't change that. All he could do now was assess the situation. His relationship with Monique was over. She didn't want to see him again. He had also tipped his hand. He had told her he knew of her relationship with Torreo. He could remember accusing her of being in cahoots with a filthy drug dealer, that little Cullomine had a plague for a dad. He could remember her face dropping. She was astounded that he knew Cullomine Torreo was senior to her son. If there was any doubt left as to whether Samuel and David's conclusion was correct, her expression removed it. The look was hurt. He had attacked her, her son and her at least one-time spouse mercilessly, as if they were all horrible people for the life Torreo led. He also showed her the money. He threw it in her face with disgust. He must have looked like an idiot falling down that hill, all worked up and emotional. He had slain the false character he had created for her. The confident womanizer unwilling to care for anyone had clearly never existed. He kept claiming she had used him in some plot they were spinning. She had to be curious now what exactly Samuel knew. Regardless, she had made her decision. It was the right one for her position. She couldn't risk him tampering with her delivery, so she had him removed from the route. Now his perfect plan for paradise was ruined. That was the real damage he'd done.

Samuel could have been grateful she wasn't trying to press charges for opening her mail, or even asking for his termination. He could have decided that when he wouldn't listen to reason that she had no choice but to keep him away from her and her home. Instead, he told himself how conniving she was. When her sweet-talking wouldn't work, she took more drastic measures; she got him suspended. She did what she wanted to get him out of her way. Samuel's villainizing of Monique worked wonders in removing any guilt he had for his behavior. All he was left with was figuring out how he could still get that money.

Fortunately, he didn't remember bringing up the big package she was expecting. He hadn't made his intentions that obvious. She was still acting to protect it, but he wouldn't give up the perfect life that easily. Why would he let someone like Cullomine Torreo walk away with a bag full of easy street when he could get his more deserving hands on it? David had wanted to acquire Lorenzo Cole's help in this situation. Before, it wasn't necessary. Now, it wasn't a bad idea. Perhaps there was still an alternate route to the end of the rainbow.

When he arrived home there was no wasting time mulling over having been suspended. He was too tired for that. He was too overwhelmed. Instead, he flopped face down on his bed and eased into unconsciousness.

CHAPTER 19: FACE-TO-FACE WITH A SERPENT

When he awoke, he felt a world better physically. Mentally, he didn't feel much at all. His mind was like an overworked engine that stalled out. It felt numb. He didn't feel the regret or embarrassment. He didn't feel anger toward Monique or himself; that was a waste of time. It didn't matter what anyone thought of him. All there was to do was finish assessing the new situation and decide his next move.

It didn't take much thought before he came to his conclusion. No longer being employed at a job he hated brought an unparalleled feeling of freedom. He decided he was going to do whatever it took to maintain that freedom. There was nothing else to fight for. With this freedom he could spend time dreaming again. He could grow his passion for life all over again. Perhaps then, he truly could step back on the playing field. He could go back to his true lost love, writing. It all added up so well. All he had to do was get that money and the rest would unfold itself. That was certainly worth fighting for, and though he hadn't in years, he felt ready to fight. He was fed up.

He had to get in touch with David, to see how this should be handled. Mouse said David wanted him to get in touch with this Lorenzo, but he would have to check with him on his own. If that was the case, that's what he would do.

Now that it wasn't obvious, plotting on how, when and where it would be best to get their hands on that money was not up Samuel's alley. That's why it was important to get in touch with David. The next few days he tried endlessly to do that, but to no avail.

After days of being cooped up in his apartment he crossed the street to the park for some fresh air. To his frustration David called in his absence. There was just a message as to when he would be released. He gave the time and location for Samuel to pick him up. Unfortunately he didn't give any details on what was to be done on the Torreo situation. He just mentioned hoping Samuel had found some things out.

That was as much waiting as Samuel could handle. He decided to call Little Lukas Bailey to set up a meeting with Lorenzo Cole. He wouldn't give away the details. He would just get a foot in the door in case that was the way David wanted to handle things. Samuel liked the idea of talking to Lukas anyway. He'd feel better knowing for sure whether he pissed anyone off.

Though Samuel had remained unable to speak with David, Lukas set up a meeting in two days' time with Lorenzo Cole. When the time came, needless to say, Samuel had his inhibitions about seeing this arch criminal. On the ride to Cole's urban palace, Lukas shared a few more tidbits of Lorenzo folklore, bringing Samuel's inhibitions up to full-scale fear. Fortunately, Samuel had always been an expert at keeping his fears hidden from those around him. Even as hard as it was to know what to expect out of this meeting, it would still assuredly be no exception.

He was battling the jitters one usually had before a job interview. He knew he would be questioned before a man of this nature would be willing to do business. On top of that, he knew this man would want to know the nature of the business in question. That was information Samuel was not yet willing to share. He knew he might have to be hard-nosed, but at the same time avoid offending Mr. Cole. Offense or not, Samuel would not be willing to give away anything until David gave the go-ahead. He could only hope he would be able to keep it from coming to a head.

As Lukas explained it, this was a privilege, getting to see him face-to-face without prior acquaintance. Usually there was a series of middle men one would have to go through before an actual meeting could be arranged. Lukas claimed it was his clout that made it possible. Samuel, however, considered it likely that Lorenzo had been hearing about David Caine for years, and with the release so close, probably thought it wise to build a rapport with someone known for being close with David, like Samuel. If David didn't accept Lorenzo's rule, it was probable that others would follow his lead. Cole could not afford that kind of division among the people he'd built his empire on. Believing that he wanted to build a good relationship with them was the only thing putting Samuel at ease.

Samuel was intrigued by this highly speculated individual. The idea that he was a gangster poet, as Lukas described it, was a contradiction of character that immediately sparked an interest. At a point, Samuel was almost excited to meet this enigma of a man, but as the merciless and perverted stories poured in, the excitement quickly subsided. Now he felt more as if he was risking misfortune by seeking the help of such a twisted soul. He feared that his thirst for freedom from his burden of a life was causing him to take a risk he would have otherwise known better than to take.

When they pulled in front of the house Samuel's intrigue was sparked again. Before, he wondered how a man who was allegedly as successful as this one could have made a neighborhood as simple as Post Edition his home. He now understood. There was a hill on the eastern outskirts of the neighborhood. It was labeled dead man's hill by the local youngsters, who commonly soared down it on their bicycles. Formerly atop this hill were three small houses. Two were side by side, while the other had its back to them. Lorenzo had apparently purchased all three. With extensive renovating they stood merged as one large house. Now it was easily the nicest house the neighborhood had to offer. Still, it wasn't so lavish that it seemed out of place.

Lorenzo Cole sat in this house like a king on his throne, looking out over his kingdom. It was purposely symbolic, and Samuel considered it as telling much about the person he was dealing with.

There were no gates around the house, no buzzer before admittance. They just pulled up the U-shaped driveway that came in front of the house, parked the car and got out. Samuel stepped back and gazed up at the home. In style it looked like a typical neighborhood home. White siding, black shutters on each side of the windows, a matching black roof and a thick oak door at its front. A common home design. It was camouflaged by its conformity to the rest of the neighborhood. Its only visible difference was its size.

After Lukas knocked on the front door, its typical mesh appearance quickly disappeared. The door was answered by a burly man in black dress pants and a tight, tucked-in black T-shirt. He looked like the Mafia's answer to the Secret Service. He had black sunglasses on and his firearm was resting quite plainly at his waist. Behind him were excessively lush marble floors. They were multiple colors and had different portraits carved into them. These elaborate carvings made them look as if they would be difficult to walk on, but at a closer look they were found to have a thick coat over them, leaving the surface smooth.

The man at the door stared at them with no recognition.

"It's me, Mouse. I'm here to see Loco," explained Lukas.

"You shouldn't refer to Mr. Cole that way. Sometimes he doesn't like it," responded the man as he rubbed at his chin. Samuel could see a scar on his face near where he rubbed. The man then punched buttons on some sort of digital planner affixed to the inside of the door frame.

"Fuck, Frank. It's me, Lukas. You know, Mouse. Shit man, how many years I been coming here? You still act like you don't know me. You punch through the list on the wall till you find my name, then you let me in. Have I ever come when I wasn't expected?" The man paid little attention to what Lukas was saying. He just continued punching buttons until he found what he was looking for.

"Follow me," he stated as he turned and headed deeper into the house.

Past the entryway, the extravagance multiplied. The path opened into a huge room with a decorative pond in the center. Each side of the room had a matching staircase winding up to the next floor. They looked like something stolen from *Gone with the Wind*. At the center of the staircases was a waterfall pouring elegantly into the pond. At either side of the waterfall were paths going under the staircases. It was the path on the left the man was leading them down. On passing the pond Samuel could see that the end opposite the falls had an oval opening allowing him to see the floor beneath. The water went through the pond to a second waterfall at this opening. There it poured down to the basement, where it met a gigantic swimming pool. Samuel could only imagine the size of the basement they had under that sizable house. He figured that was where the parties Lukas had mentioned likely took place.

As they passed the falls and continued down the hallway, he glanced back to the front of the house. There were little balconies against the elevated windows on each side. Standing in each balcony was a man in similar black attire, holding a sharpshooting rifle. Samuel figured the majority of the windows in the house had men like these. They were replacements for gates.

The hallway they were walking down was short and dark. It opened into a black room. The walls, carpet, and ceiling were all a deep shade of black. It was the office of one Lorenzo Cole. He was sitting behind a desk, also black but with gold trim. His chair had the shade and trim to match the desk. There he sat reading a book attentively.

"Mr. Cole," announced the doorman, bringing Lorenzo's snake-green eyes up from his book. "Lukas Bailey and his one accompany are here to see you."

Lorenzo smirked up one side of his lip. "I'm not sure that's a real sentence but I do catch your meaning." He then looked over them at a calm, deliberate pace. "Please, have a seat," he said as he gestured toward the pair of sofa chairs in front of his desk. He set his book down, rose slowly to his feet and swaggered around to the front of the desk, leaving nothing between him and his guests.

He was wearing a silky black robe, pants, and shirt, with matching slippers that left the top of his feet near the ankle exposed. Samuel guessed his age in the early thirties, considerably young for such accomplished surroundings.

As he reached the front of his desk, he smacked Frank on the ass like he was a horse. "Go on, I don't see why we'd need you in here. Get back to the door, and tell Stephanie to send me in a Hawaiian chicken sandwich."

Samuel looked to the corner of the desk, where an unfinished ham sandwich sat on a plate. Lorenzo noticed and seemed intrigued by Samuel's observation.

Samuel was now considerably more nervous than on the journey up here. He assumed it would be much like a visit with Monique, where the anxiety was in the wait but once in the situation it became easy. This strange man seemed to have a talent for making other people uneasy. He was leaning back on his desk with his hands clasped in his lap, twiddling his thumbs. He continually looked up and down the two, studying them as if he had something in store for them.

His hair hung shoulder-length and was almost as black as his surroundings. It was so dark, Samuel couldn't decide if that was its natural state or if it had been dyed. There was stubble across his face. He looked ethnic but not with an obvious origin. If Samuel hadn't already known he was Irish-Italian, he would have been challenged to guess it.

"So," he finally resounded, breaking the awkward silence he let fester, "what brings you gentlemen to my humble abode?"

Lukas chuckled, "Yeah, that's the way I'd describe it, humble."

Lorenzo smiled slyly at the backhanded compliment. It was clear to Samuel that this man was clever. It was also clear that he had been accustomed to dealing with people who were far less gifted than him in such matters. He still enjoyed getting others to do the bragging for him. He smiled proudly at the ease of his manipulation.

Samuel's respect for him immediately lowered. Having usually found himself mentally superior to others, Samuel still had not allowed that to make him arrogant. Lorenzo had built an arrogance of that nature to the point it seemed to dominate his whole character. That, more than the stories he'd been told, rubbed Samuel the wrong way.

He thought it safe to assume Lorenzo would attempt to assess his mental caliber during this conversation. He considered it better if he was held in similar standing as the rest of the Posties.

"Anyway, humble or not, I wanted to bring by this old friend of mine I was telling you about. Lorenzo Cole, meet Samuel Lamech." Lorenzo turned his head toward Samuel, and they both nodded a respectful hello.

"So Samuel Lamech, why is it Lukas here, along with other friends of mine from this neighborhood, know you so well, yet I've never heard of you?"

"Well, I didn't actually grow up in Post; I just did a lot of partying with them in high school and a couple years after. The party lifestyle wasn't really treatin' me too good so I haven't been around much. Old friends bring about old habits, as they say."

Lorenzo nodded in a slow, methodic pace, as if analyzing every word. It made Samuel nervous at first. Then he decided it was a ploy. He could see how if one always acted like they knew something everyone else didn't, it would make everyone else uneasy. He thought that was more than likely what Lorenzo did to keep others on edge.

"Makes sense, I suppose, except that you're back here now," said Lorenzo.

"Well, I'm sure you've probably heard of David Caine, and how he's gonna be released soon. We were always pretty tight. That and some business we're gonna be looking into has brought me back over to the East side of town."

"And am I right in supposing it's the business portion that has brought you here?"

"You're right, I just wasn't sure if this was the best time to come visit you or not because until David gets out I can't really go into any details. I just thought it'd be good for us to meet and maybe I could get an idea of what it is you do."

Lorenzo again nodded his head, this time with a hint of agitation. Samuel attributed it to his unsatisfied curiosity. He seemed like someone who always got what he wanted. He was probably a spoiled child who still threw a fit when things didn't go his way, only the fit of this man was something to be revered.

"Well, I can help you there. I do a lot. We don't want to sit here and listen to the ins and outs of every detail, but Lukas here tells me that you guys have some kind of score brewing, as opposed to an operation to suggest. So I'll tell you what it is I offer in that aspect. You see, when I got here there was one thing there didn't seem to be any shortage of: potential. On the other hand there wasn't much of anything getting done. I had to ask myself why that was. The answer I came up with . . . trust. There was no trust in this neighborhood. So, simply put, I became the trust. You don't have to take anyone's word because I am the word." He smiled at Samuel. "You look a little confused so let me clarify," he said arrogantly as he picked his book up and went to find its place in the giant bookshelf that was the wall at the back of the room. "You see, if Joe Shmoe down the street notices a kink in the chain of the security at a bank, or gets an idea on how to embezzle off his workplace, it's hard for him to get anything accomplished around here. He might try and think of some guys he can trust to do it, but eventually it gets written off as wishful thinking because he's spent too many years watching even his closest friends steal money out of their moms' purses. How can he trust them not to screw him if the opportunity presents itself? If you spent much time here you must know there's no shortage of ideas like this. People are always coming up with a good place to rob, or a good scam to run, but even the guys who will trust their friends just never got around to doing much about it. If they weren't so lazy they probably wouldn't be criminal-minded in the first place. That's where I come in. You just come to me with the information and I organize things and make sure they get done. If you don't know anyone to play the necessary roles then I find someone. If you do, you don't have to worry about a double-cross because I'm involved. If you get Sammy the pizza boy to be your getaway driver and the lick is under my supervision, then Sammy gets arrested a week later, you don't have to worry about him ratting you out. 'Cause Sammy knows that if he starts ratting I'm gonna make sure he comes up missing. If I can't get to him I'm gonna kill his mother, his kids, his friends and whoever I got to. He knows that I'll find a way to make sure it's not worth it. See, nobody on the deal has to trust each other; they just all trust me. And trusting me is easy 'cause I got a precedent set. They all know about the results when other people come to me with their ideas. They know what's happened when others tried to get greedy, and let me tell you, no one has bothered trying in a long time. It's worth it to go through me. It's like criminal insurance. I reduce all risks considerably."

"So what are the insurance rates?" asked Samuel.

Lorenzo gave another superior grin, as if amused with a child's behavior. "Well, it varies, but I usually take somewhere in the neighborhood of fifty percent."

Samuel jerked his head back in surprise, fueling Lorenzo's grin all the more before he began again.

"Occasionally I've reduced that percentage for various reasons. I wanna make sure everyone goes home happy. If a job takes six or seven people, outside my staff, I might have to come down, depending on the score. I try to make sure everybody gets their profit, but usually I take about half. That covers everything. If Frank out there has to visit a nosy citizen who saw something they shouldn't have, I don't come to you saying I need more. I pay him on my own. The only time there's a possibility of me renegotiating terms is if you actually get arrested—lawyer fees and things like that. Even then, it's not likely. I have some of the finest lawyers in the Midwest on retainer. You get picked up doing a job that I'm behind and my guys are usually at the station before you are. The only time we'd have to worry about paying them more is in the case of a long, drawn-out legal battle. That doesn't happen too often. You see up there?" asked Lorenzo as he gestured to the top of the book case. "Those top two rows there are all law books. I've read each of them, probably more than once. I rarely actually need my lawyers' advice. Half the time I'm telling them what I want done. It's just a matter of needing their reputation, like men around here need mine. See, I don't think the law stands much of a chance. In most cases across the country it's a battle between the police and powers that be, who have all the resources, and the criminals, who have almost none. The only thing the criminals have going for them is a boundless approach to the problem. They can, and usually will, do anything to get out of the bad situation. The law and its backers, on the other hand, have all those resources, but they are bound by certain self-made rules and guidelines. Being a successful criminal is knowing how and when to hide behind those rules. Use them as a shield, so to speak. So when there's someone like me, who has the boundless approach of all criminals, who knows those rules and guidelines up and down, knows all the angles to put them to use, then on top of that has as much for resources as the law, they no longer stand much of a chance. Ask around; nobody in this neighborhood is going to jail anymore. Everyone's making moves and getting away with it. I'm like the salvation of the Posties," he boasted, laughing with both hands out, as if asking who could argue his point. "Your friend David, if I'd been active here back then, he could have gotten out of that. He might not be in jail right now. You see, that is what I do, Samuel. I'm the word that fills in the blanks. I'm the bridge that allows everyone to reach their piece of the pie, and that's what I can do for you."

As Lorenzo Cole wrapped up his sales pitch, Lukas cosigned everything said with an agreeable nod. He had clearly already been sold on the abilities of this man. It was easy for Samuel to see why. Lorenzo spoke smoothly, and everything he said made a lot of sense. It was obvious he was used to talking to the hoodlums of this town. Samuel knew them well enough to know they would eat up everything this man was feeding. He had a strong presence about him. He was the sort of person one might notice come in the room even if their back was to him. It was easy to be impressed by his accomplishments, the lifestyle he lived. He was easy to fear as well. There was a twisted look hiding behind his excessively knowledgeable eyes. Just being around him allowed Samuel to feel how passionately disturbed this man was.

After listening attentively, Samuel responded, "Well, that all sounds real good. I'd be surprised if we weren't back here real soon for your help. Like I said, I gotta go over things with David before I can say anything for sure."

Lorenzo nodded his head, not nearly as upset this time by this open-ended situation. Samuel deemed him more at ease now that he got to put on his show. He was confident everyone in the room was impressed with him.

"There is one thing I'm wondering about," spoke Samuel again. "Not so much in relation to our business, but more to my own curiosity about you having tamed the wild streets of Post Edition. If that's all right?" said Samuel, knowing this man wouldn't pass up the chance to highlight his own achievements.

"No, no. I'm happy to explain," agreed Lorenzo.

"Well, it's just that having always been an outsider who spent a lot of time here, I've always been kind of a keen observer of the customs in this neighborhood. Now I can see why what you've provided has brought in all the success it has, but I'm wondering how you handle all the beefs and old grudges that used to fill the nights here. For instance, through conversation with some of the boys, I've heard that you have the Sozzollo brothers doing a lot of work for you. I hope you're not offended by me addressing them specifically, but it seems that just about everyone in Post has had a problem with them at one time or another. I just don't know how you get guys to go into business with you if they have grudges with your employees."

Lukas was looking at Samuel with pale eyes. "Hey, Samuel. . ." he interceded, not happy with the question. He'd have rather left the idea of anyone beefing with Lorenzo Cole completely out of this meeting

"Lukas," interrupted Lorenzo like a scolding parent, "he's capable of asking the question; I'm capable of answering. I don't understand what role you're playing. Why are you talking?" Lukas closed his mouth and went back to listening. "Well, you see, Samuel," began Lorenzo again, "it's those grudges and beefs you mentioned that held back so much of the progress here. Perfectly good soldiers getting killed over nickel bags. If Billy does work for me and Johnny hates him 'cause he cheated on his cousin, Johnny still can't touch him 'cause Billy's with me. If you got a problem with somebody working for me you come to me and we'll work it out. You don't just attack someone on my payroll or making me money without there being repercussions. So if Johnny can't touch Billy anyway, what difference does it make? He might as well come make money with me too. I usually keep track of who's upset with who. If it helps to keep certain guys away from each other, I do, but if for some reason I can't, they'll still behave because they know I want them to. More often than not, once they know they can't have at each other, they give up on their futile anger. Next thing you know they get along and even end up doing work together. See, most of the time they only held on to those grudges because they were expected to. Once they couldn't pursue it, the problem usually deflated altogether. Now you mention Ron and Randy; do you think your friend David is gonna have a problem with them upon release?"

"Naw, naw, nothing like that. They're just a prime example of what I was asking about. I can't tell you how many people have had it in for them over the years. I woulda guessed they'd have been more trouble than they're worth. No, David's not gonna be concerned with any grudges. He's just trying to get ahead of the game. He's been gettin' left behind in there so the only thing he's out to do is make some money." Samuel bit his tongue after giving that false description of his friend. The idea that David would give up on a score that needed settling for the sake of money was absurd. The idea that anyone in this neighborhood would didn't make sense to Samuel. It went against everything he'd learned about the Postie attitude. He found it difficult not to bicker its possibility with Lorenzo, but he knew better. He just stayed relaxed as Lorenzo began another drawn-out explanation with the self-serving undertone that seemed to be his trademark.

"The Sozzollo brothers are a perfect example of what I'm talking about as well. Two capable young men. They're rowdy, wild and have a resolve beyond measure. That could take them far in this business, but they were too wild for their own good. It was just a matter of time before they got themselves locked up. That powerful resolve kept them from respecting even the police. They were sloppy and well . . . just plain stupid at times. Now that I've given them some regulations and direction, they've done a lot of good work for me. A man ballsy enough to shoot an officer in broad daylight doesn't know when it's time to back down. But once under the supervision of someone like me, their potential is free to blossom without the drawbacks it would have brought on their own. Now they are very useful to me, and I protect them from themselves. Their reputation alone gets things done, at times without even lifting a finger. A strong reputation can get you more than a gun in the face if used properly. That's one thing I've mastered."

When the meeting was over, Samuel was pleased with the results. His foot was in the door as hoped. He had laid the groundwork for David and him to come back and do business, while avoiding giving away information. He also got to learn exactly what kind of man they would be dealing with.

Lorenzo had made an impression on Samuel in that meeting, though probably not the one intended. Samuel respected the man and what he'd done, but felt he'd bitten off more than he could chew without realizing it.

He made it clear he had little regard for the people he was working with. He seemed to look at them like children he was looking after. Samuel, too, had felt his mental superiority over the Posties at times. However, he didn't feel the need to put it to use as a self-confidence builder. He chose, rather than to dwell on their weak qualities so that he could feel better about himself, to look past them to find their stronger ones. That's how he came to see the heartfelt attitude toward life that they had. Lorenzo, by pointing out the shortcomings to remind himself of his own mental status, blinded himself to their stronger qualities. It was those ignored stronger qualities Samuel felt would catch up with Lorenzo. It was their passionately proud attitude that was a weapon Lorenzo wouldn't be able to protect himself against.

Samuel decided that if this man was really that amazing he would be back in New York doing business instead of remaining here. He looked at Lorenzo like a professional pitcher who took the petty approach of staying in the minor leagues so he could dominate with ease. Samuel could have no respect for that. Lorenzo Cole should be in the big city he was bred in, not taking advantage of these small-town criminals. Samuel didn't believe there could be any reward for taking such an easy route. Without the proper competition, there would be no genuine joy in the accomplishments. He felt that was the real sum of Lorenzo Cole's person, one who made everything so easy for himself that he couldn't enjoy life. Samuel was no longer impressed but still maintained respect for the man. It was safer to give the benefit of the doubt than to be caught by surprise.

He couldn't doubt that Lorenzo would only live off the men of that neighborhood for so long before finding repercussions. It didn't matter how much money the people made with him. There were a lot of guys coming up that had legitimate beefs with men under his protection. These were a people notorious for their lack of respect for authority. It didn't matter how frightening his reputation was; as long as he had people like Tim Russell or the Sozzollo brothers working for him, it was only a matter of time before a mutiny stirred.

The Sozzollo brothers weren't from Post Edition. They came from a rough slum on the South side of town. They were both of the most merciless nature. There weren't many they hadn't crossed at one time or another. They first got a name for themselves due to their violent business recipe. They'd set up meetings with drug suppliers at random bars or pool halls. Randy, the younger, would take the drugs and go get the money. Ron would stay with the suppliers as collateral. He'd hang out, play cards, and chat with the men like they were old friends. After enough hours would pass the suppliers would eventually suggest that Ron's brother had run out on him, leaving him holding the bag. Ron would get a sinister gleam in his eye as he explained that they had never planned on Randy coming back. He had just been waiting around enjoying himself until he killed them. After enjoying the sight of their jaws dropping, he'd empty his revolver into the suppliers, witnesses or not, and be on his way.

That's how they sprang into the drug world, by killing a lot of small-timers from around town and some trafficking through. The cold-blooded story of enjoying an evening with his victims, waiting for them to finally inquire about his brother, just so he could give his planned response and see their reaction, all for the sake of a menial purse, quickly gave them fame across town. Of course it didn't take long before no one was willing to do business with them. That's about how far ahead they looked with any of their plans. That's why Samuel couldn't believe they were still operating. They should have either been dead themselves, or in jail. They were too ballsy for their own good, as Lorenzo had said. They were either too tough or too stupid to even attempt to hide the crimes they committed.

Ballsy as they were, they still made very few moves in the East side. That was attributed to the wild reputation of Posties, along with the way they all looked after one another. To cross one of them would soon have you facing countless. They even got into a beef with one of Kris's crew but respected Kris enough not to pursue it.

The whole situation started with a small debt owed to John Brewny by Randy Sozzollo, after a series of pool games. John Brewny was Kris's closest friend, his right hand. That's why Kris never let John pursue the debt. He knew it wasn't worth how far the Sozzollo brothers would take it, and he didn't want anything to happen to his friend. John obeyed, but couldn't help the occasional drunken talk about his low opinion of the two-bit dealers the Sozzollos were. The Sozzollo brothers, of course, heard through the vine of John's speeches and returned similar insults and threats, but neither side was anxious to face the other.

However, once Kris was gone their attitude changed. It became rare to find John sober after his friend died; he was enraged by his inability to get his hands on a hidden Tim Russell. His drinking and frustrations resulted in a lot more threats against the Sozzollos.

On a Saturday afternoon two months after Kris Caine's death, Randy heard that John Brewny was shooting pool at Brownies, a pool hall down town. Excited by the idea that John was outside of Post Edition, Randy went down to see if it was true.

At seeing him, John, who was the size of an ox, began roaring threats for everyone to hear. In spite of John's obviously high number of consumed drinks and not having anyone to back him up, Randy still cowered at his massive size. He begged John not to hurt him and swore he'd return with the money.

A half hour later John could see both Sozzollo brothers out the window. They were standing in the parking lot, hands in the air, beckoning John to come brawl. John, infuriated by the insinuation he wouldn't face both of them, burst out the door hollering otherwise. Knowing the two of them weren't the type to fight with fists, when they got close enough, John pulled his renowned Bowie knife. Instead of the reaction he was hoping for, the brothers both smiled.

"I was hoping you'd have that with you," said Ron, to John's surprise.

Without warning, John felt a motorcycle helmet crack against his head and a grasp around his legs. Before he knew it he was on the ground and being held down by men he hadn't seen. Ron used his foot to squeeze the knife out of John's hand. He handed it to his little brother.

"It's time you learned," he commanded.

Randy accepted the knife like a proper student. Then, without hesitation, he stuck it near the bottom of John's gut and pulled it up to his rib cage. The boys all let go and raced across the street. When they glanced back to get a last look at their victim, to their surprise, John was back on his feet hollering again.

"Come on back! Now that I know how many of you there are! Come on! I bet I fuck up every one of you. Where the fuck you runnin' off to!?" he roared.

Bystanders claimed to be able to actually hear Brewny's blood splashing to the ground as it poured from his stomach.

The Sozzollos remained on the other side of the street, now laughing.

"Yeah, just keep talking, man. You're dying right here in front of us and you're still runnin' off at the mouth. Makin' threats—you're already dead and you're still makin' threats," they mocked.

They stayed there laughing in unison until the sirens were heard. Even after they ran off, John stood yelling, ready for a fight. He seemed oblivious to the outlandish amount of blood escaping his body.

His girlfriend he'd been there to meet arrived just before the Sozzollo brothers and company made their exit. She tried to calm him, but was herself in shock by what she was witnessing. Her gigantic boyfriend, who had seemed invincible, was dying right in front of her. Once he accepted his yells to be futile, he groaned, pulling the knife from his gullet, wiped it off on his shoulder, and handed it to her.

"Save this for me, baby. I'm gonna need it," he instructed somberly.

Soon after they got him to the hospital, doctors came out to inform the friends and family that John Brewny wouldn't survive the night.

There were a number of witnesses to the events but, as was the custom with Sozzollo crimes, they were all too scared to come forward. However, his girlfriend Jenny had seen who was responsible and told the police everything. Warrants were issued, and it took less than twenty-four hours before Ron and Randy Sozzollo were in custody.

As fearless as the two brothers were, they still couldn't help feeling nervous when, two weeks later, the charges were dropped. John Brewny, still alive, had convinced the police that the Sozzollos had nothing to do with it. He said he was a part of a drug deal gone bad. He claimed he had told Jenny a false story so she wouldn't know what he was involved in. Though anyone who knew him knew John had nothing to do with drugs, the police had no choice but to drop the charges. John wanted the Sozzollos free, where he could get his hands on them himself.

As sure as the Posties were that John would succeed in killing the Sozzollos and despite his valiant efforts, his body never returned to working condition. A year later he died, never being able to fulfill his prophecy of having need for his knife.

Every day that he survived amazed the doctors. His thirst for vengeance kept him alive, regardless of what his organs were capable of. When he finally lost his battle and didn't wake up one morning, his close friends and family were devastated. It had been a trying year of meaningless hope. His death brought an end to the reign of Kris Caine's crew. Many felt the neighborhood would never be the same. The boys who had been running things for years were suddenly gone. It was they who had kept much of the drug traffic out of those streets and the new generation's wickedness didn't seem to leave much hope.

Things weren't the same. Not for the reasons predicted but instead because of the sudden presence of Lorenzo Cole.

No one was more devastated by the death of John Brewny than his young cousin. Nathan Brewny was considerably younger but had always spent his whole life mimicking and trying to follow the footsteps of John. He was big in size as well. Most who knew him knew that he had inherited the Bowie knife after his cousin's death. They knew how he kept it on his bedroom wall. Anyone who was familiar with the Post Edition way would know it was an unwritten law that when Nathan was of age, he would be the one to fulfill his cousin's threats. One day, when they thought all was forgotten, he would catch up with Ron and Randy, and square the score with his mentor's favorite knife. He might end up in jail, or perhaps not. It was the circle of life in that neighborhood. They lived by an unwritten law book.

Lorenzo Cole stood in opposition to that law. That was where Samuel felt he had made his mistake, considering such grudges as trivial. To protect people like the Sozzollos was underestimating the resolve of a scorned family member. It wasn't just Nathan he had to worry about; there were countless others who had reason to hate those two. There were countless beefs that could come back on Cole. If it wasn't Nathan and the Sozzollos, it would be Dale Schaver and Pat Norad, or Blaine Dalley and David Bay or one of any number of unsettled scores that Lorenzo stood in the middle of. His house was built on train tracks, Samuel was convinced of that.

CHAPTER 20: THE PRINCE RETURNS

It was now back to the waiting game for Samuel. There was still no word from work. There was no more to be done in the Torreo situation until David was released. He had no interest in visiting his poker buddies. He wasn't up to the questions they'd have about his suspension. So he screened his calls, only answering the ones from Mouse. All that consisted of was confirmation of the plans for David's return. The only things he had to do to pass the time were watch TV and sip cognac. He decided to drink moderate amounts throughout the week. That way when the welcome home party arrived he wouldn't be blindsided like last time. He'd have a tolerance built up. Unfortunately, being buzzed made him anxious, which just made the time drag even more in anticipation of David's homecoming.

Finally that Friday afternoon arrived and Samuel found himself waiting impatiently in the prison parking lot. The last few days had been glum, with the rain continuing right through till that morning. The ground was still wet, but the sunshine glared, making its presence felt, boasting its escape from the relentless storms. Now the sky was clear. There was the fresh smell that usually announced the first crack of spring. The ground, cars and even gates shined as they reflected the rays of the sun with their leftover moisture.

Samuel sat on the hood of his elderly automobile, smoking a cheap factory cigar. He wore sunglasses and a lightweight rain coat that was no longer necessary but he'd yet to remove. He filled his anxious wait by repeatedly picturing David's departure from prison walls. Each time his appearance changed slightly, his reaction to Samuel and his freedom was a bit different, but he always had the same cocky David Caine smirk. Finally, in the midst of one of these daydreams, Samuel's blind stare at the ground was interrupted by a loud clank. He lifted his head to see the gate open and

David walking out with a duffle bag over his shoulder.

Samuel remained sitting, trying to be cool, but he couldn't keep his cheeks from swelling up with joy at the site of the triumphant exodus. David was facing the same struggle, trotting out at a casual place, attempting to keep his excitement from bursting into the open. Samuel put his feet to the ground and began a similar laid-back walk in his friend's direction.

Before they could reach each other, David gave in. His joy found its way free, just as he had. He threw his bag as high in the air as he could and unleashed a champion's roar. Then, he hunched down into a full-out run and dove into a hug of Samuel. There was no hand clap, no style to it, just an old fashioned hug. Samuel squeezed at his ribs like it could accomplish something, and then tossed him up a bit, before releasing him.

"YAAAA-HA-HA! I'm out that bitch," David shouted again as he looked back at the walls that had confined him. The mood quickly changed from returned camaraderie to awkward ferocity as David gained a curdle in his voice and screamed back at the building like he expected it to answer, "I'm out that bitch! You ain't got me no more. You ain't got me. You can't even touch me. You won't never touch me again. That's on everything."

Samuel could hear the rage behind his friend's anguished laughter. He sounded like he was in a personal vendetta with someone and drawing the lines of war. It struck a chord of fear in Samuel as he watched. David hopped in the air swinging his fists; Samuel held him back, nudging him toward the car as if trying to avoid a fight. The determination to remain free brought Samuel uneasiness rather than comfort. There was a time when the look in David's eyes and the tone in his screams would have inspired Samuel; these days it made him wary.

Finally David broke his fierce stare-down with the giant cage, turned and hopped into shotgun position in Samuel's car. He had the smile on his face of a child just out of school, ready for a sunny day's play. Samuel picked up his duffle bag and joined him in the car.

"Fuck it! We don't even need that," hooted David. "All I need is a drink and a fine hooch." Samuel just smiled, tossed the bag in the back, and began the drive.

They coasted in a brief silence, until David started chuckling under his breath. He put the side of his fist over his mouth to mask the joy that was leaking out. It was to little avail. "Whoooo man, I'm on the loose again. It's like somebody hit pause on my life for some years and it's finally time to play."

"It's damn good to see you out in the open, man," said Samuel earnestly. "You ain't the type to be trapped."

"Shit, you're right about that. Coming up, I was prepared to do a bid; I just thought it was one of those things that would have to happen. Not no more. I heard other cats out the joint talking 'bout it ain't that bad. They weren't even scared of jail no more, so they'd do crazier shit. That ain't me. Fuck that. Don't get me wrong, I couldn't never rat or nothing like that; I'm just not goin' back. That's high priority. But fuck all that, what's the agenda?"

"I figured we'd go down to Snickers and see if anything's poppin'," smiled Samuel. "I hear a lot of the old crew goes there."

"Oh, we gonna see what's poppin', huh. Yeah, maybe we'll see somebody," David smirked sarcastically. "That'd be lucky, huh."

Samuel grinned at his friend's inability to be snowballed. "So what's the big agenda now that you're out?"

"Shit, I should be asking you that. I gotta check in with my PO on Monday. I'll have to get a job quick or he'll give me one. Of course, the dream here is to work very little before we get our hands on a certain no-good dealer's nest egg. Then it's off to never-never land. So what's up with that?"

"Ah, there'll be time to talk about business later. What's up with your ma and sister and shit?"

"Man, don't give me that, buildin' the suspense and what-not. I've been waiting to hear from you about this for weeks."

Samuel laughed at the way he was toying with his old friend. "Naw man, where's your priorities? Family comes first. I wanna hear what's up with them. Then we can get back to that."

David tried to give a serious glare but still couldn't hide his amusement. "Yeah, right. I plan to go by there in the morning. They don't even know I'm out far as I know. I'm really not in no rush. I know I'm just gonna get pissed off at how they're living. I swear me and Kris was like both their daddies. With us gone it's nothin' but stupid choices, no question. But I'll get them out this bitch altogether if it's on. So what's up with it?"

Samuel smiled again at the impatience. "Well man, I've spent a lot of time around this Monique and . . . I'm pretty sure it's on."

"Whoo! It's on?" David asked again.

"I think it's on," answered Samuel.

"Damn, I've been waiting to hear that."

"So Mouse told me you wanted me to hook up with this Lorenzo cat. Why'd you wanna bring him in?"

"Oh, I didn't necessarily want to bring him in. I just wasn't sure how you wanted to handle it. I didn't know if you were gonna want to hold on to that bullshit job or something. So we might have needed him."

"Ah, hell no. The second I seen that sort of money I'd've been gone. I'd never set foot in this city again. There ain't shit for me here."

"Well, cool. So we just gotta wait till the package shows up."

"Well, that woulda worked."

"Woulda? What's woulda? I'm not about hearing no wouldas."

"Well, woulda is the issue at hand."

"Fuck man, explain that to me."

"I got suspended. So I got no access to packages. I don't even know how we're gonna find out if the package is in circulation."

"A-h-h-h shit, you got suspended? How the hell did you pull that off?"

"You don't want to know."

"Oh, I want to know. How did you get suspended before we pulled off the biggest score in Postie history? Of all the times you needed to be at work, this was the only time that really counted and you ain't there. That, without question, requires explanation."

"Yeah, yeah, fuck off. Look, I couldn't figure out for sure if she was his girl or not. So I had to open one of those envelopes to see if it was the support money like you said. It was."

"Well, good shit."

"Yeah, but then that night, I got senselessly drunk with Mouse and ended up at her house, cursing her out and throwing the money in her face."

David just stared with eyes wide. Samuel kept looking at the road in front of them, then back at him, waiting for a response. David continued to stare with a look of both astonishment and almost entertained disappointment.

"Shit man, what you want? I hadn't drunk in a long time. You know how Mouse and the boys are. They keep it flowing like the Nile. I was gone. Unaccountable for my actions," said Samuel.

David continued staring, now with a "don't give me that shit" curl in his lip.

"Man, she's a real nice girl. I was pissed to find out she was all mixed up with some dealer. I got blasted and dealt with it poorly."

"Yeah? Well, I guess we'll leave it at that. So I guess we are gonna need that motherfucker after all, 'cause I ain't got no idea how we're gonna get our hands on it now."

"Yeah, how sure are we that he'll even send her the money? Maybe she's just hoping and he'll really take off on his own," inquired Samuel.

"I thought about that but she's the smartest way for him to handle things. It's Johnny law's money and they don't know nothin' about her. The DC does but they don't give a fuck about the money. The second he gets that money in the mail he won't even have to worry about feds no more; he can just focus on evading the Dragons. If they agreed to give the law a few more days to find the money before deadin' Cullomine, that's the best time for him to escape. The agents won't have given the go-ahead 'cause they still won't have the loot. Trying to get out of the country with the money would be too hard with the feds watching. This way he can make his slip and meet back up with her. The only tricky part is how he's gonna get the money and get it sent out without no one seeing."

"True. But she's our safety net, regardless. It don't matter if we don't see him make the drop, we know where it's going."

"Exactly, except that some lush went to the enemy's front door and tipped our hand."

Samuel rolled his eyes before defending himself. "Naw man, I didn't say nothing about the package. She don't know we know about that. She just knows I know about her relations with Torreo."

"Yeah, she don't know but she got you suspended to make sure you don't snag it."

"Well, she has been talking about this package for a while and when she knows I opened one of her letters she probably just doesn't want to risk me opening the big one," explained Samuel.

"So she got you suspended—pretty smart."

"Yeah, she is."

"So we'll have to talk about Lorenzo with Mouse tonight at the party."

"Yeah, he's in tight with him. He'll set up an appointment."

David smiled triumphantly at Samuel. Samuel looked back and forth between him and the road, trying to figure out what the silly grin was about. Finally he realized he had just admitted to the party.

When they pulled into the parking lot the day was just losing its light. Against the dusk sky the two men exited the vehicle and approached the bar at their typical casual pace. David did not worry about going home to freshen up. He was happy in the clothes he left the prison in. His hair had grown out to the point of being bushy, but he wasn't going to see a group of people he had to worry about impressing; he was going to see his adopted family. It was perfect, like a movie star who was too cool to wear a tux to the award show. He was casual and collected. He knew his fans would love him all the more.

Upon opening the twin doors to Snickers, they were greeted by a roaring crowd, welcoming David home. He was a kid in a candy store. Everyone was diving on him, cheering him back into their lives, shoving drinks into each of his hands. Every time he turned around there was another face he had longed to see. With each one, his eyes got big and he let out a hoot that made it seem like that was exactly the person he'd been looking for. He finally made it to a barstool when he heard another familiar voice.

"Dae Dae!" it beckoned.

He turned around to see Steve Level Bradley. Just hearing his name that way got a reaction. Little nicknames were like a trademark for Bradley. He was an antsy sort. It was too tame for him to call anyone by their real name. He was always coming up with his own versions that usually consisted of the person's first syllable repeated twice. Lukas was Lue Lue, Keith was Key

Key and so on. No one minded except that if they spent much time with him they would find themselves using the names that sounded quite ridiculous out of anyone's mouth but his.

"It's good to see ya," greeted Steve.

"Fuck you; it's good to be seen. Man, I didn't think you were loose though. I heard you were gettin' all sorts of time. Somebody told me you actually escaped from the cop car?" asked David.

"Hell yeah. My little ass squirmed right through the space in the window where they talk and was out the front door while chiggy was chasing Phillip."

"Ha-ha. I bet he shit. They said the chigs caught up with you at the spot, though, and you were gettin' crazy time."

"Back on probation was all. Shit, I was facin' some years. That cat Loco can hook a brother up if you're good by him. Too bad he wasn't around for you," explained Steve.

"Right. So are you makin' it to the PO this time?" inquired David.

"Shit! I ain't seen him in months. I would have pissed dirty anyway," answered Steve matter-of-factly.

David shook his head. "Some dogs just can't get trained."

The evening continued in similar manner for hours that passed like minutes. An assembly line of people made their way to David. They all cheered at the sight of him and had a different story to remember, each person followed closely behind by another. Most, after talking to David, would finish to notice Samuel by his side. They'd show a bit of surprise and begin a similar conversation with him. Samuel was amazed at how many of the Post Edition roster he had actually become acquainted with in his few years there. The flow of old-timers seemed endless and every drink that David wasn't speedy enough to keep up with, he'd pass over to Samuel. It started as great, then should have grown tiresome, but the alcohol kept it new. It was more entertaining as the night went on. The laughs got louder and the jokes seemed wittier.

It left Samuel in a daze, loving every minute of it. He could only imagine the result if an opponent showed up in that bar. It made him feel so safe and welcome, having a place packed wall-to-wall with people who loved each other. It was inspiring to see so many loyal friends, willing to go to any limits to help one another, despite the absent time between them. He could see now how miserable David must have been in that cage. The camaraderie was comparable to the heartiest of family reunions. Growing up around that had to be part of what made David so strong. Being suddenly without it had to be much of what made prison so horrid. The void he was left with must have been crippling. It gave Samuel more sympathy for his friend's passionate fit thrown that afternoon.

CHAPTER 21: BUSINESS VS. PLEASURE

It didn't take long before things got the euphoric blur that Samuel had grown accustomed to years ago. He was surprised that everyone stayed so late. Usually when people started drinking that early they'd head home early too. The place was still packed at midnight when Samuel went to the bathroom. Having now been separated from him for a while, he was happy to see David resting casually on the sink. He had a blissful half-grin that displayed how pleased he was to be back in his element.

"Trying to get some private time to clear your head?" suggested Samuel, curious to why David was sitting on the bathroom sink during his welcome home party.

"Wa-a-gh-gh!" came a sound from one of the stalls.

David leaned his head to look in the direction of the sound and laughed. "Yeah, something like that. Actually, it's good you're here. Why don't you lock the door behind you," he instructed. "Now we can figure some things out."

"Who is that?" hollered Lukas from the stall.

"Samuel," answered David.

"This is the time you pick to go over business?" challenged Lukas as he stuck his head out the thin plastic door.

"I feel fine. How 'bout you?" David asked Samuel, making light of the state Lukas was in.

"I'm good to go. Just need to piss," answered Samuel with a smile.

"Wr-a-rgh!" returned the sound. "I don't get it," said Lukas as he gasped for breath. "You've been in jail all them years with no drinks or nothing. Then the day you get out you come back here and start puttin' 'em back like there's no problems. But I get to drink all the time and I'm the one in here

158

hurling."

David gave a bigger, more mischievous grin to Samuel, like he was getting away with something. "Sucks to be you, huh," he returned to Lukas.

"You probably dropped more back than I did. It's like it has no effect on ya."

"All right, all right. Get your mouth off my cock long enough for us to figure a few things out," interrupted David. "When can we see this hero of a man Lorenzo Cole?"

"I already took Samuel to lay down some ground. He said we can come back early this week if you're serious," answered Lukas.

"You met him?" he asked Samuel.

"Yeah, I thought you knew. I haven't told him nothin' yet. I said me and you had to talk first," he answered.

"Right. But what kind of impression did you get?"

Samuel tilted his head, hesitant to say what he wanted. "I think everyone's blowing him up a bit."

The door swung open with a smack and Lukas's head popped out with a dumbfounded expression. "Oh, he didn't make an impression?" questioned Lukas.

"I mean he's a man to be reckoned with, don't get me wrong. But I just don't look at him the way I've been hearing about him. That's all I'm saying."

"You're crazy, man. I wouldn't recommend fuckin' with dude," said Lukas as he whipped his head back to business. "A-a-hg!"

"Truthfully, I wouldn't recommend fuckin' with him either," agreed Samuel. "I just mean that it's like he's conquered a town without a lot of competition and took on the low-budget authorities to come out looking invincible. I just think if he was really that amazing he'd be back in his hometown making real waves. It's like a champion caliber boxer that decides he's gonna spend his career in the Golden Gloves so he can dominate. That shit ain't fresh, and as soon as he causes enough trouble up here that the feds get interested he's gonna end up singing a different tune. Based on what I've heard about him and my meeting with him, I'd say he's a control freak. It'd be hard to know what exactly he's gonna do. He's like a frustrated, caged animal. Only he's caged by his own boundlessness. He's always had everything with ease so he can't be happy with it. That's why he's got to keep trying all that crazy shit. He's chasing that little tingly stir in himself but he can't get his hands on it. He's a spoiled rich kid, only worse because he's not limited to the power of money but also has the power of genius and crime. He's an enigma. He can control the world but not himself. Any control freak gets frustrated the instant something seems out of his grasp. Like the spoiled rich kid who's used to getting his own way, he's probably prone to throw a tantrum the second something isn't to his liking. The scars some of his help carry account for that. Only the tantrum of this man is something to be wary of. He's a loose cannon, to say the least. I think going into business with him might be walking a tightrope. The wrong thing happens, we're in some serious shit. But for now we got nothing but mutual interests and he can help us with what we can't do ourselves. So as long as nothing goes wrong, he's the way to go. As far as taking him on goes, I'm sure you'd have everyone's support but we'd be in over our heads."

"Well, I guess what's at hand here is how helpful he can be. How much do you think he wants for helping?" asked David.

"Well, he said half is his usual but right now I wouldn't be surprised if he'd want more. We don't have a whole lot to offer except info. He's gonna want to give us a finder's fee unless we can find a way to keep ourselves involved."

"Right, right. Well, we can squeak out the details before we go," said David.

The entrance door rattled, followed by some banging. "Let me in, I got to piss," came a voice from outside.

"Yeah, yeah," answered David as he got up to head out. "Wait." David paused. "What do you guys keep talking about, 'take him on'? What beef would we have with him?"

It grew suddenly quiet in the room as Samuel and Lukas were confronted with a prime opportunity to share the news they had been dreading. Samuel wanted to restate that he just meant in case something went wrong, but he'd already paused too long. It would be obvious he was trying to cover up something. David's eyes got stern with silence and he turned to look at Samuel in request for what he wasn't being told.

"It turns out Tim Russell works for Lorenzo," admitted Samuel. "I asked a few questions to get an idea how he'd handle something like that. As far as he's concerned anyone who works under him is under his protection. He doesn't want beefs getting in the way of business and he bases his whole business on his reputation so he doesn't let anything slide. You go after Tim, you're taking on Lorenzo."

David swallowed deep and dropped back against the wall. He stood there, not saying a word.

"Bang bang!" came the pounding on the door again. "Hey, are you guys coming or what?"

David ignored it, remaining silent. His face gave no expression of his rage and frustration. They instead seemed to be spraying directly out his cold glare at the wall.

"Bang bang," came the sound again.

This time David swung his left fist like a wrecking ball, full circle, landing square in the door. "Shut the fuck up!" he screamed with a ferocity that would hold rank in the jungle. He walked toward the sink and swung again, this time at the hand drier. He caved its side, bringing it from its place on the wall, and smacked it again with his other hand before it reached the floor. He planted both hands on the edge of the sink counter, kept his arms extended with his head hanging low, as he panted heavily. Samuel could feel his friend's rage. The room was thick with a brother's wrath.

Samuel looked over at the door. There was a fist-shaped indent about a half-inch deep in its surface. The paint had chipped off, leaving the wood naked. Lukas got to his feet and joined Samuel in placing a hand on David's shoulder.

"I mean it's suicide going up against that motherfucker," began Lukas, "but fuck it, man. If that's what you want to do, you know I'll be right there with you. We can put together our own little army real quick."

David looked up into the mirror. He could see Samuel's reflection nodding in agreement.

"Naw man," said David. "That's what I did last time; I went off half-cocked to take up for Missy and we all paid for it. I can't make that mistake again. I've been gone too long for that. My sister and ma need me right now. The living gotta come first. I gotta do for them while I'm still able."

The room remained silent again as the three contemplated what was just said. To know David was to know the hardest decision for him to make was that which he just had, to swallow everything he felt, everything that burned in him for those years locked up, and to do the wise thing instead of the brave. Samuel considered it the strongest side he'd ever seen of his friend.

After a moment David threw his head back up and clapped his hands together. "All right, we got a party to return to. How 'bout it?"

Lukas and Samuel both nodded their heads, pleased to see their friend's second wind.

"I think I'm about ready for round two," agreed Lukas. "Let's shoot some stick."

When the three headed out the door, the owner of the bar was standing outside waiting. Apparently he'd been informed about the noise. Lukas went directly over, giving explanation and pulling money from his pocket, while David and Samuel continued past.

As the night carried on, naturally, so did the drinking and gambling. Out of respect there was always a spot open for David on one of the four tables. He hadn't lost his shot. He reigned on his table and even two at the same time for a while. Samuel only played a couple of games. He was so out of practice he was quickly frustrated by his inability to put the balls where he wanted them. It was a rare opportunity to have so many people to talk to so he decided it would be wasted time shooting pool anyway. Conversing or not, David continued to shoot until someone worth tearing himself away finally made their appearance.

Samuel found it nourishing to see David back in action. The zoo had returned the cheetah to the wild and it was sprinting through the fields like it was intended to. He put his balls down and his drinks back like he'd been doing the same thing yesterday. There was the constant witty razzing of someone he'd known for years. He had the same presence in the room he'd always had, the same attentive awareness of everything going on around him. He never stopped watching for anything out of place. He was back to his big brother ways. Every few minutes his eyes would circle the room to locate the people especially important to him. He'd find Lukas, Samuel and a few others to make sure all was well, then he'd go right back to what he was doing. He wasn't worried or edgy. It was just his instincts. He likely never noticed himself do it.

Samuel truly enjoyed watching the habits; it had been too long since he'd seen them. There was some behavior he was sure only he had noticed. No matter who was calling David's name or what happened, he never went near the far back corner of the pool area. In that corner was the door that opened into the scene of his brother's murder. Though it wasn't out of place, Samuel was amazed that David could spend an evening in a bar with that sort of history. It was never mentioned; he never seemed visibly bothered by it. His composure and attitude were calm and joyful but in a few instances his avoidance of that corner was visibly deliberate, at least to Samuel.

Eventually the big brother inside David came into play. Dustin Benton, who was so drunk he could barely stand, accidentally bumped into a burly man trying to shoot pool. The man was on the extra table in the back. He was with three others who made up all people who weren't there for the party. The large man didn't hesitate to jump in the considerably smaller Dustin's face. David was just as quick to come to his old neighborhood pal's aid.

"You takin' up his beef?" the man asked as David stepped between the two.

"There's not gonna be no beef to take up. I'm just lettin' you know that. He didn't mean nuttin' by it. There's no reason for this to get out of control," said David to the stranger.

"I didn't hear no apology out his mouth."

"And you're not gonna. He's too drunk for all that. I'm apologizing on his behalf. That should be good enough."

The man stared grimly at David. In the old days he was already too close and staring too tough for this not to be an altercation. David would have cracked him and at seeing that, the majority of the bar would have flooded over, swinging. Instead the man thought on David's words for a moment.

"Yeah, all right. I guess that's fair enough," he said before returning to his game.

David put a hand on the rather confused Dustin's shoulder. When David had walked him back over to a friendly table he looked up to see Lukas joining the scene with battle in his step and far too familiar fight in his eyes. David stopped him by putting a hand on his chest.

"Don't worry man, I handled it," he explained.

Lukas looked outraged. "You're just gonna let this motherfucker off?" he spouted, deliberately loud enough for the man to hear.

David gritted his teeth at Lukas's attempt to bring things to a head. "Listen. This is my fuckin' welcome home party and if I don't feel like watchin' no fights, you're not gonna make it otherwise."

Lukas obeyed his orders but spent the next few minutes pacing around the tables, making it obvious to everyone how heated he was. He couldn't grasp why his friend wouldn't handle things like they always had.

"Fuck this," he mumbled as he headed to the front of the bar.

A moment later the Snickers bouncers came and escorted the man and his friends out. They put up very little fuss. It was easy to tell they weren't the typical rowdy bunch common to that part of town.

Lukas came over triumphantly. "We couldn't let them fucks chill at our spot."

David looked up in disgust. "Why can't you ever just leave shit alone?"

Lukas returned to the look of confusion he'd had for the last ten minutes. "Did you go soft on me up there?" he challenged as he shrugged his shoulders.

David's eyes grew cold and his face hard. "You don't say shit like that to me," he stated simply.

Lukas knew he'd overstepped his boundaries and closed his mouth. He stood there looking for a way to resolve the tension that had built between him and his friend. David, still frustrated, went back to playing pool and offered none. Lukas finally walked away like an embarrassed child who'd been chastened in public.

For a group that was shrouded in trouble the majority of their lives, that was the only glimpse of it the entire night. Other than that it was the good-spirited fun of jokes, drinks and pool games.

CHAPTER 22: REUNITED

David was lining up for a lengthy shot when she finally walked in. He paused his effort when they exchanged glances. They stared for just an instant, but their eyes conveyed a thousand intentions, then David looked back to his shot and Jamie turned to some friends at a table. David continued his game and they didn't seem to pay each other any mind. Just an occasional glance as he waited for his turn or she made her way through the tables full of old friends. When David had won his game Harold handed over his lost bet.

"Man, let's run that back," suggested Harold.

"Nah, I better go mingle a bit, my party and all. Catch up with me a little while later."

"Aw, that's cool if you're letting me keep the table. I'll just win my money back off somebody else," agreed Harold.

David smiled, and then scanned the room for Jamie. Her back was to him. He walked up slowly behind her and put his arm around her waist. She looked up to him and turned, placing her arms around his neck and giving a full embrace. David maintained his bottomless cool but the strength of the moment was visible to Samuel. They began with the intention of a short hug, but neither was willing to give up the embrace that had comforted their lonely thoughts for so long. No one wanted to be obvious with their stares, but the reunited romance paused all talking in the previously rambunctious room.

Anyone who had known these two would have to be moved by the rare public display of affection. After such a long separation it was inevitable. Even when David was a free man the hidden affection was obvious to his friends. They didn't talk to each other that much. They never talked about each other. All their real interactions were behind closed doors. But to see one's face when the other walked in the room was to feel the intensity of their affection. To watch them glance at each other was an instant reminder of your childhood dream of the perfect someone.

Samuel knew David was secretly waiting for her from the moment he got there. He knew Jamie's arrival would be late, after most of the crowd had cleared, late, but imminent. He'd heard she was in some serious relationship with an uptown guy. That didn't matter. She could have been happily married with countless children; if there was a chance of David wanting to see her, she would be there. She would always belong to him, no matter how long it had been or what had taken place. Her obsession with him had no boundaries. There was nothing she would not do, if he merely asked, but David was not the asking sort, nor was he the mushy loving sort. He indeed loved her, perhaps too much.

He never spoke of it, but Samuel knew him well enough to know what the equation consisted of. He adored her, but did not think himself good enough to, partly because of his own adoration. He couldn't resist being around her but after a small dose he would distance himself again, thinking her better off without him. She would go back to passing time until he was again overwhelmed by his need for Jamie and they met up again.

For her, he was like a drug habit. She knew she shouldn't spend time with him, she knew a real and stable relationship could never come from it, but she enjoyed him too much. Their time together was so perfect everything else seemed plain and drab. Life was merely the wasted time between her evenings with David.

Married at the soul, thought Samuel. He had to feel sorry for any man who tried to win her heart. How could they know she belonged so completely to someone else? She would never tell them. David would never get jealous or mad. He liked having someone else treating her the way he knew he couldn't. But Samuel could only imagine how David would react if he couldn't have Jamie the instant he wanted her.

The two made their way to a corner booth slightly elevated from the other tables. They sat close, smiling a lot as they talked. The chemistry was visibly stronger than ever. It was surprising to see how much they said to each other in the open. Of course it went without saying that Jamie hadn't heard a word from David in all the years he was gone. Visits, calls or even a letter would be too sentimental for him.

Samuel had to wonder if David could have wondered, as he did, whether she would show up at all. Though no spectator would have ever doubted, David loved her so much it would be hard for him not to fear she'd moved on. His animated talking fed Samuel's belief he had feared it. He was so happy to have her with him. He likely doubted that moment had a chance of occurring. He hadn't been totally complete until now. With Jamie back at his side, David Caine had officially returned.

Before long, his boisterous hand gestures and storytelling died down.

The laughing had finally stopped, but the smiles remained. The two were now in a more familiar stance. Jamie lay with her feet stretched out on the circle booth and her head and back against David's chest. His arm was over her shoulder and down to her stomach, where her hands hugged it. That was more typical to their style—no talking, just enjoying having each other.

Samuel was back to staring at the pool games when he noticed David waving him over with his free hand. Somewhat surprised by his invitation to intrude, Samuel still got up and went to see what his friend wanted.

"W'the fuck man?" asked David as Samuel joined the booth. "Your boy gets freed from incarceration and you just ignore him. What's wrong with you? Order us a couple shots. In fact, where's Mouse at? I want a bottle up here. Mouse! Mouse!" he yelled. Lukas emerged from the barroom to see what David wanted. "I need me a fifth of JD up here. You think you can do that for me?"

Lukas just winked in response. A few minutes later he was up the stairs and placing the unopened bottle and three shot glasses on the table. "Three?" asked David, "Where's yours?"

"Fuck you," replied Lukas amusedly as he happily escaped down the stairs. "I'm done with shots for this evening."

"You pussy!" David yelled after him. "Fuck that dude. Pour 'em, Samuel. We're taking a drink to Jamie."

She looked up with a smile. It was the nicest thing Samuel had ever heard him say to her.

"She don't believe me. She thinks I'm bullshittin' when I tell her we got a big score coming and I'm gonna fly her away with me. Will you tell her it's on?" asked David.

"It's on," Samuel stated as he poured the drinks. "David says it's on, you know it's on."

"Shit!" hooted Jamie in disbelief at what she just heard.

David smiled and shook his head, playfully disappointed with her attitude. "Let's take these shots."

They all lifted their glasses and David started a toast. "To Jamie, who finally made it to my welcome home party. To me for finally getting to have a welcome home party, and to all of us being on some tropical island sipping margaritas in the very near future."

At that they clinked their glasses and drank their shots. Samuel was amazed by the candor in his old friend. He would have never admitted to even wanting Jamie there in the past, let alone saying out loud he was impatient for her arrival. The pleasure was written all over her face, but Samuel could still see the fear of a woman protective of her heart. It would be easy for her to accept everything being said and enjoy it as much as she wanted to, but she had to be cautious. Though it wasn't like David, she respected the possibility that it was the drinks and the moment talking more than him.

Samuel smirked at the ease with which she dropped back her shot, just like they did. She had been on this Post party scene as long as or longer than anyone. He considered it quite possible that she was the coolest girl alive. She could hang out like one of the fellows all night long, and not for one second lose her stunning beauty. If there was anyone to be envious of in the department of women, it was David. He had such a prize, completely wrapped around his finger.

"You all right, man?" asked David.

"Aw, I'm fine," said Samuel.

"Yeah right, I remember that gloss over your eyes. You get wrapped up in your own drunken thought and stop talking to anybody else. That's how we know you've had a few too many. Then the next day we're all talking about the wild shit you did."

"Not me. I'm cool as a bitch," countered Samuel.

"Uh-huh," agreed David sarcastically.

The conversation stopped and all three went into their own worlds while they stared at the pool games. Then David spoke again. "Hey Samuel, didn't you say once that we both had biblical names?"

"Yeah, I did. Actually the Samuel and David of the Bible were pretty close too."

"For real? They used to kick it and shit?" asked a surprised David.

"Well, kind of. David was anointed king by Samuel while someone else still held the throne. He served as kind of a mentor or advisor to him after that," explained Samuel.

"Advisor, huh? Not all that different, I guess. If there's something I need explained you're the one I'm gonna ask," complimented David. "Do you ever think we could have been like them, you know, back in the day?"

"I wonder about it sometimes. What kind of people we would have been in different times or cultures. I don't know, though, they were both very religious men. Maybe we could have been if we made it to church growin' up."

"Yeah, maybe. Ma took me to church once. It was Easter and my grandma insisted we go. Me and Kris got to arguing and wrestling during the sermon. The preacher stopped and gave us a look like we weren't the type welcome. My grandma was so embarrassed she never invited us again. Don't think it was no skin off Ma's nose, though," David remembered.

"Yeah, church ain't looked at the way it was years ago. Gotta wonder if that's why things are so messed up now compared to the old days. 'Course on the other hand maybe in the colonial days or Roaring Twenties people weren't no better to each other than they are now. Maybe people just think better of those days now that they're gone. Like we might look back on high school. It didn't seem so perfect at the time, but now, looking back, we only remember the good shit we ain't got no more."

"True. 'Cause in high school I remember lookin' back on junior high like it was the days. I don't think I felt that way at the time, though. I just wanted to get across the street to the high school. 'Course, I doubt it's just that 'cause I don't think you had kids running in schools capping each other in the Roaring Twenties and they still at least had actual families and shit. So I'm gonna stick with the shit's just fucked up now idea," said David.

"For behold, the days are coming, in which they shall say, Blessed are the barren, and the wombs that never bear, and the paps which never gave suck. Then shall they begin to say to the mountains, fall on us, and to the hills, cover us. For if they do these things in a green tree, what shall be done in the dry? Luke twenty-three, twenty-nine. Jesus said that just before they crucified him. He was saying if that's how the people handled it when he came, how would things be once he was gone?"

"Do you think we're to that point? I guess it's not uncommon for daddies to freak out and pay to make their women barren. But do you think people would prefer the mountains to cover them?"

"Maybe not yet. But it seems like every time period and culture you hear about there was always the common folk, falling in love, having babies, no matter how much hardship was around them. It seems to me our culture has pretty much broken that happy family idea. Relationships don't work; parents don't want to put forth the effort with their kids. We all got too many options nowadays. Nobody wants to stick with it. We're like a baby in that cradle. You put five or six toys in there with it, it starts crying, but you just give it one and it stays busy for a while. As things that people really need to be complete go away, we become more and more like robots, going through the motions to do our part to support a system of society that really just lubricates everybody's journey to eventual death. People can't exist as robots; they need more. That's why more and more kids aren't gettin' with the program. They see their parents who went for that American dream and it didn't work out so good. They look around and the four years of college and the lifetime of raking in the dollars don't seem so appealing. Without any joy in it all, what's the point? Think of how many kids who went to our school around the same time as us who have committed suicide. I don't know, man, it just seems like every bad statistic is always rising and the whole world is a part of some silent agreement to keep pretending everything's great. We just watch a lot of TV and movies where we see people gettin' on all right and we pretend we're doing the same things. I guess I'm just ranting now. I just don't know too many truly happy people is all. Gettin' by, sure, but I just can't believe that's all it's about."

"I feel ya man, but you can't think about shit like that too much. Nothing good can come from it," preached David.

"I hate to interrupt you guys' lovely Friday night philosophy session but are we gonna have another drink?" asked Jamie.

Samuel smiled brightly at David as he began pouring another round. "You're one cool gal, Jamie. There ain't a lot of girls who rush the fellas when it comes to drinkin'. It's supposed to be the other way around."

"Well, I gotta make sure this one's good and drunk so I can take advantage of him," joked Jamie.

David smiled even brighter and looked down at her from the corners of his eyes. "Well, on that note, Samuel, I think this will be our farewell shot. This is great and all but a fella's been locked up for a while, ya know."

They all laughed, then David started another toast. "Let's tip this one back to my motherfuckin' man. He might have took a little leave of absence, but for the most part he was there for me when I was locked up, he was there for me when I was handling my business to get locked up, and he's here for me now that I'm out again. Don't think it's not appreciated, Samuel."

They tipped back their drinks, and said their farewells. Samuel remained in the booth. It was just him and a tall bottle of liquor.

He was taken aback by the toast. It was another sign of the changes David had undergone in his time away. It was one thing to hear his newfound appreciation for Jamie, but it brought home the difference much more when the affection was directed toward Samuel himself. Like the rest of the Posties, David was sparing when it came to words and conversation. Any display of sincerity was easily mocked by peers. Samuel could only ever know of their bond through his actions, never his words. He never questioned David's inability to talk about his own feelings, but Samuel recognized it as leaving the people closest to him parched for some sign of affection. Apparently David now recognized that as well.

Samuel watched the couple walk away in each other's arms. It was too beautiful for him to be jealous. If it was anyone else so happy in a woman's arms the envy would have burned inside him, but he couldn't betray David in that way. He could be jealous of himself from the past, but not of David.

Though not willing to hate David's good fortune, it still wasn't long before the good times reminded him how overall unhappy he was. His inebriated view of the world stomped its way into his mind. He tried to reassure himself that the briefcase full of money would fix things, but that didn't change his lack of affection from another. It wasn't long before the relentless nostalgia and draining loneliness brought his train of thought to Susan. He remembered how in love they once were, how much she had meant to him. She had filled the void in him that every man was born with. He wondered how she could have taken those vows, how she could express all those emotions, then just run out on him, leaving him stranded in the world. How could she be that cold? How could anyone be so heartless? How could she even exist? His drunken view allowed him to wonder if she had ever existed at all. Maybe he'd just imagined her so she could embody all he thought was wrong with the world.

Over the years, he had allowed her to represent everything he hated in mankind. He believed everyone to be only out for themselves. He gave a snide expression at the thought of a person feeling upset when betrayed, as if they didn't deserve it, as if they hadn't only been interested in what was good for them all along. Everyone wanted to be loved but no one wanted to love in return. How could no one see this?

Even the camaraderie in that room was undermined by their willingness to take advantage of each other. It was a contradiction the people from that neighborhood were used to. They would take a bat to the head of anyone who wronged their neighbor, but even if Mouse were picking up a sack of weed for David, it went without saying he'd pinch some out for himself. David would know that when he sent him to get it. Regardless of whether Lukas had a pocket full of money, it was still just the way of things. It was the way they felt they had to behave to get ahead in the world. It was a protective barrier between these people. No matter how close they got to one another, it kept them from getting too close.

David and Jamie's relationship glaringly reflected that. No matter how strongly they felt about each other, they could never get as close as they wanted. David could love her with every ounce of himself, but having grown up in that neighborhood made it his instinct to keep a distance. Even if he was willing to take the risk of letting her in, he couldn't trust himself to do right by her. That was what the barrier between them was made of.

Thinking of that made Samuel sick to his stomach as they walked out the door. How could they feel the way they did and still not really be together? As he watched them, he was overwhelmed with the feeling that there was nothing anywhere that could work out for the best anymore. Society's soil no longer had enough nutrition for its plants to sprout correctly. They instead came up twisted and out of place. Bearing the fruit that should have been in their nature became difficult and improbable. Samuel's eyes scanned around the room at the leftover partiers, some laughing, some in serious conversation. He felt sorrow for all of them. They seemed like warriors and victims at the same time.

He continued tipping back the bottle in the privacy of that corner. He was now consumed in the endless, downward spiral fueled by being too observant for his own good. It was a vicious circle. He was too wise not to notice the ailments of the people around him but too weak to fight against the flow of a life he hated. He had returned full circle to the man he had tried to do away with by putting down the bottle those years ago. It was all that negative thought and restless feeling that prompted him to stop drinking. It seemed a waste now. Putting away the drink without improving the things that had made drinking so bad was pointless effort. If life had any pleasure for him, the occasional drink wouldn't have been so bad. It couldn't let the feelings he was running from in if there weren't any. Now he realized it was only a matter of time before he ended up in that corner with that bottle in his hand.

Jamie still didn't know what to think of the bounce in David's step as they gave their goodbyes to the friends still standing and made their way to the car. It wasn't the same fierce boy she had fallen in love with years ago. Then, it was undeniably his dramatic stance in life that had allured her so completely, but now she had loved him long enough, she would gladly be rid of his "blaze of glory" attitude if it was replaced by some form of contentment. She was amazed by knowing she would now rather see him cower from a brawl than to take on the world. She could have never imagined that as a girl. She never believed she could love someone when they were weak. She had always been disgusted by the sight of tears. She considered it her own weakness to need such strength in her man. She believed that made her incapable of being a proper mother or wife. She was far past all that now.

Back then, she couldn't have imagined the depth to which she could adore. She would have laughed at the idea of waiting for someone through prison, at spending all these years at the beck and call of someone with no intention of committing. That was all before she met her love incarnate; at that point she hadn't minded pursuing a relationship incapable of growing. She fell so hard for David none of that mattered. It was still her dream that they could someday become a real couple. But she had long accepted that as unrealistic.

"So you takin' me home to meet the fella?" asked David as they coasted down the road.

"Shit! I bet you two would get along real nice," joked Jamie. "I can't wait to hear how he reacts when I don't come home tonight. It could be back to old Mima's again."

"Damn, your grandma's still up and kickin'? She's gonna end up burying us."

"Burying you won't be so impressive if you don't wise your little ass up, and quit fuckin' around," scolded Jamie. "Speaking of which, what's this you and your boy are plannin'?"

"Aw, it ain't nothin' big. Real simple. Low risk and hella payoff, then it's smooth sailing. You'll never wait another table."

Jamie rolled her eyes, both showing disbelief and covering how much she wanted to believe. "Yeah, right. Just don't get yourself locked up again. I'm glad Samuel's involved. I know he'll keep you from gettin' too wild."

"Shit, you don't look at him right," argued David. "Take a minute and really look at him, you'll see he's on his last leg. If things don't get better for him soon he'll snap. Go postal would be the proper term, I guess. But why'd you roll your eyes at me like I'm playin'? I'm serious about leaving. You need to get your shit in order 'cause I could be callin' you this week, like let's go, and we need to be out with no hesitation. People might start snoopin' around for the money we'll have and we don't want to be hangin' around to get smelt. So you might as well move out on whoever this cornball you're fuckin' with is, so he don't be surprised when you stop coming around."

"Man, why you gotta start callin' him shit? You don't even know Stanton," sassed Jamie.

"Stanton! His name's Stanton. You telling me he's not a cornball?" David stared at her, waiting for an answer. She finally cracked a smile that gave it. "Yeah, that's what I thought," boasted David. "But let me clarify. Regardless as to what goes on I think you should move back to your Mima's. I'd like you to."

"Why is that?" she asked coyly.

"Why is that!" he repeated like it was an unnecessary question. "So I can see you when I want. So I don't have to worry about messin' up your game. I'm free to stop by, call, and spend time with you and all that." Jamie couldn't respond; she just gave an expression of outrage and question. "I'm telling you, I'm trying to be with you. Sittin' in that cell I had to figure out just exactly what I was in a hurry to get out for. I was missing one thing more than anything else, and that was some Jamie. I ain't trying to share you with these motherfuckers who think they're smart, but are too dumb to see how fresh you are. And as many times as I've talked down on those legit cats, calling 'em cornballs and pointing out that they're not as smart as they look, I've left myself in the same class by being too stupid to tell you how important you are to me. You deserve to have somebody who can tell you those things, and who appreciates you enough to really know you, to know you down to every little detail. A motherfucker who recognizes that half-smile you give when the joke went over your head so he can clarify for you without letting anyone else know he's doing it. A motherfucker who sees how you try and make whoever the crew's makin' fun of at the time feel better about themselves. A motherfucker who can't help but cheese when you stand up too fast after taking a shot and have to make up something to say so no one notices that you're leaning on the table until you get your balance, who can recognize when a tough girl feels insecure, who will feel it for her more than she does and try fix whatever's causing it. That's gonna be me. Whether you know it or not, or are ready for it or not, I'm gonna be that motherfucker. It's gonna be me lookin' out for you. So watch out."

Jamie couldn't look at him. Before she blew off his new affections, not taking them seriously, but now, after him pointing out all those observations of things she never thought anyone noticed, and stating so in-depth how serious he was, she could no longer ignore it. She wasn't one to lose her composure any more than he was. She swallowed deep and stared straight ahead, trying to make herself think of anything except what she just heard. After a few moments, she finally spoke. "Stouffer's."

"What?" asked David.

"You asked where we were going. I got us a room at Stouffer's," she explained.

"Damn, for real? We're livin' it up. Thanks girl. It's appreciated."

Not much was said from arrival to check in to reaching their room. They were both basking in just being together again. The feelings were too real to let words tamper with. Even looking at each other was overwhelming after years of separation, filled with dreams of doing just that.

David's time in jail made him think better of his attitude toward Jamie. It made him question his decision not to stay in contact, not to call or invite visits. He hoped she had moved on, and then he hoped she hadn't. He wished he could talk to her, find out how she was doing. Now the wait seemed worth it. Building up the moment for so long had made their reunion so powerful it was worth any amount of suffering in the past. It gave David a vivid moment of clarity. For the first time, even more than in prison, he could see exactly what he wanted. There was no doubt or need for second-guessing. He loved the girl in front of him. The only mistake in that was that he had still never told her.

When they walked in the room David flopped on the bed, bouncing into place. Jamie went to the miniature fridge next to the TV. She pulled out a bottle of champagne and began fiddling with getting it open.

"Man, I'm glad our room's so high. The view up here is real nice," said David, gazing out the window. The hotel sat in the dead center of the town. Though it was not a particularly big city, it looked more so from up there. The vast lights gave the impression it was much more significant a place than it was.

"Damn. The town almost looks important from up here," he said without receiving a response. He looked over; she was still picking at the top of the bottle. She appeared nervous and was pretending to be on a mission rather than face him. His first instinct was to say something smart aleck but he decided better. He wondered how he could still make her nervous after all this time. How could she be that taken with him? He wanted to figure out a way to make her relax without embarrassing her.

It occurred to him that she hadn't known any better than him how tonight would go. She wasn't confident that he'd grab her up and give her the attention she longed for. She had just dared to hope he would. She had hoped so much that she purchased this room without even being sure it was necessary. She could have just as easily been up here by herself, depending on his mood. A mood that in the past had been quite random, yet she still gave up her hard-earned money based on those hopes.

She had almost certainly dreamt tonight would be the one where he finally said he loved her, where he finally asked her to be a real part of his life. She probably wouldn't let herself think of it for long before reminding herself to keep her head out of the clouds. Now that those far-fetched dreams seemed a legitimate possibility, she didn't know how to act. She was scared stiff.

He could see every bit of that in her fidgeting. It was the most romantic fidget he could imagine. He rolled over to his left and switched out the light. The darkness fell over the room like a warm blanket. He could feel her tension release.

"Can you see all right?" he asked.

"Yeah, I got it."

The moonlight came in the bay window, giving the room enough blue glow that she could still pour the drinks. She came and sat on the edge of the bed, handed him his glass, then turned facing out the window. She was still too edgy to be comfortable. David scooted his sprawled-out body up against her back and put his arm around her waist.

"You're not to be out of arm's reach for the rest of the night," he reassured her.

She gave a short laugh and leaned back against him. She rested her elbows on his side, sipping at her drink. "What about when I have to pee?"

"Hmm. I guess you'll have to use the ice bucket."

They both laughed again, and then relaxed into a quiet stare out the window.

"You know, I had been in the front room for a long time before I came into the game area," Jamie admitted.

"Aw, you're stale. That's more time we could have been up there talkin'," said David. Jamie shook her head, still amazed by his referring to her like she was important.

"For a minute I thought I was gonna miss my chance to see you," she said.

"Whaddya mean?"

"It looked like you were gonna get in a brawl. I was watching through one of those windows. I didn't know if you'd have to leave after that. Depending on how bad it got, I guess. Then you squashed it. I didn't know what to think. I still don't know what to think. It feels crazy asking you this, but were you scared of that big guy?"

David giggled at the idea of fear. "Naw, girl . . . well . . . I guess. . . yeah, I was." Jamie's face scrunched, astounded at the answer. Then David attempted to explain. "I mean not of that dude, or even what could happen if I get in a fight on parole. I was scared of me." Jamie's look said her need of explanation didn't diminish, nor did David's need to explain. "Sometimes my feelings are so strong they scare me, just for a second, but I feel it. It's like my love, my anger, my everything is so potent I can't control it. Sometimes I wonder if I feel things more than other people. Like they put too big a heart in this little body and I can't keep it all in. That's why I scare myself sometimes. After being locked up for so long, thinkin' about myself, I feel like I'm destined for a bad ending, like every instinct and emotion I got is just gonna get me fucked in the end. Thinkin' about it makes it worse, so I try not to."

"Well, I for one was proud to see you not split the guy's head. I mean everyone in there knows you can do it. Mouse sure wasn't happy, though. Why does he need you to be such a bad-ass all the time?"

"I don't know. After all these years he's still insecure, I guess, still got something to prove. Maybe it's just being in my shadow. I know how that can be. I could be feeling like the Hulk until Kris walked in the room. Then suddenly I wasn't sure what I was doing. Havin' someone who looked out for me around seemed to bring out my weakest parts. It's hard to explain, I guess."

They both went back to relaxing in silence. Just being together again, being pressed up against each other, they felt full and complete.

"Tell me when you thought of me while I was gone," asked David earnestly.

"Hmm. Well, let me see," began Jamie, seeming to enjoy the question. "Last summer at my family reunion, we all went to my Aunt Linda's house on the lake. It was real nice. I hadn't been in a few years. We went out on the boat, skiing, tubing and stuff. It was a great day. Most everybody left early afternoon but a few of my cousins and me stuck around. When it was dark we floated around on the pontoon boat, drinking beers and talking. Before long we were all lying down staring up at the stars, not saying much. I just knew everyone was loving the view but I wouldn't. Watching the stars without you was like watching a broken television. I wanted to cry. Somehow I wished that, even though I wasn't capable of enjoying them, wherever you were, you were looking up at the stars, being moved. That would have been the only thing that eased my pain. It was like that a lot. If I was watching a good movie all I could think about was whether you would like it or not. I didn't feel right laughing at a joke knowing you were locked away. So in that way I thought about you all the time. I didn't feel right living a life knowing that you couldn't."

Jamie could feel the grip around her waist tighten to the point of restricting her breath. She feared she had taken his simple question too far and upset him. She looked at his face. He was biting down on his bottom lip, his nostrils were flaring as he breathed and a tear stream was running down each side of his face. He was fighting off the flood of emotions. His face hadn't lost form. She wouldn't have been sure he was upset if it wasn't for the out-of-place tears.

Her mouth hung open slightly as she stared in awe. She tried in vain to keep calm. It was overwhelming and in seconds her eyes turned red and rolled with tears of her own. She lunged into a squeeze around him. "Oh David, I'm sorry I didn't mean . . ."

He flung his arms around her and returned the embrace. "Ah, I fucked up, girl. I fucked up. I shouldn't have left you out here. We should have been together. I'm sorry. I fucked up. I left everybody. I . . . I left him and now he's dead. My family can't cope, he's dead. He was always there for me and I wasn't . . . I wasn't around. He's dead and they wouldn't even let me go to his funeral. Oh I'm sorry. . . I'm sorry, baby, I fucked up."

"No. No, you didn't. No, you didn't. You were just trying to help as best you could. It's not your fault. None of it is. Quit it. It's not your fault."

The two clung tightly to each other. Once they lifted their heads, they stared deeply into each other's teary eyes, feeling the compassion and adoration they had for each other.

"I love you," said David, just before pressing his lips to hers. She wasn't given a chance to respond so her answer was in the passion of her kiss. The barriers between them were wiped away in that instant. The two made love that satisfied a neglected hunger. In all the nights they had spent in each other's arms, they were never completely together until that one. It was the sort of coming together that could never truly be pulled back apart.

David, as with his drinking and pool games, had not lost his touch. They slept through to the afternoon.

CHAPTER 23: A NOT-SO-PLEASANT REUNION

Samuel's evening wasn't as rewarding. Fortunately, he had little recollection of it. The last thing he remembered was a foggy image of Jamie and David leaving, then him laying into the bottle they left. Things went dark after that.

The next thing in his chain of memory was waking up on a strange couch in a strange room. He sat up slowly, looking around to study his surroundings. It was nice white carpet and blue flowery furniture he was sitting on. There was a big screen TV, with wood trim that matched the end tables. He looked to the other end of the room to see sliding glass doors displaying a balcony. He was definitely on an upper floor. The layout of the home and the balcony led him to believe it was an apartment, a very nice apartment. He didn't recognize it and he'd hung out in most complexes in town. There was an obvious woman's touch. Not many men would even let their wives decorate like this.

Then a dreadful thought hit him. There was one apartment complex he knew he'd never been to. They were on the upper West side of Lakeview, the higher class portion of the city. They had a reputation for being quite nice. Samuel could picture them looking just like this one.

But he couldn't believe that . . . there was no way he . . . his thought was interrupted by a rustling noise coming from the kitchen behind him. He looked across the back of the couch. On the right side was the entry door and on the left was the edge of the kitchen. Samuel's mouth was dry with anticipation. A figure emerged to the edge of the counter where the coffee maker was. Samuel's lips separated at the sight of her.

She wore a pastel blue silk robe. Her hair was wavy, longer than he remembered it, but it was clearly her. It was Susan.

He had thought of her so many times over the years. His efforts were to not think of her at all, to pretend she didn't exist. Instead she was standing right in front of him. She stood in contrast to every time he tried to forget her, to every daydream of telling her off if he saw her and to every reassurance that he no longer had to have anything to do with her. He was dizzy with amazement that he could be sitting on her couch. What could he say? He wanted to run out the door but how would that look? He hung his head and rubbed his brow.

He was hung over and now dizzy with wonderment. How could he possibly be where he was? How could he have ended up at Susan's house? His first thought was that she went to the party, he made advances, then she brought him home. He quickly dismissed that idea. One, he wouldn't be on the couch in that scenario; two, she would never have shown up at that party; three, the bar was almost closing when David left; and finally, if he saw her, as drunk as he was, there would be no advance, only accusations of her ruining his life, even if that wasn't how he really felt. His next theory was that of a similar situation with Monique. He was drunk and angry and decided to confront her. That could not be the case because he only knew which complex but not the full address. He sat there, dumbfounded by his own presence.

"Oh, you're awake. You want some coffee?" came a stale, unenthused voice from the kitchen.

Samuel slowly creaked his head around to look at his long-absent ex-wife. She had the expression of a disappointed mother.

"Yeah, that might help," he answered. "Um . . . How did I end up here?"

"What? No how you doing, thanks for rescuing me. I didn't really figure you'd remember much. You were that level of belligerent only you could reach. Most people pass out before they can reach that point. You wrapped your car around a tree."

"What!? Where!?" he asked in astonishment.

"Over on Verona Road. You were in the back of the squad car about to be hauled off when Carl recognized you," explained Susan.

"Carl?"

"Yeah, you remember Carl from high school. He's a cop now. He's the one who showed up. Nothing had been reported yet, so he called me and asked if I wanted to come get ya. I guess he felt sorry for you. He said it looked almost deliberate. Made me promise to get you some help."

"I'm surprised he didn't take the opportunity to return that whoopin' he caught."

"Some of us have grown up. He's real religious now; he's a good man. He said you were just sitting on a curb smoking a cigarette like nothing had happened. Talking to him like it was a bright and sunny morning, as he put it."

"Well, I'm sorry you got hassled and roused out of bed. I do appreciate it," said Samuel in a not very gracious tone.

"Oh, don't do that," snapped Susan, who had joined him on the couch, delivering his cup.

"Do what?" he questioned.

"Politely insinuate that I'm a horrible person, then use that to help you pretend to yourself that you haven't done anything wrong. It was no problem getting up and coming to get you; it was what I saw when I got there that was the problem," said Susan fiercely.

"Oh, and what's that?" returned Samuel, now openly furious.

"You! You haven't made one step of progress since I left. It's been more than three years and you haven't made any changes," she explained.

"What did you expect me to change? You left, that's all that's different. You didn't exactly leave me with the means to do much."

"I left you in a life that couldn't work anymore so you'd have to move on but you're still there. You're just gonna stay there until something horrible happens and sets you free. If you can't wait any longer you just drink ungodly amounts until you can't even form coherent thought and hope something's different when you wake up, if you wake up. You made a lot of accusations at me last night. I realized that just leaving you wasn't enough. I had to come clean. I haven't been able to sleep all night."

"Again, I'm sorry for your inconvenience." Susan rolled her eyes with frustration as Samuel again exhibited the attitude of a neglected puppy. Her annoyance finally pushed Samuel too much. He gave up on avoiding the fight and pretending he didn't care. "Oh, fuck that. Don't act like anything you did was for me. However you justify what you did is none of my business, but don't throw that bullshit in front of me like I'm supposed to take it seriously. And as far as anything I said last night, you're stupid if you gave it a second thought when I was that fucked up."

"You can get as mad as you want. I'm not going to argue. I just need to say what I need to say and be done with it. I'm not like you; I don't need to justify my actions, to myself or anyone else. I do what I want, as I always have," began Susan, now in a calm, controlled tone. "You're right; I didn't just do it for you. I did things here that I'm not proud of and I can admit to that. I was greedy but that's not what needs to be addressed. As for you not believing what you said when you were drunk, I'd like to believe that was true but I know it's not. Drinking always let out the feelings you were scared to face when sober, then you'd pretend it was just the alcohol the next day. The truth is you're blaming me. Maybe you have good reason but nonetheless you're using me to hold yourself down like you always have. You hate me. I can see it in your eyes now. I didn't want to be your blockade anymore but I see I still am. You had such potential when we met. It was like you were ready to take on the world. Then you gave everything up and just centered your life around me. For a while I thought it romantic. But slowly I had to accept that it was not. It was you being scared of your own failure. You used me as an excuse to stop living your life, to hide in the little corner you built for yourself. I couldn't take that. You stopped being the boy I fell in love with and just became a spiteful, disappointed mailman who spent most his time in the bottle. The worst part of it was you were still so damn dreamy you never even looked at why you acted the way you did. You could see the world so vividly but you could never see yourself. I thought when I left you'd be forced to leave the corner, you couldn't remain there anymore. You're still there, but now you just use me to hate and tell yourself I ruined any chance for you to have a real life. But it's still just a matter of you being too scared to try. You're miserable and you won't even do anything to change that. You'd rather get real drunk and hope it will somehow change on its own. That's not gonna work. You have to be willing to try. I can't tell you how hurt I was to see you in that state, to see you hadn't gotten any better. You just got worse. That's when I decided I had to tell you how I felt. I had to."

"Oh, give me a fuckin' break!" Samuel hollered as he jumped to his feet. "I can't believe this bullshit. You're actually saying it to me like I'm supposed to believe it. You're so fuckin' deluded. I loved you. That's all I did wrong. I loved you and that's what stopped my life. Then you left. Don't try and deny that. At least live with that."

"That's partly true. I filled in the blank and it hurts me that I was the object of your affection when you made those choices. If I hadn't been there, if I hadn't pursued you maybe you wouldn't have caved in. Maybe you would have tried for the things that really make you happy, instead of pretending I was all you needed. You used me to hide behind, and don't you delude yourself, you never loved me. You may have loved the idea of me, but you never loved me."

Samuel replied with a cold, hollow stare. The life he lived was hard enough but to listen to these accusations was more than he could bear. He couldn't muster the composure to speak. He just stared in outrage.

"Fine!" she began again. "What's my favorite color?" They both stood in silence. Samuel continued his stare, but she could tell he was searching his head for the answer. "Or . . . what did I want to be when I was growing up? Who's my favorite cousin? Anything? Is there anything you can tell me about me that you couldn't tell about your average friend or acquaintances? Anything that was really about me, that wasn't just a detail of my surroundings?" Her voice cracked as she spoke. Samuel's glare softened, just a bit, when he saw her sincere emotion. "This was never an easy thing for me, Samuel. Don't tell yourself differently. I had to accept a long time ago that you didn't love me. You didn't really even take the time to know me. All the romantic things you said to me over the years, all the beautiful notions I was swept away with, could have just as easily been for anyone else. You had spent so much time dreaming of the woman who would come and love you and what you'd say to her. You had mapped out romantic scenes in your stories. I just filled in the blank. It could have been anyone who got caught up in you. You loved the idea of me. You loved having me there to show off to your friends and to be Samuel's girl. But I was never your girl. You never really let me in. You kept me at the safe distance you were comfortable with. You would never let me in. Coming to terms with that was a turning point in my life. That's when I got the strength to leave. You kept me pushed back, and the world with me. In school the world was a safe distance away. You got scared when it was over and things were getting too real. You used me to push it back to where you were comfortable again. Then you were eaten up by your own fears and disappointment. You'd drink like a fish, always want to party, but we never really even talked. Now that I've told you that's what I believe, I'm no longer responsible. I stopped letting you use me in spite of how it hurt. I now told you everything. When you tell yourself I didn't love you and I ruined you, you'll have to remember this conversation. You'll be that much closer to facing things."

She could see him wanting to crack, wanting to discuss these things further, calm and collected, the way they had been with each other so long ago, but he wouldn't.

"Well, I'm glad to see you've made a clean break. It's nice that you have at least took the time to concoct an elaborate theory as to why you left. I suppose I should be flattered that you weren't just laughing up here, counting your money. But fuck you and fuck what you just had the nerve to say to me with a straight face."

Samuel picked up his rain jacket from the end of the couch, and then walked at a cool, deliberate pace to the door. His stride pretended he wasn't affected by what was going on. It purposely made her think her efforts had been in vain, that she hadn't had any effect on him and that he was above even giving her thought. It would have been kinder for him to smack her across the face. He walked out, closing the door gently behind him.

As well as he pretended he didn't care, there was still a strong feeling churning inside him. It was how badly he had wanted to tell her he could now understand what had happened. He wanted to put her at ease, tell her there was obvious validity to her points, but that would be too close to accepting what she said and forgiving her for all the things he held her responsible for. That was something he was unable to do.

His feuding emotions kept him waiting just outside the door after he closed it. Through its seams, he could hear the light sound of her sobs. He'd heard her cry before. No matter how genuine it was, it was always unnecessarily loud. It always carried with it a request for others to hear and come play audience to her grief. But this time there was no performance in it. It was a soft, pulsating grief, echoing from deep inside her. He knew how bad she must have felt. He could feel the burden he had just left on her shoulders. He could almost taste her fear that something horrible would happen to him and she would remain eternally responsible, no matter how good her intentions had been. She too had been stuck in a no-win situation. She probably had wanted to turn back time more often than he had, so she could stop their involvement. So that she would not be in any way responsible for his life. But she was just as unable as he.

Each pulse of her sobs pounded the regret against his chest. He still had the chance. He could face the situation. He could open that door up and make things better. Even without the chance of a relationship, he could still rescue the damsel. But he didn't. He walked down the stairs and started his journey to the nearest payphone.

"Hello," Lukas answered.

"Mouse."

"Ah, what up, man? Where the hell you at? David's been callin' all over for you. We went by your house when you didn't answer the phone and your car wasn't there. I got to thinkin' about how fucked up you were when you left and we was a little worried. I knew you'd be straight, though. Nothin' new for you. So where you at? You didn't get locked up, did you?"

"Naw man, I stayed out. Just barely, I guess. I don't even remember leaving the bar. But why don't y'all come get me? I'm standin' here at the Lakeview Shell Station."

"Where's your car?"

"Out of commission, I guess. Fuck it. It was a junker anyway. Come on, though."

"Huh ha-a-ah. You're wild, man. All right, we'll be there."

About ten minutes later Samuel was pleased to see the decked-out Cutlass pull into the parking lot. Both David and Lukas were smiling and shaking their heads at the sight of their friend standing alone in the dreary, wet afternoon. It was visible in his face that the prior night had taken its toll.

Samuel hopped in the back seat with childish enthusiasm.

"Well, how'd you boys' nights end up?" he asked in falsely perky voice.

"Mine was pretty good, actually. But how the fuck did you end up out here in Lakeview?" replied David.

"Fuck, we don't even want to get into that. All that's important is I totaled my car and I don't know how the fuck me and you are gonna get around to do what we gotta do," explained Samuel.

"Well, I set up a meeting with Loco tonight. I'll be takin' y'all there. Once we know how he's gonna handle things we can figure out how y'all get where you need to go," explained Mouse.

"Cool, cool," agreed Samuel.

"It's good to see you in one piece, man. You were fucked up when I left and they said you really laid into that bottle before you made one of your famous low key exits. I been away too long, shit like that actually gave me a worry," said David.

"You should know better, man. I always land on my feet. How'd everybody else come out?" asked Samuel.

"Shit, they got Harold downtown still. He was all over the road. I don't know where the fuck he was going. He was out in Springfield. You gotta be drunk to be riskin' cuttin' through there. Must have been a fine piece of ass. Then somehow Turkey ended up in Jackson. He don't even know what he was doing on the highway. He just woke up in his car sitting at some rest stop."

Samuel laughed. "What they holdin' Harold for?"

"Guess he had warrants and shit. Nothin' major. Child support or something. They will lock you up for that shit now, though. We'll get him out once we get up on the details. Shit, Pat crashed on my couch too. He wudn't in no shape to be hittin' the road neither. You know how that motherfucker gets."

"Another one of those nights. Shit, I had fun, though. It's good to be back," added David.

"Yeah, I had fun too, for what I remember," agreed Samuel. "It was one of those rare nights when everybody is going all out getting blasted and havin' a good-ass time. No one was holding back. Those are always the best. Unfortunately, they usually end up with me trying to retrace what the fuck I was getting into after a certain hour. I swear it's like I'm something out of one of those werewolf movies."

"Shit. That's pretty much every night for you, ain't it?" suggested Lukas.

Samuel sighed to himself in response. He didn't like the observation. He thought he'd left these blackout spells in his past. There was a time when they were just part of the regular routine. He went out, partied as often as he could and occasionally he wouldn't retain what took place. He'd wake up frustrated, trying to remember what embarrassing things he did and who he might have offended. What he couldn't remember would be replaced with painful daydreams outlining the worst possible scenarios. They were a weight on his mind he'd worked hard to free himself from.

It had been so long, he believed he would never have to face those frustrating mornings again. Now, after years of success he was back to square one. All the successful time in between seemed pointless. He was in the same vicious circle as before. Just like in those mornings past, he was now teetering between making himself feel better by swearing he'd never drink again and not liking the alternative of drowning in an endless stream of boring evenings. It was the same choice that had always plagued him when it came to his drinking habits. Should he continue a life that brought about such disheartening events, or would he not live a life at all, just hiding away in his apartment? All these years had gone by and he still didn't have a proper answer.

"So where am I taking everybody?" asked Lukas.

"What time we supposed to be at Cole's?" questioned David.

"Eight."

"Shit, I guess I gotta stop puttin' it off. Take me to Ma Duke's. I'll kill the time there," directed David.

"Roll me to the crib. I need to recover before I do shit," explained Samuel.

"Cool," agreed Lukas.

CHAPTER 24: BACK WITH THE BEAST

When Samuel got home he partook of his traditional hangover remedy: a bowl of cereal, followed by a long nap. When he woke he felt better than before, but still carried the brittle weakness that followed a night of heavy drinking. He recognized the familiar drag from his binges past. He knew the feeling wouldn't completely subside until the next morning, but a shower could help. His hangover was induced mainly from the dehydration by alcohol. A glass of water would be sent back up the way it came, but a shower allowed his body to absorb some much-needed moisture through his pores.

After he cleaned and dressed himself, he found the pre-Loco visit butterflies returning to his already nauseated belly. He'd dealt with Lorenzo already, but this visit would be far more important than the last. This would be signing on to do business with a man who based his entire life and livelihood on his willingness to be wicked.

Samuel told himself there was no point in second-guessing things. Lukas and David would soon be there to pick him up. There was no chance to back out. Thinking on that only made him all the more restless. Knowing he was trapped in an uneasy situation left him feeling like a caged animal. He found himself longing to stay in his shoddy apartment. He was safe and comfortable there. Circumstances were forcing him to leave. He no longer wanted to. He would rather the meeting be pushed back to another day, perhaps forgotten about altogether. He would stay in that room, watch TV and wait for the suspension issue at the post office to be resolved. Suddenly what had seemed an abhorred life became a fluffy blanket, protecting him from the lurking monsters.

He rustled around in his chair, thinking of how much he wanted to stay right where he was. Then he remembered another time he decided to stay in that chair. It was also a time when he feared what was waiting for him.

He had stayed there to keep himself safe, but the only thing that seat had preserved was his regret. Staying in that room meant monotony. It meant sticking with a life that had proven it couldn't work. Susan was right in one aspect. If he continued, getting up early, delivering letters and coming home with no joy to be found, no matter how long he could persevere, eventually it would end in tragedy. It would likely be self-inflicted on a subconscious level, if not outright premeditated. Staying in that chair meant holding onto a life he had no use for.

He remembered a recurring dream he'd had for years, even when he still was married. It was worse than a nightmare. It was its opposite. In a nightmare the mind conjures up some horrid image or situation that frightens the dreamer to their very depths, but when they awaken they get the comfort of knowing it's gone. They are rescued by reality which lasts far longer than the dream. His dream was a portrait of the perfection he'd always longed for. He could feel the pleasures of a full life. There was the completion that came from the love of a perfect but faceless woman, there was the approval of his mother and his grandparents' pride in what he'd become, there was a nourishing feeling of accomplishment from completing the goals he set out for. Nothing in the dream was specific. He didn't know who the woman was or what he'd accomplished. There was just a blissful beauty to it all. Then, when he awoke, it was gone. The first time it came, he appreciated it for the glimpse of paradise it was. Over the years he changed to longing for nightmares in replacement. At least when they were over he would be left remembering what he had. When these finished he was left realizing what he'd given up on. The long-lasting reality was unhappiness instead of relief. His mind was taunting him with the image of the life he wanted, fading out of grasp.

That dream was trying to show him what the true price of hiding from the world was. Drinking was hiding from the world as much as staying home was. When school was gone and life came barreling at him, he had not just feared failing to become a writer, he feared he was wrong. He feared that every in-depth opinion and intricate philosophy he had built over the years would prove flawed. His very way of making decisions might not work. If he couldn't control things properly, he wasn't the person he had believed himself to be. If life was a test he might fail it. He was scared of facing that. He found a shortcut, as modern man seemed to do with everything. He would not see things through by their long and proper way. He would marry the woman he'd become infatuated with and he'd drink himself into stupors that left him with no control. Without control of himself or the world around him, he was not responsible for what took place. If he was not responsible he would not have to find out what he was made of. It was a way of living, without the burden of being in charge of his life. It was keeping his identity and beliefs intact, without putting them through the tests life would bring. When drinking and marriage didn't work, he took the second choice. He stayed inside. He still wouldn't let circumstances force him to face the world. He kept himself safe from his own fears.

Now, being safe was no longer an appealing choice. Suddenly the answer to his question became so clear. Drinking heavily or staying home waiting for eventual death were the only options he'd given himself. There was a third. Hiding away in his home had attacked him more than anything outside ever could. The emptiness of it became an anchor weighing him down. He'd spent too many years struggling just to keep his head above water. It was time to break free and swim. It was time to move on. His life was in far more peril in the comfort he'd provided it. It was time to give up the protection that came from both alcohol and burying his motivation. He could socialize without getting belligerent. He could go out and do things with a clear head. He could put forth the effort that he should have from the start. He could no longer let his opinions that nothing ever worked out keep him from trying. This was the perfect opportunity. Going after Cullomine's treasure could break him free from his past mistakes. He wouldn't have the safety of his home. He wouldn't have the luxury of knowing where this route would lead, but as long as it was away, that was all that was important.

In an instant his countenance changed. He stopped wanting to hide and he started wanting to attempt. Failing was no longer as frightening as not trying. His life was already in jeopardy. Pursuing this was worth any risk. The worst thing that could happen was getting killed. He had desired to give up on living for years. There was strength in that. He found the strength of the hopeless, the resolve of the rock bottom. Having nothing to lose made him capable of facing anything that came his way. Knowing that life couldn't do anything worse to him than he wanted to do to himself made him invincible. He promised himself that no matter what happened he would never return to this barren wasteland he'd been living in. Nothing was worse than that. As his newly discovered strength swelled up in him, the uneasiness and hesitance blew away. He would either succeed or die in this attempt. Either choice was better than staying in that chair.

Before he got a chance to let his new philosophy carry him away in a daydream, he heard a car horn informing him that his friends had arrived. He trotted out at an easy half-jog. One could see the readiness in his step. He was like a cocky ballplayer taking to the field. His decision to reach his goal by any means was visible in his contented smile.

"So how are we gonna play this?" asked David as Samuel slid into the back seat. "Do we got a strategy?"

David was a doer, Samuel a thinker. They both had great respect for the other's place in things. David, cocky as he was, still considered a battle of conversations something Samuel was best suited for. It was a rare change in things for David to be leaning on Samuel.

"If we go in there and lay all our cards on the table, he's gonna have 'em. All we are really worth is the information we have; once he has it, he might try and give us a finder's fee and take care of the rest himself. Our main goal is to keep ourselves involved from A to Z, so we get a better split. We'll tell him everything else, but I won't mention the package's description that Monique gave me. Not knowing that or exactly how Cully's gonna make his move will probably 'cause him to keep us around to help keep track of things. For instance, if he decides to just watch her house, he'll want us there to help ID the package. If he doesn't know enough to make a perfect plan, he'll want us around to help watch the angles," explained Samuel.

"You guys are talking about staking out houses and shit. I hope whatever you're after is worth it or Loco ain't gonna put forth all that effort," interjected Mouse.

"Yeah, I figured that, but once we mention the purse he'll go right into let's make a deal mode," said Samuel.

"I'm with that. But it sounds to me like you got a straight plan already. Why don't we just wait outside Monique's and snag it when it gets there?" questioned David.

"Well, for one, she'd recognize me, even masked. I couldn't go in. Plus she is gonna be very protective of this thing. She knows I know more than I should and she might change things around or at least be prepared to. Plus she'd notice anybody sitting outside her house very long. We need some people with more talent in surveillance if that's the route we're going. I think the thing to do is to get it as quick as possible. Either from Cullomine himself, or when it's in mail circulation. That we need Cole for."

"You really think she might change things around, though? That could fuck everything up," asked David.

"I don't think she can change much. This plan had to be made before Torreo even went up. She can't get hold of him now without tipping her hand. The whole key for them is that the law don't know nothin' about her. She needs to get the cash and slip away undetected," explained Samuel.

"No. She needs not to," corrected David amusingly.

As the two talked it was clear Lukas's curiosity was growing. They still hadn't shared the details of the job with him. It wasn't good criminal etiquette to ask unnecessary questions so he never did, but after hearing the name Torreo it was obvious his ears had perked.

Once in the U-shaped driveway and out of the car, the three proceeded to the door. After only a few steps David grabbed at Samuel's arm, letting Lukas continue on.

"Man, I'm not wanting to back out or nothin'," began David, "but there's part of me that wonders if this ain't all still just wishful thinkin'. I've been sure up until now but . . . once we start this thing here, we won't be able to stop it. Are you sure you wanna go ahead with this?"

Samuel looked up at the ominous house in front of them, then back to David. Still inspired by his newfound determination, and accompanying that with the strength he always got from having the Postie prince at his side, he answered, "What the hell else are we gonna do?"

David nodded in agreement and they made their way up to the door. It was the same routine. The same big lug of a man answering. The same attitude as if he didn't know who they were.

It occurred to Samuel how monotonous this man's job must be. It had the promise of excitement but was likely more drab than his daily deliveries. All the guards were large, buff men, who obviously went to lengths to keep in shape. They were armed to the teeth, but putting that to use would never come until something out of the ordinary happened. He wondered how often they hoped for an attempt on their boss's life just so that all their work and preparations could prove useful.

"Follow me," the guard said. Lukas didn't bother harassing him this time. Having his mentor here had him more down to business than before. He too probably hoped that someone might try something so he could go to the limits in helping David. It would give him the chance to display through action the feelings they were both too strong to say.

The guard led them down the same hallway as before. David didn't look around much. He didn't seem at all interested in the mouth-opening decoration and lavish design to the house. Flash never interested him much, and he too was sticking to business.

"Sit down, sit down," directed Lorenzo once they had entered the room. "So you're presumably the David Caine I keep hearing about. The tongue of these streets doesn't speak your name lightly. I've been looking forward to finally meeting you. Even more so, doing business with you. So let's cut to the chase. We're all here. There's no more need for mystery. What is it exactly we're here to accomplish?" asked Lorenzo, exposing his frustration at being kept in the dark.

David and Samuel had each taken a chair facing the throne-like desk Lorenzo was seated behind. Lukas sat on a small couch in the corner behind them. Lorenzo seemed to be taking this meeting a little more seriously as well. He wore a white button-down dress shirt not tucked into his black dress pants, as opposed to the robe and slippers on the last visit. He stayed seated instead of pacing around, putting on a show. When they arrived he used a remote to turn off the elevated TV near the ceiling behind them.

Samuel decided the difference in attitude was a result of mood swings instead of any real circumstances. He was still uneasy around this man. He could almost see the untamed restless spirit behind Lorenzo's sly green eyes.

"Well, I return the pleasure in finally having met. All my old friends seem to have the highest respect for you as well. The job's a basic snag and run score. There's just the problem of knowing where and when we'd make the snag or we'd probably attempt it ourselves," replied David. Samuel was surprised at how well his friend was handling his wording.

"I was under the impression you'd be the information holders while I'd play the accomplishing role," said Lorenzo, still impatient at the lack of details.

"I think we'll all have to play a role in both parts," started Samuel. "It's basically real simple. There's a case of money that'll be shipped through the US mail. I would have been the one delivering it, or not so as the case would have been, but for reasons beyond my control I've been temporarily suspended. So me getting my hands on it without getting the heat on me would be real rough. You know the man named Cullomine Torreo?" asked Samuel, still feeling funny bringing a daydream into reality for everyone to see. In the back of his mind he still felt like people would mock anything that was his brainchild.

"Of course," answered Lorenzo.

"Well, his parole has been approved and he'll be released from prison this week. When he does get released he's gonna be going straight for a stash of money. He's got the law and his old affiliates out to make sure he doesn't escape with that money. He's gonna have to pull some moves to get it and himself safely out of the country. We know basically how he's gonna do it. The idea is to snatch the prize up midstream and divvy it up between us without anyone else being the wiser."

"Intriguing. Very intriguing," commented Lorenzo. "How is it you two are so in tune with the dealings?"

"Well, I stumbled across the important part. Then, with the help of David and his inmate friends we've been able to dig up the rest of the information. You see, we're relatively sure he's gonna send this money to a girlfriend the law don't know nothing about. It's their money really so they're the ones he's gotta keep it away from. The cartel isn't interested in the loot. They just want Torreo but they're giving the feds time to get their money back. He sends it to her, and then she makes off with it and meets up with him later. Then he doesn't have to worry about concealing the money when he gets on a plane or does whatever it is he plans to do. See, I would have just not delivered it but we can't do that now. Now I don't know when he's gonna mail it or when it's gonna get there. I know this girl; if we were fishing around her house too often she'd spot us. We don't really know how to do shit like that. We need someone who can watch him for his move and know the best time to make the snag. The only thing is he knows the law is gonna be watching so we gotta be ready for whatever slippery moves he tries."

"As I said, it sounds intriguing. I had heard that Cullomine had been exiled by his organization. I was not aware he was being hunted as well. What I don't understand is a man like Cullomine having to trust a woman to meet him with his money. It would seem like he'd have some connection that could get him on a private plane and away to safety," said Lorenzo, seeming to want to blow off the whole situation.

"I don't think he has a lot of choices at this point. He's a man on his last leg. His Dragon Clan wants him dead. He's only alive now because the Clan is giving the law that chance to get their money back. There's likely no friend he could go to that the Clan couldn't find. Right now that money is like his bulletproof vest. He's gotta figure a way to get everyone chasing that while he escapes. I figure he's gonna pull a switch somewhere, toss the real money in the mail and get the hell out of Dodge while everyone else is trying to figure out what's going on. That's why we gotta be on top of things," explained Samuel, giving Cullomine more credit than David would like. Samuel seemed to believe that Torreo had something up his sleeve that would leave almost everyone else guessing. David couldn't give a dealer that much credit. He believed Torreo to be running scared and it was only a matter of time before the predators caught up with him.

"So how much money is all this over?" asked Lorenzo plainly.

"Somewhere in the neighborhood of twenty million dollars," answered Samuel like he was dropping a royal flush onto the table. "It was supposed to be a large-scale payoff to a team of feds. They're trying hard to get their hands on it but we got the inside track. We know that he's going to mail a box and we know where it'll be delivered to."

Lorenzo grew abruptly attentive, while Lukas almost hopped out of his seat at learning the amount of money they were after.

"Well, it's not so complicated is it?" said Lorenzo with an obvious change in attitude. "Luckily for us, surveillance is one of my boys' specialties. It pays to know what others don't want you to. So what it comes down to is this . . ." continued Lorenzo as he interrupted himself to talk into an intercom on his desk. "Send up Sylvester, would you? I'd imagine he's up at the range," he ordered before turning back to Samuel and David. "What it comes down to is you being willing to take the responsibility. We can sit here, mull through the details and plan this whole thing out, but first I have to get guarantees from you, and even more, an acceptance of responsibility. You have to guarantee me the information you give me is accurate. I'm not one to dedicate man-hours and my efforts to something that won't pan out. Every time an employee of mine drives down the road with a firearm on his person there is a risk being run. I don't run those risks lightly. The responsibility comes down on you in this case. I am gonna make moves based on the idea that what you boys are telling me is on the level. You gotta know if things go bad, if you turn out to be wrong, it's on your shoulders. It's the only way I can be comfortable. Now I'm not gonna sit here and make threats. You have heard the stories and I'm sure you're all aware how I handle those I've been made to become cross with. I don't let anything slide lest it be incentive to the next."

The end of Lorenzo's sentence was punctuated by the entrance of the man he'd sent for. He was a burly individual, not buff to the point that he was trying to impress people, but indeed big enough to make an impression. He was slightly round in face and body. It was clear that bulk and brute strength were more important to him than being toned. He had the face and disposition of a bulldog. There was no peace in his black shark eyes. At just a glance Samuel could see his hatred of play and those who were playful. He had a gruesome scar on the side of his neck and the soulless expression that held the resolve of someone who was incapable of hesitation. Handling tough situations was a way of life for this man.

"This is Mr. Sylvester Cotton," introduced Lorenzo. "I believe most people refer to him as Sly, like that actor. He's quite capable. He's the head of my more intricate and secretive operations. The military seemed to train him in just the right things for my needs. When I send you boys out, he will be the one at your side. I don't leave anything to risk. He'll be making sure you guys stay on the straight and narrow. But before we can continue, the question remains, are you willing to accept the terms I put to you?"

Samuel hadn't looked away from Sylvester since he'd entered. His very presence made Samuel nervous. Considering the amount of money involved, he just knew this was the top of Cole's roster.

David looked to Samuel for his answer. Samuel rolled his head over to look back, shrugged his shoulders as if unimpressed by the whole situation, and then nodded.

David turned back to answer. "Well Lorenzo, our information is solid and our intentions coincide, so it wouldn't make any sense to do anything but proceed. Where do we go from here?"

"How much of our surveillance team is in use?" asked Lorenzo of Sylvester.

"I'd say about 70 to 75 percent," he answered in a foreboding and raspy voice.

"We're gonna need three tail units and two SWAT, one stationary, one mobile. Keep a couple of extra guys on call in case we run into trouble. If this doesn't work out it won't be because of us." As Lorenzo spoke Sly grew more attentive. He could see the caliber of the mission by his own presence and the uncommon warning of no mistakes. Lorenzo didn't have to say much for Sly to get the idea.

He returned his speech to the rest of the room. "You see we'll put the stationary SWAT outside the girlfriend's home. That's a van with a team made up of those necessary for proper surveillance and those needed to make the snag once they're given the go-ahead. They're our safety net. The three tails will be in charge of keeping up with Cullomine. They're good at what they do. They'll never be seen by the target or the agents. Both the mobile SWAT and a car containing you two will follow only by directions given by these tails. Anytime Torreo stops somewhere he might make a move, you boys will move in. It's your place to give positive confirmation that he has the goods. Then it's up to us. The mobile SWAT will be nearby and ready to move. It's important that you two try and keep up with anything he might be pulling. You let us know everything you're thinking. Don't leave anything unsaid. Watching all the angles is gonna be a group effort. Ideally he'll lose the others' eyes as planned and make the drop in the mail. Then we can just crack open the mailbox and have it. I hope we don't have to run into the post office or anything like that," laughed Lorenzo, slightly gloating over what they were willing to do. "The more ways we have of coming up with the prize, the better. We go all out to get it as soon as possible, and then if we miss, we still have the backup of the girlfriend's house. A close second priority to getting it is not letting the feds see us get it. We don't want them snooping around town trying to find out who made off with what was theirs. Dirty law is really just a well-organized gang. We don't want to have to take them on if we can avoid it. Ideally they'll just be left not understanding what Cullomine did with it. This is gonna be a play it by ear situation; that's why everyone's going to have to be sharp at all times. Sylvester, you make whatever staff switches you have to. I want the best guys on this. I don't want any hesitations or mistakes when something needs to be done."

It frustrated Samuel to hear Lorenzo talk down to them. There was such braggadocio in everything he said. He loved explaining what his men were capable of and that he was the boss over it all. He loved explaining every little detail to them as if they were weak-minded, blessed by the all-knowing knowledge of Lorenzo Cole. But Samuel also had to appreciate his hopes and dreams being in the hands of such capable men.

"So what's the cut gonna be?" asked David.

"Well, the amount of real information you've given me here is minimal," Lorenzo began delegating. "I'm the one having to accomplish most everything in this situation, but if the money is near the amount you claim, I'll give you six million to split up how you see fit."

David and Samuel nodded to each other in silent consultation. "That sounds fair," agreed David. "Real fair."

CHAPTER 25: SECOND THOUGHTS

After the meeting the boys stopped at a small out-of-the-way pub called An Idle Hour. They wanted to avoid the crowd of Snickers so they could speak privately.

"Man, y'all sure got his attention," announced Lukas. "I never actually seen Sylvester Cotton. I just heard the stories. If Loco's puttin' dude on this, he's real serious. They say that motherfucker was discharged for conduct unbecoming of an officer. He was a sergeant or something in a technical division. I guess he killed his superior over a card game or some bullshit, but he did it smooth. There wasn't enough evidence to convict, and in the army that's saying something. I didn't like seeing dude gettin' put in the mix. I wish y'all had told me we were dealing with so much money."

"Why's that?" asked David.

"'Cause I didn't know the stakes were so high. Fuck, we're all under the gun now. If something goes bad . . . I don't know, man, I just got a bad feeling. We can't take this kind of business with Lorenzo Cole lightly. This thing could move him from the pond to pool, ya know. He's gonna go all out. If he doesn't come out with the loot and there's no one else to blame, we're gonna be the ones he takes it out on. Everything sounds simple enough but there's a lot of room for mistakes and missed opportunities. I just don't like it."

"Well, Little Lukas Bailey, I've been smackin' you around as long as I can remember. You'd think that'd make you tough, but I go up for a few years and you turn pussy on me?" accused David.

"Ahh, it ain't even like that," said Lukas, defending himself.

"It is like that. I mean I ain't mad at you. You turned scared over the years, that's your business. It's on you. But don't sit here and try and put a spin on it. I mean I respect the man, he's earned that, but I'll be damned if I ever become scared of him," continued David.

"Man didn't nobody say they was scared, it's just . . ."

"I said it motherfucker," interrupted David. "How you gonna sit here and tell me you ain't scared of him? That motherfucker is harboring the cat that killed my brother and you don't tell me. What? I was supposed to believe you just found that out when I was released? Samuel knew and I didn't. I'm supposed to think you didn't tell him? You know where Tim be at. You didn't come and tell me. You didn't see if I wanted you to handle it. You just kept it to yourself. Now that to me, knowing you as I do, could only be you being scared of Loco."

"Man, fuck you for saying that to me. You know damn well I'd go get Tim right now if you asked me to. But I know you, and you wouldn't have sent me in there 'cause then they'd be looking for me. You would go do it yourself, then they'd be lookin' for you. I'm lookin' out for . . . man, fuck that. I don't need to explain myself to you. You knew that shit was wrong when you said it." Lukas stood up and tossed a fifty on the table. "You can get a cab where you're going."

They sat silently, watching him walk out the front door. It took years to be able to recognize the different feelings behind a cool Postie stride. Samuel could see the hurt frustration in Lukas's. "You know that motherfucker was just lookin' out for you the way you've always looked out for him," said Samuel, trying to mend the wounded friendship.

David shook his head and waved his hand. "Don't even start defending him, man. I don't feel like talking about it."

"I hear ya," agreed Samuel.

"But as long as we're already all somber and serious, I think I've been avoiding really talking at you for too long. I gave you a pass for a minute, but we got to get into it after last night. You drank till you're not even sure what happened, and trashed your load." Samuel rolled his eyes like a child receiving yet another in a countless number of scoldings. "Go ahead, roll your eyes, but this shit needs discussing. You keep acting like this and get yourself killed, I'm not gonna be kicking myself wondering why I never talked to you about it. For one, it's obvious to me that as long as I've been gone you're still in the same rut. You're not doing nothing for yourself most of the time. It's like you get by for a while then you start actin' wild. I recognize that look in your eye, man, when you start puttin' your drinks back like you're on a mission. You used to get it even back when things were supposed to be going good for you. You'd be cool at times but then I'd just see it. Even earlier in the day before the parties started, I usually could tell when you was gonna have one of them nights before you could. You don't take them drinks like you're trying to have a good time; you do it like you're trying to get something done. Here it is years later and none of that shit has changed. Now you're gettin' into this thing with Loco, so I gotta question your real motives, man. You never were a big spender. You never been one to talk about what you'd do with money if you had it. I can't help but wonder if you're not just getting into this thing secretly hoping it'll go bad. Maybe you think doing this will make someone else get rid of whatever weight is on your shoulders for ya."

Samuel paused for a moment, considering what was just said. It was his instinct to dodge subjects that pertained to him, but this time he didn't. "Well, I can't argue that I've been diggin' myself into a rut for a long time. I've seen that for years but I wasn't willing to do what it took to make things better. When I look around I feel like most people are doing the same thing. They're all just burrowing themselves deeper into the same hole. But as of today I'm different from the rest. As of today they're still workin' to stay there but I'm workin' to get out. Nothing's been good for me in a long time. I'm seeing how important it is to make some changes. I'm finally able to do it. I gotta do something and this is the perfect opportunity. So don't get it twisted, I'm not in this for an ending. I'm after a new beginning, there's just no price I'm not willing to pay at this point."

"Fuck," said David with muffled pride in his smile. "That's finally the kind of talk I like to hear. Any time I've ever brought up serious shit like this, you just blew it off and changed the subject. That sounded like a real answer for once. I don't even think it was a line of shit neither. You look kind of chilled. That drink goes down at a nice, reasonable rate. Finally coming back to the land of the living. It's about fuckin' time." He paused, then decided to press his luck with another touchy subject. "So you writin' again?"

"Aw man, what do you give a fuck about that for?" asked Samuel, almost embarrassed.

"I give a fuck about that 'cause for some reason you don't. Every so often you get real drunk and start talking about a story you wrote, or just an idea you had for a story, and to me, maybe it's just to me, but you'd seem kind of excited. I haven't seen you excited too many times. If you really didn't care about it, I don't think you'd ever bring it up. From the shit of yours I read, I could see how good you were. If you're that good it makes sense you'd enjoy it. I gotta wonder if you were doing that, if you would still feel the need to get into this thing. If that's the case I don't think this money is gonna help you that much. You hear about all them people that win the lottery then end up killing themselves. You need more, know what I mean?"

"Food for thought, man, but fuck it. This'll get me away from everything, then I can see with a clear head what I need to be doing."

"Well, that sounds more like one of the answers I'm used to. Just enough to get me to lay off. A'ight, one for two ain't bad."

Samuel smirked. "So what do you think you're gonna do if this works out? I can't really see you without the Posties nearby. You live and breathe for it. I bet you put together a circle in the joint. How long do you think you can last on the beach?"

"Shit changed in the joint. When I started out you're right, I did get in a circle, started movin' up the ranks. It was kind of like the early days here. In a way I liked it. Then when Kris got killed, man, I could finally see how pointless it all was. All this we was doin' out here, earning respect livin' out the stories we heard, that wasn't gonna add up to shit. It was a whole lot of nothin'. I realized a lot, man. I'm not the same person I was back in the day. I spent so much time trying to live up to him. I spent so much time trying to protect everybody else but then couldn't protect that motherfucker. That's when I had to figure out exactly what I wanted. I put it all down in my head. I gotta get the people I care about and get 'em the fuck out of here. I just want to enjoy what time I have with 'em. That's top priority. I always thought I'd fuck around then one day get it together and do things like I ought to. But fuck, I'm already feeling old, man. There was so much I thought I would have done by this time in my life. I sit and hold my head at night. I can feel life slippin' away and the way things are here it's just gonna keep slippin' till it's gone. I gotta get it together and Loco is the fastest way to do that."

"When the hoarse voice of mortality is heard, even the most directed reevaluate," quoted Samuel.

David smiled. "You are writin' again."

"Naw, that's from a story I wrote back in the day. I swear I think I was a lot smarter back then."

"There was less to cloud the vision. You started trying to do the family thing; that can throw everything off," said David. "Did I tell you Ma got piss tested at Denzo? They fired her. Now she's at Koyoe. That pushed back any plans for retirement. She can't keep it up like that forever. I want to get her out of here. And Missy—shit, you know she didn't even show up today to see me. She couldn't face me, I guess. I think she holds herself responsible for a lot. Ma Dukes said I was better off not seeing her. She said I would flip out. Like she's a full-fledged junkie or something. Now how can I ever make her better if we stay here? I don't know how I'm gonna keep myself out of trouble, let alone clean her up. There's no way I can fix things for me, Jamie, Ma, and her if we stay here. Plus Kris's kids, Rex and Bree, they're growin' up fast. They'll be into all the same things before I know it. It's just time for me and mine to get away from this damn city, and how am I gonna pull that off other than with what we got going. We in the same boat. We gotta go all out on this."

"Man, there ain't a whole lot you can't do once you decide to," argued Samuel. "It's just easy to get worried when shit is so important. Even if this don't pan out you'll get things where they need to be. Once you put your head to it, you'll get there. It just won't be the quick fix we all like."

"Yeah, maybe you're right. Shit, we in this now, though. I gotta agree with everybody, fuckin' with Cole is high risk. It was all I could do not to puke on that motherfucker. He stands there all proud. He is in the way of what's mine and he don't give a shit. I can't even let myself really think about it or I'll give in. Lettin' Kris go without being avenged goes against everything. But I know he'd want me take up for the fam first. It's hard, though. That's really why I went off on Mouse just now. I don't want him in the middle of this shit. If it comes to it he'd want to take up for me like I do for Kris, and he ain't got the self-control I do. Gettin' 'im pissed was the only way I could think to back him away from this thing. It'll be all good when I give him his cut, though," smiled David, ready to think on the good way things could turn out.

CHAPTER 26: DRAWING LINES

It was the following Wednesday afternoon when the cell phone Lorenzo Cole provided them with first rang. They both sat in a small diner eating breakfast. It was Cullomine's scheduled day for release so the two planned on being together in preparation for the call. They were both startled by the constantly anticipated ring. Samuel answered to learn Sylvester was on his way to pick them up.

When Sylvester walked in the front door they hopped up, eager to begin the pursuit. He was wearing the same thin army green jacket and black jeans as when they last saw him. Other than his ferocious aura he didn't appear much different than a hundred other war vets who decorated the streets of that Midwestern town. He was likely unnoticed by most. At seeing them stand he gestured them back to their seats as he continued toward their table.

"We don't need to leave yet. I'll get a call when it's time," he spoke hoarsely. There was little expression in his voice. He explained in a very matter-of-fact, straight-to-the-point manner, "Torreo is driving himself in a black 98 Lincoln. It was waiting for him in the prison parking lot when he was released. We got tails following on the highway coming in this direction. We'll be getting the call when he's close to town."

"How do we keep him or anyone else from seeing a tail follow him off the highway?" inquired David.

Sylvester's face contorted slightly at just hearing the sound of David's voice. "One car follows him on the highway, while the others hang back; when the target gets off, the car that was following keeps going while letting one behind him know what exit they need to get off on. That way he doesn't see the same car all the time," explained Sylvester condescendingly.

The waitress came and Sylvester ordered off the lunch menu. The three then sat in an awkward silence.

"So I heard you were ex-military?" inquired Samuel, to lighten the mood. Sylvester looked up at him, annoyed by the question, then looked away again without answering. "So what branch were you in?" Samuel attempted again. A similar look was offered up, and then followed by the same dead silence. It was slightly more blatant this time. It left no confusion as to whether Samuel was heard.

David looked at his friend with a half-enthused smile. Seeming to enjoy the gruff attitude, he decided to push things a bit farther. "So do you do a lot of work for Lorenzo or what?" David wasn't even granted the annoyed glance. "I mean you're obviously a rather large individual. I suppose it would be right up your alley to do things in the bodyguard field. Of course you got that grisly scar on your neck; that's gotta be good for intimidation, money pickups, threats and such."

Finally Sylvester was pushed to the point of responding. He kept the same cold, hard face as he spoke. "I'm not interested in telling you the first thing about myself. My name is more than you need know. My job here is quite simple: to help connect the dots, pass on info and to kill the two of you if you act out of our best interests in any way. So before you start getting cute, know that if I get angry and decide to kill you for personal reasons, Lorenzo has been dealing with me long enough that he doesn't hassle me with a lot of questions. As far as my background, just be aware that I'm trained and experienced enough that it is small chore to handle you two jokers."

David's expression went from playful smile to the razor glare he got when challenged. Samuel watched as David's priorities visibly took precedence over his instincts. Though it was becoming commonplace, it was still impressive to see such behavior out of his once immeasurably impulsive friend.

As the waitress brought Sylvester's food, Samuel tried to help calm David by changing the subject a bit. "So how do you think Cullomine plans to ditch the feds?"

"I don't know. He must have something planned." They were both a little antsy with things finally about to get started. What had begun as a fantasy used to pass the time had become real and was about to go into action. They were creaking to the top of the first big hill on a roller coaster and after hours of waiting in line it was, at last, time to begin their rush downward.

"True, but you know how cops are. They probably think he's just gonna go get the money and make a break for it, 1, 2, 3. They never give their opponents enough credit. They probably don't figure him to even know they'll be watching, or that he's gonna try and give 'em the slip."

"True. Can't let 'em see us, though."

"If he sees someone watching he'll assume it's feds. The feds are the ones we really gotta worry about."

As the two talked Samuel was watching Sylvester eat. He didn't savor his food. He barely chewed. He didn't seem to take any enjoyment in it at all. He addressed the situation like a goal that needed accomplishing. He set out to achieve it efficiently. It aroused all the more fear in Samuel when he saw the intensity put forth in something as menial as eating lunch. It allowed for insight into the man in front of him.

Sylvester was the perfect right arm for Lorenzo Cole. He needed to put his training and skills to use in order to feel complete. He couldn't be calm without a goal ahead of him. His sadistic tendencies negated the US military's ability to employ him. However, they made Lorenzo the perfect employer. Running the surveillance teams and committing the occasional murder must have been hog heaven for this man. He got to put all his talents to use without the burden of a code of conduct.

It was clear the ferocity that was burrowed in Sylvester was great. Samuel hoped he and his friend did not end up on the wrong side of it. What's more, he knew David had made the same observations but with a completely different reaction. The apparent dominance would only entice David to battle. Samuel didn't like to admit to himself how wary that made him. It wasn't often he feared someone could get the better of David Caine.

He tried to reassure himself by seeing Sylvester's weaker side. He had a no-nonsense approach to things. Samuel considered that a weakness. Sylvester was the type to believe strength came with size, speed came with exercise, smarts came from schooling and there were no exceptions. He would likely underestimate what the small, sassy hoodlum could accomplish. But with Sylvester being trained by the government, almost twice David's size and in a constant prepared state, Samuel couldn't help but fear this man. He hoped a confrontation was not on the horizon.

CHAPTER 27: SO IT BEGINS

Sylvester wasn't finished with his food long before his phone rang.

"Yeah, we're on the way," answered Sly. "Come on," he commanded as he stood abruptly and tossed money on the table.

"Where are we headin'?" Samuel asked.

"Don't know. He's pullin' into town now. We just gotta get on the road and start in the same direction. Hopefully we can get this over with quick."

Samuel sat shotgun and David in the back of Sylvester's car. They rode along impatiently, unaware of their destination. All they had to go on was from listening to Sylvester talk into his phone. It was frustrating following blindly. Trying to make out a conversation from only hearing one side added to the frustration.

As they hung on every word, Sylvester was suddenly cut off by his phone losing signal. He didn't bother fiddling with it long before he pulled a walkie-talkie out of the glove compartment. He used it to get the final details of their directions.

"This is only for emergencies. You never know who's listening on these things. Something happens and you have to talk on this, be careful what you say," explained Sylvester as he eased to the side of the road. "He's gone into that bank across the road. You figure that's where he's got the loot?"

"Makes sense. He wouldn't have it in an account but it's probably in a safety deposit box. Hopefully he'll come out with it," Samuel thought aloud.

"You see that blue sedan over there?" questioned Sly as he gestured toward a car up the street from the bank.

"Yeah," answered David.

"That's our federal agents. Looks like you guys were right about this thing."

Samuel felt relieved to see his opponents in the beginning competition. He wasn't happy to have to compete, but they were the final proof that there was indeed a game to be played. He flopped back in his seat with a small sigh of relief.

During the wait the boys got a glimpse of how serious and capable Lorenzo's team was. For fear he might try and give them the slip, all options were quickly taken into consideration. A car was sent around to the back to make sure there were no alternate exits. Someone was sent to the roof of a building across the street to keep a bird's eye view. They didn't know how he could achieve reaching the roof of the bank but if it was a possible escape route, they were watching it.

Samuel sat back in awe at how prepared Lorenzo's team was. The second someone got an idea about a potential problem a solution was found and acted out in an instant. The efficiency was inspiring. For the first time Samuel became genuinely optimistic of their chances for success.

When quick communication became imperative, Sly plugged his cell phone into an adapter that was attached to the car radio. From then on the voices of their teammates came through the car speaker for all three to hear. He then pulled a receiver out of the glove box and put it on the dash.

"All right, we got a conference call going, so don't say nothing unless it's important and relevant to what's going on," he directed the boys. "We can all hear each other right now and we can't tie up the line with pointless chatter. The second you get an idea of something he might pull or anything else important, you speak toward this mic on the dash."

Samuel thought to himself for a moment, then spoke. "Well, I figured he might try and disguise himself in the bathroom or something. I wish I could get a better look at everybody coming out."

"You catch that?" asked Sly to the microphone.

"Yeah, we're on it," answered a voice through the speakers.

In almost no time at all there was a stocky woman in raggedy clothes, posing as a bum outside the doors. She asked everyone who emerged for change. Without bringing suspicion she was able to get a close look at anyone exiting through the front doors of the building.

Finally, with no trickery or surprise Cullomine presented himself to the crowd of onlookers. Though to their team the feds sitting outside the bank were obvious, he never glanced in their direction. To anyone who didn't know better, the black suit, the hair pulled back into a presentable ponytail and the expensive leather briefcase now in his hand would have all added up to seem like a legitimate Latin businessman. The ones surveilling saw a criminal with a briefcase that potentially held twenty million dollars for them to snatch away.

"You boys figure that money is in the case?" asked Sylvester.

"Whaddya think?" David asked Samuel.

"Well, I'm as hopeful as anyone but I don't think he's gonna be this obvious. It could be bait, while he pulls something off. On the other hand he might be that confident he can shake the tail."

"Shit, I'm startin' to think you guys are givin' this spic too much credit," argued Sylvester. "He hasn't looked at the feds' tail once that I've seen. He's probably got it in that case and is on the way to the nearest airport."

"Well, I definitely wouldn't count on that," countered Samuel. "One way or another he plans on sending that money to Monique. She's our trump card. We should be mindful of any mailboxes he passes."

"You guys got that, right?" asked Sylvester of the mic. "They say that it's probably a distraction and to watch for him as he goes by any mailboxes. . . I got my phone hooked up to this thing. Somebody call Cole and get his take."

"We're on it," explained a voice from the speaker. "Let's keep this conference call going and we'll direct Sly and SWAT as to which streets they should follow on."

The boys felt powerless as they watched Torreo pull away in the black Lincoln. They were left trusting the team they had recruited to handle things. Seeing Torreo in person for the first time brought to a head all their hopes that pended on this plan. It was frustrating having so little control in something they'd been dreaming about for so long. They felt like younger, tagalong siblings not allowed any real participation.

They watched the agents pull out behind Cullomine, but they never saw any of their own players. The derelict woman maintained her cover as she walked in the opposite direction up the street. Apart from her, the boys' only evidence of the rest of Cole's men was the voice leaking through the speakers.

After a moment another conversation began for them to hear. "Okay, this is A following the target eastbound on Capital Avenue. What are the other tail positions?"

"This B following parallel on Winding Way, which is one street to the north of A."

"This is C following parallel on Chestnut Street, which is two streets to the south of A."

"Okay, Sly and SWAT should head down Columbia Ave. eastbound and wait for directions. We just got off the line with Lorenzo; he says to continue in pursuit but not to expose. He wants confirmation but if target makes a quick move do not let him get away with that case still in his possession. Repeat, do not risk losing the case."

They rolled along in silence again. Samuel tried to keep from fidgeting as he yearned for the speaker to vibrate with an update on events. Finally the voices returned.

"This is A. Target is taking a right on Broadway Boulevard heading south."

"This is C. Let him go, A. We'll tail him."

"Okay, this is A turning right on Orchard Avenue heading south."

"This is C. The target just passed, there's a green Tercel, there's the feds. C is turning onto Broadway Boulevard. C is following target on Broadway Boulevard southbound."

"This is A following parallel on Orchard Avenue two streets to the west of C."

"This is B following parallel on Dickman Road three streets to the east of C."

"Sly and SWAT should turn back and get on Beckley Road heading south."

"Well, he's not even using the side streets," said a surprised Sly. "He's staying in traffic. I don't think he knows they're following him."

They coasted along in silence for another ten minutes before the voices returned. It was all Samuel could do to keep himself from double-checking all the connections to make sure they weren't loose.

"All right, this is C; apparently he just came to town to make that pickup because we're getting back on the highway. Can either tail turn in time to catch this exit on Broadway?"

"This is A. That's affirmative. You can let him go."

"Okay this is C abandoning target as he gets on I-94 heading toward Detroit. A is going to pick him up. Everybody else needs to get on the highway heading the same direction within the next five minutes."

"Fuck!" snapped Sly. "Where the hell is he going that we need to be leaving the city?"

They soared down the highway but in Samuel's mind they were standing still. He couldn't understand why Cullomine would be straying so far from their city with the briefcase still in his possession. Samuel was always one who tried to wait until everything important was settled before he would let himself relax. All these questions weighing on his mind left him very uneasy.

David, however, was a take things as they come sort. He had dozed off in the back seat. Sly stared coldly at the road in front of him. His determination and focus were visible in the stare.

Samuel's mind continued to spin as he tried to come up with information or even a theory he could take comfort in. Perhaps Cullomine had stashed the money at whatever far-off destination they were heading toward, but that left him wondering what they were doing at the bank. He knew Torreo would have a trick up his sleeve and he had always believed he would be the one to catch on to it. But here the games had begun and Samuel wasn't able to make any sense of the first two moves made.

What added to his frustration was his fear that the opposing teams in this game were ahead of him. There was really no way to keep track of what the feds had figured out, or what Torreo had noticed. The only thing worse than letting Torreo's money slip through his fingers would be to watch the feds snag it. He felt the players that Cole had provided were as capable as he would ever need them to be, but when it came to watching the angles, to catching on to what Torreo was planning, Samuel put that responsibility on his own shoulders. It would be more than he could handle to have the agents outdo him and be stuck watching them make off with his paradise.

He also feared that Cole wouldn't let the feds walk away with something he coveted so. He was one who was used to getting what he wanted. Samuel could see Lorenzo sending the pit bull and the rest of his dogs in with guns blazing to take the money by force. He could only imagine the heat that would come from a team of slaughtered federal agents. He couldn't put it past the arrogant Lorenzo Cole. He didn't appear to be someone who could stand the idea that anyone had more authority in a situation than him. That would likely eclipse any logic that told him not to move against the FBI if it came to it.

"You guys got any way to figure out where the feds are with all this?" asked the endlessly curious Samuel.

"All this?" replied Sly, trying to be hard to get along with more than he didn't understand.

"Well, where he's going, for one?"

Sly adjusted himself in his seat. "Lorenzo's got someone slippery at the bureau with a talent for letting him know things. He hasn't been able to get in touch with him yet. I'm sure we'll be hearing something before long."

Samuel nodded his head, slightly reassured. *Competent teammates indeed,* he thought to himself.

They rolled in silence for another hour, three highway hours in all, before the monotony was broken. They were near the top of the state and Samuel was still trying to calm his mind when the phone rang. David sat up as Sly hit the button to answer the call.

"He's getting off at exit 198. You guys are far enough back you can go ahead and get off too," resounded the voice through the speakers.

"That's the exit to the big airport, isn't it?" asked Sly.

There was a bit of rustling before the answer. "Yep, it sure is. Takes you right down to the airport."

"He might have come to this one because he thought he had a better chance to shake his tails. I'm calling Cole." Sly hung up the phone, then made the call.

"Yes," answered Lorenzo's familiar relaxed tone.

"Boss, he's gettin' off on an exit toward a big city airport."

"The second he enters the airport let the dogs loose. He's not to get on a plane till we know for sure he does or doesn't have the money," ordered Lorenzo.

Samuel was swept away in the urgency of the moment. "You know, he might just have the money in an airport locker. We don't want to give ourselves away till we have to," he said.

"Ideally we want someone to follow him through the airport till the last minute. The second he's out of that car, I want it searched. If there's an empty briefcase, we'll assume he's got the money on him and he's heading for a plane; if not, keep tailing him till we get an idea what he's doing, but giving ourselves away or not, he is not to get on a plane till we know," redirected Lorenzo.

"I'm on it," said Sly as he hung up the phone. As he dialed his next call he spoke toward Samuel. "This seems like a lot of unnecessary waiting. Looks to me he picked up the loot and headed straight for the airport. He didn't even know enough to hide it."

"Yeah, this is A," answered the voice.

"Cole said the second the target enters the airport parking lot, the leash is off. He said allow room for . . ."

"Well, I don't think that's gonna be an issue right now. He's pulled into a cheap motel and appears to be getting a room," interrupted the voice.

"What!" barked an astounded Sly.

"Yeah, he's at the front desk right now with the briefcase . . . wait . . . yeah, he's out coming toward his car . . . passing his car . . . got a key out . . . he's in room twelve."

"Fuck! All right what's your location?"

"We're about a half mile east of the exit. It's called the Park Motel."

"Okay, you boys set up shop; I'll call you when we're in the area. Try and have us a spot picked out."

It was dusk when they got the call about Cullomine renting a room. Within an hour Samuel, David and Sylvester were parked in the lot of a closed down gas station, atop a hill that gave binocular view of the cheap inn.

By then it was pitch black out. The night had taken on a darkness that didn't appear like just a lack of light but seemed to be a thick blanket of blackness covering the outdoors. The darkness looked stuck to everything they could see. The only relief for Samuel was to use the small telescope he'd been provided to see the motel. Its bright yellow sign and the surrounding street lights contrasted against the night, surrounding the motel with a glow. When Samuel looked just outside the car, it was hard to see the broken down gas pumps that weren't ten yards away from him, but he could clearly see the angelic glow of the motel so far out of his reach. It was a glow that held in it all his hopes and dreams. It embodied relief from a world that had become stagnant, useless and unbearable to him.

His mouth watered at the idea that the briefcase might already hold the new life he longed for. It was frustrating to think how close it all was, but still too far away for him to hold.

Over time, sitting on that hill, they received different reports as to where each branch of their team was located. They got confirmation that Torreo was in his room. There was reference to a heat-sensor camera that allowed them to keep track of any attempt by him to leave. The building was surrounded in case he had designs on an unexpected exit. With the airport so close, no one wanted to allow room for him to slip off in the night. Samuel still never saw his teammates. He only heard the assortment of voices passing on information.

Before, Samuel took comfort in how well they kept watch on Torreo; now it was accentuating his frustrations. Now, everyone appeared to be circling a prize they greatly desired but were all incapable of grabbing. It was the way Samuel viewed the world. Everyone was missing something, few sure what it was. People just made circles through life, never actually obtaining what they needed for happiness.

The idea that Torreo had a way to give them all the slip had become somewhat relieving. Samuel almost hoped for it. At least that would give an explanation as to why they were all the way out there. Getting that room was just another in a series of activities that Samuel couldn't make sense out of. His wit and ability to understand were the only things that had never failed him. That they were doing nothing for him now was disheartening. He tried to tell himself that Torreo had the money and a way to make them all think he was in the room while he boarded a nearby plane. Somehow, Samuel knew that wasn't true, but it added sense to what seemed senseless behavior. That gave temporary relief to his frustration.

He tried to take his mind off everything by asking Sly questions. It had failed repeatedly before but with David asleep it was his only option. "So how'd they know where we were located all the time?"

Sly rolled his eyes over to look at Samuel. "There are bugs on all our cars. The navigators' laptops show where we're all at, all the time. They just call to confirm and make sure nothing's amiss. It'd be nice to get one on Torreo's car but the feds never take their eyes off it."

"Navigators?" asked Samuel.

Sly shook his head again. He was bothered by having to explain things to someone beneath him, but he was unable to pass up a chance to describe anything that made him feel powerful. "Each tail is made up of the driver and the navigator. Navigator is the one making all the phone calls. He's also got a laptop that has a lot of map programs. They can keep track of everything and everyone. They can anticipate where they're going. All the computers are connected; they can communicate through them if they have to. It's really a flawless system. Between us having the inside loop and superior equipment, the feds don't really have a chance on this one. It's just a shame you two fucks get to get rich off us."

Samuel was astounded by the insult. Until now he hadn't seen the degree of contempt Sly had for them. Before he just considered Sly naturally poor-tempered. At hearing his anger with the size of their cut, Samuel realized the hatred was more specific. He was glad David wasn't awake to hear the comment.

Samuel laid his head to the door and tried to sleep. At closing his eyes and giving his mind free reign, it raced back to the Cullomine mystery. He mulled over every detail to no end, believing he would never be granted sleep. Then he opened his eyes and the sun was out. He had awoken before he ever realized he'd dozed off.

He looked back to see David sitting up rubbing his face. His skin had that soft disfigurement that said he hadn't been awake long.

"F-u-u-ck," he bellowed. "I'm starving."

Sly had his head leaned back. Until he spoke, Samuel could have only guessed to whether he was asleep or not.

"There's a drive-thru up the road. We're going to order a lot because we ain't stopping again."

"We're gonna eat cold burgers for lunch?" asked David.

"This ain't a luxury cruise," said Sylvester.

Samuel didn't hear any birds chirping. From the look of the day he knew it wasn't early morning. After they had obtained the food and ate their portions in silence, he asked the time.

"10:30," answered Sly gruffly.

Then the phone rang. Samuel looked at it the way a hung over drinker looked at a beer. He felt worn out from the mental roller coaster yesterday's events had put him on. He felt like he'd dreamt about the details of their situation the entire night. Still, he was eager to hear what that phone had to offer.

"Yup," answered Sly.

"He's in the car crossing the street. He just pulled into the gas station." There was a long pause, and then the voice began again. "He's pumped, paid and pulling into traffic—wait, wh-a.. he's going the way we came. He's going away from the airport."

"We're gonna sit tight and let you get some distance ahead. We'll get some gas ourselves. Let us know if he turns; otherwise, I'll call you in about five minutes," ordered Sly as he hung up the phone. Before they had come to a stop in the gas station it rang again. "Yeah."

"This is A; we're trailing the target back down the highway the way we came."

"Are you fucking kidding me?" Sly shook his head in anger. "Maybe the feds let themselves get spotted so he's going for a plan B," he suggested.

Samuel rolled his eyes at the insinuation that Cullomine didn't always know the FBI were on his trail.

"All right, here we come," said Sly.

"This is ridiculous. None of it makes any sense," said an all-the-more agitated Samuel as they began another three-hour journey.

This one went much like the first. They all watched the road as countless little lines passed them by. Samuel tried to anticipate what Torreo would do. There was no bottom to his well of daydreams and theories. There was no telling where they could be getting off next. They were all at the beck and call of this notorious drug dealer. David had described Cullomine as a rat in a maze and them the spectators. But now they were playing the role of the rat and him the cheese. He kept being pulled just out of their reach, beckoning them forward. Despite their lack of knowledge as to where they were going, they continued on in hopes of obtaining the elusive prize.

All the more to Samuel's dismay, Cullomine took the exit leading right back into town, continuing the precedent of senseless behavior.

Before he knew it the long highway drive was over. His anguish was compounded by their return to the beginning. They were back in their home city on conference call listening to the step-by-step pursuit. An entire day of following and nothing had been accomplished. The only difference was Samuel being farther behind than where they had started. What could have been in that hotel room that was worth six hours of driving? Their SWAT had raided the room once they were a safe distance away. Torreo had left nothing behind.

The pursuit was running smooth until more static hit the phones.

"My *fuzz-z-z* no connect *fuzz*," the voice attempted to explain.

Sly again grabbed the walkie-talkie from the glove compartment.

"Did everybody lose signal?"

"Yeah, this is SWAT. I know we did."

"This is team A. We're getting interference on the phones. Everybody communicate through the computers. I'll keep Sly informed on this until the phones are back up. Aw shit. He's pulling into the Dixie grocery store here on Rittenhouse. I repeat, I need everybody to the Dixie Market."

"He's a lucky bastard. He pulled off at the best possible time," said Sly to the rest of the car.

"Sometimes luck is better than smarts," added Samuel.

By the time they had neared the grocery store the phones rang again.

"Yeah."

"Yeah Sly, we're back on conference, we got SWAT following in the store with palm mics."

"This is Goose," came a muffled voice. "I'm following the target past the women's clothing department. This store is very crowded. I'm having trouble . . . I've lost visual. He was last seen moving toward the back . . ."

"Got 'im," came the triumphant tone of a woman. "This is Turtle. I'm near the target. He has the briefcase and is lingering in the produce. No signs of agents."

"This is Rhino; I have an agent here in aisle seven. He doesn't seem to be too concerned with hiding. He's staring at me now . . . he is very interested in me. I'm leaving aisle seven. I'm now in the perpendicular refrigerated aisle along the edge of the building, left from front . . . agent has stopped pursuing."

"This is Turtle; target is coming toward Rhino in refrigerated aisle. He should be in your view, Rhino."

"This is Rhino. I'm stopped and pricing cheese. Target is approaching, briefcase in hand . . . he's passed. He made no recognition of me or agent. He's continuing toward the back left corner, which I believe to be frozen foods."

"This is Goose. I'm still on the right side of the numbered aisles. I'm approaching frozen food section . . . I'm in frozen food section. Ah, I'm looking, I'm looking. Target is not here. I repeat the target is not in back left corner."

"This is Rhino, same position. I can't see him. If he's not in frozen he had to turn down a numbered aisle. I'm attempting to locate."

"This is Turtle. I'm heading up right side of numbers, I'm moving fast; it's hard to see with . . . ah. . ." There was a brief pause before the woman's voice began again. "This is Turtle; target popped out in front of me. I was startled. I think he could tell I recognized him. He looked surprised; he tried to follow me. I lost him near makeup."

"I wonder why he was so interested in her," asked Sly.

"He probably wondered why someone who didn't look like a fed or a Dragon was following him," explained Samuel.

"Fuck!" roared Sly. "You're blowing our cover in there. Has anyone located the target yet?" Their speakers remained dead with silence. "Is anyone out there!?" he yelled again.

"Yes sir, we're out here. I just don't think anyone's found him."

"This is Rhino. I could have followed him near the makeup but not without the agent seeing me. Now he's completely out of view."

"Yes sir, and in this crowd it might take a bit to find him."

"This is Snake. There're a few checkout counters in the back right of the store. He hasn't been back here. I suggest someone head toward the front exits."

"This is Goose. Turtle, you go take up for Snake. Snake, when she gets there you head to the front; Rhino and I are gonna do an organized search."

"You can put a halt on that. This is A. He just came from the front door. He's got the briefcase in one hand and a bag of groceries in the other. B and C, are either of you in view of the target?"

"This is C; I'm at the far South entrance. We cannot see target."

"This is B; we can't see him either. We're at the back doors; you're going to have to pursue, A."

"That's a negative. A is pinned in by agents. There is a car of them right by us. We cannot pursue. Target is passing his car. He is crossing the street on foot. He is heading into the park. It's a crowded park to the east of Dixie. We cannot get him."

"All right, we're pulling around to the front of the park," explained Sly, annoyed that he had to take part. "We're circling the park . . . it's a bad view . . . lots of trees."

"There he is," exclaimed David. "He's sitting on that bench."

Sly pulled out his binoculars to get a better view. "That's a confirmation. We're parking on the southern side of Binder Park. Looks like he's having lunch on a bench."

Samuel thought of all the times he sat and ate on a bench. It was always the same. He ate unappealing food dwelling on how much he hated his life and work. For only a second, he could relate; he felt just a hint of compassion for this hunted man. Here was Cullomine Torreo with his whole life in turmoil. People were out to murder him and snatch the money in his possession. Still, he took the time to pick up food and enjoy the pleasures of eating outdoors. He looked blissful, smiling, basking in the sun, peeling his orange. All the time Samuel had done it and he never derived the enjoyment this abhorred man was. He wondered if a man like Torreo would have preferred his life. If he couldn't have found enough simple pleasures that all this money wouldn't be so necessary. Maybe this man would have gladly traded all these legal woes and criminal conflicts for the calm eventless lifestyle Samuel hated.

"Are you guys regrouped yet?" asked a feisty Sly.

"Yeah, SWAT's back together and I'll come relieve you whenever you're ready."

"Ooh . . . uh . . . shit, this could be something," said an anxious Sly. "He's just been approached by a Latino woman. I can't get a clear shot of her but they're talking." Sly looked in his rearview mirror and cursed at an approaching car. "Damn! Feds are approaching from the rear. We're gonna have to move. We look conspicuous sitting here watching."

"I'll get out," suggested Samuel.

Sly looked at him, tempted but unsure.

"I'm the only one who can confirm whether that's Monique or not. If it's not, I'll walk on by, gettin' an earful on the way."

"You got that phone?" asked Sly.

"Yup."

"We'll pick you up on the opposite side. If that's not gonna work, hit memory one. Don't so much as glance at him and don't you say a fuckin' word."

Samuel hopped out casually. Sly pulled back into traffic before the agents had passed.

Samuel was fine with the idea of doing this but now that he was actually out in the open, his heart was pounding. He started up the sidewalk. The feds glared in his direction as they passed but it was only to get a look at Torreo.

Samuel began by concentrating on his walk. He didn't want to walk too urgently or too slowly. If he seemed out of place they might suspect that he was eavesdropping. Then he reminded himself that thinking about it would be the best way to do it wrong.

He instead turned his attention to figuring out if that was Monique. He couldn't let himself get close enough for her to notice him. The couple in front of him made it hard to get a clear view of the woman. As he recognized the golden brown skin, he became sure he was once again in the presence of that perfect beauty. He started to make designs on the best way to leave the park without her seeing him.

There was an assortment of people, pets and an abundance of trees. He figured his chances were good, but as he grew closer he realized it was desire to be near Monique that made him see her. This woman was plump and older. She seemed newer to the country, still foreign.

As Samuel got close enough he could hear her poor attempt at English. There was no question, she wasn't local. He turned his attention to Cullomine. He could see the sun reflect off his ponytail of curly brown hair and the bits of sweat on the back of his neck. His light gray suit was neatly pressed. For the first time he seemed real. Until now Monique's kingpin love had been merely a figment of imagination. Now, suddenly, he existed and was close enough to touch. Samuel could hear his voice as he passed. It brought home all the more that this was a real man they were dealing with. Figments had no voice of their own.

"Yeah, it's a worthwhile museum. Not a bad walk if you don't want to wait for the bus," he said with a thick Latino accent. He sounded cheery and upbeat. He was happy to be in the park with the sun beating down.

Samuel's wonderment as to how this man could be happy, made him want to turn and look at his face, but he feared it would draw attention.

As he came to the end of the sidewalk he took out his phone and called Sly. "I'm gonna walk another block in this direction in case the feds are circling. Pick me up there. It's not her. He seems to be giving her directions like she's a tourist. He's got the case by his feet. Just make sure the lady doesn't walk away with it."

"Yeah, she's gone already. Case is still there. The teams are back in position with a body in the park. I'll have you that next corner."

CHAPTER 28: WHO'S IN CHARGE?

Sly picked him up at the next corner as planned. They pulled a bit farther down the street, and then parked. All three heads were turned around watching Cullomine eat his lunch through their rear window.

"That's a cool motherfucker. Taking a time out on this thing and eatin' lunch in the park," observed David. "He's either got steel balls or a screw loose."

"I can't decide if he's clever or an idiot. He's still never showed any sign that he knows he's being followed. He'd have to be damn cocky to pull this when he knew the law's on him," said Sly.

"If he snagged that much money and doesn't think these guys are gonna come looking for it, he ain't got no sense. I don't see how a man like that could have reached the status he did," argued Samuel. "I think it's more likely he's trying to convince his audience that he doesn't know they're watching before he makes his real move."

"Yeah, but how would yesterday's drive contribute to that?" asked David.

Samuel just shook his head, unable to respond. "I don't know, man, none of it really adds up. Everything he does seems to contradict something else."

It wasn't long before Cullomine had finished his late lunch and was back in his car.

"All right, this is A. We're back on the move," said the voice, announcing the beginning of another pursuit. "Everybody keep an eye out for these feds. I think there are more of them than before. They're getting antsy. I won't be surprised if they make a move soon. There's one federal sedan two cars in front of me, and the target's directly in front of him. They're not trying real hard to hide themselves. We're turning off Rittenhouse, heading south on to Sprinkle Road."

"This is B. I'm turning south down Morning, two streets east of Sprinkle."

"This is C. I'm on Saint Joseph, heading south, one street west of Sprinkle."

"Okay, SWAT and Sly need to be heading south on Blackhawk Ave."

Samuel was slowly coming to a calm after having received some real PT. All the time he'd spent on the bench made getting in the game a powerful moment. He was taking comfort in being safely back in his position as a spectator, though a part of him longed for a bit more.

"Okay, this is A. Target is turning right onto Sunset Boulevard, which has him heading southwest."

"This is C. I'll pick him up."

"Okay, this is A. I'm turning around and making a left on Lavista, which will have me heading west."

"Yeah, this is B. I'm making a left that has me heading west. There is no parallel street to Sunset. We're both gonna have to make a lot of turns to keep in the same direction. You're just gonna have to let us know when he turns and we'll update on our exact position. But uh, B is to the south of target."

"This is A. We got that same issue as B. We're gonna be to the north of target."

"Understood, gentlemen. This is C. I'm pursuing target southwest on Sunset. I'll let you know as quickly as possible."

"All right, we're gonna want Sly and SWAT to keep heading south on Blackhawk until you reach East Avenue, at which point a right heading west."

A few more moments of silence passed.

"Okay boys. This is C. Sunset comes to a dead end up here so he's gonna be making a turn shortly. Get ready."

"All right, this is A. If you're nearing the dead end on Sunset then we're keeping up with ya pretty well. We'll be ready if he's coming this way."

"That's a ditto for B."

"This is C. He's at the stop here on the end of Sunset but he doesn't have a blinker on. I'm not sure which way he's gonna turn. Okay, he's taking off, he's not turning. He's going straight into the Pat Davis Parking Garage. Uh, this could be what we've been waiting on. The feds are waiting at the stop watching him. They're holding up the traffic behind them. The target has a card out . . . he's swiping it through a machine . . . the garage doors are opening and he's pulling in. . . .the feds are turning and parking on the side of the road here. We need everybody to the end of Sunset to the Pat Davis Parking Garage. This place has a street on each side and a garage door opening to each street. I'm gonna circle around to watch the doors until you guys get here. I don't know how we're gonna get in. It's huge. You got to buy storage time at the front desk and they give you one of those card keys. He's got four exits, a chance to switch cars, and a lot of time with no eyes on him."

"F-u-uck," roared an infuriated Sylvester as he gunned the gas pedal.

"All right, this is A. We need SWAT and Sly to get on Helmer Road and down to this garage as quickly as possible. I'm turning into the donut shop on Fremont Street, which gives me view of the east entrance of the garage. Looks like we got agents at the gas station next door."

"This is B. I'm in a deli facing the west side of the building here. I don't see any stationed agents but there is one that looks to be circling the building. This side has the entrance to the front desk as well as a garage door."

"This is C. I'm gonna go ahead and settle on the northern side of the building. That leaves the southern end where he entered naked."

"This is Sly. I'll be there in less than a minute. I want someone in there on foot immediately, and I don't care if a station wagon with an old lady driving it comes out one of those doors, I want to know about it."

Sly kept the pedal floored and yanked the wheel on each turn until they reached the parking garage.

"This is Sly. I'm parked at a flower shop watching the southern door. Where the hell is SWAT?"

"This is Goose. I'm on a palm mic about to go in the front door. I can try telling him I left my card in my car and see if he lets me in, or I can pay for a card and get a car in but that might take longer."

"This is A. I've been here before. They don't let you walk out the door until you show them your card, to make sure it's not left behind. They don't allow anyone in unless they show the card. There's usually only the one teller, though. You could probably detain them. Then there's a switch they push to open the door to the garage."

"Nah, we don't want to cause a scene yet. Try and buy a card. Keep your earpiece in; if it's taking too long I might change my mind," ordered Sly.

"This is Goose. I'm going in now. Hey, how's it going?" said the operative's faded voice now that he wasn't talking into his hand.

"Hello. What can I do for ya today?" came the sound of the teller lightly through the speakers.

"Well, I'd like to park my car here."

"Okay, just for today or would you like a weekly or monthly membership?"

"Ahh, just today is fine."

"All right, I'm gonna need a picture ID and a credit card."

"Can't I just pay cash?"

"I'm afraid not. You see, the first time you come in we take all your information and print you out your personal membership card. Then you pay for how much time you want on there. If when that time is up you decide you want more then you bring it in and we update it."

"You can head back to the van, Goose. This is C. The target has just come out the northern exit. Nothing tricky about it. He's out here plain as day. He's making a left turn heading west . . . feds are already back on his tail . . . he's taking his first right heading north on Claymore."

"This is B. I'm parked on Claymore. I'll take him."

"This is fucking ridiculous," said Sly. "How long was he in there?"

"I'd say more than five, less than ten," answered an unidentified voice.

"You guys figure there's a mailbox in there?" asked Sly.

"No," answered Samuel. "There's no route that requires a membership card to get in and pick up the mail."

"He's sure keeping everybody guessing," commented David.

"It's like everything is deliberately senseless," agreed Samuel. "Maybe it's all a diversion. Like most magic tricks, you get everybody looking at one thing so they don't notice what you're pulling with the other hand."

Once again they were back in motion riding Torreo's tail. As the step-by-step directions continued Samuel felt more and more like Cullomine's puppets. Instead of a hunted man on the run for his life, he behaved like a carefree child taunting his pursuers. Samuel could remember being a child and holding a piece of food in front of the family dog. He would move the food up and down, left to right and giggle as the dog followed it with his eyes. No matter how long he did it and how pointless it seemed, the dog would not look away. He now felt like the dog in the scenario. It was Torreo who was in charge and he seemed to be having fun with it.

Samuel no longer had the confidence that had visited him before. The way Cullomine had almost slipped away at the store, then the park, and he could have likely lost them at the garage had he made a real effort, it was like he was making his audience uneasy by showing just how capable he was of losing them.

"All right, this is A. He's pulling into a driveway . . . he's out of the car . . . he's got the bag of groceries, the briefcase and he's heading into a house. He's in. It looks like an otherwise empty house. We might need to set up shop. I'd say everybody park where they're at. Sly, if you want to continue up to South Haven Avenue and turn right, you can drive by and make a decision."

"Okay, let's cut the conference call. A, I'll call you back and get the specifics."

Once Sly turned on the street as planned, he picked up his phone and dialed.

"We're coming your way. All right, we're gonna go past," Sylvester stated before hanging up. "Okay, take a look at this last corner house on my side," he directed as he eased to a halt at the stop sign. "That's where he's at."

He continued down the street and took the next left. It was another block before he parked on the side of the road.

"We can't see from here," complained Samuel.

"Yeah, I know. They're gonna keep us updated. We can only have so many people watching on a rural street like this. We're lucky to be this close. They're trying to find out whose house it is and setting up some surveillance. If it looks like he's gonna stay in, we'll probably put you two up somewhere."

It was twenty minutes of uneasy silence before the phone rang again. Sylvester answered it in a calm, firm voice. "Yeah. Really? All right, what about these guys? Yeah." He hung up the phone and passed on his information. "They set up a heat-sensor camera across the street, next to somebody's garage. It's small enough that it could be there for weeks before anybody would notice. It gives a feed to the SWAT van a few blocks away. His body heat lets them see everything he's doing. Right now he's sittin' there watching TV by himself; nobody else is there. House is in a Carl Angelina's name. Could be an alias. Those agents are settling in for a stay. Looks like he'll probably ride out the night there. We got a room waiting for you at that hotel up on Wabash."

"Why would we be staying at a hotel?" asked David.

"We don't want any problems getting you when it's time to go back on the move. It's not like this guy's gonna give us a lot of warning," explained Sly in his trademark hoarse tone. They both nodded in agreement.

It was dusk when the boys were escorted to their room. Neither liked the idea of being trapped at a hotel but at that point, they didn't have the authority to argue.

CHAPTER 29: REVELATION

"All right, if we find something out or I'm coming to get you, then you'll hear that cell ring. If you have something important to say, dial memory one. Don't just call for any bullshit. Other than that, you guys don't leave this fuckin' room. You get hungry, order room service; they'll bring it up." Sylvester spoke like a parent to a hard-to-manage child. As soon as he closed the door that brought a response from David.

"I'm gettin' real sick of that dude. I get pissed off the second I see his mouth start to open. I'm gonna hear that raspy voice talking down to me in my nightmares. I hate him so much."

"Keep your eye on the ball, man," reminded Samuel.

"Shit, don't worry about that. Don't matter how much I hate 'im, I ain't gonna let it fuck things up. I just hope I run into him after all this is over."

"Shit, he ain't nobody I'd want to see alone in an alley or nuttin'," commented Samuel.

"Ah, don't say shit like that. That'll really make me wanna bust him, you start thinkin' I can't," said David.

"I didn't mean it like that. I just mean he looks like he can handle himself, ya know. But what is this put us in a room till you need us again shit. I didn't sign up for nothing like that."

"I feel you, but fuck trying to argue with these guys, eye on the ball and all."

"True," agreed Samuel. He then turned on the TV and the two zombied out while staring blindly at the so-called entertainment.

"How can there be so many fuckin' channels all playing bullshit," said a genuinely bothered David. "Everything on here is for special interests. Can't we have one channel that is designated to making sure there is something halfway worth watching on at all times? No fads, no news, no educational bullshit, just good old fashioned quality reruns. Just play *Cheers* or *Simpsons* all day and I'd be happy. Naw, they gotta get creative with the shit. And what's up with these hip-hop videos? Where are all these tight jeans coming from? These dudes look like they're losing circulation to their nuts. Shit wasn't like this when I went away."

"The suburban gangster movement," agreed Samuel. "They let in all these rappers who grew up safe in the wealthy suburbs. They started bringing in rock and roll trends from those neighborhoods. Now we got Mohawks, jean jackets and what not. It's fuckin' up the whole scene," he explained, happy with the baggy clothes and lower hanging pants they both wore.

"What's the world coming to?" reiterated David.

"Yeah, I don't even got basic cable no more," continued Samuel. "Shit numbs the brain, and the commercials—them things are an insult to the viewer. I stick with movies."

"Yeah?"

"Yeah, they got those cheap seats around the way. Three bucks a flick. It's the movies that left the theaters but ain't on video yet. They know me by name up there."

"We'll have to check it out some time."

"Cool," agreed Samuel before realizing that they might never get a chance for that or anything else their town had to offer. If things worked out they would be gone in a matter of days. He wondered how prepared to leave David actually was. "So you talk to Missy yet?"

David looked up somberly and shook his head. "Naw man, she ain't been home. We haven't even heard from her. I don't think she's ready to see me. She's probably keeping herself so faded that she don't have to think about it. Fuck, I can't believe that girl. This shit works out I'm gonna have to flip this town over to find her. I wasn't there for one sibling; I'm not gonna make that mistake again."

"You're too hard on yourself," said Samuel.

"Maybe, but I tell ya, if something happened to her, that Lorenzo Cole would be in trouble. He don't understand how far I'm willing to go to make things right for Kris. Lookin' out for Tim or not, if it wasn't for me wanting to take up for Missy you better be sure I'd be going after that little dog lover, and fuck Cole if he did try and stop me. I'm not scared of that twisted motherfucker. Bullet take his life as quick as anybody's. Dude be talking all that if we mess up he's gonna kill us and our family shit, fuck him. He's threatening himself when he says that. That just lets me know how I gotta handle things if it comes to it."

"Yeah, I hear you. I don't like 'im neither. He's on some delusions of grandeur trip, but I do believe he's for real. He's built his entire livelihood on doing what he says he's gonna do."

"Well, we ain't gonna be testin' 'im anyway. There ain't gonna be no mistakes," David confidently reassured.

"That's what I like to hear. But this fuckin' Torreo's really buggin' me. I can't figure how he'd expect to lose his tails with the shit he was doing, and why would he waste time sitting in that house while he's still got the loot? I'd understand if he'd dropped the prize in the mail but when did he have a chance?"

"He didn't go near any mailboxes."

"True, true . . . wait a minute," said Samuel with a returned spark in his eye. "He didn't have to. Maybe it's just like I said. It is a diversion. He's keeping everybody watching him till the money is safe. He got it in the mail from the jump and he's been toying with his crowd ever since. There was no need for him to go to a mailbox. If he did he'd have to pull some trick to make sure no one saw him put it in. That'd be risky. The easiest way for him to handle it would be to just ask the bank to put it with their outgoing mail, easy as that. He probably already had it sealed in a box and ready to send. He goes in, takes the briefcase out of the deposit box, takes the package out of the case, gives them the package to mail, maybe some money for postage, then emerges with the briefcase to keep all eyes on him. It's perfect—an alternate way to mail it. I can't believe it took me so long."

"I guess it makes sense, but how would he make his getaway?"

"Well, with everybody ogling that case he could probably use it as another diversion somehow, make them choose between him and the case. But the truth is we still don't know what his plan is but more importantly, we don't care. As long as we know how to get the money, it's not our problem; the feds and Dragons can worry about his big exit."

"This guy's a real piece of shit. Using his girl and son to take the risk of smuggling money for him. Dickless dealer, I wish I could see the look on his face when he gets to the rendezvous and there's no prize. He'll pro'ly take it out on her. If he even makes it to their rendezvous," said David, unable to take his eye off his anticipated bonus prize of a notorious drug pusher.

"I'm calling Sly. They should be aware that it's pro'ly already en route to Monique's," explained Samuel with a newfound enthusiasm. A weight was lifted off his shoulders by finally finding a way to put the puzzle's pieces together that didn't leave him confused about a leftover detail. He picked up the phone and pressed memory one as was suggested. There was barely a complete ring before Sylvester answered.

"Yeah."

"Hey man, it's Samuel."

"W'the fuck, I was just about to call you. We got a few more developments."

"Really? What?"

"Lorenzo's finally heard back from his agent friend. He's not really connected to the task force following Torreo, but he's been trying to get info and finally has. Seems you guys are right that they don't know nothin' about this Monique, and we left it that way. But it's the FBI's, of course, unofficial position that the money is in that case. We're startin' to agree with 'em. Figure he probably doesn't want to have to deal with a girl and kid on his hip if he doesn't have to. He's just going to try and lose everybody and make off on his own. He probably has sending the loot to her as a backup plan in case he runs into trouble. He told her he'd send it so she'd be ready if he did. If he's just gonna try and slip off, we don't want to wait around for his next move. On top of that, the feds are gettin' antsy and we don't want to risk them moving before us. It's on the board now to raid the house, maybe as soon as tonight."

"Ah fuck, man, if we go in now and it ain't there, we'll have blown our position completely," argued Samuel.

"Yeah, but if that's the money with him, we don't need a position; we'll have it. And where the fuck else would the money be? You think he's just going to leave it in hiding? The guy doesn't have the time for that."

"I agree, but he's not gonna go get it, then just sit in some house waiting for everyone to come take it from him. Whatever time he has is over the instant the feds get their money. To even walk out of that bank would be a risk. If it was the money and the feds snagged it he'd be easy pickin's for the DC. He doesn't want to have it on him any longer than he has to. That's why I called you. More than likely he just boxed it up and asked the bank to put it in the outgoing mail. Now everyone is distracted by him while it gets sent to her. If he left immediately the law might have snooped around and found out he mailed something. He just waits around to keep everybody interested while it has some time to safely arrive at Monique's, then he makes his move. If we go in, then he knows more people have been watching than just the law. Since he can't be sure what we know, he might give her the heads-up, or try and retrieve it himself. We like where things are at right now. We know just enough more than everybody else and it's gonna pay off. The last thing we want to do is change the course things are taking."

"Hu-g-h-h," sighed Sylvester, who didn't like the idea of more waiting. "Well, I'll call the boss and let him know what you said. If he did already mail it, how long before it gets there?"

"It could get there as soon as tomorrow and I'd say no later than three days from now. I think we should also get confirmation that he is the one settin' off those heat sensors. He could have had someone there and slipped out the back or something. Besides, I don't think we have to worry much about the feds rushing anything. They think they got him cornered."

"All right, I'll call you back," said Sly, followed by a click.

"Sounds like they're gettin' antsy," commented David.

"Yeah, but they don't want it to go wrong any more than we do. Lorenzo couldn't stand the idea of making a wrong decision. They're still listening so we're cool," reassured Samuel.

"Yeah, I hope so. I tell you I keep gettin' that feeling like shit's gonna go bad. You know, like when you'd be in a store, about to steal something and you just get a feeling like you better not." Samuel turned his head, surprised by the uncharacteristic confession by his friend. "It's just high stakes is all, man. I probably just want it to work so bad that it's making me worry. Besides, like we said what the fuck else we got to do?" said David.

Samuel turned back to facing the TV. He was becoming worn by the continuous ups and downs his emotions were being put through. One moment he was frustrated by his inability to decipher what Cullomine had been doing, the next he was enthused by achieving a working theory, which was now undermined by finding out that David was capable of worry, let alone had doubts about their success in this. It was disheartening for Samuel to see David, who commonly served as a symbol of his own confidence, be anything but cocky about his ability to come out on top.

They both watched the inane programming in a daze. It was safe to say that neither one of them were giving it any real attention. They had more interesting thoughts to occupy their minds. After a long, thick silence David finally asked another question that caught Samuel off guard.

"Do you believe in God, man?"

"Shit!" responded Samuel at the heavy subject. Then he looked at the genuine emotions stirred up in his friend's face, causing him to take the question seriously. His tone changed to a somber one as he looked up at the ceiling in search of his honest answer. "Yeah, man. Yeah, I do. It's not like I been to church in a long time or nothin' but sometimes when things were real bad, when I felt like I was gonna just cave in on myself, I'd pick up that old Bible of my dad's. The first time was because I wanted to take my mind off things and there wasn't a lot else to read. But when I'd be sitting there reading it, everything would get real chill, you know. The whole room would just seem so calm. It's like I was always on fire but for those brief moments it would cool the flames. And it's not like I'm somebody who always prays before they go to bed or nothin', but every once in a while you'll be going along and you'll hear that little voice saying do this, or don't do that, and you just know if you ignore that voice you'll officially become one of the bad guys. I could count on my hands the times in my life I actually heard it. But it's always like, oh yeah, you. I forgot about you. You never steer me wrong. It's like everything you done wrong in your whole life added up together won't be as bad as ignoring that little sound and I can honestly say I never have. I've never really decided that was God, but I guess deep down, I think it is in a way, maybe a part of him."

"Yeah, I know exactly what you're talking about. And you know, sometimes when I'd be watching the news in jail, shit would seem so fucked up out here. I guess I always felt like I was a hoodlum 'cause I liked to be, but the rest of the world was doing what they're supposed to. But then, if you take a look at the so-called good citizens and shit, nobody is doing what I at least thought good people were supposed to. You never hear anybody talking about the really important things. People's idea of a crucial news story is something that affects their pocketbooks. I feel like God is out there but nobody's paying him enough attention. He's a neglected parent. It's like today's world doesn't invite him in it, then we wonder why kids are killing each other, families can't get along and all that other horrible shit. That's what was making me ask about Samuel and David of the Bible that night. Sometimes when I'm trying to figure out how to make things better, I start to feel like whatever is supposed to be out there to make things work just ain't out there. Sometimes I wonder if that's why. Fuck if the Posties heard me saying shit like this."

"You cannot plant flowers in rocky soil and still expect them to grow right."

"What?"

"Oh, it was one of those stories I wrote in high school. It was more about how people can't grow without love. But it's the same concept. Society is man's soil. There are things necessary in it for man to grow properly, and I have to agree with you, something is missing. Perhaps it is God."

"Yeah, that's exactly what I'm trying to say. What about like karma—do you believe in karma?"

"Damn, man!" said an astounded Samuel. "What are we, in the wrong chairs or something? I'm the one who always asked the philosophical questions and you were uninterested. Besides, karma is kind of a contradictory philosophy style more than a religion. You're switching beliefs here."

"Well, I guess I don't know the actual definition of karma. I just mean some natural law that means you can't do somebody wrong without having something bad happen to you," explained David.

"Karma, God, things changed up top, didn't they? Back in the day you wouldn't even consider that there was anything out there with more control than you."

"I guess I stopped feeling in control a long time ago," admitted David.

"Shit, nothing wrong with that. Control is an illusion anyway. Some people are just better than others at fooling themselves." Samuel looked up at the ceiling again, as if caught off guard by his own words. "What you're talking about is close to karma. In Biblical terms it would probably be 'you reap what you sow'. I believe in it, but I don't really have a place for it in my life. I don't know, man. I don't really worry about how I treat other people anymore. I used to try and be a good person who looks out for others; I'd go out of my way to make sure I didn't fuck anybody else's shit up. I didn't mind stealing from a business that makes its money off the little man's sweat, but I couldn't ever steal from the little man. I ain't really like that no more. I don't worry about it. It's like I would look around and nobody was worried about me. Even more, nobody was worried about anybody but themselves. Everyone is trying to improve their own position as best they can and fuck anybody who doesn't help their cause. Sometimes it's misleading 'cause people will still get married and shit, but if you think about it, usually that's only 'cause people need interaction. It's still about what they're after. Chick falls in love with a dude, it's for her sake not his. She don't really give a piss bout him; she just needs a man in her life and thinks he can fill the void. Even in a working relationship, how often do you see two people really concerned about what the other one needs? For me now, man, I really don't give a shit 'bout most people; till I see someone who ain't just lookin' out for them, I'm not gonna. So fuck karma, Ima go for mine."

"I feel you. As far as what we're doing, though, it's cool to me regardless. Even if I wasn't gettin' the money I got no problem snaggin' it from a dealer just so he don't have it. But that's not really what I'm talking about. I'm not asking if it's okay. I'm saying can it work. I mean is it possible for us to build a happy life based on what we stole from somebody else? Can the world ever really work that way? Can the rest of our lives turn out good if we base it on this act, on taking something that ain't ours, even if it shouldn't be theirs?"

Samuel looked at David, pausing in hopes that a worthwhile answer would come to him, but it didn't. "Fuck, man. I guess we'll find out." David nodded his head approvingly, happy to see his doubts wouldn't stop Samuel from pursuing what they longed for. The heavy moment was broken by the phone ringing.

"Yo," answered Samuel.

"Yeah. It's me. You guys got it put off again," said an angered Sylvester. He didn't like being held at bay. If he had power he was one who was quick to use it. There was no desire to refrain or wait for the proper time. If they were capable of moving he wanted to. He couldn't make himself worry about whether the money was actually in the case. "This is just gonna give Torreo more chance to pull something but you got Cole all in a bunch. He doesn't like how up in the air everything is. He says SWAT is going to keep watching everything she's doing, but we're supposed to go over there every day for the mail deliveries, so you guys can ID the package if it comes. He's givin' it three days. If she ain't got nothin' by then and he still ain't made his move, we're going in. In three days, no matter where he's at, we're snagging the briefcase. I just hope we haven't missed our chance by then. We had somebody stealth to the back window of the house, 'bout an hour ago. He's definitely in there. Just him sittin' there, watching TV like he didn't have a care in the world. Cocky fuck."

"I don't think it's a good idea to have too many people around her house. She will notice anything fishy and it might tip our hand," informed Samuel.

"Don't worry about that, these guys are professionals at not being seen. We are gonna be up the street with our binoculars. She ain't gonna notice nobody. What time do you think she'll be gettin' her mail?"

"I delivered around noon; this guy will probably be a little later."

"A'ight, I'll be pickin' you guys up a little before noon, assuming Torreo hasn't gone on the move yet; then it'd be sooner. I can't see him holing up there much longer. He'll move soon."

"Well, you know where we'll be," commented Samuel. He got no response, just another click.

CHAPTER 30: DAILY DUTIES

It was a restless sleep for Samuel that night. The concerns of his friend had made their way to being the most unruly of guests in his mind. He kept trying to take his thoughts off what could go wrong, but it was no time before the concerns had completed the manifestation, as most of his feelings did, into a daydream.

It was long occupied by the David versus Sylvester scenario. It would replay a little differently each time but usually with the same theme. Things would be going just right. They would have a beautiful outlook, then Sylvester would make one too many insults and David would lose it. He'd swing a staggering blow on Sly, who wouldn't waste his efforts with a fight; he'd pull out his gun and kill David on the spot. Samuel would look around for witnesses or police or any reason why his friend couldn't be murdered so casually, but there would be none. It would rest on his shoulders to deal with it. In some versions of the story he'd make a futile attempt at Sly, who would kill him as nonchalantly as he had David. In others Samuel would keep his cool, act like he never cared for David and his impulsive ways. Then when the guard was down he'd make a go for the gun, or stick a fork in his throat during a lunch stop. But he'd never get to the gun in time and he didn't have the luxury of no witnesses at the restaurant. It seemed no matter how the story went, it went bad.

Then after that scenario had been played to its end, the merciless fantasies took a more emotional pace. They would star Monique and his betrayal toward her. He would do all he could to get Cole's men to the house at the right time. They would go in, make the snatch, then decide there was no use in witnesses and kill her and young Cullomine both. Their deaths would forever weigh on his shoulders, and the money would remove his last remnants of ambition. He would lie alone, sulking in a hotel room, until David couldn't remain to witness it. Eventually he would take his own life. The efforts he had taken to escape his suicide in turn would bring it to a head, a Shakespearean tragedy with him as the real victim. There were simpler versions as well. They would successfully snag the money and be fleeing the scene when he would look back to see Monique's creamy brown eyes staring at him in pain. He would have taken his mask off too soon and she would witness his betrayal. She would burst into tears, trying to figure out what she had done to make such a nice man turn on her so blatantly. Again his guilt would be overwhelming, eventually leading to the same end.

He continued such thoughts until eventually the negativity that kept him awake wore him out. He rolled into a broken, exasperated sleep. He was grateful that he rarely remembered his night's dreams, for they would likely surpass the pessimism that had led him there.

It was not earlier as Sylvester had predicted but close to noon when he called their cell phone. Samuel, who at hearing it became at best, half-awake, answered sluggishly.

"I'm on the way. Be ready."

"A'ight," agreed Samuel, hanging up the phone. "Yo. David!" he hollered as he threw his pillow to the bed his friend was lying in.

"What, man!" he replied frustrated by the disturbance.

"Wake up! Dude's on the way."

"Yeah, a'ight," David rustled his hands through his hair a few times, then sat up and gave an empty stare at the walls while his mind slowly gained full consciousness. "Man, we gotta get something to eat. How long before he gets here?" He turned to get his reply and saw Samuel had fallen completely back asleep.

"Damn motherfucker! How you gonna wake me up and then go back to sleep yourself?" said David, trying to mask his amusement while belting Samuel's feet.

"Yeah. Huh! What? I'm up," argued Samuel.

"Yeah, you up," agreed David sarcastically. "What'd I just say then?"

"You said . . . wake up," answered Samuel with the only thing he could think to say.

"Yeah, anyway," laughed David. "How long 'fore he gets here?"

At the close of that sentence was another ring of the phone. Samuel's eyes flung open as he looked at David like a child who was late for school.

"Shit!" He jumped up and started scurrying to find his shoes while he answered the phone. "Yo."

"Come on," the voice returned.

"We on the way down."

Both boys walked out the door still situating themselves and putting their over shirts on.

"Nice hair," razzed David as he looked up at the chaotic appearance of Samuel's head.

"Yeah, thanks. It took me all night," said Samuel, joining in the joke.

When they reached the car Sylvester shook his head at the sight of them. He had been out of the military for years but he still woke with the sun every day, regardless of how late he had stayed up. It embodied his feelings about them to see they had just got out of bed. He had countless opinions about the occupants of the neighborhood he had come to work in. To him these two were the epitome of everything he disliked in his coworkers. He considered them lazy, unmotivated, scared and weak. He wished his boss, whom he had the utmost respect for, would be slower to take jobs with these types.

As soon as they got back in the car David returned to his previous agenda. "We gonna grab something to eat?"

"You should have gotten up sooner and ordered some room service," returned Sylvester, infuriated by David's lack of focus on the job they were doing.

"Yeah, well, I didn't. So let's go through a drive-thru or something." Again David's sentence was ended with a ring. This time it was Sylvester's phone.

"Yeah. Good timing, we're on the way now." *Click.* "That was them; they just seen the mail truck pull down a side street."

David shook his head at the fact that his hunger would go on being neglected.

Samuel was made uneasy when they pulled on to Emerald Boulevard. He hadn't been there since that hazy memory of his drunken visit was formed. He felt unwelcome, like his presence on that street was a burden.

Sylvester didn't even pull on her block. He parked down farther and handed Samuel the miniature telescope. "Here, watch through this."

Though the mailman wasn't coming yet, Samuel looked through it to locate Monique's house. After some fiddling, he was able to locate her front porch and bring it into focus. It looked so peaceful, almost as inviting as it had always been. He hadn't realized until now how much he missed going there. His life had been such a barren routine just weeks ago, and going there had provided a flash of joy. That house had been an oasis in the burning desert. It was strange to him that he was now there with such different intentions.

As he continued to look around in hopes of locating his replacement, he noticed a van across the street. "Is that our guys in the van?" he asked.

"Yeah, that's them," replied Sylvester, who was looking through a pair of binoculars as well.

David rustled around in his seat, agitated by his hunger and inability to watch the show.

"Man, that's too obvious. She's gonna notice."

"It's easy to notice when you're looking for it, but when a person is going through the motions of their day-to-day routine, it's amazing what they'll miss," explained Sylvester.

"I could see where that would usually be the case. But she doesn't have a day-to-day routine. She just sits around that house waiting for her package to arrive. She doesn't have much else to think about and she's sharp as a tack. Trust me, she'll notice a van sittin' out there. Shouldn't they be using one of those cameras?" argued Samuel. David sat up in his seat, noticing how much respect Samuel had for this woman.

"Those things aren't cheap. We don't use them unless we have to."

"Well, I'd say this is one of those 'have to' times."

"That's not your department," said Sly coldly, paying Samuel's concerns little attention.

"Well fuck, I'm lettin' whoever's department it is know they fuckin' up, 'cause she's gonna notice."

Sly didn't bother responding; he just went back to watching for the mailman. He'd had enough of these boys' observations. In his opinion, they hadn't done anything but slow him and his team down.

Samuel also gave up the conversation and went back to watching, but it was a long wait before the mailman made his approach. During the wait, Samuel slowly became more comfortable with his return to these surroundings, and as he did, he made realizations about what had separated them to begin with.

The idea that he wasn't welcome was unrealistic. What Monique did was necessary to take care of her plan with Torreo, but it was almost assured she would still like to have contact with Samuel. She was a kind-hearted person. She wasn't the type who could be comfortable causing someone pain. She would probably be delighted to see him again and have a chance to clear the air. He had to think of how his drunken verbal attack on her was more about his fears and personal issues than anything she had done. She had never really rejected him or attempted to make him feel out of place. She knew it wasn't smart to begin a relationship that could never go anywhere. That was no reason for him to be angry with her. Before, he had told himself she used him for her personal agenda, but really she had no need to take their acquaintance beyond letting him know of her important delivery. Everything after that was genuine. He tried to tell himself otherwise when he had run away from her and back to his safe borough of negativity. In truth that was just an excuse to do what was easy. He wasn't living like that anymore. He no longer gave what was easy any value. He was better off facing what came his way in spite of how difficult it might be. As of now he had to face that he had been the problem in their relationship, not Monique.

When the mailman showed up, Samuel recognized him. He was a new kid named Shad Herrera. Samuel wondered if this rookie had been designated to take the route permanently. For a moment he felt like a dog needing to piss on his territory, but he quickly blew off such feelings as silly.

When Shad arrived on her porch, he began reaching toward the mail slot but instead was greeted at the front door. Samuel's heart jumped at the sight of her. He'd been trying so hard to not even think of her that it made her image all the more potent. In the way a deeply hungry person enjoys their meal, so did he enjoy the sight of Monique. She appeared as a golden-skinned angel. All at once he remembered the warmth she provided him, how kind her tone of voice was, how interested in him she had been and how accepted that made him feel. Samuel had many times described people as selfish creatures concerned with little outside their personal wants and needs, but Monique most certainly did not fit that description. It was not her selfishness that noted how quickly he drank his beverages, nor did it cause her to always come up with the proper advice to help with his problems. Many people gave advice only because it made them sound wise, waitresses brought him refills only to raise their tip, but those ways weren't Monique's. She was kind toward him without any self-serving motive behind it.

Now, it was bitterly ironic that the selfishness of man was causing him to wrong the least selfish person he had ever known. Samuel wondered how he could continue to ignore that. He was overwhelmed with a need to jump out of that car and rush off to talk to her. He wanted to apologize for how he'd behaved and enjoy another conversation over one of her home-cooked meals. Even more, he wanted to be the one to deliver her package and see her face light up when it finally arrived. It was a small step in the efforts he should take to thank her kindness and apologize for his accusations.

Then, like a rock thrown in a pond came recognition of how contradictory those thoughts were to his goals at hand. It came crashing in, disrupting the calm pleasantness the sight of Monique had given him. He quickly accepted he could not let that pleasantness enter his mind again. It would disrupt all he and David had planned. He pushed it down deep and away. He made note that he couldn't have another drink until all this was over. Alcohol always allowed the thoughts and feelings he pushed away to come barreling back in. He couldn't risk his fondness for Monique being considered again until their prize was obtained, or gone for good.

"Doesn't look like anything special, does it?" asked Sylvester.

"Nah. Just some junk mail," answered Samuel.

"A'ight, let's get out of here."

"Cool, where we going?" asked David.

"I'll be taking you guys back to the hotel. They got Torreo bugged now too. There hasn't been so much as a phone call yet. He's still just watching TV. There's nothing for us to do until he goes on the move again. If he hasn't moved in the meantime we'll just be waiting until we do this again tomorrow."

"Well, then what the fuck are we going to the hotel for?" asked an outraged David. "We got the phone and we definitely got better things we could be doing for the rest of the day. I'm hungry; I need some clothes so I can shower and change and shit."

"That's not up to you. I gotta call and check now, but more than likely you're going back to the hotel."

After passing a few blocks, Sly pulled to the side of the road and got out of the car to make his phone call in private. David stirred in the back seat, frustrated with the way he was being bossed around, even after his return to the free world.

Samuel wasn't giving the phone call or David's anger much attention. To his surprise, his thoughts of Monique were not so easily pushed aside. He could ignore a dead-end life and his own self-loathing, but Monique lingered. It was now clear what his fears consisted of the night before. He had been justifying his actions and attitude by dwelling on the hollowness of the world around him. By looking at the selfishness and individuality of everyone else, by considering how the world had disregarded him, he was attempting to condone committing a robbery to get where he wanted in life. But Monique was the contradiction to that hollowness he dwelled on. She had been anything but selfish and never disregarded even the smallest detail of him. He tried to tell himself it was the evil drug pusher Cullomine Torreo and a bunch of crooked cops' money he was taking, not Monique's. He pretended to believe that Torreo was probably just using her to get the money where he wanted before he ditched her. Deep down he didn't believe those things but it was the only way he could combat the mounting guilt.

Sylvester got back in the car. "We're taking you back to the spot. It's pretty much the same drill. I'll come get you if Torreo moves, and otherwise I'll pick you up the same time tomorrow."

To Samuel's pleasure, David didn't argue past the grim expression he planted on his face. Once they got back in their room, however, he released the fumes.

"Man, whoever said we was gonna be their prisoners for a week? We gotta sit up in here so they can keep tabs on us, fuck that. What difference does it make where we're at? You can get anywhere in this town in ten minutes. When is our timing ever so crucial that we can't spare ten minutes? Fuck, they got an eye on everybody. It's not like we're gonna lose him. Dude is just mad 'cause he can't do shit else while he's on this job and so he don't want us to be able to neither."

"I think we're right on target with the shit already being in the mail. Which means Cullomine pro'ly ain't gonna make his real move till he thinks ol' girl has the loot, which means we won't be hearing from Sly till tomorrow," explained Samuel. "You can call somebody to come get us if you want. I got the phone and all; if he does try to call, fuck, it ain't that big a deal."

David flopped down to a sitting position on the end of the bed. "Nah man. I don't want to call Mouse so he'll keep his distance till this whole thing is over and anybody else'd be curious why we're here. Nah, fuck it, I'll leave well enough alone. Sportin' dirty gear is a small price to pay for what we're after. I just need to call ol' girl, hear her voice and it'll calm me down."

"Well, I'll go down, order us some grub and shit, give you some privacy. Plus I don't wanna stink up the room so I'll use the lobby bathroom to take a dump."

"'Preciate it, man, but I think you'd be better off if you left one."

"Yeah, yeah," said Samuel as he walked out the door.

He dragged out his errands as much as he could to allow David and Jamie time to talk. It was about twenty minutes before he ran out of ways to stall and headed back to the room. He would never expect David to be able to spend that much time talking, so it made for a small surprise when he returned to see him still holding the phone.

"... nah, I'm for real. Whatever, I'm sorry I haven't seen you. It might be another day or two, but I'm taking care of things, then you won't be able to get rid of me. You gonna wish you had some time away like you got now. Yeah, right. Well, I gotta go, though. Yup, I'll be hollerin' at ya... peace," spoke David before hanging up the phone.

That night and the following day followed much of the same routine. Samuel and David wasted away the evening with television, Samuel had his now-routine trouble getting to sleep, and then they were woken by the ringing of Sylvester's call. They accompanied him to observe a relatively eventless Emerald Boulevard, and then they were dropped off to be cooped up in their hotel room for more inane waiting.

CHAPTER 31: A PRINCESS IN RAGS

About an hour into their next mind-numbing stare at the television, David picked up the hotel phone.

"Who ya callin'?" asked Samuel.

"A cab. We gotta get the fuck out of here for a while. We'll go visit Ma Dukes."

"Sounds good. Any change of scenery will help me out."

Samuel wasn't worried when they took a breather from their project and went to visit David's mother. He had become quite comfortable with the belief that Cullomine would be spending a few days in that house.

When they did arrive back at the old Caine home it was somewhat amusing for Samuel. He could look up and down the street and think of a story or time he partied in almost every residence on the block. He could see the yard where David had dealt with Tim. He could see the porch swing where Mouse lost his cherry while he and David watched from the window. He could see the front yard of Angela Arms that Kris and his friends had covered in trash, boxed up junk and street signs one drunken evening when they had nothing better to do. For Samuel, it was like returning to an old playing field for a retired football star. He was flooded with memories of good times and gossip-worthy events. He wondered if David, who had spent his whole life there, ever felt the same way. It was all so natural to him that he never seemed to consider those good times of the past worthy of much attention.

David didn't bother knocking when they approached the door; they just walked in as if returning from a daily trip to the corner store.

"Dav-i-d!" exclaimed his mother, delighted at the sight of him.

"Hey Mama," he returned as he gave her a hug.

The boys both joined her in sitting at the kitchen table, while Samuel shook his head. He was always amazed at the warm greetings this family gave one another, yet rest assured, in no time, they would take their positions on a verbal battlefield and begin arguing mercilessly.

Mother Caine was sitting at the table enjoying a beer and cigarette when they entered. After the greeting, she grabbed them each a beer out of the refrigerator without the bother of asking if they wanted them.

"Mind if I spark this joint?" David asked as he reached toward the remains of a marijuana cigarette on the edge of the ashtray.

"Don't you gotta piss for the PO?" she inquired.

"Yeah, but I know how to take seals, unlike your ass."

"David, I told you. Now they didn't give me no warning for that. It was a random surprise thing or I would have definitely drank the vinegar, took the blockers and everything else I could have thought to do."

"Mm-hmm," said David in a patronizing tone as he took a hit and passed to his mother. She accepted it while shaking her head at her son's attitude of superiority she should have long been used to.

"So you're at Koyoe now, I heard," asked Samuel, making reference to Mother Caine's job change.

"Yeah, I have been for about a year now," she affirmed.

"How do you like it?"

"It's nice. The pay isn't as good but they don't ride you like they do at Denzo. I should be hired in soon."

"Shit!" exclaimed David. "Rollin' up on fifty years old and you about to get hired in at another factory. You should be talkin' about how long it's gonna be before you retire and you just gettin' in somewhere."

"Oh, fuck you, David. You don't need to say shit like that. It's hard enough on me as it is."

David just leaned back and smiled. It was another sign of his change. In the past he would have been set into battle by the curses and it would have quickly become an all-out yelling match for the following minutes. Instead he just relaxed, accepted the joint she was returning to him and thought about what she said.

"Oh, I'm sorry," she said to Samuel. "Did you want this?"

"No thanks, I'm cool," he answered.

"Yeah, Samuel here is a nonsmoker. Even back in the day we only got him blowed a few times," explained David.

"Yeah, it wasn't never my thing," he agreed.

"He just likes drinking till he can't see straight," razzed David.

"Nah. I try and avoid that nowadays too."

"So Ma, you gonna take that trip down to Florida to see Aunty Brenda anytime soon?" David asked, changing the subject.

"Oh, I don't have the money for that right now. As soon as I win this lotto, though, I'll be down there livin' it up," she explained as she lifted the ticket that was sitting on the table. "Speaking of which, they'll be announcing the numbers here in a minute. I'll be right back." She hopped out of her chair and into the connecting living room, where she turned on the TV. She actually seemed excited, as if her chances were within reason.

"Fuck," said David as he shook his head in disappointment. "You'll never change. The list of things you're gonna do when you win the lottery is longer than you could ever remember. Everything you ever want or need to do, you put off till you win it big in the lotto. 'I'll start exercising when I have the time after I win', 'I'll spend more time with my grandkids after I win', 'I'll fix up the house after I win'. You know, some people would just discipline their spending for a while and save up to take that vacation they want. Not you. You'll just keep waitin' for that big moment before you'll bother living your life."

"Yadda yadda yadda. Don't you worry your little head about me. You just wait and see, today'll be the big day and you'll be eatin' your words," said an unfazed Mrs. Caine.

"How can she remain so optimistic about something so impossible?" said David, turning to Samuel. "It's not like she acts that way just 'cause she thinks it's funny, like some people. She really believes deep down she's destined to win. She doesn't doubt anywhere in that little brain of hers."

"Ring. Ring," came the phone on the kitchen wall.

"Can you get that for me, honey?" called Ms. Caine from the next room.

"Yeah," answered David as he picked up the phone. He suddenly appeared startled and began situating himself in his seat "Hey, how ya doin'? I was startin' to think Ma was lying about you still livin' here in town . . . right . . . yeah. Well, why don't we get together somewhere . . . He can come along, I won't sweat it. Yeah, Samuel's with me anyway . . . a'ight, about an hour then . . . okay." Samuel watched David, waiting for a description of what just happened. "That was Missy. I don't think she expected it to be me answering. Anyway we're gonna meet down at the Griffon in about an hour. I figured we could use the chance to get out of here. I'm a call another cab. You got the phone in case Sly calls, right?"

"Oh yeah, don't worry about it," answered Samuel, giving his approval to the plans.

The cab arrived in just over a half an hour, which got the boys to the Griffon pub a little early. The Griffon was a low-key bar in the center of downtown. Its location made for a large variety of clientele. Everything from local hoodlums to middle aged homemakers meeting for chit-chat to college kids pre-drinking before they crossed the street to the popular club were common attendees.

The boys didn't notice anyone they knew when they walked in. They took a seat in the corner and ordered their drinks. Samuel figured David planned to be there early so he could get comfortable with the place before Missy arrived. Samuel didn't believe he had ever seen David visibly nervous before. This was a first.

It was likely that David spent much of his incarcerated time building fear that Missy hated him because of the way things played out. When she avoided seeing him upon release, David likely took it as confirmation. That plus hearing from his friends and family about how bad a drug problem Missy had was making this a very uneasy reunion. In his mind, seeing for himself how bad she was would be seeing how bad he had messed things up. Samuel had to sympathize with David's uneasy state.

Samuel also had to sympathize with how Missy surely felt. She likely took as much or more responsibility for what took place as David did. It was over her that David had been locked up and Kris killed. The burden must have been surreal. From having known the girl in her youth, Samuel could have predicted she would drown these pains away in drugs and wild living. More frightening to Samuel now was that Missy had never been the type to admit to herself she felt guilty for anything. She was one to hide her guilt behind everyone else's wrongdoing. She probably built an explanation for her current state that largely consisted of her family's faults. Samuel feared that if things got too serious during this visit, she'd lash out at David with words she didn't really mean. She was likely as nervous as or more nervous than her brother and might take even the harshest opportunity to escape from the heavy situation. David was in no condition to handle any attacks from his baby sister.

Samuel watched his friend sip at his drink. He wanted to warn of what he felt was the likely outcome of this meeting. But what could he say? If he warned of Missy's potential emotional attack, David wouldn't attribute that warning to Samuel's acute sense of human behavior. He would consider that Samuel felt an attack was warranted and it would reaffirm his need to take responsibility for those things that were far beyond his control. This dilemma was not uncommon for Samuel. He always saw things clearer than others but usually hadn't the ability to share that insight. Not being able to show them what he could see was, at times, a torture to him.

When Missy finally walked in the front entrance both of them studied her appearance. They had heard of how strung-out she looked. She wasn't nearly as bad as they might have imagined but somehow seeing how bad she was in person was worse than the horrid sight they had pictured. She was always exceptionally thin but now it was different. She seemed withered, a bit worn away, not completely, but enough to give pain to a caring sibling.

She was accompanied by a boyfriend. Samuel could see now why David had to promise not to bother him. He was clearly not someone David would have approved of. He was a grungy type, whose pupils conveyed his years of drug abuse. Samuel could picture his kind just by a look at his face. He was one whose soul had drowned in his stupors long ago. His mind and body both behaved completely out of the system experience had programmed them with. He was like a social robot. He only reacted. He could no longer learn or truly decide. To others he might seem quite personable, but that was only because that's how a person had to behave to get along in this world. He didn't decide who he liked or disliked. He treated almost everyone completely the same. He acted only out of animal-like need. He was probably one who snorted lines and when his mind began racing he'd spout off hours of philosophical circles that added up to nothing. His druggie underlings were likely amazed by his deep understandings of the world that proved they all knew something everyone else didn't which was why it was okay for them to piss their lives away to the addictions they pretended were innocent. Spending time with them and seeing how they looked up to him probably made Missy feel she had an alpha male. In truth he was just a ringleader in a bottom of the barrel lifestyle. He was the champion of failures. His minuscule qualities were enough to lead the empty and wasted.

It was visible in how she spoke to him that he was held in high respect. He didn't seem particularly receptive to her. A man needs a woman and that was what she was to him. At times he probably rolled on about how much he loved her and at others he likely blamed her for his own faults. To her the endless circle of it would seem like a portrait of his depth, when it was actually just a product of the ramped chemicals in his system, both natural and not so. Whether he was in love or enraged was now only a matter of what scrambling enzymes had taken control at the moment. It would provide for her the conflict a person needs in life. It would give her something to deal with in the safety of her home and the simplicity of her stupor. He was almost certainly the provider of most of the drugs she used, which would be what gave him much of the authority he seemed to have. Leadership begotten by a coincidental connection allowing access to narcotics.

When the couple reached the table Missy flopped into the booth seat next to David and threw her arm around him for a welcome home hug. David, a little unsure how to take such affection, put a hand on her waist. "It's good to see ya, Sis."

She smiled back at him. "You too."

Her boyfriend sat down opposite them in the chair next to Samuel.

"How's it going?" nodded David, trying to hide his obvious disgust.

"Not bad, man, how you doin'?" returned the boy in a typical stoner tone.

"I'm cool."

"So you just out the box, huh?"

"Yeah, something like that," returned David, annoyed to have to associate with this type.

"So how have you been, Samuel?" asked Missy in attempt to evade the tension building in her brother.

"I've been all right. What about Missy?"

"As good as can be expected around here."

"What's been keeping you so busy?" asked David, unable to resist questioning her social life.

"A whole lot of nothing," replied Missy, blowing off the inquiry. "So what are your plans now that you're on the loose?" she asked in attempt to give him the same uneasy feeling he'd just given her.

"Aw, you know us Caines ain't really the plannin' types," said David, seeming to call a truce to the subtle conflict.

Samuel leaned away from the table to let the siblings talk more privately. He glanced over to get a better look at Missy's boyfriend. His greasy attempt at dreadlocks was an embarrassment. He wore a checkered flannel with the sleeves cut off and smelled of cat urine. Still, there was nothing better to do to pass the time so he put out his hand and introduced himself. "I'm Samuel."

The boyfriend smacked the hand properly and did the same. "I'm Jeremy but everybody calls me Germ."

"Well, Germ it's good to meet ya," replied Samuel condescendingly as he decided it might be fun to pose as the protective brother. "So do you work, Germ?"

"Yeah, I'm out there at the EPL parts factory."

"Hired in, Germ?"

"Nah, not yet. I'm gettin' along a'ight, though," said Jeremy, insinuating he had other forms of income as if to impress Samuel. Before Samuel could ask any more questions or find an excuse to repeat Jeremy's nickname, they were interrupted by an apparent friend of his.

"Hey Germ, how you been?" asked the boy. Jeremy turned around and greeted him pleasantly. Samuel looked the newcomer over. He was wearing a tie and dress shirt. He was certainly a Lakeview baby. The neighborhood wasn't more than a five-minute drive but you could see the difference in its residents with ease. The hair and speech gave away their pampered life without them knowing it. Samuel figured this one as an underachiever who probably got a cushy desk job from a friend of the family.

It was amusing to watch these two talk. To the eye, they were completely different, one a scrub, the other a prep, but they had a strong acquaintance between them, undoubtedly based in their mutual love for pill popping and line snorting.

Samuel looked back to Missy. He was bothered by how thin she was. What was once dainty was now unhealthy frailty. He could see she had spent time on her appearance but it couldn't mask her lifestyle's toll. She bounced with every syllable she said and her words had little space between them. Her stress in meeting David was probably what motivated her to get so high before they came. Even people who hadn't grown up around drug users could have seen the elevated state these two were in.

David had been moved by her affection when she first arrived but Samuel could see in his face that as Missy's current mind state became more and more obvious, the affection she gave became hollow to him. Seeing her this way forced him to struggle to keep his composure.

"So you tried those morphines that are going around?" asked the dressy friend, catching Samuel's attention.

"Yeah, I didn't really like 'em. Not my thing, I guess. I've been laying off pills. I took 11 Vicodins in one night a few weeks back. I figured I better take a break."

"Shit yeah, it sounds like it. Can you still get 'em, though?"

"Oh yeah, I can get 'em all day."

"Sweet. I gotta get your number before you leave. We've been looking all over for 'em. A buddy of mine wants some quantity."

"That's not a problem. Whatever he needs," accommodated Jeremy.

Samuel shook his head. This was the glamorous drug cartel in this city. One guy knows a guy who wants it for another guy. That was why it was so hard for cops to have an effect. There weren't too many kingpins or full timers around; they were few and far between. Most of the trafficking happened just like this. Two people, both otherwise employed, making a little side money moving small amounts when the opportunity arose. How was anyone supposed to monitor that? It wasn't like the movies, far more casual.

"Did you hear about Carlos and Reese?" asked the suited boy.

"Nah, what's up with 'em?"

"They got jobs working for an elderly care company. Their positions are to go clean the house up after the old folks kick it. It's like a gold mine. They get different assortments of shit every day, and nobody's missing them. Sometimes they can even get the prescription slips to go get more."

"Ah, hell no. That's too good to be true for them. I wonder who the dipshit who hired 'em was?"

As they both laughed, David, who couldn't help repeatedly looking at them over the last few minutes, gave up on biting his tongue.

"Do you fellas mind?" Both Jeremy and his friend looked up at David, unsure of what he meant. "If you two want talk about that shit, why don't you take it to the other end of the bar?"

"Oh please!" interjected Missy. "Don't start with that self-righteous bullshit. Aren't you the one who just got out of prison?"

"I really don't see what the hell one thing has to do with the other. I mean come on, Sis, gettin' drunk and smokin' weed after a day's work is one thing. I mean we've all been doin' that forever, but you've gotten into a whole different league of the sport here. That shit ain't all right. How the fuck am I supposed to sit here and pretend it's all right?"

Missy hopped up out of her seat, probably more startled by the insinuation her habits were visible than by the question. "I knew this was a mistake coming here. You don't have to sit there and pretend anything. You've been trying to play like my daddy my whole life and it's too late for that shit now. You don't get to make my decisions anymore. This is my life and you can either respect how I live it or stay the fuck away from me," she flared as she began a march to exit the bar.

Jeremy gave an awkward expression and stood up slowly. "Well, it was nice meeting you both," he said as he turned to follow after Missy.

"Ah fuck," said David as he stood up and started after her. Samuel was pleasantly surprised. It wasn't the typical mechanics of this family for him to chase her back down, but it was clear that David wanted to make an effort to repair this broken relationship. He seemed prepared to put forth the apologies he'd given Jamie and the patience he'd given his mother. His pursuit was paused by the ringing of the phone in Samuel's pocket. He whipped his head back to see.

Samuel pulled the phone out and watched the blinking green light accompanied by a chirp. "What are the fuckin' odds?" he said as looked back to David.

David watched the phone, and then turned to see Missy walking out the front door.

"Ahh, go ahead and answer it," he directed without looking back to Samuel. He watched his baby sister walk out the door without going after her. He seemed to consider his efforts to be a lost cause. He didn't believe that all the compassion in the world would make his sister forgive his mistakes.

"Yeah," answered Samuel. "Well yeah, we're ready to go but we're not at the hotel."

David could hear Sly's yells resound through the receiver.

"Well, there's not shit we can do about that now. We're at the Griffon downtown . . . yup . . . we'll be out back." Samuel closed the phone. "Man, that motherfucker is pissed," he said as he looked up at David. He could see the frustration over the fight with Missy. "Ah, don't sweat it, man. She'll come around. It'll just take some time," he reassured.

"Nah, she's right, man. I'm too late. She was already so independent before. Now that I've been gone, she ain't gonna listen to me none. She might just get worse to prove I ain't the boss. Fuck! I don't know, man. I don't know." David tossed some money on the table for their drinks. "Let's get out of here."

CHAPTER 32: CONFRONTATION

The two stood in the back entrance parking lot wandering in place. They shared a cigarette while waiting for Sylvester to arrive. It didn't take more than five minutes but from the anger in his face one would think he'd been delayed for hours.

Samuel took his usual shotgun position and David hopped in back. Sly began his drive and complaints in synchronization. "I'll tell you, I don't know how the fuck we're supposed to work with you guys. Every one of you fucks we deal with is just the same. We got the target on the move with the case and you two ain't where you're supposed to be. I hope Cole doesn't give you a cent after this shit. If we had the prize already I'd drop you both in the river right now. How fuckin' stupid can you be? I said stay at the hotel and you guys go out drinking," continued Sly in his coarse voice. It was the most either of them had heard him say at one time.

David was rolling his eyes at what he considered unwarranted reprimanding. Uninterested in hearing any more he interrupted. "So where are we heading?"

"SHUT THE FUCK UP!!!" roared Sylvester as his knuckles went white with his forceful grip on the steering wheel. "You two fuckin' clowns act like this is a joke. You act like when I said I'd take you out when I felt like it I was just making threats. Whether you're alive in the morning or not is up to me and right now it's not looking too good. When I say what you're going to do, that's what you're going to do!" His spewing rage was interrupted by his phone. He gritted his teeth and shook his head while answering it.

Samuel was stiff in his seat, though his friend's unenthused expression in the back didn't agree. Samuel believed what the man next to him was saying. He could hear the ferocity in the growls. Sly didn't sound to him like a man trying to make an impression but a man trying to keep himself contained. He believed him to be truly struggling with not taking their lives, and he knew this man had been trained by experts to be more than capable of doing it. From the beginning of this job Sly behaved as though he had a longstanding grudge against them. Samuel couldn't understand where such contempt for people he'd never met before could come from.

When Sly hung up his phone he didn't return to yelling, he just drove in silence. After what took only a few minutes, they were in parked position down the road from an all night convenient store.

"He's in that Liberty Mart right now," said Sly. He paused for a moment then began again. "I tell ya, I'm gonna be talking to Lorenzo about renegotiating after this shit you pulled. And if there's anything like it again, I'm not gonna hesitate. Fuck the money, fuck what anybody else has to say, I'll take the both of you out."

"Fuck man, it didn't take ya any longer to pick us up there than it does from the hotel," argued David, tired of what he considered being blown out of proportion.

Before his sentence was complete Sly had whipped a knife from his coat and was turned, pressing it to David's neck. He made the move so fast neither of the boys had a chance to react. It was a long blade with a decorative handle. It didn't seem to mesh with the rest of Sylvester's drab style and attire. He held it tightly against David's throat. It wasn't pushed hard enough to draw blood, but still enough to display his willingness to see his boasts through.

"This was the knife that put the scar on my neck. It's the knife that got me discharged from the military. It's claimed quite a few lives. It's the one I use when I really feel strongly about killing someone."

David's attitude hadn't changed much. He had his bottom lip stuck out to show how unimpressed he was with the gesture. He considered this a cheap maneuver to look tough when there was obviously more important business preventing a response. He thought it about as impressive as attacking a man in handcuffs.

"You know, I had a friend with a favorite knife once," he cleverly threatened.

Samuel was frozen with eyes wide at the showdown in front of him. His brain was stiff as he tried to think of something to say to relieve the pressure between the two. To his relief Sylvester's phone did the job for him.

Sly remained paused for a moment after the ring. Then he smiled to show how much he was enjoying the confrontation as he pulled the knife away and answered the phone.

"Yeah . . . a'ight . . .yup." He hung up and the car was back in motion.

Not a word was said until another ring filled the otherwise silent car.

"Yeah . . . fuck, all right." He got off the phone and addressed them.

"He's back in his house. Apparently he just went to grab a loaf of bread. I'm taking y'all back to the hotel and that's where you're going to stay until I pick you up again. I don't care if the place is burning down, you don't leave that room unless I tell you myself." Neither responded. When they arrived back at their luxury prison, they got out of the car and headed up the sidewalk. "Hey David," Sly called after him, using his name for the first time. David turned to look at him. "When this is all over with I'll be looking forward to running into you again," he said through the open window with a wicked smile, as though he believed he was oppressing an already defeated opponent.

David nodded, genuinely unconcerned with the statement, then turned back to following Samuel.

After they were both safely in their room, Samuel still found himself feeling restless and uneasy. The issue responsible for the feelings was a tossup between David and Sylvester's showdown, his guilt surrounding Monique and mounting frustration over Cullomine's long stay in that house.

Before, a contest between David and Sly had been a fear Samuel concocted almost completely without evidence but his instincts had proven correct, as it had now become a matter of how long David could contain his temper rather than whether or not they would actually clash. If Samuel had ever wondered if David would back down from the burly tyrant of a man, the questions were answered by the lack of fear when the knife was against his skin. There was no sign of being startled or intimidated, or anything beyond bothered by Sly's advance. There was no doubt that the only thing that prevented an all-out battle between the two was David's eyes on the ball. Samuel couldn't decide whether the lack of intimidation was for the better or worse.

While his mind whisked from one issue to the next he did well to keep from dwelling on Monique, but somehow, she was still present in everything he was thinking. There was a portrait of her beautiful face lingering just outside every thought he had and action he took. He wouldn't let himself focus on the pleasing features that made up the portrait, but it remained just the same. He feared it could endure the test of time and stay with him for years after the Cullomine situation had reached its end.

Staying in this room and waiting for some sign of the alleged money was taking its toll on Samuel. Before he'd been comfortable with the fact that Torreo was holing up in that house. He had decided that he was waiting on the money's safe arrival at Monique's but as it still hadn't showed up, Samuel wondered what made him so sure. How could he really know that whatever Torreo's plan was wouldn't involve abandoning Monique? If he was willing to leave her once they had safely reached their foreign rendezvous, as Samuel had tried to convince himself to ease his guilt, how could he believe that Torreo didn't have a way to make off with the money now and leave her out completely? There were any number of things he could be waiting on before he saw his mystery plan through. Along with that, how could they even be positive there was money to be snatched? Maybe he had lost it before he went up, or the DC had it all along and were just pinning it on Torreo. If the money did not show up soon, how long would Lorenzo Cole wait before he would give up and take out his anger on Samuel, David, Lukas and how many others? Samuel had begun to long for something to break the stalemate. Torreo's casual trip to the store was enough to bring question to everything. If he had put the money in the mail at the bank, it was about time to be making a move and losing his audience, not getting food to continue his marathon of television. Samuel wanted something concrete to cling to but it wasn't a concrete situation. Everyone else seemed to think Monique might easily be left out of Cullomine's plan. He couldn't help fearing that it was his own affections for her that kept him from believing otherwise.

He was again plagued with the fear he was missing something. It was something much smaller this time. But there was still need for a detail, or exposure of misassumption that would allow everything to take form in Samuel's mind once again.

"Do you remember that thing you wrote?" began David, bringing interruption to Samuel's blooming seeds of doubt. Things he'd written were usually one of the last subjects Samuel wanted to discuss, but right now he was happy with anything that could replace the subjects currently occupying his overactive mind. "It was in one of the stories you let me read back in the day. Something about plants and animals and struggling."

"Oh yeah, I know what you're talking about. It was a story I did for a creative writing class. That part was comparing plants and animals. It was saying how plants are far more efficient than animals. They don't even have to move. They get their food from the ground beneath them. They reproduce asexually. They are the perfect living machine. It then goes on into how animals couldn't live like plants because of their deeper needs that come from having a soul. We need the thrill of the hunt, the feeling of accomplishment when a goal is reached, and the effort it takes to make love, the approval you get when someone wants to make love to you. Everything in which we put forth effort caters to a deeper part of us. We could never just stay in one place, pulling our needs from the ground beneath us. The rewards would be incomplete. It's the importance of work and difficulties. The different conflicts and turmoils of the animals' struggling life feed our souls in different ways. Plants are the soulless lives so they don't need all that. It then went into how the modern way of things didn't completely work. Like how getting food from a window feeds our belly but leaves us hungry somewhere else. I don't remember exactly. The whole thing had some relevance to the rest of the story. That part was just trying to make the point of the necessity of struggle for animals," explained Samuel.

"Yeah, that's what I'm thinking about over here. The necessity of struggle. That's what I always thought that was about. And I'm over here thinking if things work out the way we hope, how would we live afterwards? I'm thinking what you said about me not being happy with all that money might be right. I could probably only be on the beach sipping drinks for so long before I'll be missing the blocks of the ol' neighborhood. I'll still need that struggle. We won't ever be able to come back here after this. Who knows how long Cully or the feds or the DC will be lookin' for the loot. I'm mean we'll be straight off in wherever land, but then what the fuck are we gonna do? Sometimes I think if I got things perfect like that I might just shrivel up and die. I don't know, man, it's just something I was thinking about," confided David.

"I hear your point, man, but this would have been shit to bring up before we signed on with Cole. It's a little late for decision making," said Samuel.

"I mean fuck that dude. I don't give a shit about him. He ain't gonna force me to do a damn thing. But the truth is I thought about this before. I still gotta get Missy and Ma and Jamie the fuck out of here before I can make things better. I want to be able to look out for Kris's seeds too. Even if Deanna don't want to move them, I'll still be able to send money and shit they might need. This is the only way I can take care of everything, and that's more important than how I'm gonna fill my days. Besides, I know if I did stay here it'd turn out bad. I grew up around here. It's a part of me, but when it comes down to it, every instinct I got, in the long run, won't bring a happy ending. Eventually the way I live would catch up to me. Truth is, when it comes down to it, I can't change. I avoided that fight at Snickers and I held myself back with Sly, but that shit was hard, damn hard. Eventually the wrong thing would happen. Even knowing that it would, I still could never stop it. Defending somebody's honor or trying to protect somebody, them instincts have been my way for so long. They take over before I even get a chance to say okay. I gotta leave 'cause I'm not strong enough to change."

Samuel shook his head. "Don't talk like that, man. It's that outdated honor and protective way that I've always loved about Post Edition. Nobody over there has today's typical view of right and wrong, that's for sure, but the way they do view it they stay truer to than anyone I see in the so-called legitimate world. That's what makes me hate that fuckin' Lorenzo Cole so much. The way he protects . . ." Samuel paused, considering that he was about to fan a flame that was better left alone.

"You can say it, I've accepted the situation. You were gonna say the way he protects Tim," reassured David.

"Right, the way he protects Tim and how many others. He stands in the way of Post Edition's justice. Without their justice the Posties just become a group of hooligans and criminals. His presence removes what was good and only leaves the bad; it makes them wretched."

David paused for a minute, thinking on how his friend saw his home. You could see his pride swell up a little that one so insightful could think so highly of his neighbors. It was also visible when he really realized how one man had changed his beloved roots for the worse and how he was powerless to stop it.

"But I lost my point there," Samuel resumed. "I can't stand you referring to the heart and soul you put into everything like it's bad. It's one of the few good things left. You can't talk like you're doomed. I've been watching you for a long time and one thing's for sure; you always land on your feet. You've come out of a lot of rough shit and you can come out of a lot more. I can't picture much that'll hold you down."

"Think so?" questioned a slightly more cheerful David.

"Yeah, I think so," reaffirmed Samuel.

"That means a lot from you," thanked David. "'Course sometimes I think you have a tendency to see things how you want to see 'em. Maybe not how they are."

"Yeah right, all you Posties just like the attention that comes from taking a dramatic pose in life," razzed Samuel. "You just don't wanna follow any logic that'll deflate one."

"Well, I can't argue with that. A good 'dramatic pose' can get you a lot of pussy." They both laughed.

After another sitcom had passed and they were back to their now official positions of an empty staring contest with the TV, David spoke again. "How can you write something like that, then not write? You explain how people need to do shit to be happy then you sit around not doin' the shit you're best at? I've been trying not to ride ya lately, but you gotta explain that to me."

Samuel rolled his eyes as he always did when David took insight into his life. "Man, I'm just not in the right position to be worried about writing. If I could get things settled then I could focus on that. We get this loot we're after, I know exactly what I'll be doin' on the beach. I'll have a portable typewriter out there. I'll be smackin' them keys from when I wake up till I fall out. I can finally get to living the way I always wanted to."

"I mean that sounds nice and all, don't get me wrong, but it also sounds a lot like my mother." Samuel's eyebrows curled as David continued, "She's always puttin' off everything she knows she should be doin' and wants to be doin'. Anything that takes a little effort and she puts it off till some make-believe moment when the world's gonna be perfect. She gets out of living for real that way. The trouble with that is, I know if my ma ever did win it big she would find some other excuse to put things off. She'd stay cooped up in that house the rest of her life where things was easy and she felt safe. You can't just wait like that. You gotta start somewhere that ain't so great and make it that way. I don't like to think of you like my mother, Samuel, but sometimes I think you'd rather let the world pass you by than go after anything."

Samuel leaned back slowly in his chair and looked up at the ceiling. "Well, you came up with something you wanted to say to most everybody while you were gone," he remarked, accusing David of not having just thought up the point.

"Shit. There wasn't much else to do on lock but think on all the people out here. I ended up with a lot of opinions," smirked David.

Samuel smiled at his friend's caring and pretended to go back to watching TV. In truth he was thinking hard on what was just said to him. David was the second person in recent days to put insight into Samuel. Both opinions seemed to share the same base, Samuel hiding from life. If there was any part of him that hadn't accepted it was his own fears to blame for the way he'd been living, that part was in conflict now. There was no question that it was fear of being rejected by people that led him to a conscious effort not to get too close to anyone. He had never denied that to himself. He also had to accept that at times he'd been moved to want to put a thought or feeling down on paper, but didn't do so. The reason wasn't really that he had to focus on work or anything else he'd claimed as blockades. Those things were what he'd always told himself was the problem anytime he took a long look at his life, but now, looking back on those instances, the only thing that could have really been responsible for his not picking up a pen was fear. Knives or guns didn't hold the same foreboding that failure of true efforts always held. It had even reached the point that he feared he'd put something on paper and realize himself that it was no good. He'd always been afraid of what others would think of his work, but it had grown to the point of cowering from his own opinion as much as anyone else's.

Now that he had this newfound strength, he considered that he needed to stand up to those fears as well. It was far past time to start writing again. It was too late now to try and work it into his old life. This thing with Lorenzo Cole had already begun, but when it was over he knew he wouldn't behave as David had described Ms. Caine. He would get that typewriter onto the beach or wherever he needed to and he would create a new story.

He could almost taste that perfect world. There would be endless sunshine, plenty of money, the camaraderie of time spent with David and family, and best of all, there would be the fulfillment of writing again. It would be his old plague of a dream coming to life. It was a nice enough thought to make him forget the things currently providing his frustration.

Having moved to his bed, the blissful feeling from picturing his utopia began to lull him into a pleasant sleep. It would be the first good sleep he had since he'd left his home to begin this quest for paradise. As he was almost there, a similar thought to ones that plagued nights prior came bursting in uninvited. He thought of how this perfect life they were after would only be achieved by taking it from another. David had brought up this idea of karma, that something of this nature could never work out for the best. He looked over at David. He knew his friend wasn't as burdened with these things as he was. The hatred for drug dealers gave him more reason than he would ever need to take this money. He hadn't known Monique the way Samuel had. He didn't have to dwell on what they were taking from her.

"David," said Samuel.

"Sup, man?"

"What are we gonna do if for some reason we decide we don't wanna take the money?" David gave a confused scowl as Samuel continued, "I mean if for whatever reason we decide we don't wanna do it. How we gonna handle that?"

David straightened his face out as he thought about the unlikely situation. "I done told you, that motherfucker ain't gonna force me to do shit."

Samuel nodded his head, slightly relieved. It was nice to hear they weren't as confined by the circumstances as he might have thought. It was enough to bring about the peaceful sleep he had long been hunting for.

CHAPTER 33: DRAGON'S JUSTICE

There were many people with interest in Cullomine Torreo's release from prison. They each had differing opinions on the actions he would take upon that release. It was likely that none of these opinions consisted of him making a series of seemingly unrelated, aimless drives, then taking solitude in an empty house and remaining there for days.

With each hour he sat there the suspense built, alongside the anxiousness of everyone with a stake in the situation surrounding him. It's doubtful that Lorenzo's cast could have held their patience so long were it not for their awareness that it could instead be Monique Romano that would hold the pending fortune. Due to that, it was agents from the Federal Bureau of Investigation who finally broke the stalemate. Coincidentally, they did it on the day Lorenzo Cole had appointed the deadline for his own team to make an advance. It was four days after Cullomine had first entered the house, the longest Samuel had predicted the package could take to arrive at Monique's, if indeed sent from the bank.

It was Cole's intention to wait for Monique's mail to arrive that day and if there was no special delivery, he would proceed by sending his men to invade Cullomine's hideout. Instead he was called that morning by his surveillance team to learn that a handful of federal agents had beaten him to it. It was now a matter of relying solely on the opinions of the boys who brought him this chance to begin with, and hoping Cullomine truly didn't have the money.

The surveillance team listened closely and monitored the heat camera for a very accurate picture of what was taking place and gave Cole a blow-by-blow description. Three agents covered the back door, while two agents and a well-dressed Latino who gave no impression of the law enforcement genre knocked at the front of the house. To the eavesdroppers' surprise he answered quite hospitably.

"Hey fellas, come on in," said Cullomine as he pulled his long wavy hair back and banded it into a tail. "Hector, my old friend! Strange company you're keeping nowadays. It's good to see ya just the same, though."

"Yeah, shut the fuck up and tell us where it's at," said the lead agent.

Cullomine had little reaction to the harsh bark. He just picked up the dress shirt on the counter, put it on over his tank top and began buttoning while keeping the casual tone he'd been using. "It? You're gonna have to be more specific."

The agent kept the same stale expression on his face and leaned his head over to his coworker. "Go let the others in the back."

He did as was told, crossed the room and opened the back door, letting in the rest of their team. The first agent spoke again. "Search the house up and down. It has to be in here somewhere."

"Again with this 'it'. Can I be let in on the particulars?" asked a saucy-toned Cullomine.

This time the agent's face moved just enough to show the disgust he felt toward Cullomine's front. "Okay, I guess I can assume you mean the money. The twenty million payoff I was supposed to drop off to you boys before I went up. Well, let me ask you a question. What in the world would make you think I would even consider lettin' you fellas have it after you let me waste such valuable years of my life in jail? I mean that's what that money is for, to keep my associates and me out of prison. I don't think you deserve it," said Cullomine as he sat in the chair he'd been in for days and began lacing up his dress shoes.

The rest of the agents continued to ransack the almost completely empty house while the one giving the orders entered the living room Cullomine was now sitting in, to continue conversation. "We were directed otherwise; now it's a simple question, Torreo. Where is it? Once you tell us we'll be out of your hair."

"Out of my hair? You mean then you'll turn me over to the wolves," said Cullomine as he glanced over to Hector. "Well, like I said, I could have saved my hide five years ago but you let me get arrested. My chances of running ended there."

"You mean running with our money," corrected the officer.

Cullomine swelled up with a smile like a child proud of his devious prank. "Well, you'll never know. You never gave me a chance to pass it over. You decided to let the John Qs snag me up and fuck me over. So if there ever was a chance I was gonna make the payoff, that's over now. I figured if I got out, picked up the loot and the coast was clear, I'd make a break, though I knew the chances of that were nil. So when I saw you guys over my shoulder I went to plan B."

"Which was?"

"Come back here, burn the money so you pricks would never get it, then sit back and watch television until you decided to come on in and get me. It took you long enough."

"Burn it?" said the suddenly more expressive fed. "No way."

"Take a look for yourself," directed Cullomine as he rose to his feet and pointed in the direction of the TV. There, sitting plainly on top of the television was the highly theorized briefcase and sitting close on the ground was a tin waste basket.

The agent marched over and opened the briefcase. The pale tan interior stared back at him. He then turned and dumped the can, pouring ashes to the floor. He swung around back to his stern stance with a now-infuriated expression. "We're not buying this shit!" he roared, more in the direction of the black-suited Hector than of Cullomine.

Cullomine was still grinning as he put on his suit coat. "Yeah, you're not gonna be buying much with that, but what's to buy? I mean, what did you think was gonna happen? I'm in an impossible situation and the only thing I was capable of doing was screwing you fucks. So that's what I did. Why are you surprised?"

"Where do you think you're going?" the agent shouted, now annoyed by Cullomine continually dressing himself.

He shrugged nonchalantly. "Nowhere," he stated as he plopped back down in his chair.

The agent turned back to Hector. "We're gonna need more time to sort this out."

Hector stuck his bottom lip out and shook his head slowly. "We've given you guys enough time. You're the ones who fucked this up and we've been as helpful as possible. But the DC is sick of waitin' on you so we can finish our business."

"We got too many people waiting on that money. We're not gonna just eat it on this," hollered the fed.

Hector smirked. "Well, if I had to predict, I'd say that's exactly what you're gonna do, but that's not my area. You'll have to talk to Carlo about that. All I can account for is what's gonna happen now. You knew how this was gonna play out coming in here. Nothin's changed."

The agent's face grew stern again at hearing the name Carlo. He was quiet for a moment, shaking his head, then finally spoke. "All right boys, let's go," he ordered to his entourage. Without hesitation they stopped their search and marched out the front door. Not another word was spoken by the agent. He followed his troops out and slammed the door behind him, leaving Hector and Cullomine alone in the house.

They both smirked at each other as old friends enjoying being responsible for the frustrations of the law enforcement that was supposed to have authority over them. But the smiles quickly faded and the lighthearted mood of the room turned hard and breathless.

Hector took a cell phone out of his pocket and dialed. "Yeah, come on. Let me know when you get here."

Cullomine remained calm and patient, looking genuinely relaxed in his chair.

"Man, you got balls of steel. I guess you always have," observed Hector.

"I think all of us in this life have come to terms with death. Even harder, we've come to terms with imprisonment. But I had never prepared myself for the mixture of the two. To take those years locked up, knowing all that awaited me when released was an ending, it was hard to endure. But to make it I had to come to terms with how this would play out. So here I am, calm and ready."

"And well dressed like you always said you would be. But fuck man, all that time you stuck it out just so you could set her up. You didn't even want to make an attempt to split?"

Cullomine's eyes grew attentive at the sound of "her".

Hector waved it off. "Don't worry. There's been a lot of changes under Carlo but he wouldn't ever challenge the rules of la familia."

"Yeah, maybe not, but if I had gotten away, it would have been a different story. Running by myself was one thing, but running with a woman and child was another. I'd be bringing too much risk to them. No, I was better off giving them the money and coming here to catch as much TV as I could while I waited for you guys to make your move. Four days in front of this thing, though, and there was never shit on."

"Never is. But you're right, with the hard-on he's always had for you, he probably wouldn't've hesitated to hurt them if it meant getting you. She'll be fine now, though. You succeeded in that. But fuck man, I guess I was always secretly hoping you'd pull off something amazing. I just never really believed it'd turn out this way."

Cullomine didn't speak; he looked at his old friend with a stare that conveyed what needed to be said. It held the tragic recognition of the fate that awaited him. Even more, it held the pride and devotion of a father and husband who protected his family by cutting off the hands he needed to defend against his predators.

"Man, you must really love her," deduced Hector.

"Was that ever in debate?" asked Cullomine plainly.

Before Hector could think of a response he was interrupted by the ringing of his cell phone. He pulled it out and looked somberly at its face before looking back up at Cullomine. He was calmed to see his mentor leaning back in the chair with eyes closed as if enjoying a blissful sleep. Hector would have hated for a man he'd spent so many years idolizing to see the tear welling in his left eye as he pulled the pistol from his coat. He twisted to tighten the silencer, pointed and put five bullets in the chest of Cullomine Torreo.

The blood began leaking down the classy shirt and Hector put fingers to the victim's neck. At confirming the death, he wiped away the tear from his cheek and proceeded out the back door to meet his ride.

CHAPTER 34: SWITCHING SIDES

When the news hit Lorenzo's ears he immediately realized that Monique Romano had indeed been their trump card all along. Samuel and David were correct; the money was en route to her home, and he already had a well-prepared team waiting outside. In his mind, the goal they had set out for was all but reached. The only detail left was for him to call his head of operations with the information and set the dominos in motion.

When Sly and the boys got the news, they were already into their daily duties of waiting for the mailman on Emerald Boulevard.

"We got an update," said Sylvester as he hung up the phone. "The ball is gonna be in Monique's court."

"What?!" questioned an astounded Samuel as he tore his eyes from the miniature telescope. "How do we know?"

"They just overheard a conversation with Torreo and a Dragon Clan affiliate. Seems the Clan was aware the money would be going to her all along. They couldn't tell the feds 'cause it'd be jeopardizing his family and breaking their code."

"Torreo was talking to a DC?" asked Samuel, even more amazed.

"Yeah, just before he was killed by 'em."

"Fuck," said David with both pride and disappointment. "I was hoping to play a hand in that."

Samuel pressed the scope back against his eye. He watched attentively, now being bothered all the more by Cullomine's behavior. Before there was any time for him to apply reason to the confusing situation, his thoughts were interrupted by the sight of his replacement pulling a square blue package from his bag. He proceeded to knock, completely unaware of the longing eyes watching his every movement.

"That's it, isn't it!" boasted Sylvester loudly.

Samuel hesitated, fearing the consequences of unleashing this group against a person he felt so strongly for. "Um . . . yeah, I'm pretty sure that's it."

At the same time, David and Sylvester jumped out of the car with excitement in an attempt to get a better look. Sly grabbed the phone in his pocket.

"Yeah! Yeah! That's it. Make the move as soon as it's clear."

Samuel tried to hold time still by clinging to each moment before the SWAT would make their move, but in spite of his efforts, it wasn't long before the mailman was a suitable distance up the street and a fleet of masked soldiers poured out of the nearby van. He reached his hand forward as if the strength of his feelings could somehow stop their progress, then he gritted his teeth at accepting that it was beyond his control. He watched the team rush her house like a defensive squadron after a fumble.

Samuel exited the car as well and looked at David for some form of consolation. Instead he saw enthusiasm, as if David were watching the hero in the climax of his favorite movie. For him it was everything he had dreamed of over these last weeks, finally coming within grasp. He could feel the perfect world he'd designed for himself finally arriving in reality.

Samuel peered at the ground without noise or gesture. For him it wasn't his paradise taking form but the guilt that came from betraying someone who had been so kind to him. How could he repay her generosity this way? She had trusted him in her home, with her son, and now he put her at the mercy of these merciless men. Despite his pain, it was hard to picture a woman like her at the mercy of anyone. Then, with that thought, his head whipped up to watch again, as he remembered what he had repeatedly predicted.

"You guys might be in for a surprise," he warned.

"I don't know what you're gettin' at, but the money will be in our hands in a matter of moments," stated Sly triumphantly.

"I warned ya. Havin' a team out here all the time was too obvious. She probably made y'all days ago," suggested Samuel.

The comfort Samuel took from his pride in Monique's ability was justified. The squadron kicked in the door and ransacked the house with no hesitation. To their surprise the woman they had witnessed just moments ago was nowhere to be seen. There was no sign of her or her child. Their search through the house was swift and thorough, but in a matter of minutes they had to accept that her escape had long been accomplished. Immediately one of the intruding soldiers sprinted back to the van to report their discovery.

Just seconds after, Sly received his call. "Yeah. . .right. . .yeah, I was startin' to worry. Do we know what she's gonna look like? Right. He should." Sly hung up the phone and hopped behind the steering wheel. He pulled up next to the boys and beckoned them into the car. "Come on. She's not in there but we got an idea where she's going and we're gonna head her off," he said anxiously, seeming to enjoy the severity of the moment.

The boys quickly got back in the car as Sly gunned the gas.

"Where are we going now?" asked Samuel.

"Gotta figure she's headin' to the airport. She's gonna want to get out of town before there's a chance for anyone to do detective work. We got a few guys watching the bus and train stations but Lorenzo wants us to head for the airport."

"I don't get it," spoke Samuel, still glossy-eyed at the sudden chain of events.

"What's to get?" questioned Sly.

"I don't understand how Torreo was just sittin' there waitin' to get deaded. I've been waiting to see how he'd escape but then he just sits there and lets them have 'im."

"As I understand it he had no intention of escaping. From what was said his whole plan was to get her the money so her and the kid could make off with it. If he disappeared, it would bring heat on them. They could have ended up dead too. So he kept everybody watching him so they could make a clean slip. Fortunately, he didn't know about y'all stumbling on to her. A noble effort gone to waste, and we'll be the ones to profit," explained Sylvester with pleasant eagerness.

Until now David had noticed Samuel's disposition was torn, but in that instant it became visibly one-sided. He could see his friend go from confused to inspired. At the same time, Samuel looked to his side mirror in search of David's reaction. Until now David had done a good job of pretending he had no compassion for the innocent woman in the situation, but as Samuel locked eyes with him, David had to lower his head to his palm and think.

Samuel could feel his friend's struggle. The money he had made such plans for suddenly felt tainted. The man he held such contempt for suddenly seemed valiant. Cullomine had been in the same struggle David was in, trying to provide for his family. Both David and Samuel had taken what wasn't legally theirs in the past, but this time was far different. It had become one of those moments Samuel had described when doing the right thing becomes so important. David never accepted the morals decided by the rest of the world, but the ones he had made for himself, despite his sordid past, had never been ignored.

He couldn't help but picture his mother before she had been worn, himself and his brother and sister as innocent children before the harsh customs of that city had taken their toll on them. He had to picture what his family might have turned out like if his dad hadn't abused and abandoned them the way he did. If his mother hadn't been emotionally raped, it's likely they all could have made something better of themselves. He had spent so many years blaming the way they turned out on the lifestyle of dealers instead of the lifestyle of his own parent. He had to accept that he had been wrong. In that moment, his dad and Tim Russell stopped being a group and became individuals. He stopped seeing it as dealers who had crossed him but as those particular people. People he could no longer put Cullomine Torreo in the same class with. It was easy to let a visible fault in one's character hide any virtue they might have. Now he had to look past whatever reason this man led a life of crime in narcotics. He had to accept that this dealer had loved his family and had made the ultimate sacrifice for them. How could he stand in the way of that sacrifice? To blockade the gesture of this man's love for his family was to demean how much the Caine family had needed that love all those years ago.

He rubbed at the scar on the top of his chest plate. Letting grudges slide was becoming a familiar habit. Finally David lifted his head to answer Samuel's requesting stare. Samuel was asking his friend's approval to feel the way he did. David slowly nodded his head to give it. They both turned from wanting to rob a dealer of his nest egg to wanting to complete his noble effort. It stopped being a matter of grabbing that money but instead interfering with the efforts of Sly and the rest of the men they had recruited to do so.

"So how are we gonna stop her at this point?" asked Samuel as if maintaining the goal.

"Lorenzo has already talked to a Postie that works in airport security. He gave him the heads-up last week. His name's, uh . . . Joney Wattley. He's already got a brief description on who he's lookin' for. We are gonna try and find her so we can give a perfect one. It's just a matter of us finding the girl and calling Lorenzo with a description. Then security will stop her, then we can make our move. We keep all bases covered," he announced smugly.

Samuel nodded his head with false approval.

Sly was at the airport in record time. Samuel figured that Monique wasn't familiar enough with the area to take the back roads. If she had to stick to the main route it was likely she had been beaten in her arrival.

"If she's not out here Samuel's gonna have to go inside while we watch people showing up," ordered Sly. Samuel hoped that would be the case, for if she was in there it would be easy to let her slip away without anyone knowing he'd done it. He had not really considered how important it was to keep their decision concealed. He was wrapped up in the feelings of being the hero as opposed to the criminal. It felt wonderful.

Sylvester drove slowly to see if he recognized anyone near the doors. When he didn't, he pulled to the nearby short-term parking. All the while he kept his head cocked back to see the people approaching the airport.

Samuel and David did the same, but with completely different intentions.

"A'ight, get in there. Wait! I think that's her!" Sly hooted after pulling into a spot. He hopped out of the car and threw the binoculars to his eyes. Samuel did the same with his telescope. "Yeah. She's in that flowery dress."

Samuel spotted Monique with Sly's description. Young Cullomine stood close, holding her hand. She wore a loose summer dress that covered her from her neck to ankles. Samuel figured the money was laced to Monique's body to avoid the luggage scanners.

"Yeah, that's definitely her," exclaimed Sly as he pulled out his phone.

Before he had the chance to dial, Samuel quickly snagged the phone and dove into a full sprint toward the doors of the airport.

Sly's smile turned to a scowl of confusion as he instinctively stepped forward and reached for Samuel. But before his arm could take hold of Samuel's collar, David swatted it into the air. Immediately Sly became aware of the extent of these boys' insolence. Without hesitation he turned with full swing into David's chin, smacking him back against the car.

Samuel didn't have a chance to look back to the fray beginning between David and Sylvester. He was focused on protecting the girl he had such affection for. He ran as fast as he was capable, with every bit of himself behind it. He was not only in the game but the star player. He felt like a child again, running for the end zone during recess football. He had the blooming joy of being the game-winning scorer and knowing the praise that would follow. He was the hero from his stories. There was nothing that could hold down his heart. In that moment, he knew they would succeed in their effort.

While racing to the doors he quickly debated how he would handle the situation. He at first thought he would dart in, and at the sight of the Postie vet give a swift swing to the jaw, but he realized the attention that would bring. He followed that thought by considering he might approach the nearest security station and claim he had been in the bathroom and seen a guard with the name tag of Wattley using narcotics. He was almost settled on that plan when it occurred to him that once Joney had been taken for questions he might still warn that the girl of Monique's description should be held.

There was still no plan made when he stepped in the front doors. He had wisely turned sprint into walk to avoid the crowd's attention. To his fortune, the first thing he saw once he stepped and began scanning the crowd was Joney on a similar hunt.

He quickly but casually made his way over to his old acquaintance. "What up, how the fuck you been?"

"Ah, I'm good. You involved in this, man? I ain't been given no good details."

"Yeah, I am and don't worry about details. That's what I'm here for," boasted Samuel with a deceiving confidence. "They sent me in here, rush delivery. We were worried you might stop ol' girl."

"Shit, I was still trying to spot her."

"Well, don't worry about it. We made the switch earlier. She thinks she's making a break and we don't want her to think no different. But Loco said there was gonna be somethin' special for you this month just for havin' looked out."

"Well fuck, that's easy enough. Send my gratitude, man. I'm always happy to help, you know."

"Oh, he recognizes that. But I'll put in the good word just the same."

"Hey, I appreciate it. And it's good seeing you again, man. It's been a while."

"Yeah, you too. I'll keep an eye out for ya. Stay up."

"Yeah, you too."

Samuel walked calmly away, with no sign of the tension there had been. As he looked back he saw young Cullomine and Monique walking through the metal detector. The boy noticed him and pointed it out to his mother. Monique looked back somberly to Samuel, as if requesting what he had already given. Samuel just nodded coolly and headed out the door.

CHAPTER 35: CONQUERING HERO

Once back into the sun, a new swarm of worries attacked Samuel. He hoped David was all right.

He headed up the sidewalk toward the parking lot from which he had emerged. His mind started to wander, debating the state his friend would be in when he returned. Though he had developed an almost unhealthy fear of Sylvester and his military background, he still maintained confidence by taking comfort in the lifetime of training David Caine had been through.

So it was little surprise when he heard a double honk and looked back to see the Caddy approaching with David behind the wheel. Surprised or not, Samuel's face lit up to see his friend in one piece. David pulled up on the wrong side and past a bit so that Samuel could hop in the back seat.

"Whooo, fuck man, I was a little worried about that one," admitted Samuel as he patted David's shoulder approvingly.

"Ah shit man, you should have known dude wasn't fuckin' with me."

"Yeah, I should have. But where's he at? You leave him in the lot?"

"Yeah, he's in the lot," said David as he gave a potent glance that suggested the severity of the situation. "He won't be leaving until somebody moves him."

Samuel's face grew stern. "Fuck man, I didn't think it would come to that."

"Yeah, well he pulled that big-ass knife he liked so much and I had to put it in his chest."

"Ah fuck, I'm sorry, man . . . "

"Now don't start talkin' like that. I was itchin' to do it since we met. It didn't have to go like that but he took it there himself. I ain't sweatin' it."

"Did anybody see?"

"Yeah, there were a few shocked faces but I don't think anybody could make the car. They mighta got the plate but fuck it, it ain't our car."

"True, one more thing Loco can be on us about," said Samuel as David nodded his head approvingly. Samuel leaned back and enjoyed how good he felt. It was almost euphoric to have all those concerns and feelings resolved so abruptly. Things had just gone very well for them, even if it were not the original plan. "Whoowee!" he bellowed triumphantly. "We handled that shit when it came up, didn't we? I ain't had to be on point like that since the old days. It was nice."

David reached back somewhat awkwardly with his left hand to request dap from his partner, who proudly gave it. "You know it, baby. That brought back some of those old feelings, and I been without 'em too long."

"True. True." Samuel paused for a minute. "So how the fuck are we gonna handle this Loco situation, though?"

David grunted a little bit as he situated in his seat. "I think I got that one figured out too."

Samuel happily raised his eyebrows, feeling that the good fortune just kept on coming. "Well, let's hear it," he requested while climbing over the seats to join his friend up front. He got situated in the shotgun position and his ears perked to hear the explanation. Then he noticed something sticky on his hand. He lifted it for examination to find moist red blood on his fingers. His head whipped to the left. There he saw David, his left hand holding the steering wheel, his right held tightly to the gash on his side in an attempt to reduce the incessant bleeding.

Samuel opened his mouth for response but was unable to speak. He had never seen a wound like that one. The inside of the car was suddenly quiet and still. All his high spirits had fled. There was no spirit of accomplishment or freedom, not even any of fear or anguish, to replace them. All those things had made way. It was like the calm just before the storm, or a still forest when the animals had all hidden from a more ferocious creature approaching. Those spirits had fled, for a far stronger one was coming. The gash screamed with a foreboding tone of death.

He looked away from the gushing blood. He felt guilty. It didn't feel right seeing his friend or anyone in that state. He felt obligated to help in some way, but had no way to do it. It wasn't an ability of his opinions or dreams to be able to fix this. The cut was deep. It was leaking out David's very life. It poured over everything. It covered the steering wheel, his clothes, and his hands. Samuel was in horrific limbo between breaking down completely and withdrawing himself so far from this reality he might never be able to return. He wobbled between the two extremes, immersed in relentless silence.

"Well, what the fuck, man, I've been away for a while; I'm a little out of practice. He got a lucky shot in before I gave it to him," said David as nonchalantly as ever.

"What the fuck are we gonna do, man?" asked Samuel with terror in his voice, riding David's break in the still.

"Well, I'm gonna take us right over to Lorenzo's front door. You're gonna pull away. When the guards see me they pull me in out of plain sight to find out what happened. When Lorenzo comes to see about the commotion, I'll give him this." David lifted his shirt to show the gun he'd acquired from his victim.

Samuel scowled. "Nah man. The second you pop him, you're dead too."

"Well, Samuel, there's really no avoiding that now."

"Nah, fuck that . . . You ain't no doctor. You can't be sure."

"Yeah, I'm pretty fuckin' sure, but even if I'm not, what would we be rushing off to try and save? Motherfuckers have just seen me dead some dude; I'd probably get locked back up and all y'all would be easy pickin's for Lorenzo. Even if I didn't get locked up, how long do you think I can go without violating probation back in Post? I ain't no good if we staying here. Besides, what it really comes down to is this might be my only chance to get at Loco, especially once the news of what just happened gets back. I ain't leaving y'all to the wrath of that man . . . we've been kidding ourselves. This was what I was supposed to be doing from the second I got out. That's the way of things. We all knew that; we just didn't want to face it. He's protecting Tim. Can't nobody get to Tim till I get to Cole. Didn't shit change, that's been what had to happen all along."

"Man, you can't be talking like that. You . . ."

"YO!" interrupted David. "I can't waste energy arguing with you. You gotta respect the choice I have to make. There's no room for debate. There ain't no way out of this thing for me now, but I can get everybody else out. After the way this went down today Lorenzo is gonna be comin' after my family, Jamie, Mouse and anybody else that means anything to me. This is the only way to protect them. Fuck it! I'm lucky. At least I get to die with a purpose . . . my life didn't have none."

Samuel was without words again. His head dropped into his palms and he clawed at his own temples. There weren't even any tears. Neither his thoughts nor feelings could come to a head. What he felt was too overwhelming; it would take longer to manifest itself. But for his friend's sake he found strength. It was the endurance that had carried him through all those years. If David was able to make this decision, he must in turn be able to accept it. He had no choice.

"That fuck is like a dragon up in his cave, frightening the town folk to make them serve him," began Samuel, using the storytelling skills he knew David appreciated. "He set up shop; makes a living off all the Posties' sweat. He ain't never had no respect for who he was working with; it was only a matter of time before the town's valiant knight had to go slay the dragon. If anybody's gonna save Post, it should be you. A perfect finale to the Caine boys' legend. The prince goes up the mountain to conquer the beast and free the people under its thumb."

David grinned proudly. "You know that's right! Fuck this dude! He picked the wrong town."

They both gave deep chuckles as if hearing their favorite classic joke that only they were in on. Samuel couldn't let himself think on the life that was being lost; he instead dwelled on the heroism in his friend's action. It was just another of those stories that had drawn Samuel's interest in Post Edition to begin with. Focusing on that did well at blocking out the approaching force.

Not much was said after that. To try and apply words to what was going on would be almost demeaning. Samuel wouldn't let himself look at David's wound. He didn't want to see everyone's big brother in this mortal state. The blood continued pumping out. There was so much. It seemed to be purposely making its way toward Samuel, trying to force him to look at what he didn't want to see.

His instincts approached and he wanted to stare off into the sky to pretend it wasn't happening. He wanted to compose a dream that would fix the flaws of the world around him, but he wouldn't let himself. This would be the last time he would be with this man who had often represented his own strength, his own heart and soul. He couldn't let his mind run away from this. He would not spend the rest of his life regretting this moment. He would not regret having needed to say something.

"Is there anything you want me to do for you? Anything you want me to tell your family?" asked Samuel, letting David know his support was there in spite of this choice.

"There's not much to be said. But if you could be around them, pay 'em visits from time to time, I think you just being around would be a good influence. As far as letting everyone know, leave that to Mouse. He's gonna want to do it anyway. But tell him what I'm doing here is just the start of something that he's gotta finish. He'll know that, but tell him anyway. Tell him I'd be honored to have him finish this for me."

"I'll tell him, and I'd be honored to spend time with your family. Rex and Bree will know every Caine boy story there is before they hit double digits."

"That's good; you're the one to tell 'em, too." David gave a low, quiet giggle at that appealing thought. "Listen, when you leave here go straight to your apartment. Park down the block at that grocery store and leave the car in the back of the lot. Take off your over-shirt so people don't notice the blood while you're walking, but take the shirt with you. As soon as you get home call Mouse and let him know where the car is. He'll take care of it." Samuel nodded his head obediently, listening closely to every detail of the directions.

It was dusk when they pulled up the U-shaped driveway that led to

Lorenzo Cole's castle. Samuel looked over to his friend. His face had grown peaked and the blood had soaked all the way down his pants. His plan was perfect. David's obvious need for serious medical attention would remove any appearance of threat. The guards' monotonous days would fuel them to get caught up in the drama; their minds would shift from protecting their boss to getting help for David.

Samuel watched as his old friend selflessly opened the door and rolled out of the car. He looked as if his legs would give way but, almost visibly, he reached down deep to find the extra strength needed to get him to that door. To Samuel, he looked like a poem.

David looked back at his partner. "You get out of here quick. I don't want them to see you pull away."

Samuel looked up, trying to find the right words in departing from someone who had meant so much. They weren't to be found. His face contorted as his strength cracked.

David was never one with a lack of something to say. "Hey man, we made the right choice and . . . you're one of the people I'm going in here for, don't forget that. Stay up." At that, he shut the door and hobbled back into the shadows from which he had come to Samuel so long ago.

Not wanting to be a part of any error, Samuel quickly slid to the driver's seat and rolled into motion. His rush kept him from looking back. His fearful curiosity had grown to a towering height by the time he'd reached the stop sign at the corner, but was quenched in an instant with the resounding cracks of gunfire. His head snapped back, startled by the coarse echo that would linger in his mind for a lifetime. He paused in hollow silence, and then pulled out into traffic.

CHAPTER 36: STRENGTH

Samuel followed his instructions to a T. He ditched the car at the nearby store, wiped away any obvious blood and continued on foot.

Night had arrived by the time his walk began. The void that David would leave was slowly taking form. One who had been the strength in Samuel time and time again was gone. It wouldn't be like his prison term. As hard as that was for Samuel, there was comfort in knowing eventually he would see him again. That comfort was nowhere in sight now. It was enough to make Samuel's legs quake as he forced himself to keep walking.

He looked up to the night to see its glowing darkness. The abundant city lights gave a crimson hue over the deep, endless black hole lingering above. It seemed as if the world was on fire and the red from the searing flames was reflecting off the sky.

He wouldn't let himself cry but his emotions filled him up so much that there didn't seem room inside for anything else and thin layers of moisture had made a place on his cheeks. The earth breathed softly with a slow hum of wind, working against the uphill walk to his apartment. It dried the moisture into a crust. Like reinforcements, a more full, real set of tears trickled free and the continued wind sent them back on his face instead of down.

He arrived home safely and cleaned himself up. The day's events were still too real to fully comprehend. He knew it would be months before it had all completely sunk in.

He hadn't even time to settle in before a ringing phone was followed by Lukas Bailey's voice cursing in the answering machine. Samuel quickly made his way over to pick up.

"What the fuck happened?" asked Lukas in both anger and panic.

"What?" said Samuel, not understanding how he could be aware of anything.

"Turn on channel 8."

Samuel did so to find the local news already reporting what had happened.

"Wealthy businessman Lorenzo Cole was slain today in his suburban home. His home security team reports that a severely wounded David Caine, recently released on parole, came to their door in request of medical attention. Once in the home Caine fired three shots into Cole, killing him instantly. Security returned shots, slaying Caine as well. Police say there will be a further investigation as to Caine's motives for the killing. This is Suzy Geeha reporting."

Samuel turned the television back off and returned to the phone, where Mouse was still waiting. They kept the conversation brief, so as not to lose composure. Samuel just confirmed what the news had already said, explained about the car, and dropped a hint as to what David had wanted. Lukas said he would take the news to Jamie and the remaining Caine family. Samuel agreed as he had been instructed to.

At hanging up the phone Samuel played the other messages on his answering machine. It felt strange doing something so mundane after such tragedies, but there seemed no right way to behave and he was in desperate need to occupy himself. There was an assortment of salesmen and other junk messages, followed by his boss at the post office.

"Hey Samuel, it's Bob. I got some real good news here. That girl that made the call left another message today. She said she decided she'd overreacted and wanted to withdraw her complaint. She said she hoped she'd see you on the route again soon. So that's that. I never even had to make a report for the higher-ups. You can come back tomorrow if you're ready. Give me a call and let me know what you're thinking. *BEEP*"

So there was Samuel, back at his apartment as if returning from just another day's work. Things were the same. The world had not changed as he tried to make it. The door to his old life was open again; it was now just a matter of walking back through.

He flopped to a sitting position on his bed. As he rested his head in both palms his circling thoughts came flooding in. He was going to have to return to the life he had tried so hard to escape. All they had been reaching out for was gone, and even more had been lost: David was dead. He had come full circle and still there was nothing to live for.

He heard himself sobbing before he realized he was. The pulsating rhythm of his own tears baited him to let go completely. His hands were soon holding puddles of the doubts, fears and sadness that had made him their slave for so long. They were now punishing him for his absence. They were raining down at an extreme beyond what they'd ever reached in the past. His very soul was roaring in anguish, deep inside him, and still there was no one to listen. As he'd always feared, his head was hanging in misery with no one to care. He was alone again.

The boiling pain lifted his hand over to the night stand and pulled out the gun that had long embodied his agenda to give in. He whipped his head back up, forced his face into composure and sniffed the drizzle from his nose. Then, from the same vein of valor that kept David standing a few hours before, Samuel's body lifted itself off his bed and took heavy, deliberate paces to the kitchen. Slowly, he opened the cupboard under the sink. He lifted the gun and held it over the waste basket, paused briefly, reflecting on the decision, then let it drop with a low *klunk* that exclaimed its final banishment. The sound was the last voice that gun would ever have in his life. He in that moment ceased to be two sides and instead was one coin. He would now be the man he had long needed to be.

The decision was made. David's sacrifice had partly been so that Samuel would live. There was no longer the option to long for death, and he no longer had the right to coast through his life without pursuing enjoyment. To do so would be spitting on what David had done for him. It would no longer just be a waste of Samuel's life, but of David's sacrifice. Every moment that pain festered inside him, there was no happiness in sight and he relaxed in spite of it was an insult to his friend. It was an insult to the way David had lived. He had been more alive than the rest of the world. His soul never rested from seeking. His shining heart was the reason men lived in the first place. He traded that in for Samuel and the others. Samuel had to shine like David, had to make the trade worthy. Whether he could accomplish it or not, he could never stop trying. As much as Mouse had to complete David's revenge, Samuel had to complete David's trade. That was how life would be continued. He would find happiness for David's sake.

Samuel walked over to the chair that had been a part of so many pivotal moments within himself. He lay back, resting his eyes as the inner struggle he'd been confined to for so many years melted away like snow in the rain. In his youth, he had made a picture in his mind of what life should consist of, the way he believed things would be. Over the years he tried to mold the world to fit that picture, but circumstances were stronger than his intentions. When he failed, it broke him. He couldn't stand not having the authority over his life he had believed himself entitled to. He tried to take that authority by killing himself. When he couldn't, it left him teetering between being unwilling to accept the way things had turned out and being unable to pursue the only alternative he could see. He was like a child who had plans for a sunny day but awoke to discover rain. The rain poured down in the way of his agenda, and rather than making a new one, he sat at the window sulking. In doing so he let that rain become a tyrant over him. It stayed and abused him. It would not leave for as long as he remained at that window, and he wasted countless years there. That was over now. David pushed him forward. There would be no more sulking. He accepted things for what they were, but he would live life in spite of them. That decision brought an end to the reign of rain over Samuel.

As a forgotten bliss drifted over him and he found the contentment of a baby in the womb, he tilted his head back, considering. He considered that Monique had probably planned to make that call all along. She only needed him gone until she safely received her package, then she did her part to put his life back to normal. It was proof they had done the right thing in letting her go. She was not the type of person who deserved to be robbed. David would not have been David had they made a different choice. He had always used his strength to take up for those who weren't so strong. He had done that today. He had likely seen his cowering mother, scared girlfriend and broken sister in Monique at that moment. There were men far stronger than her in pursuit. The man responsible for protecting her had been killed, leaving her vulnerable. David saved her in his stead. He had been a big brother to the end.

Samuel then moved to considering the strength that would be in Lukas's stride when taking the news to David's friends and family, the pride involved in handling the funeral and keeping the pressure off the bereaved. He considered the reactions of Jamie, Missy and Mother Caine when they learned of David's death. He could see Ms. Caine's heart split when hearing she had lost another boy, Jamie's composure crumble at hearing the day she had long feared finally arrived, Missy's ferocious and teary-eyed Caine tantrum at hearing something she would be unwilling to accept. The crippling pain and regret he pictured in their faces brought lines of tears back to Samuel's face. But these tears did not have the longing like the ones just moments before; they were purely tears of goodbye that conveyed how much his old friend would be missed.

CHAPTER 37: MAKING GOOD

The following day Samuel returned to work. It brought memories of that first morning after he met Leah, but this time was very different. Then, he had returned as a way to pass the days in hiding from his own pain and the world with it. Today he returned to face that world, get past his pain and begin a real life. He was no longer the walking dead making his way through his mail route. He didn't let dreams eat away his days like before. Instead, he found himself nodding to people as he made their deliveries. After only a few days the nods became greetings, then brief conversations. The scenery was the same but in truth, his work day was entirely different from before. Now, fulfillment was coming from the service he provided, and there was a subtle pleasure in speaking with the residents.

At the end of the week he attended David's funeral. The friends and family buried him with heavy hearts and still tongues. As loved as Samuel knew him to be, he was still surprised by the turnout. Everyone David had touched, everyone who heard of the Caines and everyone who had a grudge against Lorenzo Cole came out to pay the Postie hero his respects. It was right that so many would miss one who so deserved to be missed.

It was two days later when Samuel heard of Tim Russell's murder. The local news station reported him being gagged and bound, then beaten severely with a blunt object. He endured multiple broken bones and ribs before being tossed face first from a tenth floor apartment balcony. Samuel saw Lukas frequently afterwards but never brought it up. He knew without asking that Post justice had returned to that neighborhood.

At the funeral Samuel had made arrangements to visit David's relatives the coming Sunday. That visit led to others and in turn his presence in their lives quickly became routine. He was surprised at the way they accepted having him around. Samuel wasn't the typical personality for Posties to take in. It was that something special in David that took a liking to him. To the Caines, Samuel represented that part of David they had all loved so much, despite their unwillingness to voice it. Having Samuel there was a way of keeping a last little fragment of David around.

Samuel remembered how his friend had asked that he look out for them. At times he felt obligated to force his opinions of their flaws on them, but never did. As David said, just his presence would be a good influence. That proved correct. Without Samuel ever having to confront an issue or point a finger, Ms. Caine, Missy, Jamie, Deanna and even Lukas got used to asking his opinion. He quickly became the source of advice for them that he had been for David.

Then, a few months after the Cullomine situation had come to an end, a final chapter unraveled. When sorting his mail one morning, he spotted an out-of-the-ordinary letter. It was addressed to Samuel Lamech at 5002 Emerald Drive. It was Monique's old address. He opened it feverishly. As he suspected it was her clever way of getting in touch with him.

Dear Samuel,

It's weird writing you this way. I can only hope that you are indeed back on your route and receive this. I felt it was important and right that I contact you. I couldn't leave things unfinished.

When you came to me that night all I wanted to do was explain and try and help you. But, probably for the best, you ran off before I could. Before long I realized as much as I wanted to, I couldn't explain yet. It would jeopardize too much. You obviously knew something of what was going on but I didn't believe you could stop things from proceeding, especially if I had you suspended, which I did in spite of the pain I felt in doing so. It was then I decided I would write you this letter once we had arrived here safely. And when I saw you at the airport I knew you had done something to help little Cullomine and me. That reinforced my decision. I want to thank you for that. It made me feel more than ever that you are owed an explanation.

I must first admit that I grew up as an orphan. I never had any brothers, sisters, or even parents. Please understand I didn't lie to you for the sake of trickery or distrust. The mother and family I spoke of is a fantasy world I've made for myself. It's always allowed me to escape the harshness of the real one and at times, avoid the shame of the discarded. I've done it since I was a little girl in my orphanage. The one who comforted me during storms wasn't my brother but Cullomine Torreo. My dance lessons were the flailing about I did while he beat drum sounds on the wall, and the movies I watched were shown on the back of the church by the town projector. Somehow getting others to believe in my perfect family fantasy always made it more real for myself. Cullomine would often play along for me. For a brief time it let me escape the loneliness of an orphan. Playing it with you did much the same. It let me pretend I led a typical life, full of stability and loved ones. I'm sorry to have lied to you. I hope you can understand.

It's clear you figured out about my relationship with Cullomine. It seemed as if you considered it lowly. I suppose Americans have just cause to hate drug dealers and what they've done to your country. But I knew him long before he was a part of that. In truth it's hard to remember the time before I knew my Cullomine. He was sent to my orphanage when I was eight and he eleven. We took to each other right away. He looked out for me as an older brother would. I never knew why, but he helped me whenever I needed it the most. We were all we had. Eventually that relationship bloomed into something beautiful. We loved each other as much as I can imagine any two people ever have. Those who knew us always knew that.

Where we grew up, there weren't many career choices or jobs at all. It's hard to tell someone what it's like living in a third world country if they've never been to one. For Cullomine to be recognized by the DC was a dream come true for us. For him to find his way into the drug cartel was being accepted by an elite group that lived far better than the rest of the world. Food was in our bellies and clothes on our backs. My Cully was never as smart as people gave him credit for, but he was strong and determined as a bull. It was his fierce determination that I believe always impressed Vincent. That was why he took Cullomine under his wing. When Vincent rose to the head of the Dragon Clan he had Cullomine as his right hand, but Vincent had an envious nephew, Carlo, who had acquired clout by his own means. His methods were usually of the most ruthless manner and due to that, Vincent tried to keep his authority limited. He never trusted someone of that nature. Carlo turned that into a rivalry with Cullomine and though the feud did not appeal to him, Cullomine was incapable of backing down. It became a chess match between the two, with respect and accomplishment the pieces. It continued that way for years.

Everyone always knew that when it came time, Vincent would pass the reins of power to Cullomine, but it was never made official under their regulations. So when the sudden stroke took Vincent's life, Carlo was able to snatch control by the same ruthless means he had always used. Without Vincent, Cullomine had little way to protect himself from his enemies, and once in power, Carlo didn't wait long before setting him up. With lies and allegations he was able to get the backing of the Clan to murder my love. Most knew the bitter rivalry was the cause and not the substance of the accusations, but there was little to be done. The title Carlo had acquired made him difficult to challenge.

Many thought Cullomine could maneuver his way out of the impossible situation, but his reputation for being crafty had always had little basis. Trying to outfox the feds and DC at the same time was far beyond him, so when I saw what was coming I knew it was only a matter of time before he left me. I would have done anything to stop it but he would never let me get involved and there was little that could be done. Once he knew his fate was sealed he came up with a way to set his wife and son up for life. He would not trust Carlo to follow the rules of the family code when it came to us. He knew his arrest was eminent as well. That's when he took the money. He was right that if he was arrested while the feds still did not have their payoff, it could postpone his execution by the Dragons. He would take that time to make sure the law had no knowledge of me or our son. If they did not, then we would continue the plan as he had explained to me. If they did, he would get a signal to me to get out of the country with what we already had.

I was never that concerned about the money. I would have gotten by regardless, but it was the last thing Cullomine could do for us, and it was important to me that he was able to. So for that sake, I waited and saw his plan through. I would do anything to bring him back to me, but it was beyond us. We were out of our league from the beginning and it eventually caught up. I miss him so much. Even with him being gone in prison all that time, it's still very different now. Knowing I'll never see him again seems like more than I can bear at times, but I do, for little Cully's sake. Cullomine would want me to take care to keep our son from the life he led. It's a purpose that gets me through. We have a nice home here and we're safe at last. I know it consoles my husband's spirit to have accomplished that before his demise. That eases my pain.

I don't know why I tell you all these details or what it was about you that I got caught up in. I think partly it was because I saw my Cullomine's strength in you, and eventually I saw my own loneliness as well. I realized on that late night you came over so upset that our not being involved physically allowed you to become closer to me than you had let yourself be with a woman in some time. I didn't mean to make you vulnerable. I'm sorry if I mistreated you. I had been alone so long. I'm sure you know about that, but you've always had your flings to get you by. I suppose a fling to ease my loneliness had gained appeal. But you weren't like that for me. My feelings for you were stronger than that. You're a good man, Samuel. I would have loved to have known you longer. Under other circumstances I would have pursued what we started on the blanket that afternoon. I hope my stopping didn't hurt you but I could not betray my Cullomine. I'm sorry for any trouble I caused you. I hope you don't think ill when you think of me.

I remember when you spoke of the hovel you lived in. It's not charity but it's a waste for my old house to sit there unused. I want you to live in it or sell it or whatever you prefer. I signed the deed over to you. It sits in a desk drawer in the living room. There is something else I left for you on that desk as well. I can only hope you use it. The key to the house is in the flower pot near the back door.

I can only hope I'm forgiven in your heart for not being honest with you. I lied about what was being sent to me in fear of jeopardizing the efforts of my love. I hope you understand that. I can never thank you enough for your help in my escape. I don't know where the extra people came from or what your involvement with them was; I only know I wouldn't have evaded them were it not for you. I could feel the aggressors at my heels and didn't know comfort until we saw you at the airport. I knew then we'd be all right. Now, I can only wish you the best and hope you find what it is you're looking for. Hopefully my gift will help.

With love and humble gratitude,
Monique

Samuel was taken aback by the letter. He hadn't felt bad before reading it, but somehow he still felt much better once it was read. It resolved something inside him. There was a definite ending to what had happened.

Monique and her son had safely escaped and she reaffirmed through her kind words that Samuel and David were right in looking out for her.

He was too anxious to continue working. The mystery and joy of receiving gifts filled him with schoolboy excitement. His deliveries would have to arrive a bit behind schedule. He was going directly to Emerald Boulevard to see what awaited him.

When he arrived he made a half-jog to the back of the house, where he found the key in the location described. Samuel proudly let himself into his new home. He took a long whiff to breathe in remembrance of Monique Romano and the way she had made him feel there. It was as if a small part of her remained there for his sake. He was already more comfortable in his new house than in his old apartment.

He made his way to the living room, where a desk was sitting dead center. On its surface was a computer. Intrigued, Samuel sat down and moved the mouse to interrupt the screen saver. It disappeared, revealing a high quality writing program already opened. At the top of the otherwise blank page was one sentence. In bold print it read "WRITERS WRITE."

He was moved by the insightful gesture. It made him later to his deliveries than anticipated. At seeing the empty page and the stagnant keyboard, the creativity he'd been bottling up for years on end came spewing out. His fingers overwhelmed the keys and the page was quickly covered, as were its followers. Just brushing the beginning of a new story opened a joy in him he had almost convinced himself had never existed. He felt full in a part of him he had never realized was empty. It was the intrigue of witnessing a gossip-worthy event at a party, the fulfillment from handing a child a mail-order present he'd been counting the days for and the resolution that came from accepting something important about himself all rolled up into one.

After finally tearing himself away and returning to the duties of a postal worker, he spent much of the remaining work day composing where he would take his new story. He was anxious just to get home and return to typing. It made the time roll by but also gave him enjoyment while at work. He had no need to finish his story, so there was no hurry. Thinking of it did not disrupt his newly obtained conversations with the people on his route. He was free to come and go from his imagination as he pleased. He had no reason to rush; he just enjoyed.

Over time, it became therapeutic to him. Things that had frustrated him in the past could be vented in his stories. Without having answers to the questions that assailed him, they still lost their power at his finding an outlet. More important to him, David's heroics and way of life would be forever remembered in his writings. His friend would take form in character after character. He would be the inspiration for countless stories. The warped wickedness of Lorenzo Cole would often be characterized as well, so that David could thwart his evil time after time.

Samuel no longer wondered where his writing could go or how others would feel about it. Writing felt good to him. That was enough. At first touching the keyboard, he knew there would never again be a point in his life when he wouldn't have something in the works. As he had advised others, he now finally accepted himself that he could never feel complete without doing what always made him happy. For him that was writing. He felt silly for having not listened to David and the others when they told him to go back to it. He had known they had a good point in what they said, but he hadn't realized how on target they'd been. He wished he could tell David he was right, and at times on paper, he could.

So was his new life filled with the joy of doing what he'd always loved despite the imperfect circumstances. He was no longer waiting for things to be just the way he wanted them before he would go forward. Instead he was willing to struggle to move forward, regardless.

Over time Missy, Lukas, Mother Caine, Rex, Bree, Jamie and Deanna all became quite important to him. They too, grew accustomed to his presence and advice. Before long Missy let up with her campaign to inebriate herself. The frequent gatherings at Ms. Caine's home gave her a far more beneficial way to spend her time. She eventually got a job at the same factory as her mother and her junkie ways dwindled into nonexistence.

At times Samuel would find himself quoting his own stories to better make a point when conversing with Ms. Caine. As she was getting on in years her life consisted of little more than work and visits from those willing. Samuel's peaceful nature appealed to her and she made him feel welcome as if he were her own. After enough quotes from his stories she finally demanded to see one. After that, reading his books quickly became a habit. She loved what Samuel had to write and the rarity with which she left the house gave her ample time to read. The instant she finished one he picked out another for her, but stipulated that she not share them with anyone unless given his permission.

Jamie was around quite often. She kept everyone well informed on her life. There was always a description of the new beau playing the part. She'd give them updates but never brought one around. In that home she was still David's and always would be. She liked that about her visits.

Lukas's life didn't change much. He made side money where he could but was never overly risky. He liked being part of the family they had built through time at the Caine home, but he remained a textbook Postie. To him he was carrying on David and Kris's torch. Through partying and wisecracks and strength of character he represented them in the most simplistic of ways. He would keep them alive by continuing the attitude and behaviors they had brought to that neighborhood.

He would occasionally coax Samuel into joining him in a trip to Snickers or whatever pub was expected to have the crowd that evening. Samuel would drink but he made sure to keep it at moderate pace. He never gorged himself as in the past. It wasn't that hard for him; he no longer had the desire of old to escape from life. He could put down a drink when it started to get to him, and in a way taking charge of drinking helped him keep charge of himself.

It was nice to get the occasional night on the town. It was nice to be out with people he enjoyed. Once in a while he would even pick up a girl. He never forced a relationship with them. He took it as it came. They rarely lasted long but he accepted it when they didn't. He couldn't make it into more than it was. He could only enjoy it for what it had to offer. It hurt sometimes, but the pain never got the better of him. As a broken bone that remains unused can keep its malfunction or an overused bandage can keep out the necessary air to coagulate the blood in a cut, so would keeping a hurt heart away from the world maintain its wound. So he would move on and the pain would play out its course. In that aspect he lived the fantasy he had conjured for Monique, having flings to tide him over until a meaningful relationship came along, but he didn't hide his heart from them as Monique had feared. He could only hope she had achieved some portion of the fantasy world she had created as well.

More enjoyable than the times out at the bar was the family time when they were all at Ms. Caine's together. Lukas, Missy, Ms. Caine, Samuel, Jamie and Deanna could all sit around and share what was going on in their lives. They would laugh at the amusing behavior of the children, Rex and Bree. And somehow David and Kris were there with them as well. Though rarely spoken of, the impact they had was in every smile, the comfort they provided was in all the camaraderie and the despair they caused was subtly behind every gesture and conversation.

At times there would be a pause of silence. It was always heavy. They never said it but they all knew they were thinking of the past. There was no expression of grief or lines from tears. The strong women never let their faces show their woe but Samuel didn't need them to. He could picture with his own heart what they felt, better than their faces could ever express. He could vent those things on his keyboard, along with so much else.

With his words he would paint a picture of all those things he never actually got to see. He could describe what Jamie's reaction must have been when Mouse arrived at her door with news of David. He would change the names and circumstances but it was them just the same. He would try to describe the sorrowful passion David was overcome by when he heard of Kris. More enjoyably, he would write of blooming love. The motivation would vary from Susan and him to Cullomine and Monique, but most often it was David and Jamie. Different mixtures of those romances made up some of his favorite moments in his stories.

So Samuel's personality bloomed in the new soil. Eventually even his work friends saw him differently and forgot the broken man of the past. Now, when people spoke to him they would likely hear an in-depth opinion instead of just what he thought sounded good. His walk had strength in it and people on his route knew his name. He became a popular man whom people respected. The Cullomine situation had made him rich in things other than money.

His opinion toward people had changed. Though there was still much ill he could say against his fellow man, he found himself better off to focus on what was good in them. He enjoyed them for whatever they had to offer instead of what he wanted.

His life was better and it didn't take the things he had believed it would to make it so. He didn't get the extra time he told himself he needed, nor the money necessary to provide it. He didn't have the unconditional love from the perfect woman he'd always dreamt of. People had not changed in nature the way he believed they had to. Instead he had just accepted things for what they were. Doing so brought about people he enjoyed spending time with, nourishment from mentoring Kris's children and watching them grow, and it re-opened the door to writing, which gave his creativity the room it needed.

Then one deceptively snowy day a man was walking up the slushy sidewalk. The snow indeed delivered the damp chill it was expected to, but it was in its threat of imposing a murky spirit that it fell short, at least for this man. The day marked the end of a pleasant and colorful fall, preceded by a glowing, eventful summer. For many the onslaught of snowfall was like banishment from the Garden of Eden. It was the sort of day that no one wanted to be a part of. It made the most active want to stay inside and hide themselves away until better circumstances came.

This man had more reason than most to hate the thick weather that could slow him in his duties, but still he maintained the same pace he had used throughout the joyous summer. His movements had strength behind them. His face held a contentment and easiness not commonly found in these days. So his stride did not reflect the abusive temperature or empty sky; it instead might cause a viewer to forget the downtrodden feelings the day had inflicted on them, even if for just a moment.

The man made his last delivery on that street and was back in his truck when he noticed a familiar street walker he had seen many times over the years. The derelict woman was treading up the street with a cardboard sign that read "Will shovel snow for food." Samuel watched somberly for a moment, then dug up his sack lunch and made his way over to greet her.

"Here you go, ma'am."

"Oh, thank you. Thank you so much."

"Ah, don't sweat it. I gotta stop eating the same thing every day anyway."

"God bless you, son. God bless you."

Samuel's experiences had not so much made a new man as uncovered one who had been buried by events and lost affections, and they didn't so much teach him things as they did remind him of important things forgotten. He was alive again. Perhaps not as alive as David had been but there was a bliss about him and a portion of it seemed to spread to anything he touched. David had saved his life in more ways than one. He had removed the threat of Lorenzo Cole and at the same time gave Samuel strength one last time. A last time that would continue the rest of his days. He couldn't live with the lack of dignity he had before. He never did anything he believed his old friend would have been ashamed of. David, in many ways, had become his conscience, watching his every move and keeping him in proper ways. Samuel no longer pretended he could control the random circumstances the world was full of. He instead enjoyed what he could with little anticipation. There would be no decisions about what he thought his life needed to consist of and thus no fear or disappointment when plans took a turn. Happiness had been found. He had accepted that he could not control the outside world; he could only control how he would respond to it.

Made in the USA
Coppell, TX
13 September 2020